HIGH PRAISE

"Cotton Smith is one of [...]
of the American West."

—Don Coldsmith

"Cotton Smith's is a significant voice in the development
of the American Western."

—Loren D. Estleman

"Cotton Smith turns in a terrific story every time."

—*Roundup Magazine*

"In just a few years on the scene, Cotton Smith has made
a strong mark as a Western writer of the new breed, telling
it like it was."

—Elmer Kelton, Seven-time Spur Award–winning
author of *The Day It Never Rained*

"Cotton Smith is another modern writer with cinematic
potential. Grand themes, moral conflicts and courage are
characteristic of his fiction."

—*True West Magazine*

"Hats off to Cotton Smith for keeping the spirit of the West
alive in today's fiction. His plots are as twisted as a gnarled
juniper, his prose as solid as granite, and his characters ring
as true as jinglebobs on a cowboy's spurs."

—Johnny D. Boggs, Wrangler and Spur Award–winning
author of *Camp Ford*

"These days, the traditional Western doesn't get much better than Cotton Smith."

—*Roundup Magazine*

"When it came to literature, middle-age had only three good things to show me: Patrick O'Brian, Larry McMurtry and Cotton Smith."
—Jay Wolpert, screenwriter of *The Count of Monte Cristo* and *Pirates of the Caribbean*

"From his vivid descriptions of a prairie night to his hoof-pounding action scenes, Cotton Smith captures the look and feel of the real West."

—Mike Blakley, Spur Award–winning author of *Summer of Pearls*

"Acclaimed novelist Cotton Smith is a Western legend."

—Recorded Books Direct

THE END OF THE RANGERS

"I'm going to have some breakfast," Lady Holt said. "You find out when the hearing is scheduled."

"What if the judge hasn't set it yet?"

Her stare made Tanner wish he hadn't said that.

"I'll get it done," he quickly added.

"Good," she said. "Then ride to the ranch and tell Paulus to drive those rebranded cattle to town. Fast. We'll turn this thing around real quick."

She smiled a wicked grin that caught her eyebrows and cocked them. "Tell Judge Opat to expect a telegram from the governor."

"Citale?"

"Do we have another governor?"

"No, of course not." He returned the cigar to his mouth and his hat to his head.

"Tell Jaudon his defense remains the same. Exactly the same. This will be the day the Rangers will never forget." Her laugh was more of a snort.

Tanner spun and left.

"Iva Lee, by tomorrow the Rangers will be history!"

Cotton
Smith

Ride for Rule
Cordell

LEISURE BOOKS NEW YORK CITY

To Margaret and Margaret

A LEISURE BOOK®

April 2010

Published by

Dorchester Publishing Co., Inc.
200 Madison Avenue
New York, NY 10016

ISBN 10: 0-8439-6201-1
ISBN 13: 978-0-8439-6201-7
E-ISBN: 978-1-4285-0843-9

RIDE FOR RULE
CORDELL

Chapter One

Texas Ranger John Checker saw the two gunmen coming in the darkness before they saw him. Like a cat, he dove toward the short buffalo grass pushing against the right side of the ranch shed. He rolled until he was lying chest-down in a shallow creek fifteen feet away. His long black hair brushed along the shoulders of his Comanche tunic.

Moonlight shivered on the dark water that fed upon most of his pants. He laid his Winchester against the edge of the creek itself. Hidden from the gunmen until they got close. Swiftly, he lifted the thong from the hammer of his short-barreled Colt carried in a reverse holster on a double-rowed cartridge belt. His hand gripped the black handles, carrying an embedded elk-bone circle on each side, and drew the fine revolver.

If they saw him, the short gun would be faster to bring into action. He froze in place as they came closer. He was certain they hadn't seen him. A shooting encounter now might prove fatal for his old friend, Emmett Gardner. The smarter move was to determine what exactly was going on and where.

He and fellow Ranger A. J. Bartlett had come as soon as

they received the wire from the gray-haired rancher. The two Rangers had hit town and learned from a loose-lipped cowboy that Lady Holt riders would descend on Gardner's ranch tonight. They stayed only long enough to get fresh horses.

Right now, Bartlett was somewhere on the other side of the ranch yard, waiting for Checker's signal to close in. If he wasn't fussing with his new socks; things like that mattered greatly to his partner. He even kept a detailed journal of recipes of meals that could be prepared on the trail. Probably the result of growing up with schoolteacher parents.

So far, there had been no shooting. Most likely, this meant the old rancher and his sons had been surprised and subdued. Or it could signify something worse. A lone light in the ranch house gave no clue to what was happening inside, but Checker thought it was encouraging. He wasn't certain how many gunmen were at the ranch, but guessed it was ten to twelve. Bartlett was uncomfortable with any estimate, especially one like that; Checker reminded him they wouldn't know for certain until the attack was over.

The two gunmen finally stopped and stood above him on the grassy bank. Their rifles were carried casually in crossed arms. Both were looking back toward the ranch house. It appeared their only objective was to stay out of the way of others.

Checker dared not lift his head enough to see them any better. He had learned well from Stands-In-Thunder how a man could remain unseen by his enemies when actually in plain sight. No movement was the first requirement.

Courage was the second.

Third was to avoid staring directly at the person; such eye contact would often make the man realize he was being watched.

Ranger reports indicated Lady Holt had forty gunmen in

her employ, including the notorious Tapan Moore and the half-breed Luke Dimitry. Were they all here? He didn't think anything near that, but wasn't certain. So far, his first guess of ten to twelve seemed right. Forty gunmen didn't count all the regular cowboys who handled her vast herds. There was little in this part of Texas the English woman didn't own—or control. There was talk of her employing the new devil's rope to stop open grazing. Barbed wire would change everything, most agreed—and few liked the idea.

The two gunmen's conversation was casual in the tense darkness.

"Looks like the ol' lady's gonna get her wish. Gardner's spread'll make it just about complete. The ol' man's got some fine water. Grazin' land ain't bad, neither. Sil said he's gonna make him sign over his place—or start hangin' his sons."

"I was kinda hopin' we'd just hang 'em all an' get it over with. Hazel's waitin' for me in town. Damn, don't know what Sil's waiting for."

"Lady Holt wants it this way. Nice an' legal. Heard Sil's gonna give him a thousand dollars for the ranch." The taller man rubbed his chin. "'Sides, Hazel ain't waitin' for ya. She'd spin anybody who's got silver."

The shorter man flinched, but didn't respond. Checker heard a match strike and saw the glow against the tall man's face as he lit a cigarette. Tobacco smoke drifted down to him.

"Damn it to hell, you're right about Hazel."

"'Course I am. You oughta try that new blonde-haired gal." The tall gunman grinned; white teeth gleamed in the night.

"Good idea. Thanks."

"Say, how'd Rikor—and the kid—get away?"

"Wilson's fault. Let 'em go piss—an' Rikor jumped him. Took his guns."

"Rikor any good with a gun?"

"Doubt it. Figger he's a cowman. Like his pa. But so far, he's been real quiet. Smart, I'd say."

"Hey, Charlie's got some who-shot-John in his saddlebags. Saw it. What say we go back an' have at it? Nothin's gonna happen around here. We can tell Sil we were checking on some noise. Thought it was Rikor."

"I like the way you think."

Neither heard the swift movement behind them. Checker's gun barrel cracked hard against the taller man's head and he shivered and crumpled. The shorter man spun toward Checker, trying to swing his rifle toward the Ranger. Too late. Checker backhanded him in the face with his Colt and he staggered backward and collapsed. The tall Ranger hit the stunned gunman again in the head; his hat bounced from his head. A soft groan was the only response.

With a quick look for assurance, Checker holstered his Colt and yanked the two unmoving bodies down into the creek bed. He threw their weapons into the night, grabbed his own Winchester and began crawling slowly through the creek bed. Where the creek turned sharply to the south, he climbed out and looked around. At least, he now knew why gunmen were stalking through the night around the ranch. Gardner's oldest son, Rikor—and his youngest, Hans—had somehow escaped. Emmett Gardner and his middle son, Andrew, were being held in the ranch house, as he suspected.

Only the dark shapes of trees and rocks greeted him. Yet the darkness could easily hide armed men. His reputation for tracking outlaws at night was well-known. His visual intensity grew with the darkness. It had always been so. Seeing color and measuring distances were the only things that he could not do well at night. Several outlaws had been surprised by his sudden appearance at their nighttime camp.

He slid into the dark. All of the night sounds had disappeared. All of this was definitely a confirmation of Emmett Gardner's wire for help. The two Rangers had been riding hard since the old rancher described a massive land grab under way with small ranchers being squeezed out or overrun. County law was worse than useless; the sheriff was in Lady Holt's employ. Emmett said he feared his ranch was the next target.

It made good sense. This was fine cow country with lots of water—creeks and ponds born of a fat river—and hilly with fine stretches of grazing land in between. Along the waterways, oaks of every kind, cottonwoods, and large pecan and walnut trees were in charge.

Captain Harrison Temple readily agreed to their going. He was growing suspicious of the activity in the region. There was little in this part of Texas not under the control of Lady Holt, an extraordinarily wealthy rancher. There were even rumors of the notorious New Mexico hired killer, Eleven Meade, being in the area.

On top of that, Captain Temple worried about the rumors of her alliance with Governor J. R. Citale. The governor was a corrupt man, pushed easily by money. The rumors seemed to coincide with the growing gap between Captain Temple and the governor.

Checker touched the small buckskin pouch hanging from a leather strip under his shirt. A gift of wolf medicine from Stands-In-Thunder. The old war chief, then on a reservation, said the Comanche warriors called Checker *Tuhtseena Maa Tatsinuupi*, Wolf With Star, because he came after them like a fierce wolf. The wolf was the young Ranger's *puhahante*, spirit helper, the old man had said. Checker wasn't certain how the old man had determined this, but had decided not to question the tribute. Choosing, instead, to enjoy the older man's companion.

According to the Comanche, the mysterious beast gave

him courage and was the reason Checker could see well in the night. Inside the small pouch, according to the old war leader, was strong *puha*, strong medicine, including a wolf claw, powder made from the wing of a night owl and the howl of a wolf.

To his far left, gray shadows along the dark trio of cottonwoods introduced more gunmen. John Checker took a deep breath, drawing in the velvety cool air, and flattened himself with his rifle aimed in their direction. He wiped each hand on his pants, as if to help him pierce the darkness to determine how many were there. Less than fifty yards away from his position, the shadows were moving. Moonlight washed stingily across them. Six. Yes, six. They were obviously searching for the two Gardner sons. Shadows told him more men were searching on the other side of the ranch. His estmate was too low; there must be closer to twenty gunmen.

Behind came soft movement from beside the shed and Checker spun to meet it.

A yellow cat.

Checker shook his head and returned to watching the gunmen.

"You look over there, Vince. By that shed." A tall man with a full beard pointed in the direction of Checker's position. "Eilert, you go there. The bastards have to be here. Somewhere. Remember Rikor has Wilson's guns."

The Ranger watched the lone gunman advance. Everything about the night was bothering the man. Slightly built, he wore a derby over long, stringy brown hair. A long coat glistened with remains of a greasy dinner. It looked as though he was wearing two belted guns; both were tied down. He held a Winchester tightly with both hands. Cocked. His finger was on the trigger. Checker watched him from twenty feet away, careful not to look him in the eye.

The gunman was far too jumpy.

If Checker attacked him now, there would be a good chance the man's finger would squeeze the trigger the instant Checker hit him, but he didn't want to leave the man in a position to shoot at him as he advanced.

Silently, Checker left his Winchester propped against a tree, circled to the outside and edged himself directly in back of the gunman, and in line with the bunkhouse. It would appear he had just come from there. The move was risky, walking in the open for a few seconds, but he thought no one would pay attention to another man walking in the darkness. He pulled his hat brim lower to cover his face and drew his short-barreled Colt. Even in the dark, it was easy to see the trigger guard was half cut away, the section gone nearest the barrel and the filed-away barrel sight. Both were designed to help the Ranger shoot faster.

The brown-haired gunman remained with his back to the bunkhouse and had not heard Checker's careful repositioning. Instead, he was watching the same yellow cat that had surprised the Ranger. Rubbing its back against a tree, the scrawny animal was a welcome diversion. The man's cocked rifle was cradled in his arms, but his right hand was still wrapped within the trigger guard.

Checker declared his presence in a friendly, offhand manner, "Evenin'. Don't shoot, partner. The boss sent me. Found them yet?"

The nervous gunman flinched, but the reassuring voice was a comforting sound in the lonely night. He turned and said, "Glad to have the—"

"If you whisper, I'll blow your head off," Checker snarled. His Colt barrel lifted the nervous man's chin to attention as Checker's left hand slid between the rifle's cocked hammer and the readied bullet in its chamber. His move was a blur. The hammer hit the back of his hand hard, pinching it against the steel frame, but keeping the strike from reaching its intended target. It was the reflex action he had anticipated.

"Let go of the rifle real easylike. Wouldn't want that hammer to get any farther, would you?" Checker growled. "Because if there is any noise to bother your friends, you won't be around to see the fun. Now move over here in the shadows. Walk naturally. That's it."

Holstering his revolver, Checker's hand pulled the rifle from the shaking fingers of the gunman with his right hand; the Ranger's left hand still blocked the hammer's path. Carefully removing his hand, he recocked the rifle and returned its barrel to the guard's neck.

"Tell me what's going on here. I'll know if you're lying."

"Y-you're a Ranger, aren't ya? I'm just doin' what I was told. P-p-please, mister, I—I—I'll tell ya the truth."

In a frightened staccato, he told Checker that Sil Jaudon, Lady Holt's right-hand man, had led a night attack on the Gardner ranch house. They had taken the youngest when he was milking and used him to get inside by threatening to kill him. Jaudon and three others were holding Gardner and the third son in the ranch house now. Jaudon expected to get Gardner to sign away his ranch.

"What are they waiting for?" Checker asked.

"Oh, two of that old man's sons got away. They're around here somewhere, I reckon," the shaking man said. "Sil's mad as hell at Wilson for letting them escape."

He further explained Jaudon and his men would take over the Gardner herd later, probably tomorrow or the next day at the latest. Satisfied the man couldn't tell him more, Checker delivered a blow to the back of the man's head with the barrel of his Winchester and he crumpled to the ground.

Checker's eyes quickly searched the yard for signs of discovery. Nothing. He breathed a deep release of tension. The men were spread out, most of them looking north. He dragged the immobile body behind the shed and into a shallow ravine that ran parallel to the ranch house, so it wouldn't be discovered easily.

Quickly he removed the man's pistols, shoved one into his own cartridge belt and threw the rifle and the other revolver into the darkness. He considered slowly eliminating Jaudon's men as he had the first three. But the other searchers had left the area, moving toward the barn and the main corrals. It would be difficult to do without being discovered. A shootout with those odds wasn't likely to end well.

He heard someone coming through the brush. From his left. He crouched to wait.

It was his partner, A. J. Bartlett, a medium-sized man in a short-brimmed fedora. He held a double-barreled shotgun. A three-piece brown suit looked as if he had just bought it. His bullet belt and a holstered Smith & Wesson revolver were strapped over his coat. But everything—and every way— about him was precise. Or as precise as he could make it.

Even the shotgun had been carefully chosen because of its firepower and its threatening appearance. He wasn't nearly as good with a handgun as Checker. Few were. Supposedly, the Confederate cavalryman-turned-outlaw, Rule Cordell, was. So were John Wesley Hardin and Clay Allison. Rule Cordell wasn't dead as previously reported and was now a preacher, or so Ranger reports had confirmed. Facing each other wouldn't be anything any of them would want.

"Saw you introducing the fellow to the stars," Bartlett said, pointing with the gun at the unconscious gunman. "Thought I'd see what you had in mind—and introduce you to a couple of lads I just ran into."

The Ranger waved and an eight-year-old boy and a lanky young man of eighteen appeared from the darkness. The young man held a Henry carbine in his hands; he looked comfortable with it. A long-barreled Smith & Wesson revolver was shoved into his pocket.

"You remember Rikor, John. And this fine-looking lad is Hans. Looks just like his pa, I do believe." He continued telling Checker about the situation, then expanded his assessment to tell how much the boys had grown since the last time he had seen them, then wondering if Emmett Gardner's herds were safe, and then wondering if cattle prices in Kansas were holding up. He finished by saying that his socks had gotten damp and were troubling him.

Checker stopped his wandering assessment by greeting the boys. "Well, good to see you, Rikor. You, too, Hans. The last time I saw you, you were just getting into everything you could reach." Checker held out his hand to greet both.

Rikor, and then Hans, accepted the handshake enthusiastically. The smaller boy looked him straight in the eye. "They've got my pa. An' Andrew."

"Yes, I know," Checker said, and leaned forward. "How many are in the house—holding them?"

Hans glanced away as if seeing the inside of his house once more, then looked back. "Four. Two inside—and two more fellas watchin' the front an' back doors. Standin' outside." Checker nodded; that matched the number given to him by Vince, the gunman he had just dispatched.

"There were five. One less now," Rikor said with a grin reaching the corner of his mouth. "These are his guns. Jumped him when we went outside to the outhouse. He's behind it now."

"Heard about that," Checker said. "Good work. You gave your pa time. Us, too."

Rikor's eyes brightened with the compliment.

In spite of his favored choice of weapons, the older Ranger was actually much less intense than his younger fellow Ranger, now a gun warrior known throughout Texas. He loved to talk and usually it seemed to fill the silence left when he and Checker rode together. Now it was getting in the way.

"How do you want to play this, John?" Bartlett grinned and recited, "'How dull it is to pause, to make an end, to rust unburnished, not to shine in use, as tho' to breathe were life!'"

Checker glanced at his older friend. "I think you made that up."

"Ah, no, my friend, 'tis *Ulysses*, one of Tennyson's best."

Alfred, Lord Tennyson was Bartlett's favorite poet and he quoted from his works often.

"I like it."

Checker looked at Bartlett, then back to the two Gardner sons. "Got an idea of how we might get close. Maybe even inside. But it will take being very brave."

"What do you want me to do?" Hans blurted, and crossed his arms.

Chapter Two

Minutes later, Checker walked with the boy toward the house. The tall Ranger had switched hats and pulled down the brim of the derby taken from the downed gunman to help keep his face covered. His rifle was cocked and ready, carrying at his side one-handed.

Bartlett and Rikor were headed for the back door, using the same approach with Bartlett appearing to bring in the oldest Gardner son. Rikor's pistol, taken from the gunman earlier, was stuffed into his back waistband, so it wouldn't be seen.

Checker straightened, lowered his rifle to his side, and pulled again on the brim of his adopted hat. He needed to get close. Pretending to be one of Jaudon's men made the most sense. He hoped. He didn't like using the boy for bait, but couldn't think of a better way.

"Well, well, lookee here," a yellow-haired gunman with a scrawny mustache and a leather vest greeted them at the door of the house. He stepped onto the porch to get a better view of the shadowed man advancing with the boy.

Checker kept walking, easing Hans to his left, so he could step in front of him if necessary.

"Hard to find a little bastard like that. Where's the big one?"

"Don't know." Checker's voice was little more than a hoarse growl. "Got any smokes? I'm all out."

"You bet." The yellow-haired gunman reached for his shirt pocket.

Checker drew closer, passing Hans.

"Keep your hands right there."

Grim-faced John Checker shoved his rifle into the man's belly. Moonlight shivered, for an instant, along its barrel.

"Wh-what? Who are you?"

"I'm Ranger John Checker and I don't like what's going on here." Checker pulled the man's revolver from its holster. "Turn around."

"Why?"

"Because I said so. Ask another stupid question and I'll go ahead without you." The arrowhead-shaped scar on Checker's cheek flamed with his anger.

"You're buttin' into somethin' you shouldn't, mister. This is Lady Holt's business." The yellow-haired gunman pushed out his chin and straightened his back.

"When I see her, I'll tell her you were clear about that. Turn around."

Slowly, the man turned. Checker handed the gun to the boy and told him to empty out the cartridges. He pushed against the gunman's back with his Winchester as he waited. Hans completed the task and held out the gun. In his other small hand were the cartridges. The tall Ranger took the handgun and shoved it back into the man's holster, then received the handful of cartridges and put them in his pocket.

"Now lower your hands and walk inside. You're going to tell your boss that the boy's been found. Say it wrong and you won't know what happens this night."

The house consisted of four rooms: a living room, kitchen,

and two bedrooms. Pine floors were freshly swept; Checker had been here several times, as had Bartlett. The house had the feel of a woman's care, even though Gardner had been a widower for nearly six years. Framed pictures of the family sat atop a cabinet in the corner, along with a kerosene lamp. The stone fireplace was the centerpiece of the main room; a small fire was mostly ashes.

Emmett Gardner stood near the fireplace, his face hard and drawn. Hands at his sides, both clenched into fists. A blooded gash on the side of his head spoke silently of an earlier attempt to fight back. On the other side of the fireplace a white-faced boy of fourteen stood. Beside him an ugly brown dog waited for instructions.

Sitting at a large brown sofa that was pushed against the north wall was a half-breed gunman drinking coffee. His wide, moon eyes never left the old rancher. The half-breed grinned a mouthful of missing teeth, bright against his skin, in response to a joke only he knew. A torn spot on the side of the sofa looked as though someone had tried to sew it together unsuccessfully. The half-breed's face was a constant smirk. It pleased Checker to see that the sofa-seated gunman wasn't holding a gun. A rifle lay at his feet; a holstered handgun was barely visible under his worn Navajo coat. Checker knew the gunman. Luke Dimitry. Some said he had killed twenty men.

At an adjacent table, a large, pig-faced man in a three-piece suit sat in one of the four unmatched wooden chairs. His hat brim was pinned to its crown in the style favored by some Civil War officers. He was holding two gold-plated revolvers with ivory handles, both aimed at the old rancher. His eyebrows were plucked clean like a Cheyenne warrior's, giving him an even more sinister appearance.

Checker guessed this was Sil Jaudon, the transplanted Frenchman who led Lady Holt's gang, according to Ranger reports. Jaudon had supposedly come from New Orleans, where he had been involved in a number of killings.

"*Quoi?*" Jaudon's guns swung toward their entrance, barely missing the blue flower vase, filled with dried wildflowers, in the middle of the table

"B-boss, h-he found the b-boy," the yellow-haired gunman announced stiffly as they entered and motioned toward Checker and the boy behind him.

Wagging its tail, the dog trotted across the room to greet Hans.

Jaudon's face became a smile and the guns returned to their position of aiming at Emmett. "*Bien! Bien!* Ah, now we vill see how tough this old rooster is."

The tall Ranger stepped forward from the shadows, pushing the guard to the side, and swung his Winchester toward Jaudon.

"Drop your guns. Do it now." Checker pointed at Jaudon, then spoke to the gunman in the sofa. "Dimitry, don't move. Keep your hands where I can see them."

"S-sorry, boss. He got the drop on me. He's a R-Ranger," the guard said, his shoulders slumping in shame.

Grinning savagely, Sil Jaudon kept his revolvers directed at the old rancher. "*Salut.* Ranger. If *vous* shoot, *mon* guns, they vill go off. An' *mon* boys'll know *vous* are here. Both *beaucoup* bad. For *vous.*"

"I've taken lead before, Checker," Emmett growled, and straightened his shoulders.

Checker raised his gun to fire. "A shot to the head usually stops such a reaction. Let's find out."

Jaudon hesitated, as if waiting for something or someone.

Emmett waved his arm toward the kitchen. "There's another o' them bastards outside the back door."

"He's got a rifle," Andrew, the fourteen-year-old son, volunteered, pointing in the same direction.

Bartlett and Rikor stepped through the small kitchen into the main room, almost on cue. In front of them was a disarmed gunman with eyebrows that sought to live together. His pockmarked face was more yellow than tan and he wore a long red silk scarf around his neck; its silk ends dangled near his belt.

"There isn't any more," Bartlett said. "Wilson's down, too. But you already knew that, didn't you, Frenchie."

"You all right, Pa?" Rikor asked, and knelt to pat the dog. "How about you, Andrew?" He looked down at the animal. "And you, Hammer, how are you?"

"I be fine, son. Jes' fine. Now. So's Hammer."

"Yeah," Andrew said, then hurried to hold his father.

Shaking his head, Jaudon muttered something in French, released the hammers on his guns, and laid them on the table. His hands slowly rose; the movement caused his ample belly to shake like waves on a lake.

"You learn well. Might make it through the night if you stay that smart," Checker growled. "Now get rid of that other gun. Behind your back."

His face blossoming into an eddy of angry wrinkles, Jaudon slowly withdrew the third weapon and laid it alongside the other two. The gun was a match to the first two. Checker had seen its shape in Jaudon's coat when the fat man moved.

"You, unbuckle that belt and shove it to the floor." Checker motioned with his rifle toward the seated half-breed. "Then get rid of that pistol in your boot. Do it real slow. I'm getting really tired of this."

Nervously, the seated half-breed released the gun belt and holstered revolver and shoved it off the sofa as if it were contaminated. He reached down to his boot, looked up, and slowly withdrew a double-action Webley Bulldog pocket gun. His eyes flirted with shooting.

"Ah, lad, ever have your belly turned apart by one of these?" Bartlett said, his eyes squinting at the man as he motioned with his shotgun.

Jerking, the half-breed, Luke Dimitry, dropped the weapon and raised his hands.

Hans ran for his father and the gray-haired rancher held both boys tightly. "You've been real brave, sons. Real proud o' ya."

"Thanks, Pa. I was scared, though," Andrew said, shaking his head.

"I was . . . a little," Hans added, looking away.

"That's what brave men do, boys. They do the ri't thang even when they're scar't." The old rancher's wrinkled face became boyish as he looked at the two Rangers. "I knew ya Ranger boys would come. I knew'd it. These sonvabitches snuck up on me. Sorry to say. Got my youngest when he was in the barn. I couldn't . . ."

Jaudon coughed and explained, his eyes glowing from hate, "*Vous* do not have ze chance, *monsieur*. *Mon* men are everywhere out there. But I vill let *vous* go. *Vous* are ze lawmen. No quarrel I have with *vous*." He motioned with his head. "Only want this ol' man. *Sacre bleu*, he has been rustling our beef—an' the other ranchers, too." He grinned again; his mouth twitching at the right corner. "All Madame Holt wants—is justice. *Oui*, justice."

"That's a goddamn lie—an' ya knows it, Jaudon," Emmett growled. "He kills an' steals for that witch. Give me a gun, boys, an' I'll settle this crap, once an' for all."

Jaudon's face was white, the corner of his mouth trembling.

Stepping away from his sons, Emmett rushed toward the fat man and spat. Brown liquid slammed into the outlaw leader's face and rushed down his cheeks and mouth.

"Damn *vous*!" Jaudon wiped at his stained face. "I vill kill *vous*. I vill kill *vous* with *mon* hands bare."

"If'n ya don't shut up, I'm gonna spit ag'in," Emmett growled, half smiling. "What ar' we a-doin' with these hyar clowns, Rangers? Shoot 'em?"

"That would be the fastest, but no," Checker said with the hint of a smile. "We're taking them into town. To jail. They'll stand trial for attempted murder."

Jaudon's face brightened.

"That damn, no-good judge is in cohoots with Lady Holt. So's the sheriff. They'll just let 'em go," Emmett pleaded.

"Emmett, we're taking this bunch to town. For trial." Checker's voice was low and even. The soft yellow of gaslight draped across his tan, chiseled face with its once-broken Roman nose for an instant, making him look like a wild Comanche warrior in war paint.

The old rancher frowned and shook his head. "How we gonna do this?"

"The Frenchman is going out on the porch and calling in his men," Checker said.

"This vill never work," Jaudon snarled.

"Better hope it does," Checker said. "Or you're dead. Got any rope around the house, Emmett? I'd like to make sure the rest of this batch aren't a problem."

"Sure do. In the kitchen." Emmett headed toward the back, paused and chuckled. "Most folks don't keep lassos in with their cookin' stuff. Almina wouldn't have allowed it." He bit his lower lip. "It's new. Bin a-workin' it some to get it nice an' smooth."

"Rangers, *vous* are new to ze region." Jaudon put both large hands on the tabletop. "Madame Holt vill understand this. She is a grand woman. She vill own this part of Texas. But *vous* have got to stop now. She vill reward *vous* . . . greatly. She knows ze governor. She can be most helpful . . . to your careers."

"Jaudon. I'm real tired of your jabbering," Checker said. "I don't want to hear anything more from you. 'Til I say so. Out on the porch."

In minutes, the half-breed and the other two gunmen were tied and kerchiefs shoved into their mouths to keep them quiet. To make certain the new ropes would be taut enough, the men's belts were added as restraints. The old rancher relished the task, tightening the cords and retightening them.

Checker motioned with his Winchester. "Emmett, take two of his fancy pistols. A.J., you're going to need that rifle." Gaslight danced again along the Ranger's derby hat, then sashayed with his black hair moving near his shoulders.

Staring at him, the old rancher said, "How long ya bin wearin' that . . . derby, John? Don't look like ya."

"About ten minutes, Emmett. My hat's outside. Thought it would help us get close." Checker grinned and pulled on the brim. "Why? Don't you like it?"

"Jes' ain't you, that's all."

Picking up the discarded rifle, Bartlett added, "Ah, Frenchie, we know how many you have with you tonight." He started to indicate how many and where they might be, but Checker's eyes told him this wasn't the time to elaborate because they didn't know.

Emmett retrieved Jaudon's golden revolvers and Rikor took the remaining handguns and shoved them into his belt.

Looking at the old rancher, Checker said, "A.J. and Rikor will head out the back. A.J., you take the side of the house closest to the barn. Rikor, you've got the other side. Stay out of sight, both of you. Emmett and I will escort Mr. Jaudon to the porch."

Hans Gardner pursed his lips. "What about me, Ranger? What do you want me to do?"

"And me?" Andrew pouted.

Checker turned toward the boys, whose faces were filled with determination. For an instant, the sight of the boys took him back to Dodge City, where he had been forced to flee as a fourteen-year-old, leaving his younger sister with neighbors. Their mother had just died of whooping cough. Neighbors took in Amelia, but young John Checker posed too much of a threat. Pent-up anger at the way his mother had been treated in life by the merciless J. D. McCallister broke loose after his mother's terrible death. The boy had gone to his uncaring father's saloon to confront him and ended up fighting some of his men, wounding one with a knife. A sympathetic prostitute had helped him escape.

He shook his head to drive the memory back.

"We need you two to watch the back door," Checker said.

"Do I get a gun?" Andrew asked

Glancing at Emmett and Rikor, who both nodded approval, the tall Ranger agreed and the older son pulled one of the hideout guns from his waistband and held it for the younger son.

"It's double action, Andrew. You don't have to cock it," Rikor said as the fourteen-year-old took the gun.

"I know. Pa showed me lots of times."

"How about me, do I get a gun?" Hans asked, his eyes bright with eagerness.

Checker shook his head. "No . . . I need you ready to run to the porch and tell us what's happening." He patted the boy on the shoulder. "Watch through the back door, but don't stand where you can be seen. If anyone comes, you hurry back. It won't be A.J. or Rikor."

"Should I shoot if they come?" Andrew asked.

"Yes. Once. Then get away from the door. Ah, take Hammer with you."

The boys beamed with the responsibility given them and

solemnly headed for the back door with the dog trotting obediently between them.

Nodding, Checker turned toward the sullen Jaudon. "If anything goes wrong, Emmett, shoot the Frenchman."

The French outlaw leader walked toward the front door; his eyes avoided looking at anyone. His face was a deep crimson; his ample belly jiggled with the movement. Hatred poured from his eyes and his fists opened and closed to release some of the anger building within him.

Chapter Three

Renewal of the threat straightened the pig-faced man's back and he began to walk stiffly as if precision would fully indicate his desire to comply. A few shadows lined up to support his compliance. Shifting the shotgun to his other hand, Bartlett grabbed the rifle as he and Rikor followed the boys to the back.

A dozen steps later, John Checker, Emmett Gardner and Sil Jaudon stood on the wood-planked front porch that covered the entire front of the ranch house. Four posts supported the overhanging roof, but provided little cover if needed. Shapes moved in the darkness. The Ranger could see two men standing under a thick cottonwood near the edge of the open ranch yard. Others were moving near the barn where he had seen them earlier.

If the Ranger report was correct, Lady Holt—and Jaudon—had at least forty gunmen working for her. Checker guessed there were twenty there tonight. Four were down and three were in the house under control. That left thirteen. If his speculation was right. Being only one off would be enough to cause trouble, though.

Without looking, Checker knew Bartlett had taken a position near the front of the house, crouched behind a scraggly bush. The barn and corrals were to their right. He couldn't see where Rikor was hiding on the other side closest to the shed.

"Rikor, keep your eye on the shed and the trees around it. All right?" Checker said quietly. "I've got the front."

"Got it."

"A.J., there were men around the barn earlier," Checker cautioned. "Most will be coming from that direction, I think. I've got the front. Two are there, for sure."

Bartlett's response was lengthy as usual, pointing out the difficulty of seeing anyone in the shadows around the barn, and wondering if the gunmen Checker had knocked out would be found. Before Bartlett could continue with a meandering speech, Checker told him to watch for movement in the darkness.

"All right, Jaudon, call in your boys," Checker said. "If you say anything I don't understand, I'll assume it's ordering an attack. Make sure nobody is slow coming. If one lags behind, you won't like what happens."

Jaudon's shoulders straightened. "*Vous* are through, Gardner," he finally blurted without looking at him. "Wait an' *vous* vill see. I vill watch *votre* . . . your sorry ass hang. I vill be the one pissin' on *votre* face."

"Emmett, stand behind Jaudon. You know what to do if his men don't come in quietlike."

"Be my pleasure," the old rancher growled. "Got these two fine pistols cocked an' ready."

Remembering his medicine pouch, Checker touched the small lump under his shirt and tunic. Somewhere a wolf cry haunted the land, as if his touch had brought the response. His rational mind told him it was just a coincidence. They had been hearing wolves off and on all day.

Jostling his shoulders to rid the nerves taking over, the

Frenchman called out, "*Venir* . . . come in! Come in! *Venir!* Ve haff them. Ve haff them. Come in. Now. Ve haff much to do." His voice was packed with anger, but he made no attempt to start anything. His fat face was like a red pumpkin.

Across the darkened ranch yard, voices carried Jaudon's relayed command. So far, the others hadn't discovered any of their downed associates. Checker told himself the darkness was helping, but he had dragged them out of the way, too.

Jaudon muttered something French under his breath.

"Remember, I want English when they get closer, Jaudon," Checker said.

Emmett chuckled.

"Keep those pistols out of sight, Emmett."

"They'll be behind me back. A-waitin'."

"Good."

Supportive grunts and calls popped through the night. Dark shapes began to emerge from the blackness and head toward the house. Checker's dark eyes assessed the advancing twosome. "I think the yellow-haired fellow is Whitey Wesson. He's wanted in El Paso. Murder."

"I did not know this," Jaudon volunteered.

"Of course you didn't. You were just hiring boys who were good with ropes, right?"

"Hey, boss! Vince's been coldcocked. Over here, behind this shed!" The cry came from the area where Checker had dragged the unconscious gunman earlier.

Checker froze. He should have expected the reaction. "Jaudon, tell him it's all right. You've got work to do." He jabbed the fat man in the stomach with the butt of his rifle for emphasis.

"Rikor, keep a close watch," Checker cautioned.

"I have him. There is only one."

"Leave heem. Ve vill care for heem later," Jaudon yelled loudly. "It is *bien*. Come on. Ve haff work to do."

"B-but he's hurt. Head's bleeding real bad."

"I said come." Jaudon's voice bit hard into the night.

"Yeah, yeah."

From the other side of the ranch yard, two well-armed men appeared from near the corral and strolled toward the porch. The shorter gunman with an oversized handlebar mustache stopped and squinted.

"Wait, Tapan. That man with the boss. I know him," the gunman gushed. "Saw him in El Paso. Last year, it was. That's John Checker, the Ranger."

"John Checker, damn! What's he doin' here?" Tapan Moore said, his breath coming in short bursts.

"Well, it ain't to help us. Let's get closer and then take him," the short gunman declared softly, "before he knows we're on to him. Remember that sonvabitch is a heller with a gun. Saw him in action in El Paso. Never saw the like. Maybe better'n you—or Luke. Be careful, though. The boss is standing right next to him."

"All right. I'll take Checker an' you get ol' man Gardner. He must be carryin', I reckon." A toothy smile from Tapan Moore followed.

"No, we'd better both take Checker."

"Oh, all right. But I don't like that ol' man."

"You can have him next."

"Sure."

They walked toward the porch, trying to act nonchalant, as the other Jaudon gunmen did the same. Neither saw Bartlett slip behind them at a comfortable distance and check out the barn to determine there were no gunmen waiting. Satisfied, he turned his attention to following the two gunmen.

At the porch, Checker focused on the gunmen sidling

toward them from the cottonwoods. He was glad they didn't look around while they were standing there. The creek where he had dragged the two men earlier was only fifteen feet behind them.

Halting twenty feet from the porch, the gunmen from the barn swung their rifles into position.

"Drop 'em, boys." Bartlett's command was like a lightning bolt out of a clear sky.

Tapan Moore dropped his rifle, jerking his arms into the air as if they were being pulled by unseen strings. The shorter man hesitated, then swung his gun toward Bartlett.

The Ranger's rifle barked twice and the gunman yipped, dropped his gun and went to his knees. The exchange surprised the two gunmen coming from the front and both swung their guns into firing position. Checker's Winchester roared into the night. Three times. Answering fire clipped the porch and one bullet thudded into Checker's left thigh.

Jaudon flinched as Emmett Gardner drove the nose of a revolver into his back. "Better hope this gits dun quick an' ri't, Frenchie."

Waving arms, Jaudon yelled out, "S'arrete! Stop this! Stop this! Come in. These are Rangers. They vill kill me." His face indicated he believed the statement.

From inside the house came Andrew's scared voice. "Pa, there's someone at the back door!" Hans's voice was right behind his older brother's. "Shoot him, Andrew!" Hammer growled as if he were much bigger than he was.

Emmett spun toward the door as two shots cracked into the night. He entered the house to see Rikor standing in the back doorway.

"It's all right, Pa. Rikor got him," Hans said, appearing calmer than his brother.

Andrew's gun was in his hand at his side. It hadn't been fired. He was shaking and close to crying. Both younger sons stood near the tied gunmen, whose expressions were unreadable.

On the floor in front of a grim Rikor was an unmoving body.

The older rancher's shoulders heaved with relief.

"That's the guy who was yellin' from our shed, Pa," Rikor declared, holding his smoking Winchester with both hands. "Watched him curl back to the house—an' followed him. He was the only one over on this side. Where do you want me to go?"

Emmett motioned toward the front window and returned to the porch.

"Did ya miss me, Frenchie?" he growled, jamming Jaudon's pistols into the fat man's back. "John, Rikor got the bastard tryin' to come in our house. Nobody's on that side now. He's at the window. To my right."

"It was his bullets we heard?" Checker said without turning his focus from the ranch yard.

"Yep. Rikor don't miss much."

Slowly, the remaining gunmen came to the porch, all realizing the situation had changed. One of the two gunmen coming from the front was down and not moving; the other held his arm. The curly-headed gunman from the barn left his companion and hurried toward the porch. Bartlett stopped and disarmed the short gunman, telling him in detail that he wasn't hurt badly, that it only was painful.

Checker was bleeding from the upper thigh of his left leg. He recognized the advancing gunman. It was Tapan Moore. The Ranger report had been correct.

The old rancher was the first to notice. "You've been hit, John."

"Yeah, I know."

"You're bleedin', man."

For a vicious moment, Checker saw his father's face in the one of the man advancing. He always realized, without wanting to admit it, that his own face carried much of the same look. Anger snarled within him as the memory barreled through his mind. J. D. McCallister was slapping his mother as she fought to keep him from the tent where they lived.

Once more he saw himself as a small boy diving into this man who was his father, but never admitted it, to save his mother and be beaten bloody himself. The evil man never came to their tent again. Ever. His mother's health deteriorated steadily after the beating and she died from whooping cough a few years later. A fourteen-year-old John Checker blamed his father, the man who never recognized him or his sister as his.

His attempt to kill J. D. McCallister at his saloon resulted in his being chased out of town by McCallister's men, after Checker wounded one with a knife. A sympathetic prostitute had helped him escape. Neighbors took in his eight-year-old sister and raised her. They hadn't seen each other since; he wasn't certain she even lived in Dodge anymore.

The hole in his heart had been filled with hardening as the young man fought his way through life, becoming one of the Rangers' best men, dangerous and fierce.

"John . . . you all right, boy? John?" Emmett's concern and the touch of his hand to Checker's shoulder broke him out of the momentary nightmare.

"Oh. Yeah, I'm all right," Checker said, flinching slightly from the rancher's concern. "That fellow out there, that's Tapan Moore. Heard about him down in El Paso. He's a bad one, Emmett."

Bartlett yelled orders, standing near the fallen short gunman, "Drop your rifles. Unbuckle your handguns. Get rid of those hideaways—before we do it for you. We're Rangers and you're all under arrest."

Chapter Four

An hour later, all of the Jaudon gunmen were tied with Emmett, Rikor and the younger sons standing guard over them in the ranch yard. Even the three gunmen from inside the house were led outside. Moonlight washed across the strange gathering as the captured men muttered and swore. Before going inside, Bartlett pointed out the two most dangerous, Luke Dimitry and Tapan Moore. Both grinned as Emmett agreed.

Only Jaudon was completely silent.

Inside the house, Bartlett brought a surgeon's tool from his saddlebags and began probing Checker's leg for the bullet. The tall Ranger had been reluctant to have the wound cared for, but his partner had assured him that it was necessary they do so now.

A bright orange fire in the fireplace heated the foot-long instrument. It had been used many times over the years, whenever a doctor wasn't close. With Checker stretched out on the kitchen table and his bloody pants pulled down, Bartlett began to probe and root for the embedded piece of lead in his leg. Checker had refused any whiskey, believing he needed to stay alert. Instead, he bit down on a stick while his friend sought the bullet.

Trying to keep from thinking about the jabbing pain, Checker took his watch from his pocket. He popped open the lid and sought the memories within its tiny, cracked photograph of his mother with her two small children. Bartlett glanced up once and smiled grimly; he knew of Checker's sad childhood in Kansas. Taking a deep breath, the gentle lawman squinted and began to probe the bloody cut in Checker's thigh. He had seen this reverie before.

Checker remembered his mother being so proud as she guided them into the photographer's studio. It took a long time for him to accept the fact that she had probably paid for the expensive session with her body. It didn't matter, he told himself. It was the only record that such a family ever existed. Except in his heart. And maybe Amelia's, wherever she was. He let his mind wander again to the awful parting of Amelia, his little sister, and himself. There was no other choice; neighbors were willing to take the girl, but not him. Not with McCallister and his men seeking his head. As the two children said their tearful good-byes, Amelia had sought his promise to return. The neighbors had given him an old brown horse, a sack of food and a silver dollar.

From a jammed-away corner of his mind, his sister came running with tears washing across her face.

"I—I—I want to go with you, Johnny!"

Trying to act stronger than he felt, the boy said, "You can't, sis. But I'll come back for you."

After her insistence, he promised to return for her.

"Say you promise."

"I promise."

As he turned to leave, Amelia asked that he give her something of his to keep until he returned. He had nothing, except the knife in his belt. She had grabbed his shirt and pulled free a button.

That was the last time he saw her.

His trail had taken him east and then south, through all manner of jobs including making money fistfighting, until his skill with a gun took precedence. A short stint as a Yankee sharpshooter. He had even ridden the outlaw trail for a short while before becoming a Ranger. His promise to return to his sister had faded into the place where other broken promises went.

It hurt too much to think long about what might have happened to her.

The pain from Bartlett's probing jerked him back to the table. Checker bit hard on the stick, nearly breaking it, and his Ranger partner held up the piece of lead triumphantly.

"Got it! Got it. John, it didn't hit anything bad, but you'll not be riding for a while—until it heals," Bartlett said, wiping his bloody hands on a towel from his saddlebags.

"No, I'll ride now, A.J. We need to get that bunch to town."

"But—"

"I'll be fine."

Running into the house, Hans brought Checker's wide-brimmed hat, at his father's suggestion. The boy beamed proudly as the tall Ranger thanked him and returned it to his head. The derby remained on the kitchen counter where he put it.

In spite of Bartlett's concern, the two Rangers were soon riding to town. In front of them were Jaudon and his remaining men mounted on their horses. Their hands were tied behind them and each man's saddle horn was connected to the next with rope. Two other men with bloody kerchiefs around their heads rode silently; another had one arm bound in a makeshift sling, but his hands were still tied together. Bartlett had tended to them somewhat. Behind Bartlett and Checker were three horses, each carrying a dead gunman.

Dawn was flirting with their alertness as the Rangers and their prisoners rode into Caisson, Texas. The growing town showed few signs of waking. Except for a well-dressed lawman who immediately left his office and confronted them in the street. It was Sheriff Allison Hangar, who served as the law in both the county and the town.

"What is all this?" Sheriff Hangar demanded.

In his crossed arms was a double-barreled shotgun. His pale, narrow face looked as if it were cut in two by the over-sized mustache. His clothes were freshly pressed and his shirt collar looked new, holding in place a dark silk cravat. Unseen, but obvious, was a gun belt. He was hatless with closely cropped hair.

"These are our prisoners, Sheriff," Checker said, forcing himself to be more alert than he felt. "They are under arrest for the attempted murder of Emmett Gardner and his family."

"Oh, that can't be," Hangar growled.

"Sheriff, we've been riding most of the night," Checker said. "If my partner and I hadn't been there, the Gardners would all be dead by now. Are you questioning my statement—or our authority?"

Sheriff Hangar glanced at Jaudon, who nodded slightly. Checker caught the exchange, but let it go.

"Neither, I reckon," Hangar replied. "There's a drunk in my jail now. I'll let him go an' you can pour this bunch in." He paused. "Guess I'd better fetch Doc—and George, George Likeman, he's the undertaker. Well, he's that and the town cabinetmaker an' a few other things."

Checker motioned toward the two wounded gunmen. "They've already been treated by my partner. But you're welcome to bring the doctor if you wish. The state of Texas will pay for the burials." He rubbed his chin. "But I reckon bounty money is there for, at least, Dimitry and Moore."

At the jail, Bartlett watched his friend dismount. As

usual, Checker's face was unreadable. Bartlett knew his friend was hurting from the wound. Had to be. Checker had struggled with himself about dealing with evil; something within him wanted the evil to go away and leave him with a normal family. And it wouldn't. Evil had a way of transforming everything.

Bartlett unlashed the ropes connecting the riders and began ordering them to dismount, one by one. He liked the precision of the order.

Across the street, a small gathering of townspeople had stopped to watch, uncertain of what had transpired. A well-dressed man in a charcoal-gray suit and a slightly tilted, short-brimmed hat announced they should go over and arrest the two strangers, certainly the town didn't need their kind around, that Jaudon worked for Lady Holt and was a fine, upstanding citizen.

Murmurs of agreement followed, interspersed with brash comments, but no one moved. Especially not the well-dressed man. A frail-looking woman with snow-white hair harrumphed and crossed the street to ask what was happening. Her face went as white as her hair when Checker informed her of the situation. Her chin rose in defiance and she spun to return to the group and relate the details.

The tall Ranger wasn't sure if he should be pleased or concerned.

As she retreated, the sound of peeing reached Checker's ears. In the alley between the jail and a saloon, a silhouette weaved as he attempted to relieve himself. The tall Ranger returned his attention to the arrested men. His leg was throbbing and forcing pain throughout his body. Reacting to it would have to wait; sleep would have to wait. Until Jaudon and his men were safely behind bars. He barely heard the sheriff say they would have to cram the gunmen into the five cells, but Jaudon would have one by himself.

"We're not through, Checker," Tapan Moore yelled, and flashed a wide, toothy smile.

"Another time. Another time."

Standing next to him, the half-breed Dimitry made a slicing motion across his neck with his hand.

Chapter Five

Above them in an apartment over the town bank, a green-eyed woman faced the scene in the street. She didn't like being in town that much, but she wanted to be close when Jaudon brought the news of Gardner's death, trying to escape. She was also looking forward to some special time with Tapan Moore. The sound of horses had awakened her immediately and she watched from the small window, dressed only in her nightgown of deep emerald.

Anger brought her skin to contrast her gown. It was obvious the night had not gone as planned. At first she thought Jaudon had brought Emmett Gardner in for the law to deal with. That wasn't her instruction, but it was all right. A closer look told a different story: Jaudon and his men were bound. Tapan was among them; she grimaced and wanted to blow him a kiss. She recognized one of the dead gunmen draped over a horse as working for her. Two strangers had apparently brought them in. Who could they be?

Moira Holt, or Lady Holt as she insisted being called, told herself to be calm. This was not a time for her well-known temper. She must first learn of the situation. It appeared

Jaudon and his men had been surprised at the Gardner Ranch. Surprised by two men she didn't know. Even from here, she could tell the two were well armed; it looked as though the taller one had been wounded in the leg. She didn't see Emmett Gardner or any of his sons, so either they remained at their ranch or Jaudon's men were successful before these two arrived. She doubted it was the latter.

As she spun away from the window with its green curtains, her mind was whirling with questions that needed answers. The best way to do that was to meet these two strangers. As soon as she had bathed.

Her long red hair cascaded along her shoulders as she walked across the green-walled apartment, dropping her night garments as she walked. Lady Holt was a mature woman, born in Canterbury, England, and given a good education— and one with a fine face and figure, as she often reminded herself. Governor J. R. Citale definitely thought so. Her smile was vicious.

Two hours from town was her ranch headquarters, a stately mansion she had purchased from an old Mexican rancher. She had bought the spread shortly after arriving from New York. Her stay in the East had lasted long enough for her to decide Texas was the place to be. The old man had been shot on his way to town with the money she had given him for the ranch.

No suspects were ever found. Or the money.

That was six years ago. Since then, she had bought five other ranches in the area. In the same way. Only three remained that she was interested in. Emmett Gardner's was the most important because of his water. Charlie Carlson owned another small spread and the third was owned by a young widow, Morgan Peale.

"That old fool has no business owning such land. I can turn it into gold. And power." She stared at the empty room.

"Iva Lee, I can do it. I can own Texas. You know I can. And you'll be with me all the way."

Iva Lee was her long-dead twin sister. Lady Holt often talked to her. Iva Lee was Moira's twin, older by minutes. She died from cholera, when only twelve, back in England. The disease took their parents, too, and Moira grew up in an English house for orphans. During her early teens, it wasn't long before her looks turned into a significant asset as men, young and old, sought her favors. Some of them didn't live long. She left Britain a few steps ahead of the law; a sea captain was enamored with her ways and gave her passage in exchange for herself.

On the way to her dressing table, she touched the painting of a phoenix dominating the north wall. She had been fascinated with the legend of this supernatural bird since she was a child. She knew the story well. A phoenix lived for a thousand years, then built a fire and burned itself up in the flames. Out of the ashes, the creature is reborn to live another thousand years.

She had heard the story first from the man who ran the orphanage. He was a practical man who thought the legend had probably been started when someone saw a large bird, like a crow or raven, dancing in a dying fire. He said it would sit and spread its wings, to enjoy the heat and kill feather mites. But flapping its wings might cause the fire to flame up again and the bird to fly away. Suddenly one had the impression of a bird rising from the flames and ashes. He had been very nice to her, enjoying her young body when he pleased.

She preferred the legend to his explanation and endured his passion as long as necessary. He had been dead ten years, dying in a fire that consumed his estate in London. Before the fire, Moira Holt had stolen the gold and currency kept in the estate—and this painting—deciding the phoenix was her good-luck charm. A slight scar near her right eye served as a physical reminder of her first criminal endeavor.

Since then, like the phoenix, she had been reborn and now owned the biggest ranch in this part of Texas and controlled thousands more acres of grazing land.

Her apartment was stylishly decorated with the latest in French furniture; she owned the building. Slowly she dressed for the day, deciding on having an early breakfast before determining what had gone wrong. Her eighteen-inch corseted waist was something she was quite proud of. A dark green dress with a matching coat that flared at the waist was selected from her wardrobe. Her pale green blouse was buttoned high around her neck. On her lapel, she pinned a small gold bird, a phoenix, she told herself. A dark green hat with a short veil was the last touch.

Methodically, she had used her newly acquired ranch as a base to build her empire. It had been a slow process, quietly pushing her neighbors into forced sales. At the same time, she had supported the new governor in his political goals, providing money, men—and herself. Governor Citale had been eager to return the favors.

"Iva Lee, it won't be long before we truly control Texas. I will be its queen. Yes, the Queen of Texas! The governor is already ours—and the power of his office. Yes, it is!" She spoke evenly, staring at a wall. "It is good you are here with me. I need your strength."

A knock at her door broke her reverie.

"Yes, who is it?"

"Tanner. We've got trouble."

"So I see. Just a minute."

Opening the door, she greeted the well-dressed lawyer tersely. He had watched the arrival of Jaudon's men. Removing his hat, he stepped inside.

"What's our next move?" she asked.

Wilson Tanner wasn't surprised by her blunt approach. No "good morning" or "how are you?" or even "what went wrong?" He had worked with her for five years, representing her interests in all manner of legal concerns. She was smart, thorough and ruthless. Time wouldn't be spent worrying about what had already happened; her focus would be totally on what they could, and should, do next. He loved her for it, but that emotion wasn't returned. Their arrangement was strictly business. Although he had tried and tried.

Removing the thin cigar from his tight mouth, Tanner explained what had happened, as it was related to him by Jaudon, adding that he had gone to the jail immediately, announcing himself as the man's legal counsel. He reminded her that several of her gunmen were in the No. 8 Saloon, as she always stationed them. She owned the saloon, but no one in town knew it. Of course, the task was one of the gang's favorites and volunteers for the task were considerable. Until it was made clear no one was to drink. They were in town to provide any quick reaction.

"I know where my men are, Tanner," she said coldly. "Now is not the time."

"Of course."

"I'm going to have some breakfast," she said, patting her hair to make certain it wasn't disturbed by the introduction of her hat. "You find out when the hearing is scheduled."

"What if the judge hasn't set it yet?"

Her stare made him wish he hadn't said that.

"I'll get it done," he quickly added, glancing at his polished boots and avoiding her gaze.

"Good," she said. "Then ride to the ranch and tell Paulus to drive those rebranded cattle to town. Fast. We'll turn this thing around real quick."

She smiled and it was a wicked grin that caught her eyebrows and cocked them. "Tell Judge Opat to expect a telegram from the governor."

"Citale?"

"Do we have another governor?"

"No, of course not." He returned the cigar to his mouth and his hat to his head, adjusting it to tilt slightly.

"Tell Jaudon his defense remains the same. Exactly the same. This will be the day the Rangers will never forget." Her laugh was more of a snort.

Tanner spun and left.

"Iva Lee, by tomorrow the Rangers will be history." This time her laugh ricocheted around the room.

Chapter Six

Weary Rangers John Checker and A. J. Bartlett walked into the restaurant after seeing Jaudon and his men secured in the jail's cells. Checker's leg was stiff and aching, but he tried not to favor it. A hearing would be set as soon as convenient with Judge Opat, the sheriff advised with little apparent interest in the matter.

They were soon enjoying ham, eggs and potatoes, washed down with hot coffee, when Lady Holt entered the restaurant. Her presence stopped the filled eatery for an instant as men and women throughout the room watched her grand entry.

The restaurant owner rushed to greet and guide her to a table kept exclusively for her use when she was in town. The table was adorned with a green cloth, laced around the edges. She thanked him in French as he helped her into the high-backed chair. A china cup and saucer, filled with fresh coffee, appeared in front of her from a wide-eyed waiter. A second cup and saucer were placed across the table, as she always insisted. No one knew why. A second waiter presented a china cream and sugar set. The china was hers, not the regular restaurant fare.

After ordering, she asked the bushy-headed owner with eyebrows to match about the two men on the far side of the room.

"They're Rangers, Lady Holt," he said, swallowed and added, "Ah, they brought in Mr. Jaudon and his men. Some kind of problem at the Gardner Ranch. A misunderstanding, I am certain."

"I would like to talk with them, please."

"Certainly."

Straightening his narrow shoulders, the owner walked to the table where Checker and Bartlett were finishing their breakfasts. He didn't like being in the middle of this and bit his lower lip to control his anxiety.

"Rangers, Lady Holt would like a word." He rubbed his hands together nervously. "Ah, she's over there. At the green table." He looked away toward the wall. "Lady Holt is . . . a very powerful woman around here."

"Is she, now?" Checker said, cutting his ham.

A. J. Bartlett looked at John Checker, smiled and said, "'A daughter of the gods, divinely tall, and most divinely fair.'"

The owner frowned, not understanding Bartlett's quote from Tennyson's "A Dream of Fair Women."

"Please, sirs. I don't want any trouble . . . with her. Please."

"I'm sure you don't. Tell her we'll come over. After we're through eating."

Checker's eyes indicated there was no need for further discussion.

"Ah, certainly. I will tell her. Certainly."

Checker took another sip of his coffee. "An' bring us some more coffee."

"Oh, certainly, sir. Certainly."

As soon as the excited man left, Bartlett said quietly, "I'm kinda excited about meeting her. What do you think she wants?"

"To warn us."

"Oh yeah. Guess so."

Bartlett started to add more, but the owner returned with a fresh pot of coffee. Both Rangers thanked him and completed their meals in silence. Finished, they stood, dropped coins beside the empty plates and headed for Lady Holt's table.

Checker's leg wouldn't take pressure for a few steps. Finally, he was able to slide it along as he moved the other. He didn't like the adjustment and quickly forced his wounded leg to walk normally.

"Ma'am, you asked to see us?" Checker said, holding his hat in his hand.

"Oh yes, thank you. Please sit down." She motioned with both hands toward the chairs on either side of her intentionally empty chair across from her. A quick flip of her hand brought fresh coffee cups from a nervous waiter. They were her china.

Bartlett started to sit.

"No, thanks, ma'am. We'll stand. Got work to do," Checker spat.

Lady Holt studied Checker appreciatively. "Well, your choice. I was hoping you might be interested in knowing the truth."

"Always interested in the truth." Checker folded his arms.

She grinned. "Good. Then you should know Emmett Gardner is a rustler. He's stolen some of my beef. Under my orders, my men went to bring him in for trial. If you ask the sheriff, you will find they acted under his approval."

Checker shook his head. "No, ma'am, Emmett Gardner isn't a rustler—and you know it. Or should. He's a good man. Working hard to help his sons grow straight and tall. Working hard to make that small ranch pay."

She lifted her coffee cup slowly; her eyes locked on to his.

"Jaudon has been arrested for attempted murder. He and his men," Checker spat. "That is the truth."

Bartlett cocked his head and added, "'Is it so true that second thoughts are best?'"

"Shakespeare?" she asked without taking her eyes off Checker.

"Tennyson, m'lady."

"Oh. Of course."

In an instant, her mouth became a slit; her eyes narrowed. Bartlett thought she looked like a cougar about to pounce. "Have you gentlemen ever heard of a phoenix? It's a wonderful tale of everlasting life." Her voice carried the hint of an English accent.

Bartlett said, "Yes, I have. The story is old. A fictional bird that gets burned up and returns to life. Something like that. Many think it came from seeing a large bird stomping on a dead fire's ashes to warm himself—and causing the old fire to flame again."

"I find it quite comforting. Like Christianity's myths are to others," Holt said.

Both Rangers frowned.

She laughed heartily. "I see I hit a chord. A 'myth' is simply a story that has grown large around some key principle or fact." She studied them for an instant. "Pardon me for saying so, but you gentlemen don't strike me as the churchgoing type."

"What is that type?" Checker said with an edge to his voice.

She changed the subject abruptly. "How much do you make . . . as Rangers? I'll triple it. I need good men." Her eyes measured Checker.

"You have a good day, ma'am." Checker returned his hat to his head and headed for the door, trying not to let his wounded leg be so apparent.

Bartlett joined him as Checker reached the door. Behind them came Lady Holt's now sweet voice. "You take care of that leg wound, Ranger. Texas needs men like you."

Chapter Seven

After seeing the doctor about Checker's leg, the two Rangers wired Captain Temple with a report of the situation, checked into the hotel and immediately went to sleep in separate rooms. Checker was washing up in the late afternoon when the sounds of cattle, being driven down the main street, drew him to the window.

He studied the cattle moving toward the far end of town, toward a corral used for gathering beef for local transactions. He didn't know the men driving them. The brands caught his eye. Each steer was carrying Emmett's brand. He knew what this meant.

The steers would be shown as proof that Emmett Gardner was a rustler! If necessary, one would be killed and skinned to show the original brand underneath. The Phoenix Ranch brand, Lady Holt's.

Dressing quickly, the tall Ranger went to the next room and knocked. Bartlett, too, was already dressed.

"That's real trouble down there, isn't it?" Bartlett said as he opened the door

"Yes. Emmett warned us about Judge Opat and the sheriff,"

Checker said. "Now they'll have all the justification they need to have Emmett arrested."

"And hanged." Bartlett cocked his head.

Checker frowned. "You ride for Emmett's place. Tell him what is happening. Tell him that he and his sons need to get out of there. Go where they can't find them until we can get this cleared up."

"What if he won't go?"

"Stay with him, then. I'll join you as soon as I can."

"I'm on my way. Where are you going?"

"I'm going to make sure no posse starts out there—until you've had time to move."

Bartlett's eyebrows arched.

Behind them, footsteps on the planked stairway caught their attention. A teenage boy in a too-tight shirt was bounding up the stairs two at a time. Catching his breath, he looked at the Rangers and said, "Are you Ranger Checker and Ranger Bartlett?"

"We are, son."

"Got a wire for you from a Captain Temple. Said it was urgent you get it."

Checker reached into his pocket and handed the boy a coin. "Thanks, son, appreciate the fast delivery."

"Yes, sir, that's what Mr. McGraffin insists on."

"Give him our thanks, too."

Checker unfolded the telegram, read it and handed it to Bartlett.

The older Ranger gulped and stammered, "Wh-hat is this? Th-this cannot be. It cannot be."

Tugging on his hat, Checker read the wire again:

RANGERS CHECKER AND BARTLETT . . . STOP . . . GOVERNOR HAS ORDERED ME TO REMOVE YOU AS RANGERS . . . STOP . . . HE

IS NOTIFYING CITIES ACROSS TEXAS OF HIS
DECISION . . . STOP . . . DOES NOT LOOK LIKE
WE CAN STOP THIS MOVE . . . STOP . . . TOO
MUCH POWER . . . STOP . . . APPEARS LADY
HOLT BEHIND THIS . . . STOP . . . SHE CLAIMS
YOU EXCEEDED YOUR AUTHORITY AND ARE
PROTECTING RUSTLERS . . . STOP . . . WATCH
YOURSELVES . . . STOP . . . EXPECT LOCAL
LAW TO TRY TO ARREST YOU . . . STOP . . .
REGRETFULLY CAPTAIN TEMPLE

"That lady makes things happen, doesn't she?" Bartlett
said, shaking his head. "Wonder if the sheriff—and the
judge—know this yet?"

"Of course they do."

Checker's hands went to his gun belt. "We still need to
warn Emmett. You ride. I'll try to delay Hangar and his
posse."

"You think there won't be a hearing?"

"Not one that's going to help."

Bartlett patted his gun belt. "You want to take 'em right
here?"

"No. We've got to let them have the first move. They are
the law. It won't help anything to challenge that right now,"
Checker said.

After seeing his friend ride off from the livery where their
horses were stabled, Checker saddled his own mount, in
case he had to leave town in a hurry. He expected the sheriff, with the judge's support, to release Jaudon and his men—
and deputize them to bring in Emmett Gardner. What
should he do? What could he do? He was certain the two
local authorities would already know the Rangers had been
dismissed.

What would Stands-In-Thunder do? The aging Comanche

war chief had become the father he had never known and the great warrior saw him as a son to replace those lost in war. They had met two years ago when Checker was trying to find a half-breed accused of robbing a bank and suspected of hiding on the Fort Sill reservation. He found the old man, but not the half-breed, and a strong friendship began. Whenever possible, Checker went to visit the old man, both enjoying the company of the other.

Stands-In-Thunder would attack, he told himself. Attack. He rolled his shoulders, took a Colt from his saddlebags and shoved it into his back waistband. Then he pulled the Winchester from its sheath on his saddle. He hurried along the planked sidewalk toward the jail, passing several couples and one whiskered gentleman smoking a pipe, who stopped to watch him after he passed. Coming from the other direction was a harried Sheriff Hangar. Checker guessed he had just left the judge's office.

"Where are you headed, Hangar?" Checker barked.

Checker's voice jolted the lawman from his focused destination. He shuffled his feet and stopped. His hand began an instinctive move toward his belted handgun; then his mind rejected the idea.

"Well, well, look who's here," Sheriff Hangar snorted. "You're just in time to help me let Mr. Jaudon and his men go. Judge Opat ruled they're innocent." His smile indicated a return of his confidence. "Oh, and I've been authorized to deputize them. Your buddy, Emmett Gardner, is wanted for rustling Lady Holt's beef."

"Since when does a judge have a hearing without the prosecution present?" Checker barked, closing the gap between them.

Hangar forced a laugh. "Guess he didn't think it was needed. You see that bunch of steers come in? They're all

Lady Holt's animals your friend stole an' stuck his brand on."

"You know that's a lie, Hangar." Checker's statement was a bullet.

"You callin' me a liar?" Hangar's eyes reddened and his cheeks flinched.

"What do you think I'm calling you?"

Hangar hesitated, unsure of what to do or say. He was certain that to move for his gun was to die.

"Turn around," Checker ordered, "and bring the judge here. Do it now."

Biting his lip, Hangar spun and retreated his steps, yelling over his shoulder, "Won't change nothin'."

Checker watched him go, then strode the remaining yards to the sheriff's office and stepped inside.

"*Sacre Bleu!* What the hell? Where is Hangar?" Sil Jaudon snorted, his heavy jowls shaking with the words.

Without speaking, Checker strolled over to the growling stove where a blackened coffeepot gurgled. He leaned his rifle against the wall, took a cup from the gathering of mismatched cups on the adjacent counter. Looking around, he spotted a rag that had been used as a handle buffer. He poured himself a cupful; a thin line of steam sought freedom. Sipping the hot liquid, he returned to the marshal's desk and leaned against the corner of the well-worn surface as if no one else were in the jail.

"*Vous* vill die, Ranger Checker," Jaudon said. "*Vous* an' that stupid Emmett Gardner. An' that other Ranger."

The men in the other cells watched mostly in silence. Even Jaudon seemed mesmerized by Checker's nonchalant style. Only the curly-headed gunman was unimpressed.

"Hey, Checker, what are you going to do when the judge lets all of us go?" Tapan Moore said, grabbing the cell bars.

"All of us. Think you can stop us? We're gonna pour so much lead into you that you'll draw magnets from the general store." He looked over at Dimitry. "Then this half-breed's gonna scalp you. How 'bout that, Ranger?"

Without responding, Checker drank his coffee, then took out the silver watch from his pocket and flipped open the case lid. On the inside lid was the tiny cracked photograph of a young woman with two small children, a boy and a girl. He shook his head. That was a long time ago. His sister might not even be alive now.

Banter began to come from the other men as their courage propped their words. Finally, Sheriff Hangar banged open the door with Judge Opat a few steps behind him. Checker's rifle was pointed casually at the lawman as he entered.

"Here you go, Checker. Here's the judge."

"Come on, Hangar, get us outta here! You heard the judge before," Tapan commanded.

Other voices joined his declaration.

"What is this crap?" Judge Opat snarled. "I already ruled on this. They're innocent, protecting their own property. I issued a warrant for Emmett Gardner's arrest. For rustling."

Checker thought the skinny magistrate looked like a rooster with his narrow, curved nose. A lock of brown hair even perched on his head like a rooster's comb. His too-big suit coat made his thin frame look more so.

The tall Ranger kept his rifle pointed at Hangar, but his attention moved to the judge. "Interesting decision, Judge. You didn't hear the testimony of the two lawmen who brought them in. How convenient."

"Didn't need to. I saw them steers. Outside in the corral," Opat declared, raising his chin defiantly.

Checker described the rebranding. The original Lady Holt brand was a symbolic fire, a jagged line with an *H* above it.

Most called it the "fire brand." In quiet circles, it was referred to as the "hell brand." The rebranding to look like Emmett's mark was as good as possible. The "fire" had been blurred over. Above it was a single line. The *H* had been turned into the *EG* with the backward *E* covering the *H* as best it could to represent Gardner's Bar EG.

"In the first place, did you ask Mr. Gardner if he had a bill of sale for those animals?" Checker asked.

"No, I—"

"Wouldn't a real judge do that? Did you look at the brands at all? Do you think anyone could see those altered brands and think they weren't changed? Did you ask where these steers were found? Were they bunched together? Do you think it makes any sense that a small rancher would take on the most powerful rancher in the region? Why did Holt's men take this long to bring those cattle in? Why didn't they come to the sheriff here first?" Checker's questions were strung together like a Gatling gun in full fire.

"A sorry excuse for a judge you are, Opat," Checker concluded.

"You don't have any authority, Checker," Opat shouted. "Or haven't you heard? Governor Citale just had you and your partner dropped as Rangers. Good riddance, I'd say."

"All the authority I need is in this gun."

Hangar froze.

Opat licked his lips and folded his arms. His face narrowed and his eyes sought Checker's. "Matter of fact, you're under arrest, Checker. For the murder of three innocent men last night. You an' that partner of yours."

From the cells came an outburst of laughter.

"*Au revoir*, John Checker," Jaudon spat. "I cut out *votre* eyes when I see *vous* next."

Checker said, "You bring in real law an' we'll give ourselves up to him. But not to you. Or Hangar." He stared at

Jaudon. "Jaudon, you talk better than you do. I'd be careful of that." He motioned with his gun toward the far cell. "I want both of you in there. Hangar, get rid of your gun belt. Judge, take that derringer out of your pocket."

"What! How'd you? You can't do this. I'm the law in this town," Opat snorted, and withdrew the small gun and laid it on the desk. "Me an' Hangar."

"No, you're not. Lady Holt is—and you're dancing to any tune she happens to play. I feel sorry for you, Opat," Checker said, watching Hangar unbuckle his gun belt and let it slide to the floor.

At the doorway, Checker turned back to the cells. "Now you listen. All of you. We're no longer Rangers, so we don't have to bring you in alive. You come after our friend Emmett and you're going to die."

Chapter Eight

John Checker rode hard toward Emmett Gardner's ranch. Behind his bay was a sturdy packhorse carrying a load of supplies and ammunition. The general store owner had been helpful, but careful no one from Lady Holt's ranch was close when he was. Checker's mind was whirling with what they must do. Now they didn't even have the law of Texas riding with them. They were outlaws.

Outlaws. He had been on that side once. A long time ago. When he was a young man riding with the burn of Dodge City in his heart. But that was a long time ago and Texas had held his loyalty—and his gun—since then.

Now? Swirls of childhood memory worked across his mind. His real father had been a gang leader with a disreputable saloon in Dodge, a corrupt man who took what he wanted, when he wanted it. J. D. McCallister had two legitimate sons, Starrett and Blue. The evil man's blood ran through Checker's veins even though the man wanted no part of him or his sister. Maybe that's all Checker was, really. Maybe he was nothing more than McCallister's blood and the evil man's temper boiled easily within him.

He shook his head to clear it. He was a Texas Ranger. A

good one. A proud one. He would act like one, even if the governor had fired the two Rangers. His mind slid to Lady Holt; she was older than he was, but she was very attractive. To any man. More importantly, she was powerful. Powerful enough to get the governor to have them dismissed as Rangers. Just like that.

Easing his horse into a smooth lope, he followed the narrow stream that led toward Emmett Gardner's ranch and tried to think of their next strategy. Emmett had been right about the judge—and the sheriff. Still, what the two Rangers had done was the right thing, bringing Jaudon and his men into town to stand trial. That was the way they were trained, use the local law whenever possible.

Would he stand trial for murder?

No. He would not give himself up to Hangar or Opat. Or anyone else under Lady Holt's control. Not even the governor. Citale was a cheat. A weak man swayed by any sign of power. Or money. But that didn't matter now. The only thing that mattered was helping their friend. He was certain Emmett wouldn't leave his home. The old rancher would choose to stand and fight. Lady Holt would count on that.

"Emmett needs to do what she doesn't expect," he muttered to himself, and surveyed the plains ahead.

His horse's ears twitched to determine if the words had significance to his performance.

"Sorry, boy, I was just jabbering to myself." Checker patted the horse's neck and the animal refocused on the trail.

It was good grazing land with long gramma grass. Dark cattle pockmarked the green as far as he could see. It was land worth fighting for—and dying for, if it came to that. Lady Holt had already made it clear she favored the latter—for his friend and anyone else who got in her way. Rumors were sliding across the region that she intended to fence in her land with that new Glidden's fence; "the Devil's hat-band," some called it. Barbed wire.

Overhead, the sun was losing its fight with the sky and three brave stars had already slid into the north sky. To his left he could see a small pond shimmering yet from the weakened sunlight. Shadows were gathering around the water to celebrate.

Checker reached into his pocket and felt for the small white stone he knew was there. His fingers curled around it and he smiled. It had been a gift from Stands-In-Thunder. A rock, the old man said, that carried much power. If one listened closely. Checker had always brought tobacco, cloth and a fine hunting knife as gifts when he visited the Fort Sill reservation. The old war chief had proudly given him the white stone, a war club and the medicine pouch Checker wore.

He rubbed the medicine stone with his fingers. "I need you to talk to me."

After a few seconds, he released his grip. Stands-In-Thunder had told him the stone talked to only a few, and the song came directly to the warrior's heart. But the more he rode, the more waiting for Jaudon and his men to attack didn't make sense. Maybe that was the song he sought.

He had bought Emmett some time and they had to use it wisely.

First, with the imprisonment. But that would last only until someone heard them yelling.

Second, his warning would make them wary. Maybe make some of the gunmen decide to ride on. The end result, though, would be a larger force coming at them. Lady Holt would supplement Jaudon's men with more gunmen or more of her regular cowhands.

What if the governor ordered in Rangers? He wouldn't put it past him. But that would take time. The closest Rangers, he thought, were working along the border under

Captain Temple's direction. Would their Ranger friends actually take action against them? What if she was able to secure federal troops?

He rode without paying attention to the trail or its surroundings. It was unlike him, but his thoughts were on what they were up against. His mind acknowledged he was lonely and had been since he was forced to flee Dodge City as a boy. A few years ago, he had bought a house for a widow and her two small children because they reminded him of his own childhood. He was not interested in the woman—as a woman. Only as a mother who needed help and he had the means to do so. His fellow Rangers couldn't figure it out; Bartlett knew without asking.

Maybe his own loneliness made it so important to see Emmett and his boys secure. That and the fact that he hated the kind of corrupt power seeking to consume them. Maybe his loneliness made him a better Ranger. Maybe.

With a shrug of his shoulders, he realized he was closing in on a buckboard ahead. The driver had the two-horse team trotting well. From the looks of the wagon bed, it was nearly filled with supplies. The driver was a young woman with a determined look on her face. Her range clothes couldn't conceal her figure. A wide-brimmed hat concealed most of her face, except for long brown hair.

His gaze shifted to the older black man riding a paint horse alongside the rear of the wagon. Gray had worked its way into the black hair visible under a weathered hat. He was heavily armed. At the rider's left hip was a short-barreled Colt, holstered for right-handed use. A longer-barreled revolver rested in a saddle holster in front of his leg. A double-barreled shotgun hung from his saddle horn by a leather strap.

Their eyes met briefly. Checker knew the man from years ago. London Fiss. He'd done a prison term for robbing banks and stagecoaches. Checker had been one of the lawmen who brought him to justice. What was Fiss doing with this young woman? Riding bodyguard? Did she know who he was? Her father might have seen the need for Fiss, especially now. Why did he not want to say her husband saw the need?

Swinging easily around the wagon, Checker pulled alongside the wagon and touched his hand to his hat brim. She glanced at him, dark eyes investigating his hard face, then returning to her horses. Fiss tensed. Checker nodded a greeting and the black gunfighter returned it and almost smiled.

The Ranger galloped on, pulling on the lead rope of the packhorse. His mind returned to the woman for a few moments. She was quite beautiful, in spite of her frown. She must be headed for one of the other small ranches in the area. The wagon turned east and headed down that trail. A string of dust followed. He rode on, watching her.

She turned to look at him and smiled. He returned the smile without looking at the black man.

Who was she? he wondered as he nudged his horse into a hard run.

Chapter Nine

After Checker rode on, the buckboard and its outrider continued in silence for several minutes. Finally, Morgan turned toward the black gunman.

"You know him, don't you?"

Fiss nodded without looking at her.

She wasn't satisfied and reined the wagon to an abrupt halt. Fading sunlight sought her face; bright eyes sought the black man's face.

He grinned and knew they weren't going any farther until he shared more. He eased his horse alongside the wagon seat and reined it to a stop. She had hired him only after he made clear she knew of his past. As the problems with Lady Holt had increased, Morgan relied on his protection more and more—and sought his counsel often as well. Her husband had been killed from a kick in the head by a horse he was breaking. She had held the ranch together by sheer grit.

"Mrs. Peale, he is John Checker. A Ranger. One of the best. Not a man to mess with." Fiss ran his fingers along the butt of the hanging shotgun. "He's the one who brought me in."

"You hate him, then."

"Suppose I should. But there were a lot of lawmen closing in on me." He looked away. "I was cornered. In a tiny adobe hut. Checker told the others to wait a quarter mile back and he came in alone." The black man licked his lower lip. "He rode up to the door. No gun in his hand. Reined up, leaned forward and said, 'Awful hot. Too hot for a gun battle. What say you ride back to town? With me. You'll be safe. You have my word.'"

Her face was a question as Fiss continued. He surrendered and they rode back to the posse. Checker made it clear to the waiting lawmen that the black man was not to be harmed. A wild-eyed deputy pulled a gun, yelling Fiss had taken his family's money from the bank.

"Checker drew on him, faster than you could hiccup. Made the deputy drop his gun—and nobody tried anything after that. Rode into town real peaceful-like. He and the Rangers stood guard until the district judge came in."

"Why do you think he did that?" she asked.

Fiss told her about a small boy getting away from his mother and running in front of him as he escaped from the bank robbery. He swerved his horse out of the toddler's way, stopped and went back. He reached down and pulled the boy onto his saddle. Then he rode over to the distraught woman and handed off her crying child.

"Checker heard about it. Told me so. Thought I could be trusted—and deserved a break. He made sure the judge heard that story, too."

"Interesting man," Morgan said. "Wonder if he'll stick around?" She snapped the reins and the wagon moved again.

Chapter Ten

Nightfall wasn't too far away. As he entered the ranch yard, Checker saw a silhouette on the barn roof.

He waved.

A slim figure waved back. It was Rikor. A smart location for the young sharpshooter, Checker thought. The young man was as steady and brave as his parents.

Reining up, he yelled, "Emmett! A.J., what's for supper?"

Emmett stepped into the doorway, holding a Sharps .50 buffalo gun that would tear a man apart. He patted the gun and smiled.

"How long we got, John, 'til they come?" Bartlett appeared from his position on the west side of the house. In his hands was another Sharps carbine.

Checker swung down, wrapped the reins and the lead rope around the hitching rack near the front porch and told him what had happened without directly answering Bartlett's question. Hammer barked his greeting and Checker gave him the attention he wanted.

The two young boys were setting the table and talking as if it were an ordinary day.

"John, there ain't no way I branded them beeves," Emmett

declared. "Hell, a greenhorn could see a smoke-over like that a mile away." He shook his head. "Guess it don't really matter. That she-devil's got her cap set for my place—an' that's that."

"I know you didn't steal her cattle, you old cougar. If you want, I could try to negotiate a sale," Checker said, studying the rancher's wrinkled face.

"What? Are you tryin' to insult me?"

Checker pushed his hat back on his head. "No, Emmett. I'm trying to do whatever you want to do. It's your place."

"Right. That's what it is. My place. Me an' my boys. We ain't movin'." He patted the rifle again. "My Almina's buried hyar, by God. A.J. told me what ya said. That we should run. I cain't do that, John."

Checker nodded. "Figured you'd say that."

"Come on in," Emmett said. "Got supper near ready. Ain't much, but it's fillin'." He motioned toward the packhorse. "What ar' ya carryin'?"

"Food. Bullets. Thought they might come in handy."

Emmett grinned. "We'll give 'em what-fer. Rikor's up on the barn roof an' he can see if they start a-comin'—from anywhere."

Bartlett bit his lip and asked again, "When do you expect them, John?"

Checker hitched his heavy gun belt and said there was no way to know for certain. They could come right away. They could wait until they had reinforcements. He thought the latter was most likely, guessing Jaudon's men would be reluctant to face them this soon. Without a pause, he said there was a real possibility that Rangers or troops would join the effort. Or both. Lady Holt had that kind of pull with the governor, he thought.

Emmett and Bartlett were stunned at the likelihood of Rangers being involved, or cavalry. Neither had thought of that.

"My God, you don't think Rangers would come at us, do you, John? Not really?" Bartlett asked. He rolled his shoulders to let the tension escape.

"I wouldn't put it past her, A.J. All she has to do is convince the governor that it's the right thing to do," Checker said, and added, "You know Citale."

The studious lawman stared at Checker without speaking. "That would mean we'd be shooting at . . . our friends."

"That's what it would mean," Checker said. "And they would be shooting back."

"They might refuse."

"Might. Then they would be fired. Like us."

"Damn!"

"Yeah."

Emmett looked at both men. They were longtime friends. "Hey, I don't expect you boys to do nothin' like that. You've already done a bunch. We'd never made it through last night without you showin' up." His shoulders rose and fell. "That devil Englishwoman got the governor to take away your badges. That's more'n anyone should have to pay. On my account. You boys ride back an' patch things up. We'll get along. Honest."

"Now you're trying to insult us, Emmett," Checker said, and placed a hand on the rancher's shoulder. "We're here—and we're staying."

Emmett Gardner looked away for a moment. "Let's eat, and then I'll change places with Rikor, so he kin git some chow. He'll be wantin' to hear what's up."

They walked inside and the two boys eagerly greeted the tall Ranger and he returned their enthusiasm.

"Are they comin' back?" Andrew asked.

Checker studied the boy. He deserved more than a fairy tale. "Yes, Andrew. They'll be comin' back."

"Figured." The boy looked down at his well-worn boots, then back into Checker's face. "I can shoot."

Checker patted him on the shoulder, then Hans's shoulder.

Hans looked up. "I can fight, too, sir."

"I know you both can."

Emmett joined them and changed the subject to eating. They ate in silence as most western men did. Downing a venison stew, biscuits and coffee. The boys drank milk, fresh from their milk cows in the barn. Hammer enjoyed some leftovers in his bowl in the corner.

When they were finished, Checker said, "When I was coming here, I passed a fine-looking woman. She turned off. West."

"That'd be Morgan Peale. Owns a little spread just on the far side of my pond," Emmett said, savoring the last of his coffee. "She's a widow. Real looker, she be. But tough as old leather. Kept that ranch a-goin' after her man was killed. Hoss kicked him. Two years back, it were." He took another sip. "We try to help out when we can. You know, spring roundup an' such. Charlie Carlson over north o' hyar, he does, too."

"A.J., she's got London Fiss riding for her," Checker said.

Bartlett looked puzzled. "Wonder if she knows?"

To Emmett's question, Checker explained Fiss had done time in prison for robbing banks and stagecoaches. The old rancher watched the Ranger closely as he spoke, then added, "You like that black man, don't you?"

"Yeah, I do."

"Any riders workin' for you right now?" Bartlett changed the subject; his interest was obvious.

"No. Not now. I always hire short riders when we need 'em. Can't afford no regulars. Not yet anyway. She's got Fiss.

Charlie's got a few." He looked around the table. "'Sides that, I'm growin' my own."

Both boys smiled and agreed.

"We work our beeves nice an' slow. No need for them to wander. Good grass. Good water." Emmett grimaced. "That's why that devil woman wants our place. She'll be after the others soon as we go down."

"Got an idea I want you to chew on, Emmett," Checker said, and pushed his chair away from the table. "But it's one we'd have to act on quickly."

"Well, I'll sure listen. Andrew, ya call in Rikor, an' stand lookout. Would ya do that, son. Shoot in the air if'n ya see anybody comin'."

"Yes, sir."

The three men walked into the main room and Checker outlined what had been forming in his mind. It was the same idea, but with more reasoning behind it. Waiting for Lady Holt to attack—in whatever way she decided—was not what they should do. Instead, they should leave. It would mean leaving the ranch and herd unguarded and accepting that the buildings would probably be burned. He thought the cattle would remain where they were; there was no advantage in moving them at this time. If they stayed here to protect the ranch, they would eventually be killed. All of them.

Emmett shook his head. "Worked awful hard to build this place." He looked around the room. "Lot o' memories here."

"I know, Emmett. But we can rebuild it when this is over—an' make a lot more memories," Checker said. "First, though, we need to move the boys to a place safe. Away from here. Until we can figure out how to win this thing." He glanced outside. "Thought about asking Mrs. Peale to watch them for a while. But I don't think it would be right. That might bring her trouble."

Bartlett settled into a big chair that had once been blue and was now mostly gray. He said nothing. Waiting.

"We'll take 'em to Rule Cordell. He's my nephew, you know. On my sister's side," Emmett declared, jutting his chin out in determination.

It was obvious he had agreed to Checker's plan, in spite of his earlier statements. "Lives over in Clark Springs. Him an' his wife. Raises horses. Does some fine preachin' on the side. Or did. Think he's outta that now." He rubbed his unshaven chin. "His pappy were my sister's husband. Cruel sonvabitch. A preacher, but I don't think he knew much about God. Not really. Beat Rule somethin' awful when he was a young'un. My sister left him finally. Ran off with a farmer."

"Didn't Rule ride with Johnny Cat Carlson's outfit after the war?" Bartlett said, sitting up in his chair. "Thought he was dead."

"So did the rest of Texas fer a piece. But he's mighty alive and well. He gave all that up. Years back." Emmett rubbed his chin. "Well, there was a mean spell there after the war. Captain Padgett and his Regulators went after friends o' his'n." He chuckled and shook his head. "That brought out the old Rule Cordell. That's when he took down that Lion David Graham feller." He shook his head again. "Governor gave him clemency a year or so ago. Not that clown Citale, but the feller previous."

"Howard Short."

"Yah."

Both Rangers nodded. The Rangers had been disbanded after the conflict and the state police, Regulators, created by General Sherman's appointed governor. Sherman had a force along the Rio Grande to assist in keeping Texans from resuming the fight. Rule Cordell's name had been one tossed around with King Fisher, Clay Allison, Lion David Graham, Ben Thompson, John Wesley Hardin—and John Checker.

"Didn't I hear where he created this fake battalion that stopped a sneak Union advance? In Virginia. Near the end." Checker rubbed his chin. "Seems to me, he and a few others were on a scouting patrol when they came across a Union force, Humphrey's Two, heading right for the Confederates' open flank. Hill's Third. Boydon Plank Road, it was. The way I heard it, Rule saved them from being surprised. Probably kept them being overrun."

"Yeah. That's Rule. Made one o' them empty Rebel breast-works look like it was full o' soldjurs an' ready fer a fight. Even created cannons outta tree trunks. Made it to look like they was a-firin'. All kinds o' stuff that wasn't real. Scarecrow soldjurs. Set up a way to fire a bunch o' guns at the same time."

Emmett grinned and continued. "Hid sacks o' powder to blow up . . . an' put some sacks with cannonballs that were left behind. Put 'em up in the pine trees whar them Union boys were a-comin' through. Ya know, so's Rule an' his friends could shoot 'em down an' make it look like they was a-firin' cannon." He chuckled. "Fooled 'em somethin' fierce an' gave the boys in gray time to stop 'em cold."

Nodding appreciation for the strategy, Checker glanced at Bartlett and cocked his head. "We should go tonight, Emmett. Soon as it's dark."

Rikor come into the house and the three men turned to watch. The oldest Gardner son reminded both of Emmett's late wife. His young face was determined, but strong; his blue eyes sought understanding.

"Rikor, it's good to see you again. You're quite the young man," Checker said, and held out his hand. "Wish the reason was different."

"Everything quiet up on that roof?" Bartlett said with a forced grin.

"Yeah. Only Ranger Checker coming in." The young man returned the handshakes. "When are they coming?"

Emmett told his son about the situation and Checker's idea.

Rikor looked around the room. "We can rebuild, Pa. But it's your call."

"No, son, it ain't. We're in this together." Emmett frowned. "What do you think about taking the boys an' leaving 'em with Rule?"

Glancing at both Rangers, Rikor said, "Maybe Uncle Rule'll help us, too. One of these days, we're going to have to stop that awful woman. We can't just keep walking around her."

"Maybe. You go in an' git somethin' to eat. Then we'll pack the wagon."

"Sure." Rikor walked into the other room and sat down at the table.

"You've got three sons to really be proud of, Emmett," Checker said, ignoring the oldest son's comment about Lady Holt. "They're going to do good things."

"If'n they get the chance." The rancher's mind drew into a hard line.

"They will, Emmett. They will." Checker crossed his arms to reinforce his thought.

Turning toward the dining table, Emmett said, "I reckon the boys'll want to ride alongside the wagon. Think that's all right?"

"Sure. Do we have to cross Holt land?" Checker said.

Emmett closed his eyes for a moment as if thinking through the route. "Yah, the fastest way'll go across her land."

"So, how do we win this, John?" Bartlett asked, his mind on Checker's earlier statement.

"Good question. Stir up enough trouble that a real judge—and real justice—are brought in." Checker moved to the corner table where a small framed photograph of Emmett and his late wife posed for their wedding day. "Probably . . . we're going to have to get rid of Lady Holt."

"You mean killing her?" Bartlett raised himself halfway in the chair.

Checker stared at him without seeing and didn't answer. "Right now, we need to buy time. We can figure the rest later."

Bartlett knew his friend had no intention of answering his question.

"We could be across her land in two hours, John. It's just a corner piece." Emmett added, "Should be at Rule's by noon or so, I reckon."

Chapter Eleven

An hour after Checker rode out of town, Sil Jaudon was in Lady Holt's apartment. The shouts of the jailed men had finally brought curious townsmen. His face was a red ball of crimson. Outside on the street, his men were saddled and ready to ride. He sat at a small table where she had directed his presence. In his hands was his hat with one brim pinned to its crown.

"*Je suis desole*, Madame . . . ah, I am sorry," he spat. "I will bring back ze heads of theez Rangers—and ze old rancher."

"You didn't do so well the first time." Lady Holt's eyes almost snickered.

"*Oui*, that was so. They were cunning. Surprised us. That will not happen again," Jaudon said, his face draining of its color. "*S'il vous plait*. . . . Ah, please, let us do our job. Is that not *tres bien?*"

She stood, walked to the window and stared into the street. Dusk was taking over the day. "I thought the idea was for you to surprise them. Here's what you're going to do." She spoke without turning around.

"Madame, but I—I want to bring *vous* . . . theez treasure. Theez rich land. *Merci.*"

She turned toward him and the soft light from outside hovered about her shoulders. "I know you do, Sil. And I have great confidence that you will." A smooth smile matched her sparkling eyes. "But when you ride, you will lead the Rangers as their captain. It is perfect."

Jaudon's shaved eyebrows tightened over his eyes. "*Sacre bleu, vous* cannot mean this."

"You doubt my word, Sil?"

"I do not understand, Madame." He shifted his wide rear in the chair, deciding it was sturdy enough to support him. His hat fell off his lap, but he dared not try to lean over and retrieve it.

Haughtily, she explained that she wanted Jaudon to send his remaining gunmen to watch the Gardner Ranch. They were to spread out and keep them bottled up, but not attempt to attack. She expected the two Rangers and the Gardner family to be waiting for their advance.

. She walked to the table where he sat and put her arm on his shoulder. "Sil, we shall have some brandy. To celebrate my wonderful idea. Then you go find Tanner. He will know how to contact the governor."

Jaudon licked his lips. "*Je comprends.* I salute *vous*, Madame."

"This will be the end of the Rangers," she said, walking toward a cabinet. "Their captain will refuse to ride against these two." She withdrew a filled glass decanter and two glasses. "The governor will have no choice but to fire him."

"*S'il vous plait*, but they will only replace him with another Ranger."

She smiled. It was a wicked smile.

"Ah, no, Sil. The governor will pick you." She filled the glasses and handed him one.

"*Merci beau coup!* Captain Jaudon," he said with his eyes sparkling. "*Oui*, Captain Jaudon has a nice ring to it."

She went on to explain Jaudon would then be able to pick his own men as Rangers to ride with him—and that he would likely want to add a few good guns to replace the men killed.

He stood and bowed as deeply as his thick waist would allow. "Madame Holt, I bow to *votre* . . . your brilliance."

They clinked glasses and downed the brandy.

Jaudon laid the glass on the table and then returned to the earlier subject. "Am I to assume Eleven Meade is to be one of my Rangers?"

"No. That would be too much to ask of the governor. Even I have limits," she said, and smiled. "His job will be to take care of this John Checker, the Ranger."

"I want to do that."

She smiled. "Of course you do." She stood and walked to the window again. "When he is dead, you can piss on his body."

Jaudon's eyes flashed. "You do not think I am good enough to take him?"

Turning from the window, Lady Holt snarled, "If I did, do you think I would have said what I just said?"

"*Non. Non.*" Jaudon waved his fat arms in front of him. "Pardon, Madame, I was just trying to help . . . you." He swallowed his reaction and added, "You know, he is so strange, Madame. Always with ze white cat. It is . . . not natural."

"Eleven Meade is a killer. For now, he is my killer." She flitted her eyes. "Do not feel badly, Sil. I do not think Tapan or Luke could kill him, either."

"*Oui*," he said, shook his head and asked, "How did Eleven get such a strange name? Is it . . . how you say, ze nickname?"

She refilled their glasses, took hers and sipped it this time.

"No, it's his real name," she said. "He told me his mother was into astrology—and numerology. The number eleven is, ah, the master number, the symbol of the light within us. Very spiritual stuff."

Jaudon shook his head. "What's he say about all theez?"

"That his mother was a fool. A much better name would have been Harold." She leaned over and picked up his hat and handed it to him.

Chapter Twelve

False dawn was filled with the sounds of creaking saddle leather and snorting horses as Emmett Gardner, his sons and the two Rangers moved east toward Clark Springs. The old rancher drove the loaded buckboard with the milk cow and Checker's packhorse tied behind it, moving east.

With a rifle across his saddle, Rikor rode the point, knowing the land. The two other boys rode flank on one side of the wagon; Bartlett and Checker rode drag, pushing the handful of Emmett's horses.

As expected, leaving the house had been teary for the two smallest children. Each got to bring along his favorite treasure; Andrew had a small frog in his coat pocket; Hans carried a cigar box filled with rocks and a few marbles. In the wagon seat, alongside Emmett Gardner, was Hammer. Beside the sleeping dog was a yellow cat.

All of the family were solemn; all were fighting the lack of sleep. They had left behind everything that was home. When they left, Emmett tried to remind them that home was wherever they all were. Together. The old man choked when he spoke, then said they had to be brave.

On the ridge to their left, the figures of three riders appeared in the night sky, then vanished.

Checker nudged his horse and galloped beside Emmett in the wagon.

"That's trouble. Most likely it's Holt riders. Coming after us."

"Yeah, we're 'bout halfway across't their land," Emmett said.

"I'm going to ride toward them," Checker said. "I'll try to keep them away from you. And busy."

Bartlett rode alongside him. "What's up, John? I saw the riders. The lady's boys, I'm sure."

"Just told Emmett the same. I'm going to ride that way. Discourage them from trying to stop us."

"I'll go with you."

"No, A.J. If they get past me, your gun will be needed," Checker said, and turned in the saddle toward the wagon. "Emmett, push through the Holt land fast. We don't want to get boxed in there."

"We won't, John," Emmett said, licked his lower lip and added, "You be careful."

"Sure."

Checker spun his horse and rode first to Rikor to inform him, then galloped toward the ridge. He wasn't certain what he would do at this point. All he knew for sure was that he needed to delay them. At least until they crossed Lady Holt's land. If he could turn them around or put them afoot, that would be perfect. He pulled his Winchester free of its special saddle horn sheath and cocked it. There was a reassurance in the *click-click*.

If he was right, the riders had come to the house, discovered it empty and begun trailing them. It wouldn't have been difficult, even at night.

Ahead was a long ridge composed of boulders, trees and

weary buffalo grass. On its far side was a stream that stayed strong most of the year. He guessed the riders would follow the stream and attempt to get in front of Emmett's family before showing themselves. Getting close enough would require his being skylined for a minute when he crossed the top, but he didn't see any other way.

He nudged his horse into a lope over and down the other side and onto an Indian pony crossing, narrow but defined, separating the higher bank to his right from loose gravel and rocks to his left. Nearby a mockingbird made fun of the world. In the uneven morning light, he could make out six riders ahead. They were concentrating on the trail in front of him and didn't see his approach. None looked like Sil Jaudon. Or Tapan Moore. Checker guessed the fat man wouldn't care too much for riding a horse—or the horse, either, for that matter. He didn't have any idea why Tapan wasn't with them.

Luke Dimitry! He was one of the six. The wild half-breed was riding on the farthest side of the group, probably acting as the scout.

They were following the stream and the ridge toward where they assumed Emmett and his family were headed. He reined up, kicked his right leg over the saddle and eased to the uneven ground. Pain shot through his left leg and he knew it would be difficult to run. Getting too close would only expose him to six against one. A large rock outcropping with two hearty pines guarding the projection would serve well to cover his horse.

He tied the reins to a low branch using a one-pull hitch. A swift getaway would be likely, especially when he wasn't likely to get there fast. Clucking its annoyance, a prairie sparrow scurried away from the thick brush around the trees. A shoot-out against six gunmen wasn't anybody's idea of a good time. But he needed to delay them and give Emmett and the others time to push across Holt land.

He was counting on the fact that they wouldn't be expecting anyone to be *trailing them*. Studying the ground near and below him, he decided on three moves to give the illusion of multiple shooters in the grayness of the new day. But he had to take into account that his wounded leg was stiff and unlikely to respond well.

Adjusting himself into position behind a bump in the ridge, he kept his leg straightened to help silence the painful throbbing. His first three shots with his Winchester intentionally cleared their heads by several feet; a fourth spat at a boulder ten feet from the first rider. Their reaction was what he had hoped for; they jumped from their horses and sought cover among the ridge's welcoming boulders.

Overhead storm clouds were waiting for an opportunity to take over the sky. He guessed rain was only hours away. It would mean Emmett and his sons would be caught out in it, but there wasn't anything he could do about that. However, if he was lucky, he could stop the six riders from reaching them. Or at least delay them long enough; it wouldn't matter.

Now he would shoot to stop them. They had been sufficiently warned. One of the hidden riders groaned as his exposed arm and shoulder became Checker's target. Another stood to fire and Checker's bullet stopped his intent. The Ranger decided to shift to his next position, about twenty feet higher, and try to get their horses running. Likely, one of the riders was holding the reins of all of the mounts. It was a typical cavalry tactic. Crouching, he ran as best he could to the fairly secure position behind a large cottonwood. His leg ached, but he ignored it. The new angle was what he had hoped for. He could see enough of the rider holding the horses to get a good shot at him.

Four shooters were concentrating their bullets on where he had been. He shoved new loads into his rifle, took aim and levered five quick shots. The first caught the man holding the horses in the arm; he yipped and grabbed it, letting go of the collected reins. The second pushed him to the ground and the third caught the saddle horn of the closest horse.

The fourth and fifth spat at the ground around the six animals. The horses snorted and reared.

Dimitry spun toward the wild-eyed horses, but Checker's clipped shots returned him to cover as the animals shook themselves and ran. The other gunmen were silent, keeping out of sight.

Time to move again.

He looked down at the crumbling rock shale beneath his boots. Assessing his footing. His next position would be closer to his own horse, then away. A first step didn't hold and he slid a foot in the loose rock. A rifle shot sang over the top of his left shoulder. Instant pain grabbed his lower back and he almost dropped his Winchester from his left hand.

From behind him! The shots came from behind him!

A shot, from the direction of the riders, grazed his arm as he scrambled to return to his horse. He was caught in a cross fire. How foolish to assume all the riders were together.

If he stopped, he was dead.

He half ran, half stumbled back, firing his pistol with his right hand wildly in the direction of the new shooter. Enough to give him some time. He didn't dare hesitate long enough to fire his rifle.

The Lady Holt gunmen realized what had happened and began to fire at the fleeing figure. Bullets bit the ground and snapped at rocks and boulders. The only things saving him were the trees and the uneven light. And his own movement.

His horse's ears were up and the animal was frightened and skittish. He forced himself to swing into the saddle as bullets sought them from both directions. It took every bit of his strength. There was time for only one attempt. Yanking on the reins to free them, he kicked the animal hard, but it was already running all out. Neither boot was in a stirrup as they bounded across the top of the ridge.

John Checker was dizzy from the loss of blood, but knew if he fell off now, he would be dead. He might be anyway. With bullets seeking them, horse and rider galloped up over the ridge and disappeared.

At a well-hidden position twenty-five yards away, Eleven Meade fired his special Evans lever-action repeating rifle once more and cursed. How lucky could one man be? Behind him was his carriage with its black horse; reins tied to a tree. Resting on the carriage seat was his white cat. He stood and brushed the dust off his gray frock coat with its velvet collar. Gray-striped breeches shoved into knee-length boots were complemented by an evergreen embroidered vest and a matching silk cravat.

He levered a fresh round into the gun and patted it; he liked the unusual weapon that used a short .44 cartridge and had a huge magazine of thirty-four rounds in the butt. The gun was too delicate for most, besides requiring an uncommon bullet. The company had gone under a few years ago for that reason; Meade had long since been making his own ammunition. He enjoyed the solitary precision of the task as well as the nightly ritual of cleaning his guns.

John Checker had been hit. Of that, he was certain. Hard, he thought. But a man like John Checker didn't die easily. Of that, he was also certain. He hadn't planned on following Jaudon's riders after they discovered the Emmett Gardner Ranch was deserted. He wasn't paid to chase after them. At the last minute, he decided to follow along, to get a better idea of what was happening.

Meade pulled on the brim of his black bowler as he

climbed back into the carriage, pushed his cat over and carefully laid his rifle on the seat next to him. He didn't hurry. That was for amateurs. Hidden by his coat, a pearl-handled Colt, with strange red markings in the grip, was carried in a form holster with the butt forward, readied for a left-handed draw. The gun itself had been modified with a left-handed loading gate. He had named it "Light-Bearer," a designation related to meanings given the number eleven.

It was his real name. He was the eleventh child and last of a high priest and priestess of a small religious sect built mostly on astrology The other children were similarly named, one through ten. Both parents and six of the children died years ago from pneumonia.

Under his coat in a shoulder holster, also set for left-handed use, was a second revolver, a short-barreled Smith & Wesson. It, too, was pearl-handled with similar strange markings and a left-handed loading gate. He had named the gun "Illumination."

His lean face was reddened, partly from the sun, but mostly from a condition that left it that way most of the time. Light blue eyes were accented by his skin color and a well-groomed mustache. His face and hands were as delicate as a city woman's. Blond hair washed along his thin shoulders. Across the bridge of his carrot-shaped nose was a scar, the result of a whiplash.

It wouldn't be hard to track Checker—or his horse—in his condition. He expected to see the Ranger lying on the plains. Or staggering ahead on foot. Certainly his horse had wounds that would stop the animal soon. Jaudon's men could find their own way back to town or recapture their mounts by themselves. They weren't his problem. John Checker was.

He smiled and patted the rifle beside him. The same markings seen on his pistols were engraved into the rifle stock. It, too, had a name, "Master Vibration," but there had been no loading modification.

"You will die today, John Checker," he declared, patted the white cat lying on the carriage seat and snapped the reins of his horse. "You will die."

His chuckle was drowned out by the clatter of carriage wheels.

Chapter Thirteen

Clearing the ridge, Eleven Meade saw nothing, except cattle, on the grasslands ahead. He shrugged and eased horse and carriage down the rocky slope. Going around would be much easier, but would take too long. He wanted to see John Checker die, not find him dead.

He hated this kind of endeavor, preferring the excitement of towns. Waco and Denver were his favorites, followed by Santa Fe. However, the law in New Mexico had made his life there uncomfortable, to say the least. Lady Holt's offer had been both timely and generous.

Staying at Lady Holt's magnificent ranch headquarters was a pleasant surprise, however, enjoying her excellent French wines, Cuban cigars and meals prepared by superb Italian cooks and a polite waiting staff. On those matters, he agreed completely with Lady Holt's right-hand man. However, Sil Jaudon was no match with a gun—and the fat man knew it. About Tapan Moore, he wasn't so sure.

Trotting across the rich grazing land, he spotted two silhouettes against the horizon, partially blocked by steers working their way through breakfast. The sight confused him. Had some of Jaudon's men recaptured their horses and gotten in front of him? Couldn't be. More likely, it was Emmett Gardner and one of his sons. How nice, he thought. Lady Holt would pay well to have this problem removed as well.

The shapes ahead of him began to form into people and horses as he neared. He moved the Evans rifle to his lap and cocked it. A black man and a woman. The black man seemed vaguely familiar to him. He assumed the woman was Morgan Peale. He had been told this was her land. Beside them, a horse was down and unmoving, presumably Checker's animal, dead or nearly so. She was kneeling beside a man. Beside John Checker, he figured.

Alertly, the attractive woman with a leather vest stood and turned toward the incoming carriage. In her hands was a cocked Henry rifle. She said something to the black man that Meade couldn't hear. She took the reins of their horses and held them as the older man spun smoothly to meet Meade's advance. In the black man's hands was a double-barreled shotgun.

At that moment, Meade made the decision not to reach for his own rifle. John Checker might choose to go against six guns, but he had no intention of attacking a man with a shotgun. That's how a man got killed. Like the Ranger.

"Mister, you've come far enough," she said. "Turn around and ride away. Do it now."

Meade reined in his carriage horse, keeping his hands in full sight. The horse stutter-stepped to comply. His cat meowed its discomfort at the sudden change. The shootist was confident they couldn't see the rifle on his lap from this distance.

"I don't understand, ma'am," Meade said. "I am taking a morning ride. With my cat. What is the problem?"

"Take your ride—and your cat—somewhere else. I'm Morgan Peale and this is my land—and I don't want you, or your kind, on it." Her voice was hard and thick. "You work for Holt. She buys your gun."

Meade shrugged his shoulders. "I shall leave. I shall leave." He motioned toward the downed Checker. "Is that man hurt? Is he dead? Is he a friend?"

"He is a Ranger, but you already know. That's why you and your friends shot him. He's everybody's friend who obeys the law." Morgan cocked her rifle. "But you wouldn't understand, would you, Eleven Meade?"

The well-known shootist was mildly surprised to see he was identified. And pleased.

"You look familiar, sir," Meade said.

"I've heard that," Fiss growled. "Don't all black men look alike?"

Meade chuckled. "I meant, have we met, sir?"

"No."

Meade cocked his head and decided not to pursue his curiosity further.

From over the ridge, three Holt riders appeared, mounted on recaptured horses. One was Dimitry. Meade glanced in their direction and turned back.

"You are outnumbered, sir," Meade declared.

"Ever see what nine slugs does to a man? And that's just one barrel," London Fiss replied. "You will die first. Mrs. Peale will get at least one of your friends. We'll put lead in the other two before we go down. How's that for numbers?"

"Your acumen with arithmetic is most impressive, sir," Meade answered, biting his lower lip, raised his shaved eyebrows and declared, "Lady Holt will triple whatever she's paying you. Triple. If you ride away now."

"Ride on before I unload this scattergun."

Without another word, Meade turned his carriage around, snapped the reins and the carriage headed away. Behind him, he heard the woman give orders about watching them leave.

Halfway across the open grazing land, Meade met the three riders and told them what had happened. Only Dimitry seemed interested in seeking a closer look, casting a quick look in the direction of Morgan Peale and Fiss, then deciding against the idea.

Meade didn't look back, smiled and said, "You can forget about John Checker."

"That him on the ridge earlier?" a bearded gunman asked.

"Yeah—and on the ground back there. He's dead—or dying."

"Where are the rest of 'em? Emmett and his boys?" a second gunman asked.

Meade clicked his horse into a walk again, pulled on his bowler brim and said, "That's your problem. I took care of mine."

Dimitry laughed. "Ah, it has been your day."

"Always is."

"If you have killed the big Ranger, the half of me that's Indian will sing songs about you."

Chapter Fourteen

"Governor . . . Captain Temple of the Rangers is outside. To see you, sir. As ordered." The stocky assistant stepped into the governor's office and pushed the thick wave of dark hair from his forehead as he spoke.

"Good. Show him in." The balding, narrow-faced governor said. "Bring me some coffee. Two spoonfuls of sugar."

"Two cups, sir?"

"Just one. Captain Temple won't be staying long." The gaunt politician brushed his fingers along the neatly trimmed mustache.

The assistant spun on his heel and left, impressed by his own precision.

Governor J. R. Citale grimaced. He had been paid well for this move. Very well. Of course, U.S. Senate campaigns were costly. The incentive had come with the tacit understanding there would also be a sudden Senate seat opening whenever he was ready.

Still, it was a sensitive matter that needed handling well. He was good at that, in spite of what some were saying about him. A newspaper story would be placed tomorrow, positioning the Ranger leader as corrupt and under arrest.

A secret bank account in his name would be discovered as proof of his guilt. It was one of Citale's with the name changed. The whole thing was well planned. In one stroke, Lady Holt would gain part of the law enforcement in Texas.

"You ordered my appearance, Governor," Captain Harrison Temple said as he strode into the office.

His wide-brimmed Stetson was held in his tanned hands in front of him. A brown coat and vest showed signs of hard riding; his white shirt and paper collar signs of much wear. The governor's order had not been unexpected, but he thought it would have to do with the charge of murder against two of his best men. The crow's-feet around his eyes were deep with his focused intent to make it clear they were innocent men. His gun belt had been left on his saddle horn of his tired horse.

"It's good to see you, Temple," Governor Citale said without standing. His pale eyes took in the cluttered desk and did not seek the Ranger leader's face. "I have new orders for you and your men that will require immediate attention. For your full force."

"We'll do our duty, sir."

"I'm counting on it."

The governor proceeded to tell him that he and his Rangers were to find and arrest former Rangers John Checker and A. J. Bartlett for murder. They were to be brought directly to the governor's office for a subsequent hearing.

Captain Temple's face exploded into a rainbow of emotions, from surprise, to annoyance, to frustration and finally, to anger. He had never liked Citale—and never trusted him. Now he knew why.

"That I will not do. Nor will any of my men," he said through clenched teeth. "Rangers Checker and Bartlett are two of my best. They are lawmen, not murderers." He pointed his finger at Citale. "How much did Lady Holt pay you for this slimy act?"

A tense silence took over the room.

Without looking at the enraged captain, Citale removed a cigar from his desk humidor and rolled it in his fingers. He bit off the end, spat it toward the floor and lit the cigar.

After a long drag, he studied the cigar again in his hand, letting a ribbon of smoke find the ceiling through his teeth.

"Do I understand it correctly that you are refusing my direct order?" Citale said, glancing up.

"I am refusing to bring in two innocent and fine men," Temple said, barely containing himself. "Two of Texas's best. And you know it." His jaw pushed forward and his fist curled around the hat brim.

Governor Citale cocked his head to the side and grinned. "You, sir, are no longer a Ranger—or one of its captains." He leaned forward on the desk, pushing papers aside. Two sheets fluttered and fell to the floor. He pointed his finger to a small opened area. "Leave your badge. Right here. Now." He returned the cigar to his mouth.

"You son of a bitch."

"Maybe so. Leave the badge."

Stunned, Temple pulled the Ranger badge from his vest and tossed it on the desk. The star shape bounced and slid off.

"I will appoint a new captain immediately," Citale announced, leaning back in his chair and drawing on the cigar.

"My Rangers won't ride for one of your . . . appointments."

"Your men will be notified their services as Rangers are no longer needed, either."

Slamming his hat on his head, Temple declared, "You won't get away with this, Citale. You and that Holt woman."

Governor Citale stroked his mustache again. A confident

smile slowly took its place under the hair as he removed the cigar from his mouth. "You, sir, are under arrest."

From a side door, Sil Jaudon sauntered into the room and pointed a gold-plated revolver at the former Ranger leader. It was a preplanned move.

"Take him away . . . Ranger Captain Jaudon," Citale spat.

"*Qui*, my Governor. It shall be done."

Temple folded his arms. "This is ridiculous. What's the charge? Putting on a hat in the governor's office?"

The fat Jaudon's smile matched that of the governor's. "*Je regrette*, but it is much more than that. You are accused of doing ze bad things with Ranger money."

"That's ridiculous, you fat bastard."

"Ah . . . but it is true," Jaudon said, reached inside the captain's coat and yanked the Colt from his shoulder holster.

Chapter Fifteen

Inside her magnificent and sprawling ranch house, Lady Holt impatiently awaited word on the tactical moves she had put into place: the governor's appointment, Eleven Meade's ambush and the gunmen sent to pin down Emmett Gardner and the Rangers. To help keep her nerves from taking control, she undertook her daily ritual earlier than usual, standing in front of a large crimson bird figurine.

"Glorious Phoenix, you ever are my guide. Lead me to your Father, the Sun. As it dies each eve and is reborn each morn, so you direct me to become invincible," she intoned, and continued in a mixture of Spanish and English ritualistic phrases.

The statuary was an odd combination of an eagle, a heron and a pheasant, carved from cottonwood and adorned with paint and feathers. At its base smoked a small mixture of aromatic herbs settled in a gold dish.

A knock at the door with its walls of red snapped her from the ceremony. She jumped up from her chair. Her eyes were dark with fury. Her servants knew she didn't like being disturbed when she was in the Phoenix Room.

But the knocking continued.

She walked across the red-and-gold Mexican rug to the door and opened it, prepared to give the servant a severe tongue-lashing.

Blinking widened eyes, the black man stuttered, "M-essenger c-came from t-town, Lady Holt. Y-ya be sayin' ya wants ta know. R-right away. *Ab inconvenienti.*" His occasional use of Latin phrases had endeared him to her, even when he didn't always use them correctly.

"Of course, Elliott."

He handed her the telegram just delivered by a messenger from town.

"Have you paid him?" she asked.

"Yes, m'lady. From the money's bowl. *Veritas odit moras.*"

She smiled at his use of the Latin phrase "Truth hates delay."

He bowed.

"Excellent. You may leave me now."

"Yes'um."

She returned to the Room of the Phoenix, sat in her chair, unfolded the paper and began to read.

AM NOW CAPTAIN . . . STOP . . . TEMPLE
CHARGED WITH FRAUD . . . STOP . . . ALL
AS PLANNED . . . STOP . . . AWAIT YOUR
COMMAND . . . J

Her gleeful laugh bounced around the crimson room, creating its own echo.

"Iva Lee, we've done it! We've done it." She laughed again, letting the sound join her first outburst. "Beautiful. Absolutely beautiful. That fool Citale. Beautiful." She turned toward the large bird statue. "Thank you, Great Phoenix. Thank you."

Her entire body was warm, so warm she ripped off her

clothes, walked over to the small walnut desk and sat naked on the ornate chair. She took a piece of paper emblazoned with a small phoenix crest at the top and began to write with a grand flourish. Her pencil broke from the intensity of her effort and she cursed, took another from the red glass holding fifty sharpened pencils. Her ritual was forgotten for the moment.

Shoulders heaving, she read again what she had written, decided it was wrong, wadded up the paper and threw it. A second note was more calmly written and more succinct:

> To Mr. Sil Jaudon, Hotel Blake, Austin, Texas
> Good work. Newspaper here will carry story. My job. You stay. Make sure Captain notice sent to Hangar and Opat. Nowhere else. I do not think Poe will react. He is a political man. See Temple arrested. Keep me informed about Poe. I have a plan. H.

After completing the telegram message, she wrote a succinct offer to buy the Morgan Peale Ranch, another to buy the Charlie Carlson Ranch and a third to buy the Gardner Ranch. All four messages were folded, placed in separate envelopes and sealed. She stood and shook her freed hair, letting it sway on her shoulders. Slowly she redressed as if it were an everyday occurrence. Leaving the room and locking it behind her, she found Elliott and told him to find Tapan Moore and have him come to her immediately.

While she waited, Lady Holt strolled over to the liquor cabinet and poured herself a small glass of brandy. It was, indeed, a day to celebrate.

It wasn't long before the curly-haired gunfighter strolled into the main room. A toothy smile brightened his square-jawed face. His confident walk told everything about him.

He was as good with a gun as he was as a lover. Lady Holt's current lover.

"Mornin', m'lady," he said cheerfully, and smiled.

"And to you, Tapan." She laid her glass on the cabinet shelf and studied his handsome face. "I have an assignment for you."

His face showed disappointment. Their private times had always been in the crimson room.

"Whatever you wish. I shall do."

She smiled, ran her fingers through her long hair and told him what he was to do. First, he was to deliver the message to the telegraph office for transmission and wait for a reply. Afterward, he was to go to Judge Opat and show him the three letters, then ride to each ranch and present them.

"You think they're going to sell?" he asked, taking the envelopes.

"Of course not. But I want to be on record having offered."

"Sure. Makes good sense," Tapan Moore said, backing toward the door. "Should I stay with the boys . . . guarding Gardner's place?"

"No. Come back when you're finished." She licked her lower lip. "So we can celebrate." She pulled him toward her, kissed his lips gently and smiled. "Oh, by the way, you're now a Texas Ranger. Jaudon's captain of the Special Force. When he returns, we'll take that old sonvabitch's place by force."

Moore shook his head and whistled.

"Yes, ma'am!" He grinned and spun around, closing the door behind him as he left.

Slowly, she returned to the phoenix display and sat down. Another knock on the door brought a smile this time, instead of anger. Probably Tapan wanting another kiss before he left.

"Oh, all right. Just one more. Come on in—" She opened the door and stopped midway through her sentence as she realized Eleven Meade was standing there, not Tapan Moore.

His light blue eyes sparkled from realizing whom she had expected. He had passed the young paramour in the hallway; her affair with Tapan Moore was well known on the ranch. Meade touched his mustache with his delicate fingers. As he removed his bowler, blond hair washed over his shoulders.

Physically, he resembled his father; both looked like blond scarecrows. His stern manner, like his mother's, made him a difficult man to like, but he didn't care. Any sense of humor he might have was kept well in check. As did his mother. As if to show a smile was to reveal a weakness of character.

"I came for my money," he said with no thought of apologizing for his interruption. "John Checker is dead."

She bit her lip again, not believing her wondrous luck this day. "John . . . Checker . . . dead? Come in. Come in. I want to hear all about it. Don't leave out a single detail."

She poured him a brandy and another for herself. Contemptuously, he recounted the unexpected opportunity, first making it clear the men she had sent to keep Emmett Gardner's family and the two Rangers surrounded had failed, that they had escaped during the night, headed west.

When he finished, her face was stone. "So my men let that old fool get away? How can that be? They had their orders. My God, doesn't anybody know how to do anything right?" Her fists were clenched at her sides. Madness slid into her eyes.

"Don't know about that. I followed their tracks from Gardner's and Checker had them pinned down. Never saw the family. That's when I killed him. You'll have to wait for their report," he said. "My guess is that they lost them in the rain. That was Checker's objective. To give the rancher time to get away."

"Don't guess. I don't like guesses." She cocked her head. "Speaking of guesses, you didn't get close . . . to Checker's body, I take it."

"Well, no, I didn't. That colored fella would've cut me in two with his scattergun." He twirled the bowler in his hands. "But I didn't need to. John Checker is dead. He must have five or six bullets in him. Mine. And a couple of your . . . men hit him, too."

"I suggest you return to the Peale Ranch and find out, Eleven. For certain. I don't pay for 'maybes.' Or 'guesses.'" She drained her glass. "Oh, and find Tapan. He has an envelope for Mrs. Peale. You can take it instead."

Chapter Sixteen

By the time Emmett Gardner and his family got to Clark Springs, the day was well past noon. Rain had delivered on its threat and soaked them thoroughly through the morning and midday. All, except Emmett, had nodded off a few times in the saddle, napping for a few minutes at a time.

In the distance was a well-built, adobe-and-timber house. Nearby were a sturdy barn, a windmill, a blacksmithing shack and three corrals. Horses of brown, black and tan milled about the enclosures. Rain caught their backs and made them glisten. A large brown-and-white dog barked his warning.

Reining up the wagon, Emmett yelled through the thickening rain, "Rule! Aleta! It's me, Emmett. Me an' my boys. We got trouble."

In the shadowed doorway of the front porch stood a familiar figure with a chiseled face and a lithe frame. Dark eyes studied the scene. Long brown hair touched his shirt.

"That's all right, Two. It's all right. They're family," Rule Cordell said, and whistled at the dog. "Come here, boy. Here, Two."

With his tongue hanging out, the dog hurried to the

porch and stood beside Rule. He leaned over to scratch the animal behind its ears. A silver cross tangled free of his opened shirt from a leather cord around his neck. Under his shirt was a second symbol of spiritual attention, a small medicine pouch also hung from a leather cord. It was a gift of an aging Comanche shaman named Moon before Rule left for the war.

Both tributes to spiritualism he usually wore.

His days as a preacher were over now; he had declined the town's offer to become the full-time minister. His experience in fighting the Regulators had convinced him that his calling was in raising and training horses. Moon had told him a man could serve the Great Spirit in many ways. Mostly, if he was doing what he really wanted to do. His feelings for God were better expressed in working with a fine horse, he thought, and being outside in His creation than bottled up in some building. Regardless of how beautiful the structure might be. That kind of spiritual guidance was best left to someone else.

The revolver in his fist lowered as he turned toward the inside of the house and said, "Aleta, it's Emmett—and his boys. Come quick. Something's wrong."

At Rule Cordell's side soon appeared a stunning, doe-eyed Mexican woman with long black hair. She, too, had ridden with Johnny Cat Carlson after the war—until she met Rule.

A boy and a smaller girl appeared at her side; the older boy looked like his mother, the younger girl more like her father. Their eyes lit up when they saw the Gardner boys climb from the wagon. The older boy said something to his younger sister and they ran out to meet their cousins. The dog followed.

In minutes, the Cordells had welcomed the soaking-wet riders into their house, helped the Gardner boys shed their wet slickers and guided them to stand in front of the stone fireplace. A fire warmed and brightened the main room. The Cordell children and the Gardner children began talking and laughing as if it were a summer picnic. Wagging its shaggy tail, the dog joined them, licking an occasional face or hand of the four. Strutting carefully, the yellow cat also joined the group, but chose to make himself comfortable near the fire. Andrew's frog sprang from his hands as he tried to show his special friend.

Laughter filled the house as everyone tried to catch up with the springy animal. It was Rule who finally secured the pet and returned it to Andrew.

Everything in the house was clean and in its place. The curtains were freshly washed, still smelling lightly of soap. In the adjoining kitchen was a large table with Mexican designs carved into the heavy legs. Matching chairs stood silently around it. A tablecloth of simple blue finished the presentation.

Emmett introduced Rule to Ranger A. J. Bartlett, who greeted him warmly. Rule introduced his wife, Aleta, and son, Ian, and daughter, Rosie, then said, "And this is Texas the Second. We call him 'Two' for short." He patted the dog's head and left unsaid that the name was a tribute to the first "Texas," a cur he found during the war. The dog's death during a battle nearly unraveled him.

"Mr. Cordell, I am glad to make your acquaintance, sir," Bartlett said, "and yours, Mrs. Cordell. But I must excuse myself and return to find my partner. John would've caught up with us . . . if he could. I fear . . ." He didn't finish, not liking his words.

"Please call us Rule—and Aleta. What happened?"

Bartlett explained with Emmett joining in. Rule glanced at Aleta, who excused herself and left for the kitchen. Rule had heard of Lady Holt and knew Texas Ranger John Checker by reputation. He said Comanche warriors called him *Tuht-seena Maa Tatsinuupi*, Wolf With Star, because he tracked them like a fierce wolf. He also knew Eleven Meade, Luke Dimitry and Tapan Moore, but not Sil Jaudon.

After listening, Rule said quietly, "Ranger Checker wouldn't necessarily have followed your same route, A.J. He might have ridden in the other direction. To make sure they didn't find you. He'll catch up later. That would be savvy."

"Well, he's that. In spades," Bartlett replied; his expression was one of a man who wanted to believe what he had just heard but couldn't quite. His thinking tended toward the negative—and to worry. Almost the opposite of his Ranger partner. But this time, his concern seemed justified.

"There you go. Please eat first, and then I'll ride with you . . . if you will allow me the honor, Ranger. We'll find your friend, I'm sure," Rule said. "You'll need a fresh horse, too."

"Thank yo . You're very kind. My horse thanks you, too."

"I cain't be askin' ya to do this, Rule," Emmett said. "I'll be ridin' back with A.J. This hyar's my fight—an' now his. Leastwise to find John."

"It's my fight, too. I'm going with you, Ranger Bartlett." Rikor's eyes were bright; his frown was keeping sleep from getting any closer.

Bartlett bit his lip. "I'd like that. Up to your pa, though."

The young man was silent, looking at his father for approval.

The statement brought a clearing of Emmett's throat. "Yas, son, I reckon ya'd better go with us. You're already actin' a warrior." He shook his head and looked at Rule. "Don' know what I was a-thinkin', Rule. I may be bringin' hell ri't to your door. Forgive me. After we done et, we'll be pushin' on." His face wore weariness and, for the first time, a lack of confidence.

"You'll do nothing of the kind, Uncle Emmett. You're most welcome," Rule said. "You are my family. No one does this to my family. No one." He glanced at a window to see the lessening rain outside.

"Wall, thank you, son, them's the purtiest words I ever did hear." Emmett shook his head. "If'n you could jes' watch the two young'uns I'd be in your debt. Keep 'em safe for a while."

Aleta hurried back into the main room, bringing mugs of hot coffee. "Of course we can. As long as it takes. Our kids would like that a lot." She handed a mug to Emmett, the other to Bartlett, then returned for more.

As they sipped the hot brew, the older rancher explained more about what had happened. A hot meal of tortillas, slices of beef and eggs soon followed. Aleta served the food with a wide smile, observing that it had been too long since they had seen Emmett's sons and how they had grown. Little else was said during the meal as everyone ate heartily. Both the Gardner boys and Cordell's children sat around the hearth to eat.

When they were finished, she invited Emmett's two smaller sons to get some rest in their main bedroom and asked Ian to show them. They followed eagerly with Rosie, Hammer and Two trailing after them.

Returning to the table, she said, "You have ze *mucho* fine sons, Emmett."

The tired rancher hunched his shoulders and told her about each. He was obviously proud of them and she said he should definitely be.

"Not so sure I'll git to see them growed up, though." Emmett bit his lower lip. "This hyar Lady Holt's just about got every-thin' bottled up her way. Wants my land—an' the few others left—for herself. Got the law ag'in me. Even got that chicken-livered governor in her pocket."

Watching his children return from the bedroom, Rule

took a deep breath and looked at Bartlett. "And you haven't seen Ranger Checker since he rode off to stop those men?"

Aleta rose from her chair and directed the children outside to play, noting first that the rain had completely stopped.

"No, we ain't. Must've stopped 'em for a piece anyway, I reckon. Heard gunshots an' nobody showed up to stop us," Emmett said, rubbing his unshaven chin. "He wanted us to keep goin'. Made that real clear. So we did."

"One against six . . ." Rule didn't finish the thought and avoided looking at Bartlett.

The Ranger's response was to take another gulp of coffee and stand. His action was an indication of the desire to leave and look for his partner. Guilt and pessimistic thoughts about letting his friend take on Holt's men alone gnawed at him, even though Checker had insisted.

"Better get riding," he said, pushing away the chair. "Thank you for the fine meal, ma'am. It surely tasted good."

Aleta smiled. "I weel geet some food together for you to take." She paused and brought up a new idea. "Mío love, maybe you should buy ze ranch from Uncle Emmett." She winked. "Until thees ees over. Then he buys eet back. That weel make eet mucho tougher for them, I theenk."

His eyebrows raised, Rule turned to the old rancher. "Makes good sense, Emmett. Keep them off stride. They wouldn't be expecting anything like that."

"Yah, it do."

Rule looked at Rikor and the young man nodded agreement.

Rule looked across at the standing Bartlett. "What do you think, A.J.?"

"No offense, Rule," the Ranger said, "but your past—as an outlaw—will be dragged into this if you do. This Holt woman's ruthless—and she's got the governor's office in her fist. She'll get Citale to revoke your clemency sure as can be. You'll be charged with being a part of the rustling."

That brought the room to silence.

"Maybe. Maybe not," Rule said, "but I like the idea anyway. We'll ride to Clark Springs first. I've got a friend who runs the land office there. He can be the witness and make sure the paper is in order. We'll take it to Caisson. After we find your friend."

Emmett chuckled in spite of the seriousness of the moment. "I'd sure like to be thar when that awful woman hears the news." He found himself saying, "Yu're gonna like John Checker, boy. The two o' ya are cut from the same tree."

Rule nodded and stood as well. "Let me get my war clothes on." He put an arm on Emmett's shoulder. "After we find Ranger Checker, we'll figure out our next step. All right?"

His comment was far more confident than he felt. Why wouldn't John Checker have caught up . . . if he could?

At the other side of the table, Rikor struggled against the lack of sleep, but wanted to show his maturity. His eyelids blinked rapidly as he resisted the urge to shut them for just a minute.

Stiffling a yawn, he finally asked, "Should we get our wagon out of sight? You want us to put our milk cow in your barn?"

"Good idea, Rikor," Rule said, walking toward the bedroom. "We'll take care of it before we leave. You've done plenty, son. Maybe you should stay behind and get some sleep. We'll be back in a couple of days."

The young man shook his head negatively and asked the questions hovering over the room like vultures. "What if John's . . . dead? What's going to happen to our ranch?"

Softly, as if it were a song, Bartlett said, "'Cast all your cares on God; that anchor holds.'"

Rule stopped in the doorway to their main bedroom. "Tennyson, if I'm not mistaken."

"Yes, he's rather a favorite of mine, I must say."

"I like 'If God be with us, who can be against us?' Romans, chapter eight, verse thirty-one."

Bartlett smiled. "Hard to trump that, I suppose."

"Rikor, your ranch is going to be yours for a long time," Rule added. "Why don't you pick out some horses while I get ready? Everything in the big corral is saddle good. Twenty saddles each—and slicker and rope broke. Aleta did the final polishing, so they handle good—and can run all day."

Bartlett nodded.

Emmett tried to smile.

"Be real quiet, *mío* love, the boys are in the bedroom. Sleeping," Aleta urged.

"I will."

Inside his bedroom, Rule dressed quickly in a black broadcloth suit and white collarless shirt. On the bed, Andrew and Hans were soundly sleeping. Beside the bed was a handmade, waist-high cabinet, accented with hand-carved flowers. Once it had been a strange display of guns when he first began his new life as preacher, leaving the vestiges of the war and the lost time as a renegade gunfighter behind. The placement of pistols and rifles had been a measured one, almost ceremonial.

Now the guns were kept in his closet, high enough to avoid the curious hands of his children. He stepped past the half-century-old cabinet now displaying a Bible. Beside the book was another gift from Moon. An eagle feather fan.

Inside the closet, on a high shelf, were seven .44 revolvers of mixed origin and a five-shot, Dean & Adams pistol. Two of the big pistols were settled in holsters with their bullet belts wrapped around them. Another brace of pistols were silver-plated and pearl-handled. They were Aleta's guns. Stacked on each side of the cabinet were two Henry rifles, a Winchester and a shotgun. All were cleaned regularly.

He strapped on one gun belt, checked the .44 revolver and reholstered it. A short-barreled Colt was shoved into his waistband, then the Dean & Adams pistol into his back waistband. Carrying four or five pistols was something he had learned in the war; it always seemed comforting.

Into his mind sneaked an ugly memory. It was a few days before he left for the war and he had caught his father, the Reverend Aaron Cordell, hiding money from the donation plate. His mother had long since left the clutches of this terrible man. The evil preacher spun toward his young son, spitting righteous phrases that meant nothing and raising a silver-topped cane to strike him. The look in Rule's eyes had stopped him.

Later, his father ridiculed Rule's leaving to fight for the Cause; the evil man showed up once more in his life, siding with the Regulators. That Sunday had brought many surprises and much pain. His best friend died, trying to protect him. His mother, long gone from his life, appeared in church to ask for his forgiveness. His father ran—and hadn't been seen again. An entire congregation stood up and shouted they were "Sons of Thunder." He announced to them that he wasn't James Rule Langford, he was Rule Cordell—and they didn't care.

He recalled a strange Indian woman, Eagle Mary, telling him, "You are thunder. You are lightning. You are the storm to clean the land. *Nanisuwukaiyu*. Moon is watching over you."

He shook his head to clear away the awful cobwebs.

After putting on his riding coat, he grabbed a Winchester from the rifles, then stopped. Laying it against the wall, he went to his drawer and withdrew a small stone earring.

A medicine stone from Moon. A piece of Mother Moon herself, the old man had said.

He slipped the leather thong over his ear and let the stone settle beneath it. Nodding approval to himself, he left the room. The tiny symbol had gotten him safely through the war, the anguish of postwar Texas and his earlier fight with the Regulators. He had only spent one day with the dying Comanche shaman, but it was enough to give him much to remember. God was everywhere and in everything. Seeing miracles in everyday things. Resurrection was not uncommon; a man just had to look for it. Just as every man could be his own priest. The highest calling was to care about others.

In that strange encounter, they had become as father and son.

Without thinking about it, he touched the small medicine pouch under his shirt; the shaman told him that it carried the medicine of the owl, the moon's messenger. Yes, Moon had watched over him.

Aleta was waiting in the main room; the others were outside, selecting new mounts.

"*Hasta luego, mío* love," she said. "I know you must do thees. Eet ees family. Hurry back to us."

"I will."

"I see you wear the strength of Moon." She glanced at the stone earring. "That ees good."

"Yeah. I thought it would help bring me back quicker."

They kissed and held each other tightly.

She stepped back and her hand touched his cheek. Her words were of war. "You must geet them off balance. Attack where they don't expect eet. You must become a son of thunder. Again."

From her pocket, she withdrew a slim stem of what had once been a rose. Without asking, she pinned it to his long coat lapel. "Theez weel bring you back *pronto*."

The rose stem had long ago been a rose given by the widow of General Jeb Stuart to his officers at his funeral. He had worn it through the rest of the war and into his nightmare in Texas, refusing to take it off long after the petals had fallen away.

"I didn't know you had this. Where—?"

"Adios, *mío* love. Ride hard and come back to us soon."

Chapter Seventeen

Ranger Captain Hershell Poe sat behind his desk in Ranger headquarters and reread the governor's directive. It was the sixth time he had read about the firing and arresting of Captain Harrison Temple, the subsequent release of the entire Special Force of forty Rangers and the appointment of Sil Jaudon as the new captain with the authority to hire his own Rangers for that group.

He and Temple were equals, although some perceived Poe to be the superior officer. Temple was a fighter leading a squad of fighters; Poe was a politician managing a squad of fighters. A considerable difference. Temple never did understand the need to pay attention to the winds of politics. Or the newspapers. He attracted men like John Checker and Spake Jamison, who would rather charge than discuss.

"Just like that," he muttered. "I should have seen it coming." He knew Governor Citale was easily encouraged by money. So it was only a matter of time.

"But the entire Special Force?"

He looked around for his pipe, filled the bowl from a small leather pouch and lit it. Smoke slid from his clenched teeth and toward the ceiling.

The Special Force was the unit charged with protecting the border from rustlers, bandits and Indians. His own force, the larger one, was charged with protecting the rest of the state; his men were spread out in all corners of Texas. He was good at keeping them where they needed to be. At least most of the time. Texas was a huge place and no one could be everywhere at once. He had done a good job of securing credit for their efforts; most often with him making the statements.

Puffing on his pipe helped him think. Should he inform his own men of this abrupt change? Regular wires kept his Rangers moving on their assignments—and their return telegrams kept him informed of their progress. What would they think? He knew what they would think and didn't like it.

"Temple should have known better than to send Rangers into Lady Holt's territory," he declared. "And John Checker no less. Damn."

He hadn't seen any of Temple's Rangers since the word went out. Nor had he seen Temple waiting in jail for a hearing. Without knowing the details, he understood the charge against Temple was false. If anyone could be trusted with public money, it was Temple. The charge had to be political, an easy way to get rid of him so this Sil Jaudon could take over. He didn't know Jaudon but knew who he worked for. It wasn't hard to figure out where this whole mess had come from. Lady Holt. She was scary. There were whispers that her empire might even become greater than the huge King Ranch one day.

Still, Captain Poe worked for the governor and at the governor's request.

What should he do? He pushed himself away from his desk and went for more coffee. No one was in Ranger headquarters today, except him. There were rarely a handful at any given time. A majority were on the trail somewhere, bringing justice. He liked it that way. A good time to catch up on paperwork and redirect his forces. He had no illusions about his job; it, too, was political. So far, he had been able to keep it in spite of two governors. The trick was to compliment the leader every chance he got—and to keep him informed of things happening around the state. It wasn't really his job, but it made good sense.

The door to the small office opened and three Rangers stepped inside. All three were Temple's men. Each had just received a wire notifying of his immediate release.

"What's going on?" the chunky lawman yelled, and waved the wire over his head.

"I just heard Captain Temple's been arrested," the bearded Ranger said.

The third Ranger, a lanky man with mostly gray in his close-cropped hair, rubbed his unshaved chin and shoved his wide-brimmed hat back on his forehead. His left eye was covered with a black patch, a result of the war.

"This is Citale's doin', ain't it?" he asked without expecting an answer. "Somebody's shoving gold into his pocket real deep this time. That no-good sonvabitch."

Captain Poe stood and removed the pipe from his mouth. He didn't like this Ranger. Spake Jamison was a hard man and a longtime Ranger. A tough older breed of lawman. A lot like an older John Checker. Honest and no-nonsense. An eight-gauge, sawed-off shotgun was carried in a quiver over his shoulder to go with his belt gun.

"I'm as shocked as you are, men. Harrison is a good friend—and, I thought, a good Ranger. I intend to talk with the governor about this. I'm sure there's a reason we're not privy to," Poe declared without looking at Spake.

"Is the whole Special Force gone—or just us?" the older Ranger asked, heading toward the stove and its waiting coffeepot. Next to it was a short shelf littered with coffee cups, spoons and half-filled ashtrays.

Poe noticed he was holding a small sack in his left hand. Most likely it was licorice, Spake's one vice. He didn't drink or gamble. Supposedly, there was an older woman he kept company with from time to time. His long coat carried three old bullet holes and many trails; it hid a holstered Colt and a bowie knife. His shotgun chaps had seen long wear as well. And he moved like a man who had been in the saddle too long.

"I have been informed that is so," Captain Poe said, pointing to a paper on his desk. "Sil Jaudon is the new Special Forces captain—and he has the authority to hire his own Ranger force. He is doing so."

"That's nuts. Just nuts," the bearded Ranger declared, not moving from the doorway. "Doesn't that damn governor understand what we do? Who the hell's this Jaudon fella anyway?"

Poe returned the pipe to his mouth without answering.

After pouring a full cup of steaming black coffee, Spake Jamison blew on its surface and tasted the brew. "Got any sugar, Captain?"

"Over there. In that blue bowl."

"Thanks. Didn't see it."

Laying his licorice sack on the shelf, he grabbed the bowl from its corner spot on the shelf. After pouring a short stream directly into the cup, he returned the bowl. He took a sip and asked, "What are ya gonna do about this mess, Captain? You know damn well our cap ain't playin' games with money. If'n anybody is, it's that damn Citale."

The chunky lawman shoved both thumbs into his gun belt. "You said you were gonna see the governor. You want us to go with you?"

"Say, I heard John and A.J. were fired—and charged with

murder. That right?" the older Ranger asked, enjoying the sweetened coffee. "Sounds like somebody's been drinking too much—or smoking too much opium. Reckon the idea is to get rid o' us." It was clear the last statement was what he thought.

Poe placed both hands on his desk and frowned. "I'm afraid what you heard is true. John Checker and A. J. Bartlett have been dismissed from the Rangers—by the governor—and charged with murder. I don't know any of the details."

The older Ranger shook his head. Pointing a finger at the captain, Spake Jamison said, "What the hell's going on, Captain?"

"Sadly, I don't know. That's why I'm going to see the governor."

"What should we do?" the stocky Ranger asked, his face a tanned puzzle.

"For now, nothing. I don't need trouble from . . . Rangers. I need time," Poe said, sitting down again. "Now if you'll excuse me, I'm going to finish this report—and then go see him."

The older Ranger drained the cup, set it down on the shelf, grabbed his sack and headed toward the door. "Well, I'm not waitin' around to find out. Headin' for Houston. Always liked that town. Should be able to find work there. Those ranchers'll be worried about not having anybody around to stop those Mexicans coming across an' gettin' their beef."

He stopped and held out the sack. "Almost forgot. Have a licorice, Captain. Just bought it. Good 'n fresh."

"Ah, no, thanks. I'm just fine."

The older Ranger held out the sack for the other two and both took black candy pieces.

"You're gettin' too old to be a Ranger anyway," the bearded Ranger said, and laughed.

"Stiff-legged an' all, I can whip your ass any day. Never forget that, boy." Spake patted him on the shoulder and continued walking.

Captain Hershell Poe didn't look up as the three men left. He drew on his pipe, but it had gone out. A swift pop of a match returned the tobacco to life. He didn't like this situation at all and wondered if the governor realized what kind of repercussions this move was going to bring. Ranchers along the border would be howling. He knew what Jaudon was going to do, clean out the region for Lady Holt. That was obvious.

At least, John Checker was charged with murder and wasn't nearby to cause more trouble. He didn't know the famed Ranger well, but respected his fierceness. The thought of Spake Jamison and John Checker being teamed up made him shiver. A. J. Bartlett was a good Ranger, but nothing like either of these fierce warriors.

Straightening his string tie, he recalled hearing about a battle Checker and Spake had fought against a band of twenty Chiricahua Apaches three years ago at a stage station. The two Rangers were en route to El Paso and were riding to the station to get a meal. Three women and five men were riding to Santa Fe; one woman had three small children with her. The Apaches killed the stage guard and the station keeper before the two Rangers got there. Checker and Spake drove off the Indians, killing eight, then took the stage and its passengers safely to the next station.

He shook his head and shivered. There was no way he could have done that. But things were changing. Fencing was coming to Texas. Slowly, but it was coming. Already several big ranches in the Pandhandle were exploring cost-effective ways to control their lands and end free grazing. He had it on good authority, the governor's, that Lady Holt's empire would eventually be fenced as well.

He smiled and wished he had invested in one of the fencing companies popping up. Maybe there was still time. First, though, he had to assure the governor that he was with him in this latest decision. He fingered the pipe bowl, pushing in the tobacco shreds to make them fit better. It was a process he enjoyed, almost as much as the smoking. He relit the pipe and returned to the report he was finishing when the three Rangers interrupted. It was too bad, he thought, but one couldn't always stand in the way of change. At least not and have a job.

Chapter Eighteen

An hour later, Captain Hershell Poe eased out of his carriage at the governor's office, told the driver to wait and walked in.

"Governor . . . Captain Hershell Poe of the Rangers is outside. He requests a brief meeting, sir." The stocky assistant tried to keep his forelock in place as he entered, but failed as usual.

Governor J. R. Citale looked up from his desk. "What kind of mood is Captain Poe in?"

Turning his head to the side, the assistant replied the captain seemed in a good mood, but he wasn't a good judge of such things.

"Excellent. Show him in," Citale said, and raised his hand. "Get a new box of cigars and bring them. You can interrupt us."

"Yes, sir."

The balding politician knew there would be repercussions from his firing of the Special Force. If Captain Poe objected, he had already decided to replace him. Only this replacement would be a political friend. He looked upon the expected uproar of ranchers along the border as a marvelous opportunity to raise more funds for his planned Senate race.

He would point out to them how someone like Lady Holt was helped when one was helpful in return.

"Thank you for seeing me, Governor. I appreciate it very much." Captain Poe bowed slightly, his narrow-brimmed hat in his hand. "I just wanted you to know that I support your decision . . . concerning Captain Temple and his men—and will do whatever is needed to make the transition to Captain Jaudon a smooth one."

"I was hoping I could count on your loyalty."

"You can, indeed. Thought you'd like to know I've also been notified of John Checker's death."

"That's a shame." Citale blinked his eyes three times.

Captain Poe shook his head. "Oh, he was too violent for my taste. But my reason for coming . . . I have some ideas to minimize the reaction from, ah, the ousted Rangers," he said, smiling. "In fact, I have it on good authority that Spake Jamison is heading for Houston. To find work there. Made me think."

"Glad to hear about Jamison. Let's hear your ideas."

Licking his lower lip, Captain Poe paused. "Well, you're going to get some hollering from ranchers, down on the border. They want Rangers to control those Mexican rustlers. And you've got out-of-work Rangers angry as hell."

Governor Citale cocked his head.

"Maybe you should contact the big ranchers along the border—and send them their own ex-Rangers. Might solve two problems at once." He motioned with one hand to suggest a wide group. "Offer to pay the ex-Rangers' salaries. For a few months."

"I like that." The governor frowned. "But don't you think these ranchers . . . ah, should pay for this service? Instead of the state?"

"Oh, you're right. You're right, Governor."

Citale's assistant entered with the box of cigars.

The governor nodded. "Excellent, Jeffrey. Captain Poe, would you care for a good smoke?"

"That's very gracious of you. Certainly, sir."

Chapter Nineteen

Emmett Gardner and Rule Cordell rode silently from Clark Springs, both lost in their own thoughts. Rule carried the signed and witnessed bill of sale to Emmett's ranch as planned. Emmett carried another signed bill of sale, returning the ranch to his possession. The precaution was Rule's idea in case something happened to him before they could act.

Weary, but reenergized from the action taken in town, Emmett rubbed his unshaven chin and rolled his head to relieve the fatigue. To ease the tiredness, he rode with his boots hanging free of the stirrups. It gave some relief to his legs. His mind raced from his children sleeping at Rule's house and wondering what would happen to them if he was arrested and hanged as Lady Holt planned, to the ranch he'd worked so hard to build, to his late wife, to wondering about John Checker, to wondering what would happen when Rule presented the new bill of sale.

Rule's thoughts were more focused. Determining what had happened to Checker was first; then establishing some kind of surprise in Caisson was next. It was time to put this evil woman on the defensive for a change. At least for the moment. Surprise was the only significant weapon against a superior force.

As the sun bled into the horizon, they caught up with Bartlett and Rikor at the agreed-upon site. It was a good camp for the night. They had brought Checker's packhorse with more food added.

Slightly elevated, the flat prairie ran into a steep bluff cutting north and south for two hundred yards before disappearing into rocks and shale. A creek with a reputation for occasional water staggered past, flirting its wetness with the land. No one could approach from three directions without being seen from a considerable distance—and coming slightly uphill as they did. The bluff itself ensured that there would be no threat from behind. Especially since they would camp close to its steep sides.

Rikor was asleep. Their horses were picketed next to the three mesquite trees clustered a few yards from the bluff itself. Bartlett had made a small cooking fire that was virtually unseen until they rode close. Boulders had been pushed around the tiny flames to further keep it hidden. Smokeless wood had been carefully gathered. A coffeepot was gurgling at its edges. Several more large rocks had been rolled into position farther away to provide better firing positions if they were attacked. Rule noted the protective action to himself, acknowledging Bartlett's thoroughness.

"Good to see you boys," Bartlett said, looking up from the fire. His Winchester lay on the ground a few feet away. "I'll get some bacon on. And some potatoes. Aleta packed us some fine grub."

Without being asked, the high-strung Ranger explained there were no tracks left of Emmett's wagon. The rain had taken care of that concern. The last time Holt men could have seen the Gardner family they would have been traveling east, toward Austin. A feint Checker had advised Bartlett to take, before going after the gunmen.

Bartlett's pained face told the story before he did. There were no signs of Checker, but he had not ridden as far as this ridge when they last saw him. Bartlett had searched this part of the region for as long as daylight allowed, looking for places where a man might hide. He hadn't seen any Holt riders, either.

"Couldn't see out there any longer," Bartlett mumbled. "John's the one who can see in the night. Like some Apache. More than a handful of outlaws have been real surprised to have him come up to their night camp. Really something." He reached for a potato and began carving off the skin.

Rikor stirred, then jumped up, grabbing for his rifle.

"It's fine, son. It's your pa—and your uncle," Bartlett said. "You go ahead and rest. I'll wake you when supper's ready."

The young Gardner stood, cradling his rifle. "N-No . . . I'm . . . ah, I'm . . . just fine. Evenin', Pa. Uncle Rule."

Both men returned the greeting as they unsaddled their horses.

"Quite the animal you gave me to ride." Bartlett pointed at the grazing buckskin with the knife he was using on the potatoes. "Could've gone a lot longer. Runs real smooth, too."

"Well, thanks," Rule answered, standing his saddle on its end and pulling free his rifle. "Aleta does the last rides on all of them." He held out his hand to take the reins from the tired rancher. "Emmett, I'll walk your horse—with mine—over to the stream. You find yourself a good sittin' spot."

"Thank you, son. I'm gonna do jes' that."

A sadness swept onto Bartlett's face. "John's hurt bad, isn't he? I should've been there. I should've." He looked away, dropping his knife and the half-skinned potato.

Rule stopped with reins in each hand. "Your friend knew what he was doing. It was a smart strategy. You achieved what he asked you to do, get Emmett and his sons through. Safely. You did well, A.J."

He couldn't bring himself to say Checker was not hurt. It was likely he was.

"Thank you. Doesn't help much, though." Bartlett shook his head, picked up the fallen potato and rubbed off the bit of mud that had attached itself, then resumed his trimming.

Rule couldn't think of anything else to say and began walking the horses to water again. Emmett took a tin cup from his saddlebags, strode over to the fire and poured himself a cup of steaming coffee. Steam plastered the cool air. He tasted the coffee and decided it was too hot. The smell of bacon frying filled his nostrils and he inhaled deeply. Bartlett was cutting up the potato and an onion, letting the pieces fall into the sizzling pan.

"Cain't second-guess yourse'f. Ain't useful." He tried the coffee again. "'Sides, Rikor an' me could've stopped jes' as much as you'n. Ya ain't the only one a-worryin'. But if'n anybody's all right, it's John Checker." He swung his free left arm. "Damn that awful woman! She needs killin'." He shoved his tongue into the side of his cheek. "Don't think I said that 'bout anybody a'fer." He shook his head. "I believe I'd do it myse'f."

Supper was a mostly silent meal. Aleta had packed fresh biscuits and jam to go with the bacon and potatoes. In town, Emmett had bought cans of beans and peaches; they decided to share a can of the fruit. After eating, they put the fire out with handfuls of dirt and most of a canteen. Emmett and Rikor were quickly asleep; Bartlett was very tired but too tense to sleep. Rule offered to keep watch until two o'clock. He assured them that his horse, a mustang, would warn them if anyone came near.

Sitting down beside Bartlett, who was cleaning the dishes with ashes from the dead fire, Rule asked, "What kind of man is John Checker?"

"Known John a long time," the lawman began. "A hard man, I suppose you'd say." He stared into the darkness. "But he cares real deep. About a lot of things." He fingered the spur on his right boot, adjusting it slightly. "Like he was friends with an old Comanche war chief. Stands-In-Thunder was his name, I think. Yeah, Stands-In-Thunder, that's it." He told about Checker's relationship with an aging Comanche war chief who lived on the Fort Sill reservation and that they had met when several Rangers were chasing a half-breed murderer trying to hide in the reservation.

Rule was immediately interested, shifting his rifle in his lap.

"All of us Rangers were real surprised," Bartlett said. "You know, John wears a Comanche tunic. Took it off a dead warrior. After they fought. Hand-to-hand. Don't remember that fellow's name." Bartlett pulled on one of his boots to remove it. "The old war chief told John it was right for him to wear the tunic. A 'remembered fight,' he called it."

He completed the removal of the first boot and started on the second. "John said he told the old war chief that was where he got the scar on his cheek." The second boot came off quicker. "When the old man died, John got permission from the army to bury him the Comanche way. Out in the hills somewhere. Nobody knew where. Not even me."

Rubbing his chin, he added, "John wears a little pouch. Around his neck. Like yours, Rule. At least, I suppose it is. That old war chief gave it to him. All kinds of thunder medicine inside, he said."

Bartlett placed his boots carefully side by side. "Oh yeah, he told me the old man gave him a white stone once. Said it sang to the right man. Don't recall John ever saying if it sang to him or not. I think he still carries it." His shoulders rose and fell. "Most of the time, though, they just talked and laughed. Smoked cigars and drank the whiskey John brought to him." He shook his head and massaged his socked feet.

"John knew some Comanche. The old man could handle some English. They got along fine. Real fine."

Touching the pouch hanging from his neck, Rule asked if all the stories about the famous Ranger were true. He checked his Winchester, wiping dust from the brass with the corner of his coat. After cocking it, he eased the trigger down so the gun was ready, but wouldn't go off if it fell over.

"Can't say for sure," Bartlett said, blinking his eyes to push away the desire for sleep. "But I suppose they'd match up with the ones about you. For truth—and for stretching."

Rule smiled. "I heard he tracked Mexican bandits right to the Rio Grande. They were crossing, so he threw down his badge and went after them. Killed two in the river. Brought the others back for trial. All wounded."

"Yes, sir. That's sure true. Several of us were only a few hours behind." Bartlett crossed his arms. "I can tell you the one about bringing in the Trimmel Gang by himself was true. I was there when he brought them. The three he hauled in were glad to be away from him, I'll tell you for sure. The other three tried to shoot it out. They lost."

Rule shook his head in amazement. "Heard he made Clay Allison back down."

"Don't know about that. Heard the same about you."

"Never met Mr. Allison."

"There you go." Bartlett cocked his head. "I'll tell you one story about him that most folks don't know—or those that do, don't understand. He bought a small house. For a widow with two children. Didn't know her real well—and wasn't interested in her, you know. He just said she reminded him of his mother." He added that Checker was the bastard son of a Dodge City gang leader and that his mother died when he was fourteen.

"The way I heard it, John tried to kill the man—his father—after his ma died. From the way he treated her. Beating on her and all. Had to leave Dodge fast and leave his little sister behind. With an aunt and uncle or something. Hasn't seen her since. Kinda grew up the hard way. Fast."

Rule shifted his feet. "The way of the gun is a lonely way."

With prompting from the Ranger, Rule shared his own upbringing, about his evil minister father and his mother, who ran away when he was young. His mother now lived in Clark Springs; he had no idea what had happened to his father, but had a feeling he was dead. He told about his new life as a minister and the confrontation in the church with his father and the state police.

Bartlett looked at him. "No offense, but you've been lucky. Most gunfighters end up with a bullet. Somewhere. Nobody caring."

"None taken. I didn't seek the reputation, A.J. Tried to avoid it, in fact," Rule said quietly. "But I don't think men can stand by and let others take away the homes of their friends. Or their lives. My guns will come out for that."

Laying his rifle against the closest rock, he yanked free the revolver from its holster, removed the cartridges and began wiping it clear of dust.

"You and John will get along real fine."

For the first time, the Ranger noticed Rule was wearing a stone earring, a small thong held it in a loop for his ear. He wanted to ask about the item but didn't. Instead, he told about the time Checker and Spake Jamison fought off a band of Apaches trying to take a stage station. He added that Jamison was a hard-nosed Ranger, a lot older than most.

"I look forward to meeting John."

Neither said what he thought, that it might be too late.

"Say, if you don't mind my asking, how did you come by the name . . . Rule?" Bartlett asked, then adjusted the boot closer to him, sensing an imaginary difference in their alignment.

Rule chuckled and said his mother wanted her son to become nobility. His father hated the name, which made him like it more.

Bartlett nodded and smiled.

"Well, Ranger, while we're at it, what does 'A.J.' stand for?"

Bartlett shook his head. "Not many know. It's Augor Josiah. Supposed to be a name of one of my kin. Always thought my ma wanted to tag me with something different just to be ornery. She was a real whip of a gal."

Rule studied the moon for a moment, then changed the subject. "Did John give you any idea of what he thought you should do, after Emmett's boys were safe?" Rule leaned against the rock and studied the night sky. A handful of stars were gleaming proudly.

Bartlett folded his arms. "Yes, make enough trouble that real justice is brought in." He paused. "Lady Holt herself would have to be arrested. Ah, John always likes to be attacking."

Rolling his shoulders, Rule nodded agreement.

"While I'm thinking about it, I want to thank you. For stalling Humphrey's Two. At the end. Of that awful war," Bartlett said, changing the subject in his mind.

Rule frowned and looked up from his cleaning.

"I was with Hill's Third. We would've never seen them coming 'til it was too late."

"That was a long time ago."

"Like yesterday. To me. In some ways," Bartlett said. "Marshal Spake Jamison, he rode with Hood. Still doesn't think the South should've quit. Lost an eye to shrapnel. Mean as a cold day. One of our best deputies."

Rule shook his head. "Understand his feelings. Took me a long time to come to grips with losing." He returned the revolver to its holster and drew the short-barreled Colt from his waistband and started the same cleaning ritual.

Bartlett shifted his weight against the rock and recited, "'Blow, bugle, blow, set the wild echoes flying. Blow, bugle; answer, echoes, dying, dying, dying.'"

"I don't know that. Tennyson, I presume."

"Yes. From 'The Princess.' One of my favorites."

Bartlett licked his lower lip. "Guess I'm not like you—and John. Or ol' Spake, for that matter. You boys would charge hell . . . and bring back Satan in handcuffs."

Rule smiled. "I think you misread the value of attacking. Can't speak for the Rangers . . . but most of the time, the advantage goes to the attacker."

"Well, maybe. Sounds like something John would say. Or Spake. He's a tough old rooster," Bartlett said.

Rule smiled. "Heard of him. Like John Checker." He shifted his boots and looked at Bartlett. "John Checker is alive, A.J."

"Well, maybe."

Both were quiet again, retreating to yesterday in the shadows of their thoughts.

"Was John in the war?" Rule spun the gun in his hand and was satisfied with its handling, then began reloading it.

"Not like you or me. Younger than us to begin with." Bartlett rubbed his stockinged feet. "Boy, there's nothing like a good pair of socks, is there?"

Rule grinned, ignoring the break in thought.

Movement among their horses brought both men to alertness. Rule jumped to his feet and walked over. The sounds weren't those of his mustang trying to warn him of someone coming; rather they were nervous sounds. Maybe a wolf or a mountain lion prowling.

A few minutes later, Rule returned, guessing there was a lion around. He suggested they move closer to the horses. Grabbing his boots and rifle, Bartlett walked over to the mesquite trees where Rule was already sitting. The famed gunfighter had already returned the Colt to his waistband and withdrawn the Dean & Adams revolver from his belt in back.

"Almost forgot what I was telling you about," Bartlett said as he squatted beside the middle tree, set his boots carefully beside him and explained Checker had been in a squad of Union sharpshooters but didn't like taking orders from officers he didn't respect. After his tour of duty was over, he left.

"Had plenty of those on both sides."

"Yeah, that's sure the truth."

Bartlett rubbed his feet again, brushing off pieces of dirt and sticks that had attached themselves to his socks when he walked over. Checker had run with a bad bunch for a while, with the outlaw Sam Lane before he straightened himself out and became a Ranger. He wanted to compare it to Rule's time with Johnny Cat Carlson but didn't.

"'Howe'er it be, it seems to me, 'tis only noble to be good. Kind hearts are more than coronets, and simple faith than Norman blood.'" Bartlett recited another Tennyson line and shifted his rifle to a more comfortable position on his lap.

"Easier said than done, my friend."

They talked a few minutes longer with the Ranger sharing the fact that Lady Holt was fascinated with the myth of the phoenix. He thought it was something she had learned while she was in England. Rule listened and mouthed "fire." Bartlett yawned and apologized. Rule told him to get some sleep; tomorrow would likely be a long day.

"Say a prayer for John, will you, Rule?" Bartlett said. "Figure you're a might closer to the right fellow than I am."

"I will do so, A.J.—but not for that reason. He listens to everyone the same. Give it a try."

Bartlett blinked his eyes. "I will, Rule. Thanks."

After a few more minutes of discussion about the phoenix myth, Lady Holt and the governor, Bartlett said he had better get some sleep. Soon the Ranger was stretched out on the ground under his blanket, using his saddle for a pillow. Next to him were his weapons. He was snoring softly.

Rule stood among the trees, letting their trunks provide additional cover. Here he was. The former, intense Confederate warrior. His name alone had brought fear to many Texans after the War, expecially Union soldiers and sympathizers. He watched a half-moon take ownership of the dark sky. In his thoughts, he was riding again in the Virginia woods. It was a cold February in 1865 and the collapse of the South was near. He was scouting alone and suddenly heard a Union battalion marching ahead of him along the Boydon Plank Road.

Behind that piece of yesterday came the Sunday morning when he challenged the Regulators and the "Sons of Thunder" came alive to stand with him. Men and women of his parish refusing to bow to their evil tyranny. Of course, the name itself had been a fake one he had used to make the state police think there was a whole band of guerrillas after them, when it was only one. Well, actually two. A traveling peddler had helped him greatly. Caleb Shank. Now a good friend. Folks called him "the Russian," even though he wasn't.

He jerked his head to send the memory into the shadows of his mind. Tomorrow they would have a better idea of what they were up against.

"I am a son of Thunder," he muttered into the night.

Rule studied the dark land, glad to hear night sounds that should be there. Whatever was bothering the horses earlier had left. For the time being anyway. Their horses were standing three-legged and quiet. Another good sign. If anything was to come close, they would warn him. Moon had told him silence was sacred, a time when man listened to the Great Spirit talking to him.

A strange contentment was settling within him, a feeling

he tried to ignore. He had felt the first sensation soon after Emmett and his family arrived. It was the contentment a warrior felt in battle or on the eve of it. Being a preacher had been an important transition in his life. A time for him and Aleta to begin their life together. A time to show his soul that his maniacal father was wrong. A time to put the wildness of the postwar years behind him.

Yet something was missing. He wasn't meant for the pulpit. Or training horses. Not really.

He felt a certain rightness within when he undertook bringing the Regulators down to save friends.

He was good with a gun. Very good. Few could match him, especially in battle. The life of a gunfighter was not something he sought. He didn't see himself as that. Rather, it was a strange sense God had placed him here—and now—to help those who couldn't help themselves. War and its aftermath had sharpened him, but not hardened him, to caring about others. He hated the likes of the old Regulators, the former state police, who ran roughshod over Texas after the great war. He hated the likes of Lady Holt—and Governor Citale—who sought power and riches through the destruction of others.

Yes, this was what he was born for. He was a man of the time, a man of the gun. A Son of Thunder. Aleta knew it better than he did. She had encouraged his participation in Emmett's battle.

"Yes, I am a Son of Thunder," he said softly, and added, "And, Lady Holt, I am the fire you should fear. A fire you won't rise from."

Chapter Twenty

Spake Jamison walked into the large jail and slammed the door behind him.

"I want to see Captain Temple." His graying eyebrows arched in held anger.

The intense arrival startled the deputy in charge. He jumped and his hand reached out for the shotgun on the desk. His arm cuffed his coffee mug and spilled hot liquid over the desk.

"Ah . . . sure. I guess. Aren't you a Ranger?"

"Was. Here are my guns, boy." Jamison shoved the sawed-off shotgun and his belt gun on the desk. Chuckling, he added, "You need to write down my name, boy. You can clean up that spill later. It ain't going nowhere."

The round-faced deputy glanced at the spilled coffee, then at the entry log. It was, luckily, spared from the splatter.

"It's Spake Jamison. One m."

"Ah, sure. Jamison."

"Where do you want me to sign?" Spake said.

The deputy pointed beside where he had written Spake's name. The old Ranger took a pencil resting in the middle of the log, stuck the lead point in his mouth and wrote an X where the deputy had pointed. Regaining his poise, the deputy stood and told Spake to follow him. He unlocked the outer steel frame and they walked past a second fuzzy-whiskered guard sitting on a straight-back chair, cradling a double-barreled shotgun.

"Hey, Spake! Shoot anybody lately?" a gritty voice called from the third cell.

Without pausing, Spake said, "Should'a shot you, Henry."

Over his shoulder, the deputy asked, "How do you know Henry Nawell?"

"Brought him in two weeks ago. He killed a family in Waco. Mother, father and two little kids. Hanging's too good for the sonvabitch."

"Oh."

They walked in silence down the row of cells; most were unoccupied. At the next-to-last cell was Captain Harrison Temple. Spake saw the tired man before Temple saw him. Temple looked weary, sitting on his cell bed.

"Afternoon, Captain."

Temple looked up and a thin smile entered his face. "It's good to see you, Spake. They fire all you boys?"

"Oh yeah. Couldn't wait to get rid of us."

Temple shook his head, stood and held out his hand through the cell bars and Spake shook it warmly.

"You've got five minutes, Jamison," the deputy said, walking away.

Spake turned toward the departing guard. "When I'm ready, I'll come. Not before, boy. Don't press it."

The deputy bristled, but kept walking.

Spake's questions triggered a terse recital from Temple. His hearing had been conducted in private and he was being held for trial. The evidence against him was so phony the judge had had difficulty with the charge. It looked as though someone had changed the governor's name on a bank account and inserted his. The governor's direct plea had secured a trial.

"Doesn't really matter," Temple added. "All they want is time."

"I'm gettin' too old, Captain. What is all this crap?"

"Lady Holt."

"Damn. Women are gonna be the death of us." Spake grinned wolfishly.

Temple explained the situation, how he had sent Checker and Bartlett to protect Emmett Gardner, a small rancher, from the Holt attempt to take his land. He rattled off the incidents that had occurred since then.

"Poe said John's dead."

Temple's eyes widened. His mouth opened, but no words would come. He stumbled back to his cot and sat. Finally, a rush of "Oh my God" found a strained voice.

"Nobody's immune to a bullet, Captain. Not even John Checker." Spake's own face was taut. "A.J.'s wanted for murder. That woman works fast."

"I heard."

The grizzled Ranger glanced at the seated guard down the hallway, then back to Temple, who was struggling with his emotions. The old Ranger stepped next to the cell bars and leaned his face into the cell.

"Captain, we can get you outta here. Piece of cake."

Shaking his head negatively, the Ranger captain told Spake he didn't want that. At least not yet.

"All right, what do you want us to do?" Spake asked. "About a dozen of us are in town. Or close. More coming in, I hear." He stepped back.

"Don't worry about me, Spake," Temple said. "I can handle the court. I think." He paused. "Anyway, there's no time to do both." He stood again and walked to the front of the cell.

"I want . . . no, I can't say that, I'd like you to ride for A.J.—
and Emmett Gardner—and those other little ranchers. Before it's too late."

"You're still our captain."

"You'll be riding outlaw."

"Done that before. But let's see how big an asshole Poe
really is."

Spake Jamison turned and headed back down the hallway. As he passed the seating guard, he growled, "Anything
happens to that man down there—an' I'll find your silly little
ass an' kill you with my bare hands. You understand, boy?"

The long-faced guard jerked in the chair and started to
raise his shotgun.

Spake spun, grabbed the gun and yanked it from the
startled guard. The old Ranger stared at him.

"Didn't like your reaction, boy. Want to try again?"
Jamison said, holding the shotgun at his side. "I asked you a
question. I want an answer."

The guard's eyes were plates. "A-ah . . . I'm s-sorry. I'll
make s-sure nothing happens to . . . Captain Temple. I—I
p-promise."

"Good boy." Spake handed back the shotgun and left.

Chapter Twenty-one

Early morning the next day found Eleven Meade pulling up his carriage in front of the small adobe ranch house belonging to Morgan Peale. He had overslept and blamed it on too much of Lady Holt's fine wine.

"Aho, the house! Anyone home?" he yelled, and scratched the back of his white cat's head. The little animal squirmed happily in response to the attention.

A dark figure came to the doorway; the shotgun in his hands was casually pointed in Meade's direction. "This is Mrs. Peale's land. Get off."

"Sure and I will. First, I have a letter for Mrs. Peale. And I want to check on the condition of Ranger Checker," Meade said. "Sheriff Hangar asked me to do so. The Ranger is wanted for murder, you know. Can he be moved to town? Does he need a doctor?"

A slow smile found the black man's mouth and disappeared. "Too late for a doc. He's dead."

Meade tugged on his bowler hat brim. "I'd like to see the body."

"Why?"

"He was a wanted killer. Sheriff Hangar will want to no-tify Ranger headquarters, you know. And the other lawmen in the area."

"I just told you. He's dead."

Meade looked down, realized his action might be mistaken for an aggressive move to his gun and expanded his hands to grip both sides of the carriage.

"I know you did, sir, but you know lawmen. They want proof."

"Tell him to come out an' see for himself, then." London Fiss turned to leave.

"I think you should know, sir, Sil Jaudon is the new Ranger captain for the Special Force. Governor Citale ap-pointed him."

Meade's words stopped Fiss in midstride.

"The previous captain has been arrested. Some kind of financial matter as I understand the whole of it. Sad, really."

As he spun around, Fiss's tightened mouth flickered at the corner. He knew what Meade's announcement meant to his boss. His words were a snarl.

"Tell the fat Frenchman that he'll have to come through me, badge or no badge."

"I believe he looks forward to that . . . sir." Meade's eyes sparkled with challenge.

"So do I," Fiss stated without emotion, and slammed the door behind him.

Meade looked down at the envelope beside him. He would need to get the black man out again. Oh how he hated doing things he wasn't hired to do.

Before he could call out, Morgan Peale emerged from the ranch door. Her face was pale, but determined. In her hands was a rifle. He noted it was cocked.

"Tell Sheriff Hangar that we buried Ranger Checker.

Under that string of cottonwoods. To the south. Nice an' shady there." She paused and added, "You can dig up the body yourself if you want to. But I want him reburied."

"Certainly, Mrs. Peale, I appreciate the information."

"I understand you have a letter for me."

"Yes, ma'am. Here."

She opened the envelope, read the letter and threw both to the ground. When she looked up, her face was hard. "You tell that woman you work for . . . to go to hell. I'm not selling to her or anybody else. Now get off my land—and don't come back!"

She didn't wait for his response and spun around, heading back inside.

Meade watched the door for a few moments before taking the reins and clicking his horse into trotting away. Minutes later, the gunfighter reined his carriage to a halt beside a freshly dug mound with a small wooden cross placed at one end. He studied it, rubbing his cat's back, and decided there was no way in the world he was going to dig up the body. Lady Holt would just have to take Mrs. Peale's word for it. Why would she lie?

He laughed out loud, drowning out the morning's songbirds, and urged his horse again into a trot. Important news shouldn't be delayed.

Not long afterward, four riders reined up on the ridge overlooking Morgan Peale's land. The sun was struggling to gain control of the sky. Vultures hovering in the gray sky saddened them. It was a sign they hadn't wanted to see. A sign of death.

Spurring their horses forward, A. J. Bartlett, Rule Cordell, Emmett Gardner and Rikor Gardner cleared the ridge and trotted across the grassland. A dark shape became a downed horse. Huge birds and a coyote were enjoying themselves.

Bartlett groaned, pulled his rifle from its scabbard and

fired three times. Two birds flopped to the ground and the others fled skyward. The lone coyote yipped and scooted away. Bartlett's fourth bullet dusted the ground behind the fleeing animal.

"I'm sorry, Rule," Bartlett said, lowering his rifle. "I—I . . . well . . ."

"Don't apologize," Rule said. "I would've done it, if you hadn't."

Their advance to the dead animal was a silent one; their horses were skittish, not wanting to get close to the stench of death.

Rule reined up and pointed. "Was that Checker's horse?"

"Yes. The right flank had a small white splash." Bartlett's face registered the sadness his entire body felt.

"Well, A.J., somebody took away the saddle and bridle. See?" Rule pointed. "And there's no sign of a body. That's good, A.J." His eyes searched the open area for sign. Any sign of a man. Nothing. Yesterday's rain had taken away all traces of the violence, except the dead animal itself.

Emmett made a sweeping gesture with his right arm. "We 'uns rode ri't down thatta way. With the wagon an' all."

Rikor nodded agreement, nudged his horse into a lope and rode out toward the ridge where Checker had gone.

Bartlett's shoulders rose and fell. "Probably some bastard needed the saddle."

"Maybe. But there's no reason for Holt's men to take the gear. Why would they?" He looked over at the distraught Ranger. "Maybe somebody came to help him. Took the saddle with them—and him."

Bartlett listened and finally muttered, "Maybe . . . they took him . . . to town."

Rule rode in a wide circle around the area of death, continuing his assessment. "Rain took away all the signs of a fight. But somebody came by this morning. In a carriage. Came and went. From town. Any idea who that might be, Emmett?"

"No, cain't say as I do. Wilkerson, he drives a carriage. He's the banker. Mayor, too. Figger he's owned by Lady Holt. Might be he was headin' to Peale's place." He shook his head. "Holt's gonna want it, too. An' Charlie's."

"Whoever was in that carriage knew there was a dead animal here." Rule reined his horse and studied the land.

"What?" Bartlett's attention was returned.

"Look." Rule motioned toward the lines in the land. "There's no pause. No stopping. Just a wide loop around it."

Bartlett licked his lower lip. "Maybe he thought it was a dead steer."

Rule waved his hand toward the ridge. "Wouldn't you be curious if you saw a dead horse? Wouldn't you want to see if there was someone hurt?"

Bartlett struggled with the reality lying in front of them. It was hard to believe so much had happened so quickly. He and Checker were Rangers one minute and wanted murderers the next. Now his mind was churning and replaying the time when Checker left the wagon. He shouldn't have let his friend go alone. He shouldn't have. Was his friend in jail? Wounded? How badly? Where was he? Was he . . . dead?

"Yeah. Could be. If it was Wilkerson, though, that ol' boy wouldn't like bein' close to no dead animal," Emmett declared.

"Maybe. It still looks to me like he knew the horse was there. John's horse."

"Why don't we ride into town? Might find out who belongs to that carriage," Bartlett said. "Maybe those bastards took John to jail." Bartlett didn't believe his own statement.

Rikor rode back and reported there were no signs of

Checker or anyone else along the ridge. No one had expected any; the rain had done its job in that regard.

Rule pointed in the direction the carriage had been heading. "You say there's a ranch that way, Emmett?"

"Yes, suh. Morgan Peale's place ain't too far from hyar. She's gonna feel that bitch a'fer long, I reckon. Don't reckon the black feller's gonna be able to stop 'em for long."

Rikor nodded agreement.

"I think we should head for town. This man in the carriage knows something, I think," Rule said.

"Yu're a-thinkin' the doc came to he'p him some?" Emmett asked, staring toward the horizon as if he could see the Peale Ranch. "Ol' Doc Curtis, he rides a buggy, ya know."

"Could be. I don't know. Just seems like we should try there first. What do you think, A.J.?" Rule asked, leaning forward on his saddle horn.

Bartlett swung his horse toward the west, trying hard to clear his mind of the guilt sitting there. "It's worth it. Let's go."

Outside Caisson, Rule wanted them to wait, near a small grove of pecan trees and a sometime spring. They would be able to see in all directions a long way. It made sense to stay out of town, but all three refused. Bartlett said he had let Checker talk him into staying with the wagon and now his friend was hurt or worse. Emmett agreed. So did Rikor. Rule Cordell understood their concern, but pointed out that their arrival in town would make it more difficult to determine what had happened to the Ranger.

Reluctantly, he agreed Bartlett could go along, but he would have to alter his appearance. He convinced Emmett and Rikor that he needed them to wait, in case they had to make a run for it from town. Splitting their resources made sense. Besides, the old rancher and his son were well known in town; Bartlett wasn't.

A short ride later, the two entered the south edge of Caisson. Bartlett wore Rikor's battered chaps and Emmett's coat and hat. It was a long way from a perfect disguise, but it might do the trick. No one would be expecting the Ranger; that was in their favor. No one knew Rule. At least, not by sight.

Midday activity was brisk. No one seemed to notice the arrival of the twosome, and for that, Rule was grateful. A freighter rumbled beside them with the driver yelling at his mules. He waved, between curses, as his wagon headed out of town and Rule returned the greeting.

They passed the hosteler leaning on a pitchfork at the Howard Livery and Grain.

"Wonder if the fellow with the carriage stopped there?" Rule asked.

The ears of his mustang sprang up to determine if the words were for him.

"Let's find out." Bartlett reined his horse.

They swung their mounts around and returned to the livery.

"Howdy. Didn't happen to rent a carriage this morning, did you? Rode east an' back this morning," Rule said, leaning over the saddle. He smiled; his manner was nonchalant.

The bald-headed liveryman studied the former gunfighter for an instant, then looked at Bartlett, trying to place them. He spat a thick brown stream into the worried ground and said, "Why ya askin'? Are ya lawmen?"

Rule laughed. "No, I'm not. This is my friend Bart. Saw the tracks coming in. Been thinking about getting one, a carriage like that—for my wife and me. Thought I'd see if that carriage fellow liked it."

"Don't figger a fella like you'd like ridin' no carriage." The man rubbed his bald head and looked down at the pitchfork. "There's a few round, ya know."

Without a pause, he rattled off six names of men in town who owned carriages; none had used them this morning, including Alex Wilkerson, the town mayor. Rule tried to think of a tactful way to excuse himself as the man continued describing each owner without seeming to take a breath or even spit.

Finally, he said, "Ya might be lookin' for Eleven Meade, though. He rode in not long ago, left his carriage hyar. Didn't rent it. It's his." He motioned with his free hand toward the stable. "Reckon he wouldn't care if ya looked it over. It's a good 'un." He rolled his eyes. "Strange name. Eleven. Don't tell him I said so. He's that, ah, shootist. From over New Mexico way."

"Oh, I won't. Sure, I'd appreciate taking a quick look." Rule swung down and handed the reins to Bartlett. They exchanged looks that indicated their hunch was right.

The gunfighter knew of Meade; he was a ruthless backshooter who killed easily for money. Rule didn't care about seeing the carriage, of course, but it made sense to act that way. Bartlett said he would wait outside.

The liveryman followed Rule, eager to point out aspects of the carriage. "See them fancy wheels? Mighty fine. Got a fine top, too." He spat again and added, "She's got a crank axle. It's bent twice . . . ri't thar an' thar. That gives it a low sit, ya know, makes them wheels look even bigger." He shook his head in support of his statement.

Rule nodded, eyed the white cat resting on the carriage seat and leaned over to examine the underframe. He couldn't care less, but it made sense to follow through with his story. The bald hosteler kept jabbering, pointing out the dirt board that kept dirt from the axle itself and other structural details.

"That thar drag shoe looks like it needs some work."

"How's the ride?" Rule asked, standing again, rubbing his horse's nose.

Cocking his head, the liveryman gave a long answer that basically meant he didn't know. Without being asked, he said Meade went to the sheriff's office, but he didn't know if he was still there or not. He added that Hangar had county authority as well as being the town law.

Rule thanked him and declined the man's offer to see Meade's horse. He said he understood when the liveryman told him the cat wasn't his, that he didn't let cats sit on his carriages. The offer to order him a carriage was also declined, with Rule saying he would talk with his wife about it. With the liveryman still talking, Rule walked outside and swung back into the saddle. He waved good-bye and loped away.

His mind had already settled on the interesting coincidence of Eleven Meade riding near the dead horse and not pausing to see what had happened. It meant the shootist already knew. Meade had either shot Checker or been involved in the shooting.

A few minutes later, they reined their horses in front of the Hires & Ludlum Land Attorneys and Real Estate Agents office. Rule eased down, flipped the reins around the hitching rack and strode quickly onto the planked boardwalk. His spurs rattled their agreement. Bartlett was a few strides behind, looking at both sides of the street as he moved. Two couples passed with only perfunctory greetings, as were his.

Elrod Hires looked up from his cluttered desk as Rule stepped inside. In the uneven light of his small office, he examined the stranger, wondering what he wanted. That the man was armed was evident by the bulges under his long black coat. It was against the law to carry weapons in town, but Hires didn't intend to bring up the matter.

His eyebrows arched haughtily as he looked up from his desk. A half-finished cup of coffee, a partially eaten donut on a saucer and a stack of papers occupied the polished walnut desktop. The desk itself was the only thing in the crowded room that spoke of quality. A gift of appreciation from Lady Holt.

Rule folded his arms. "Am I speaking to Hires—or Ludlum?" Reaching into his coat pocket, he withdrew the contract.

"Elrod Hires, sir. How may I help?" The businessman with the wide mustache made no attempt to stand or hold out his hand in greeting.

"Bought the Emmett Gardner Ranch and I want to register the ownership," Rule said, stepping forward and laying the paper on Hire's desk. "You'll find it's been witnessed by Lawson Docher. You may know him. He's the land agent over in Clark Springs."

The businessman stared down at the papers, then lifted them, acting surprised at what he saw. He shivered, dropped the paper and picked it up again. He saw the second stranger come inside, nearly close the door, then stand beside it, looking out through the crack at the street.

Taking a deep breath, Hires bit his lip, pulled on his right ear nervously and said, "I believe I should inform you that Mr. Gardner is suspected of rustling. A warrant is out for his arrest." He forced himself to look up into Rule's face. "You would be doing your duty to inform Sheriff Hangar of his whereabouts."

"What I do after registering this purchase is my business, Mr. Hires," Rule said without raising his voice.

"Y-yes, of course. Of course it is." Everything about the manner of this stranger bothered Hires. He didn't like surprises, to begin with. Who was he? The stranger's long black coat added to an ominous look. Did he know this man? He didn't think so, yet there was something familiar about him. Who was his companion?

Rule folded his arms. "Mr. Gardner was riding on. Headed for Nebraska. Had his family with him. Told me about the problem with what's-her-name? Holter?"

"Oh, that would be H-Holt. Lady Holt, sir."

"Never heard of her."

Hires straightened his collar and said a wire, from Ranger Captain Sil Jaudon, had come to the sheriff and the town council yesterday. In a self-serving style, he pointed out he was a member of the council. The message said Jaudon and his fellow Rangers would be coming from Austin to rid the area of lawlessness. The wire said Emmett Gardner, John Checker and A. J. Bartlett were wanted dead or alive.

"Of course, the Checker fellow is already dead. He was shot yesterday, resisting arrest," Hires added.

At the window, Bartlett jerked in reaction to the awful news and spun around. "John killed? Oh my God!" he blurted. "He stopped all those Holt gunmen with his life. Oh my God!"

The rest of the statement caught up with him.

"Captain . . . Sil Jaudon?" he asked. "How the hell could that happen? He works for that witch Holt." He shook his head and his shoulders shuddered. "Reckon they've got us coming and going." His face was torn with agony.

"Who are you?" Hires asked.

"I'm Rule Cordell. He's my friend," Rule snarled. "Both of us know what's going on around here—and we don't like it."

"I-s he . . . R-Ranger Bartlett? Ah, A. J. Bartlett?"

"Who's that?" Rule asked.

"Oh, sorry. I just thought . . ."

"Are we finished, Mr. Hires?"

"Just about, sir. Just about."

Rule's mouth was a narrow strip, barely holding the anger he felt. "Let's get it done, Mr. Hires. We're in a hurry."

After the recording of the transaction was completed,

Rule and Bartlett left, swung back into their saddles and headed down the street.

Rule put his hand on the Ranger's heaving shoulder.

Bartlett looked up and his face was filled with fury. "I'm going to kill that woman. Her and her fat Frenchman. All of them!"

Chapter Twenty-two

Quietly, Rule Cordell let A. J. Bartlett vent. It was needed and the former outlaw knew it. He had lost a stray dog during the end of the war and didn't think he would recover from the dog's death. The loss was bad, but his reaction made no sense in light of the fact many fellow cavalrymen were dying around him. Still . . .

"A.J., when we're finished here, we'll find your friend."

"He's dead. You heard it."

"I heard he was reported dead," Rule said quietly. "I was dead, too, remember? Maybe he's hurt and needs our help. But I don't believe he's dead." He paused. "We've got a little more work to do here. Are you up to it?"

"I am. Thanks. Think Hires'll go see Hangar?" Bartlett said.

"Oh yeah. Has he left yet?"

Bartlett pulled on his hat brim and glanced back. "Yeah. Looks like some lizard in heat. Yeah, he's definitely headed for the sheriff's office."

"A lizard with a mustache."

Bartlett tried to smile.

"Let's go to the saloon and see what's new. I have a feeling we won't be without company long."

"Sure."

"And deliver some news." Rule's face took on the hint of a smile.

"Even better."

Rule and Bartlett rode down the main street and reined up at the Bar and Billiards Emporium. He shifted his backup gun to his long coat pocket. He wasn't sure what to expect, but it didn't seem prudent to be unarmed, even though he planned to appear so.

"Wait a few minutes before you come in," Rule said. "Stay away from me. In case."

Bartlett nodded as he swung down. Rule walked inside and the closest handful of customers looked up, several offered greetings, as he headed to the bar.

Hesitating, Bartlett took off his gun belt, hung it over his saddle horn and pulled free the Smith & Wesson revolver. He carefully placed the gun in his coat pocket. Adjustment of the weapon took a few moments until he was satisfied with its placement in Emmett's coat and followed Rule into the saloon. Walking in Rikor's battered chaps gave him a forceful stride.

After ordering a beer, Rule deliberately unbuckled his gun belt and laid it on the bar. Bartlett passed him and went to the far end of the bar.

"I'm new to town. What's going on?" the gunfighter asked casually.

The long-faced bartender delivered the heavy mug with only a hint of foam and told about Mrs. Cunningham's difficulty with her firstborn, about the coming celebration of the town's founding and the arrival of a new attorney from somewhere in Ohio.

"Sounds like Caisson is growing," Rule said. "That's good. I'm planning on ranching near here. Good-looking land. Hear anything about a railroad coming through here?"

The bartender gave him a look that indicated he wanted to tell him something, then decided not to do so.

"Any trouble with rustling around here?" Rule asked, then took a sip of the beer, holding the mug in his left hand. His right slipped comfortably into his coat pocket.

Next to him, a clerk with lamb chop sideburns and a dirty shirt and paper collar stopped slurping his own beer, glanced at the bartender, then said, "Oh yeah."

With another gulp for courage, the clerk told about Emmett Gardner being charged with stealing some of Lady Holt's steers, and two Rangers being charged with murdering some of her men. He shook his head, looked around to see who was listening and decided against making observations about the situation.

The bartender leaned against the bar and quietly told about a wire coming yesterday, alerting lawmen in various towns. The wire said Emmett Gardner was to be arrested if seen and Sheriff l   ar was to be notified. Former Ranger A. J. Bartlett was wa ed for murder. The wire had been signed by Texas Ranger Captain Sil Jaudon, now head of the Special Force. A second Ranger, John Checker, also wanted for murder, had been tracked down and killed.

Rule ran a finger along the side of his whiskey glass, trying to keep the emotion of again learning about Checker's death from showing. "Sil Jaudon, you say? Don't think I know that name," Rule said, sipping his beer again. "Thought Temple was the captain. Special Force, right?"

"Yeah, Temple was," the clerk said. "Some kind of money problem, I hear. Word is the governor kicked him out." He adjusted his collar. "Jaudon, ah, works for Lady Holt."

"I see."

"Probably not, mister. You're not from around here," the bartender said softly.

Rule smiled and noticed three men enter the saloon and

slide along the far wall. All wore gun belts. He noticed the bartender motion toward the stack of gun belts in the far corner of the back bar.

"Guess it doesn't really matter," Rule said casually. "I own the Gardner Ranch now. Bought it from him."

The look on the faces of the clerk and the bartender was what he expected the news would do.

"Are you sure that's a good idea, mister?" The bartender's glance behind Rule told the gunfighter what he suspected was coming.

Rule felt a hard grip on his right shoulder. He continued to drink as if the connection hadn't occurred.

"You insulted my woman, mister. Turn around," the tall bearded man behind Rule commanded from a foot behind him. His ugly breath snarled against the gunfighter's neck.

Later, it would be argued by saloon patrons as to what actually happened next. Rule's movements were one continuous blur. He tossed his beer over his shoulder, making his adversary blink, gasp and drop his hand from Rule's shoulder. Spinning around, Rule swung the empty mug in his left fist and slammed it against the man's beer-drenched face.

The would-be assailant crumpled to his knees and fell over like a shoved statue.

Rule's gun appeared in his right hand and roared. He dropped the mug and yanked free the holstered gun from the unconscious man at his feet.

Standing across the room, the yellow-headed gunman staggered, groaned and buckled over. His dropped gun slid across the card table in front of him, spraying cards, chips and money. The cardplayers yelled and dove for the relative safety of the underside of the table.

"Barkeep, I wouldn't do anything that would make me use this." Bartlett swung his revolver onto the bar's shiny surface and cocked it.

The bartender froze and slowly lifted his hands. Along the bar, the string of customers snapped from watching Rule to realizing there might be a closer problem. The three standing closest to Bartlett spun away with their drinks untouched and headed for the back door.

The remaining gunman's face turned white. He was young and full of himself. But this wasn't the way it was supposed to go. Word had come from Hires immediately after Rule had left. A sweat bead slid from his forehead down to his chin and dangled there for an instant before dropping. The stranger hadn't reacted as he was supposed to. Sheriff Hangar told Vincent to get Rule Cordell into a fight and the other Holt gunmen would kill him.

It would be easy, over with in seconds. The infamous Rule Cordell would be dead and the immediate ruling, by Hangar, would be self-defense. He had been thinking to himself how he would tell the others at the Holt Ranch how well he had handled himself.

Now he shivered and hoped he wouldn't die. Not here. Not today.

"Drop your gun," Rule growled, "or use it."

The young man swallowed. He didn't dare look down at his groin where his pants were turning wet. He unbuckled his gun belt and let it drop.

"There's more." Rule's eyes tore into the terrified man.

A Colt appeared from the man's back waistband and was discarded as if it were hot.

Four businessmen broke for the back door and disappeared to safety. A drunken cowboy yelled a tribute to the Confederacy. Most of the remaining patrons were hiding behind overturned tables; a few remained seated as if nothing had happened.

Noise at the doorway became Sheriff Hangar. The look

on Hangar's face was shock, then annoyance, as he entered. He had expected to see a dead Cordell.

"What's going on here?" the lawman demanded, waving his hands. "You're under arrest."

Both of Rule's handguns swung toward him and Hangar was unsure of his next move. He looked around the room for signs of support and saw only frightened faces. He regretted not bringing a shotgun, fully expecting the three men to have eliminated this new owner and what he meant.

"No, Hangar. Not today. Go play Lady Holt's game somewhere else," Rule said.

"We know who you are. You're Rule Cordell. No wonder you're mixed up with Emmett Gardner and his damn rustling," Hangar said, trying to keep his voice as low as possible. He wanted to draw his holstered gun, but it didn't seem like a wise thing to do and managed to fold his arms.

"Yes, I am Rule Cordell."

Hangar frowned at the admission. "Rule Cordell is an outlaw. You're under arrest."

"Better check your facts. I got a pardon from the governor. A long time ago," Rule snarled. "I'm a rancher. Just bought Emmett Gardner's place." His stare made Hangar look down at his boots.

"A rancher who doesn't want any of Lady Holt's nonsense about rustling," he continued. "Do you really think there's a real man in town who believes Emmett Gardner rustled any of her beef?" He waved the gun in his right hand for emphasis. "Did you see any of those rebranded steers, Hangar? Did you? Do you think a savvy ol' rancher would do something so goofy looking? Why would he?"

Rule Cordell's face tightened. "No, he's a man of honor . . . like Ranger John Checker and Ranger A. J. Bartlett. You wouldn't know much about those kind, would you, Hangar?

Everybody knows they saved the Gardner family from being murdered by Jaudon and his bunch. You do, too."

"Gardner has the right to a trial. Tell him to come in." Hangar found a little courage and lowered his hands slowly to his sides and stared at Bartlett. "You, you're Ranger Bartlett, aren't you, mister? You can give yourself up, too."

"I'll wait for a real judge," Bartlett barked.

"Don't tell us about justice, Hangar. You don't have any idea what it means," Rule said. "But you will. And you won't like it. Neither will Opat or Jaudon—or that woman you all work for."

The room jingled with murmurs of concern.

Sauntering into the saloon came Eleven Meade, his long blond hair swishing along his collar. Rule guessed the man's appearance wasn't planned, judging by the look on Hangar's face—and the amused expression on Meade's. The New Mexico hired killer stopped beside Hangar and, in a stage whisper, asked the sheriff if the man at the bar was Rule Cordell.

The sheriff nodded his head, then grimaced.

Meade's toothy grin reminded Rule of a mountain lion seeing an easy prey. Rule didn't know the well-dressed man, but recognized the slight bulge under his coat, at his hip, was a gun. It looked as though another bulge would be a shoulder-holstered weapon. Who was he? Surely not a deputy. Most likely, one of Lady Holt's gunmen in town for some reason.

Bartlett knew and stated his recognition clearly. "Well, well, Eleven Meade. I see Lady Holt is paying well for her guns these days—or did the New Mexico law finally chase you out of there?"

Any noise in the room was sucked away by the challenge. Another table was overturned and four men scrambled to huddle behind it. Somewhere a man was trying to sing "Nearer My God to Thee."

Meade studied Rule as if trying to determine where they might have met. His grin transformed into a cruel sneer.

Bartlett demanded Rule's gun belt from the bartender, slipped it over his shoulder and stepped away from the bar. It was a smart move, Rule thought, separating the two of them if shooting started. Rule's only interest in Meade was his hands. Right now they were at his sides.

"Well, who'd you come to shoot in the back, Meade?" Bartlett yelled as he stopped beside one of the overturned tables. "Emmett Gardner? Morgan Peale? Charlie Carlson? Someone in this room? Who did Lady Holt pay you to kill?"

On the other side of the table, one man prayed and another told him to be quiet.

Smiling evilly, Meade patted his coat where the gun rested. "I came to kill John Checker—and I did." His cackle rattled around the intense saloon. "He tried to escape from me, but I am too good."

It was Rule who responded first, but both guns remained pointed at Hangar. "No, you're known for shooting opponents in the back. You ambushed the Ranger while he was fighting Holt gunmen to keep them away from Emmett Gardner and his family. There's no way a piece of scum like you could face him. No way."

"He was wanted, dead or alive. For murder." Another cackle followed Meade's first.

Two cowboys slipped out the back door; one hesitated and looked back before going on.

Sheriff Hangar nodded. "That's right. Now he's worm meat. Morgan Peale—an' that black shooter of hers—took his body an' buried it." He avoided matching Rule's hard stare.

"I dug it up just to make sure," Meade giggled, and waved both arms. "He was bloody and full of holes. I added another. Just for the hell of it. Right between his eyes." The giggle became a hearty laugh that surprised even Hangar.

Unable to hold back his anger any longer, Bartlett screamed from across the room, "You bastard! John Checker was the best Ranger Texas ever had. You murdered him—and all of Texas will know it." His eyes were wide and hot. His gun swung toward Hangar and Meade.

For an instant, Rule thought the distraught Ranger was going to shoot.

So did Hangar, who flinched and ducked.

So did Meade, who stepped behind Hangar and slipped his right hand inside his coat.

Blinking, Bartlett caught his fury and turned it aside. Rule glanced at him and was proud of his new friend's determination. Killing the two men now would only complicate their task, not ease it. Lady Holt had the upper hand and they needed to leave without more violence. Their appearance— and the news of the new Emmett Gardner Ranch ownership— would rattle the region.

The handful of men remaining in the saloon would tell everyone what they saw and heard. It was enough for now.

Swiftly, Rule shoved both guns in his pockets and moved toward the bent-over Hangar and Meade to block Bartlett's view, in case he decided to fire after all.

Stopping within two feet of the shootist, he folded his arms. "You're a really tough man, Meade, aren't you? Next, maybe you can shoot one of the kids outside. Of course, you'll need help from Hangar here. Maybe he can rig up some kind of phony rustling charge. Better yet, a phony murder charge. Ask Judge Opat to help. He'll be glad to."

As Hangar and Meade straightened, a pearl-handled gun appeared in the shootist's fist. "No, I'm going to shoot you, Rule Cordell."

Taking time to announce his intention was a mistake. Rule's left hand was a blur that shoved the gun hand sideways. A bullet smashed into the far wall. Rule's right fist was an eyeblink behind, slamming into Meade's face and sending blood onto both of them. The shootist's gun thudded on the floor.

From behind them, Bartlett hurried across the room, shifting the shotgun to his left and drawing Rule's pistol with his freed right fist.

"Give me a reason, Hangar," he bellowed.

The sheriff backed up, holding his hands away from his side.

Meanwhile, Rule drove his left into the gunman's stomach. Meade bent over in agony, trying to find breath. A right uppercut sent the gunman flying backward. Unconscious, he slid on his back and stopped with his head against the door.

"When he wakes up, tell him to run—and run hard." Rule turned toward Hangar and shook his fist to rid it of the pain. "I don't like people who shoot people in the back."

Hangar's face was a snarl.

"And tell this Holt woman that the fire has come to town—and she isn't going to rise. She'll just be another fried bird, if she doesn't stop."

Rule yanked Hangar's gun from its holster and pointed it at him. "You aren't going to like the fire, either. Neither is Opat."

Hangar glanced down at the groaning Meade as Rule took the shootist's handguns and shoved them into his waistband beside Hangar's. Swallowing, the sheriff managed to say, "Cordell, you and Bartlett will be sorry when Lady Holt hears this. She'll come after you with all of hell. You have no idea what's going to happen. I don't know why you're here, or why you bought that old man's ranch, but it was a big mistake."

Returning to the far side of the saloon, Bartlett retrieved the weapons of the standing gunman and the wounded one.

He quietly told the young gunman that it would be wise for him to get out of the region. He walked over to the wounded gunman, lying like a child on the floor. Wimpering. A patron squatting behind the upturned table motioned toward the gunman's revolver a few feet away.

Bartlett thanked him, picked up the gun and checked the wounded man for any hideaway weapons. After removing a second Colt from the man's back waistband, Bartlett shoved it into his own with the others and strode toward Rule. Everything in him wanted to kill Meade. The bastard had killed his friend. Killed John Checker!

"Leave this piece of scum, A.J. Justice will get all of them." Rule stepped past the dazed Meade to the door, recognizing the feelings of the Ranger.

Halfway through the door, he stopped and turned back toward the inside of the saloon.

"Gentlemen, tell your friends justice is coming to Caisson. Tell them Lady Holt isn't going to run things anymore."

Tossing the retrieved guns into the street, Rule Cordell and A. J. Bartlett rode hard until they cleared the town, both taking turns at checking behind them as they galloped out onto the prairie. Satisfied they were safe for the moment, the two eased their horses into a walk.

Shaking his head, Bartlett said, "Well, that's one way of letting folks know." He chuckled. "Why did you put your guns away?"

"It wasn't my smartest move. I didn't think Meade had the nerve to pull on me. I knew Hangar didn't."

"You wanted him to, didn't you?"

Rule rode without speaking for a few heartbeats. "I guess I did. It gave me an excuse to hit him."

"We'd better get your hands into some water. They'll swell."

"There's a spring where Emmett and Rikor are waiting."

Bartlett held his hand to his forehead and studied the horizon. "What'll Lady Holt do . . . when she hears?"

Rule patted the neck of his horse. "She has to send Jaudon and his men after us. I'm guessing he's coming from Austin."

"That'll be more than a handful. What are we going to do?"

"First, we're going to ride to this Morgan Peale's ranch and find out what happened to your friend," Rule said, glancing back over his shoulder. "Then I think we should pay a visit to this lady."

Bartlett adjusted his gun belt because it didn't feel right.

"Then we need to see the governor."

Bartlett's shoulders rose and fell. "You mean, kill him?"

"No, I mean . . . get him to resign," Rule said. "Something's happened to your captain, too. We need to find out what."

"I forgot about Captain Temple." Bartlett licked his lower lip and stared at the land ahead.

Minutes later, they reunited with the two Gardners and shared the news with them. With Bartlett's reminder, Rule soaked his hands in the cooling spring water. Emmett Gardner was visibly upset and slammed his fist against his thigh; Rikor walked away for a moment to hide his feelings. They agreed to ride for the Peale Ranch and see what had really happened to Checker.

Chapter Twenty-three

Eight well-armed men burst into Ranger headquarters. Captain Poe jumped in his seat.

"Mornin', Captain. We need to see you." The gray-haired man's mouth was loaded with licorice "Got any coffee, boy?"

Without waiting, Spake Jamison walked over to the stove, grabbed a cup from the shelf and poured a cupful.

"What can I do for you men?" Captain Poe asked, sitting down again, glad he had worn a dark suit today as it hid the wetness around his groin.

"We're headed for Caisson." Spake poured sugar into his coffee.

The other seven men spread out in the room. One was also eating licorice. The shortest Ranger walked over to the stove and helped himself to coffee as well.

"Caisson? Oh, going to work for Lady Holt, huh?" Captain Poe asked. "I'm a little surprised, but I'm sure she pays well." He pointed to his desk. "Been working on getting jobs for all of you Special Forces men. You know, with ranches along the border. It'll take a few days, but you'll like the pay, I'm certain. Better than Texas pays, that's for sure."

Spake walked over to the desk, swallowing the licorice before washing it down with coffee. "Wrong. Again, Poe. We're headed to Caisson to help A.J. and those little ranchers. Gonna stop that damn woman."

Captain Poe wasn't sure how to react. He looked over at the other former Rangers; each man stared at him. None smiled. The shortest man stirred his coffee with his finger.

"Reckon you didn't have much of a meetin' with Citale." Spake reached inside his shirt with his free hand and pulled out a wrinkled sack of candy. "Licorice, boy?"

The Ranger captain shook his head. "No . . . ah, no, thank you." He rubbed his cheek. "I thought my meeting with the governor went quite well."

Spake grinned; his single eye glared at the lawman. "So you got our jobs back—and Temple's our boss again."

"What?"

"You know. Our jobs? As Rangers? You just said the meeting went well," the older Ranger said. "Maybe you define 'well' different than we do." He cocked his head to the side. "That's how I'd describe getting our captain out of jail—and his and all of our jobs back. How would you define it?"

The other Rangers supported his comment with strong grunted agreement. Another walked over to the stove for coffee. Captain Poe didn't like where this was going at all. He didn't like Spake's insubordination. Spake didn't understand how difficult it was to stay on top in Austin. He remembered the old warrior mentioning he was headed for Houston the last time they talked.

"Thought you were headed for Houston, Spake?"

He hadn't answered Spake's question, but this might get him off the subject.

"Changed my mind." Spake took a piece of licorice from the sack and tossed it toward the bearded Ranger. "I asked you a question, boy. I don't like folks not answering my questions. I always have the feeling they've got something to hide."

"Is that a threat, Jamison?"

Scratching his chest through his shirt, the old Ranger thought a moment. "That was a statement of fact, Poe." He adjusted the shotgun quiver strap on his shoulder.

Trying to deflect the intensity of the older man, Captain Poe turned in his chair toward the other former Rangers. "Well, how'd you men like the idea of getting good pay?"

"Poe, let's quit dancing here. We came for one reason. So you could make us Rangers. Again," Spake said. "Like I told you, we're heading for Caisson. So let's do it. We've got some hard riding to do."

Frowning, Poe threw up his arms. "Make you Rangers? I can't do that. I've already got my full battalion. You know that."

"No. We don't."

"I—I don't have that kind of budget. The state of Texas isn't very generous, I'm afraid."

"You aren't listening, boy. We want our badges, not money."

Captain Poe stood, pushing back his chair. His hands trembled so much he held them behind his back. This was idiocy. Didn't these men realize how things worked? Didn't they realize no one could just do what they wanted when they wanted? A grim smile reached his mouth and vanished. Maybe someone like Lady Holt could. But not ordinary men and women.

"Look, men. If I did what you ask, I would be directly insulting the governor." Captain Poe reinforced the statement with a wave of his right hand and quickly returned it to his back to rejoin the other.

"Harrison Temple refused a direct order from the governor. He was insubordinate and had to be removed," he continued. "That was before all this money fraud stuff surfaced. Understand?"

Without thinking about it, he brought both hands forward and waved them wildly. "I am not about to be removed by the governor. You and I don't know that Jaudon might be a fine Ranger captain with an excellent force of men. We don't know that."

He stopped and took a deep breath; most of his fear left with the following exhalation. "I am sorry Jaudon didn't see fit to ask you to stay on. But that happens. Men are hired—and fired every day. Please. I am trying to find jobs for you on ranches that need protection. It's the best I can do."

With another deep breath, he sat in his chair and looked down at his desk. He didn't look up again until he heard the door slam. They were gone.

Chapter Twenty-four

"Do not talk to thunder and lightning. Do not challenge thunder and lightning. There is no pity, no caring, no understanding. I do so as a young man only because my vision showed me the Thunder Beings were there to guide me, not hurt me. Few are so chosen," Stands-In-Thunder said to John Checker in the dark dream that engulfed the Ranger's wounded body.

In the world of dreams, the old man told Checker part of the war chief's spiritual connection included never to eat any raw meat, to sing a special song during all storms, always to carry white stones and a hard ball from the buffalo's stomach into battle and to paint his face and body with lightning bolts and hail marks. His medicine also came from the Sky Beings—and the great Thunderbird itself. Few Comanches would ever challenge the Thunderbird as the old war chief had done.

Suddenly the dream turned ugly and one of the Indians standing beside the old war chief pulled a gun from his robes and began shooting at Checker. Then another pulled a gun from a pipe bag and fired at him, too.

"*Tuwikaa*, the raven, no longer tells us where the buffalo have gone," Stands-In-Thunder pronounced as if nothing were happening. "White soldiers have burned our lodges, and killed our women and our children. You are a white man. You are to blame."

In his dream, Checker pleaded with the old man as the other Indians began to shoot at him. "I buried you, my father. With your best horse and your finest weapons. I prayed and sang for your spirit passage. I watched your spirit ride toward the great valley of wonder and youth."

From somewhere came an old brown horse. Someone pushed a sack of food and a silver dollar into his hand and told him to run. Once again, his sister was beside him, wanting to go with him, tears filling her pale face. He promised to return when he could. She wanted something of his, a tangible thing to be his promise.

"Wait, Johnny . . . please," Amelia said, her face wet with despair, her eyes bright with fear. "I want something of yours. To hold. Please."

Grabbing his shirt, she pulled free a button from it. But this time it wouldn't release and she was swept away into the shadows. Even in his dream, her face was a mere blur now. The only place he could actually see her—or their mother— again was in the small photograph pushed in the lid of his pocket watch.

Over his shoulder, a dark shadow appeared. It wore a bowler hat and held a rifle. Beside the looming shape was a carriage and a single horse breathing fire through its nostrils. The horse burst into flames and became a giant bird.

Checker was suddenly awake.

Where was he? Where were his guns? He shook his head and the ache came back. He was in some kind of sleeping clothes and his wounds were cleaned and wrapped in bandages. He heard voices in the other room. Was it A.J.? Had the Gardners made it safely to Rule Cordell's house? How long had he been here?

He looked at himself and remembered getting shot and trying to escape. What happened? His body was weak and pounding with pain. He looked down at himself again and was comforted to see he was wearing Stands-In-Thunder's medicine pouch.

Lying back on the bed, he drifted again into another tortured dream. His sister was gone, as were his father and his two sons. Only Stands-In-Thunder remained. Checker touched his hand to his cheek and mumbled, "Yes. We fight in . . . *Llano Estacado*. It was many years back. Don't you remember?" He used the Spanish name for the Staked Plains where the Comanches once were the lords. The rest of his words were nonsense only his sleeping mind heard.

In the other room, Rule, Bartlett, Emmett and Rikor were talking at the same time, almost delirious about discovering John Checker was not dead but wounded. Emmett had introduced Rule and Bartlett; Morgan had introduced them to London Fiss. Morgan and Fiss explained they thought it was the only way to protect Checker; they didn't know exactly what had happened or where the Gardners had gone. All of the group were thankful for their help and their smart decision.

The Peale Ranch house was small, but sturdily built from a combination of rough-hewn logs, adobe bricks and flat boards. Two bedrooms were in the main house; London Fiss slept in a room built out from the barn even when Checker wasn't there. Inside the main house the feeling was warm— and definitely a woman's.

Fiss studied Rule as the group described what had happened on the trail and in town. Finally, the black man said, "Believe I know you, sir. Or of you."

The other conversation stopped.

"My cousin, Alexander Morrison. Lives over your way. He told me about you and your wife helping . . . us. Teaching our children. You stopped one of those awful clans that killed Suitcase . . . Mr. Eliason."

"Thank you, Mr. Fiss. Suitcase was a good friend," Rule responded. "My Aleta enjoyed her time with the children. She said they were bright and eager to learn."

"It was very much appreciated," Fiss said, "and please call me London."

"I'd like that. My name is Rule."

Rule shared that Eleven Meade said he had dug up Checker's grave and shot at the body. The gunfighter cocked his head slightly and added that he didn't think the killer had done so, because it would have taken some serious work.

With a wistful smile, Fiss said, "I was watching him through my field glasses. If he had started digging, I would have killed him."

The statement was matter-of-fact.

"John Checker saved my life a few years back. I owed him that," the black man continued, and motioned toward Morgan. "Mrs. Peale, she gave me a chance. I owed her, too."

Conversation among the group grew once more, mostly about Lady Holt and what was happening. They avoided the subject of Checker's condition.

"Can we see him?" Bartlett finally asked. His face was years younger in its relief to know his friend was alive.

Morgan frowned. "I don't know. He's been asleep since we found him. Or nearly so. Woke up briefly last night. Said something about Apaches. Then a woman . . . ah, named Amelia, I think. I couldn't make out the rest."

"Amelia, that's his sister's name," Bartlett said. "Hasn't seen her since they were little. Awful tale."

Morgan smiled at hearing the woman was Checker's sister

and said, "Mr. Fiss has been treating him with some family remedies. We were afraid to ride for the doctor."

The black man nodded. "Good remedies, they are. Especially with bullet wounds." He paused and added, "The only lead in him was in his lower back. The rest were scrapes and burns. Really lucky. None caught anything vital. Got a wound in his left leg. Not from this gunfight. Looks like it's been treated. Before." He grimaced. "He's got some old bullet scars. Not the first time he's been hit."

Emmett nodded. "Yeah. Got that hole in his leg fightin' off Jaudon's bunch. At my place."

"The bullet in his back was a short .44." Fiss put his hand against the lower left corner of his own back. "You don't see many like that."

"Eleven Meade." Rule's declaration had an ominous ring.

"Yes. I saw one of those Evans rifles in his carriage." Fiss added, "Shoots a short .44. Shoots a lot of them."

"How long before John can ride . . . again?" Bartlett asked.

Fiss looked at Morgan before responding. "He's a tough man. You know that. But he lost a lot of blood. Awful weak."

Almost crying, Morgan blurted, "He needs to sleep. To rest."

"We owe both of you a lot," Bartlett said. "How can we ever thank you?"

Morgan smiled gently. "Win this war against Lady Holt. Or we all go down." She told about Eleven Meade delivering a letter from Lady Holt offering to buy her ranch for a cheap price. "I imagine that's so she can tell others that she tried to buy it . . . before we got wiped out. I figure Charlie Carlson got the same letter. Got one for you, too." She swung her fist in the air and grimaced.

Before anyone could respond, she invited them into her

small kitchen for coffee and freshly baked donuts. Rikor was particularly pleased with the offering and had to be reminded by his father to only take one.

Morgan heard the whispered direction and said, "Rikor, there are plenty. Please help yourself. I would feel insulted if you didn't."

Glancing at his father for approval, Rikor thanked her and immediately took two donuts.

As they enjoyed the refreshment, Rule turned to Fiss and Morgan with a response to her earlier statement. "A few minutes ago, you said we needed to win. I agree. But that's going to be more easily said than done, ma'am. We're going to have to do what she doesn't expect—and do it swiftly. And we're going to have to be lucky."

"What do you have in mind?" she said, putting her coffee mug down on the table.

Rikor sneaked another donut while the others were concentrating on Rule.

"As soon as this Jaudon returns from Austin, she'll send him and his men on a sweep through here. Emmett's place. Yours. Carlson's. She'll figure this Ranger setup won't last long—so she'll strike and strike hard," Rule said softly.

No one spoke.

Emmett downed the last of his coffee and declared, "Why don't we jes' go an' see that damn governor an' send him skedaddlin' out o' Texas?"

After taking a bite of his donut, Rule responded, "Uncle Emmett, I think that's a good idea."

"Ya do?"

"Yes, I do." Rule took another bite. "But we need to do some changes in Caisson first. Get those arrest warrants changed. Get Captain Temple back in charge of his Ranger force so we've got some men to go against hers."

"I imagine there's a good bunch of former Rangers all

spitting and fuming right now," Bartlett said. "Maybe they've already started something."

"Maybe so. We're going to need them." Rule took a long swig of coffee and pushed his hat back on his forehead. He wanted to say they were going to need John Checker but didn't.

Morgan licked her lower lip and looked away. "I don't see how that's going to happen. Governor Citale is dug in deep. His alliance with Holt has made him a rich man. Others, too. Railroad men mostly."

"I didn't say it would be easy," Rule said. "But if we stay here, or at Emmett's, her men will eventually overrun us. Our only weapon is movement and surprise."

"Doesn't sound like we've got much of a chance," Emmett growled. "I'd jes' like to wring . . ."

He didn't finish the statement.

"All right, I'm in." Morgan folded her arms. "Tell me what to do."

Fiss walked over beside her. "I ride for Mrs. Peale."

"Mr. Fiss, I don't expect you . . ."

"I know you don't, but I must."

Rule frowned and sipped his coffee. "You know they might burn your place, Mrs. Peale. And make you an outlaw again, London."

A noise in the other room stopped the conversation.

"What's that?" Bartlett said, and spun toward the unseen disturbance.

"It came from John's room!" Morgan headed in that direction before the statement was completely out of her mouth.

Everyone hurried toward the bedroom where John Checker had been sleeping. Rikor hesitated and grabbed another donut before leaving the kitchen. In the narrow room, Checker, already in his pants and boots, was putting on a shirt. His medicine pouch, dangling from his neck, bounced against his chest. His Comanche war tunic lay folded at the top of an old dresser, along with his rifle, gun belt and hat.

"John, what in the hell are you doing!" Bartlett said, and hurried into the room, passing Morgan. "You've got no business being up."

Checker stared at him and frowned. "A.J., it's mighty good to see you, too. I'm all right. A little stiff, that's all. Where am I?"

"You're in my home." Morgan rushed past Bartlett and stood beside the wounded Ranger. "John Checker, you get back in bed." She touched Checker's arm and left it there.

Smiling weakly at her, he continued to put on his shirt.

"He gonna be all right?" Rikor asked, poking his head into the room and munching another donut.

"Guess that's gonna be up to the good Lord—and Mrs. Morgan an' Mr. Fiss hyar," Emmett said.

Ignoring Morgan's concerns as well, Fiss told Checker what had happened, including the news of Sil Jaudon being named a captain of the Rangers and of Captain Temple being dismissed and arrested—and the faking of the Ranger's death to give them some time for him to heal.

Waving her arms in frustration, Morgan told him again to lie down and rest.

Stepping into the room and standing next to his father, Rikor grinned awkwardly and mumbled Checker wouldn't get any donuts if he didn't do what she said.

Shaking her head, Morgan took a step closer. "You need to rest, John Checker."

"No, I need a horse. Mine's dead. I remember that. I can pay."

"Don't be silly," she said. "You're lucky to be alive. You look like you've got a fever." She reached up to touch his forehead, but his smile stopped her.

Edging closer, the black man explained how Rule expected Lady Holt to send her men to check out the Peale Ranch, that she wouldn't take Meade's word for his death. He thought they would move on Emmett's ranch and take control of it.

"Meade? Eleven Meade? The New Mexico gunman?"

"Yes, that's the one. He even came to Mrs. Peale's ranch and delivered a letter from Lady Holt. An offer to buy her place. An insulting one, of course," Fiss said. "He also wanted to know about you."

Checker asked, "He's the one . . . who got behind me . . . isn't he?"

"Yes. He's the one. Quite proud of telling people in Caisson that he killed you. Sheriff Hangar backed him up, saying you were wanted dead or alive."

Checker tucked his shirttails into his waistband. "Where are my guns?"

Fiss pointed at them.

Stepping toward his weapons, the Ranger stopped. "Instead of asking questions, I should be thanking you—and Mrs. Peale. You saved my life."

Morgan turned toward him and smiled. "That's not necessary. You Rangers are trying to save all of us from that awful woman."

"I'm not a Ranger. I'm an outlaw."

Her mouth opened, but she didn't know how to respond.

Checker buckled on his gun belt, shoved his second gun into his back waistband and looked over at Rule Cordell, who was standing quietly, with his arms crossed, in the doorway.

"You must be Rule Cordell," Checker said.

"I am, John Checker. Been looking forward to meeting you."

Rule held out his hand and Checker shook it.

After putting on his Comanche tunic and grabbing his

hat, Checker turned to the exasperated ranch woman. "Mrs. Peale, I can't thank you—and London—enough for what you did. You made yourselves a big enemy in Lady Holt. But I reckon you know that—and that you already were." Removing the bandage tied around his forehead, he returned his hat to his head.

"Only a fool wouldn't want to stay here and be waited on by such a beautiful woman," he continued, "but I've got work to do."

He patted Rule on the shoulder and they walked together into the next room. As they did, Rule touched the medicine pouch under Checker's shirt and then his own medicine pouch under his shirt. He said something no one understood. Strange words.

Bartlett thought it was a Comanche blessing, but the only two words he knew for sure were *muea*, Comanche for "moon" and *rami*, Comanche for "brother." He heard Checker repeat the message.

As he followed the two gunfighters to the doorway, Rikor turned toward Bartlett and, through a mouth of donut, asked him what they had just said to each other. The Ranger explained it was a Comanche warrior blessing he had heard a long time ago. It connects the power of the moon to a man's heart and makes it strong, he said.

Rikor stared at the gunfighters as if not believing, but not daring to challenge the statement.

Fiss watched him and shook his head. "I don't think that Englishwoman has any idea of what she's stirred up. John Checker and Rule Cordell."

Chapter Twenty-five

Lady Holt had just finished her phoenix ritual when Sheriff Hangar and Eleven Meade arrived at her ranch house. She was strolling from the red ceremonial room when she heard the knocking at the front door.

"I'll get it, Elliott," she yelled, and strode to the heavy wood entrance. Looking away, she said softly, "Iva Lee, do you think it's Emmett Gardner giving me his ranch? Or that foolish Peale woman?" Her laugh followed her approach.

"Well, good afternoon, Sheriff, what brings you to my land today?" She glanced at Meade holding his white cat. "I'm sure you're here to collect your money—or advise me of the status of your assignment."

Meade managed to say, "Checker's dead" before Hangar declared, "Got some bad news. Somethin' nobody expected."

"You mean *you* didn't expect," Lady Holt said. "Come in. I was just about to have my afternoon tea." She looked again at Meade. "Or do you need to be traveling? Elliott has your payment. I'll call him."

Eleven Meade bit his lower lip and smiled, more of a thin grin. "I'll stay if you don't mind, m'lady. You might have another assignment for me."

"I see."

He leaned over and let the cat loose. "Discover the world, my precious."

Sitting around the elegant mahogany coffee table in the main room of the house, the threesome enjoyed hot tea and dainty cookies made by her chef. Elliott served them on fine Italian china. Hangar asked for three spoons of sugar, Meade a squeeze of fresh lemon. Lady Holt's tea was laced with a spoon of sugar and a touch of cream, before presenting it to her; Elliott didn't ask.

In the center of the table was a fresh display of prairie lackspur, rain lilies, scarlet pimpernel, Mexican gold poppies and wisteria. She loved the mixture of color and insisted on her considerable garden being harvested for the best blooms each day.

The quiet black man said something to her in Latin; she nodded and he left. She studied both men before finally asking what the problem was.

"Rule Cordell."

"Rule Cordell?" she repeated. "If memory serves me right, he's dead. One of those wild pistoleros who popped up in Texas after the war. What's that got to do with me?"

Sipping the tea, Hangar explained about Cordell and his appearance in Caisson. Her lack of reaction surprised him. He was expecting a vicious outburst.

"So, Rule Cordell now owns Emmett Gardner's ranch," she said, more to herself than to either man. "And Gardner has left the region."

"Looks that way." Hangar reached for another cookie.

"And you were afraid to kill him. This Rule Cordell." Her cold words stopped his advance on the plate.

Meade snickered. "No, he tried. Cordell was ready—and too good. For three of your men. That other Ranger . . . Bartlett . . . he was with him."

"I see. And you?" She stared at Meade.

The hired killer's face was taut. "Actually I *was* going to kill him. For you. But I wasn't going up against two guns."

"That isn't how it happened, Meade," Hangar said. "Cordell knocked your gun away and hit you to the floor. It was something to see. Slammed him silly."

"I didn't see you trying anything." Meade stared at the lawman.

"Gentlemen, I really don't care—or have time for this," Lady Holt said, waving her hands for emphasis. "Do you know where this Rule Cordell was going? You said he left town. Was he headed for Gardner's ranch? I assume you checked on the validity of his claim."

"Yes to both. Hires said it was all legal and buttoned up. He left town with that other Ranger, but I don't know where they were going."

"And you didn't follow him." Lady Holt's eyes tightened around Hangar's face.

"I . . . ah, I . . . no, I didn't," Hangar said. "Thought I'd better come out here to make sure you knew about him."

Lady Holt sipped her tea. "And you thought I'd rather hear about him coming, than hear you took care of him."

Meade smiled.

"Well, ah, no, I . . . ah, I . . ."

"Never mind. Jaudon should be back from Austin tomorrow. All of his men are officially Rangers—or we can say they are. I'll have them take out this Rule Cordell and take over the Gardner Ranch at the same time." She placed her teacup on the table. "Eleven, did you deliver the letter to that Peale woman as I asked?"

"Of course."

"Tell me how you know John Checker is dead."

Rubbing his hands together, Meade explained what had happened at the Peale Ranch and his subsequent inspection of the Checker burial, ending with his shooting into the dead man's face.

She stood and looked down at the killer. "So you always carry a shovel with you?"

"What?"

"I asked if you carry a shovel in your carriage." Her mouth was a slit with a snarl appearing at the right corner. "Surely you didn't dig him up with your bare hands."

Meade glanced at the amused sheriff and said, "No, I don't—and I didn't. I made the colored man do it. The one who works for the Peale woman."

Her smirk disappeared.

"He didn't want to . . . but he did." Meade patted the holstered pistol at his hip.

Lady Holt ran her hands over her gold-striped blouse, looked down at herself and said, "You think she beds that black?"

Meade was happy to have her attention on something else. But how would he know if the woman was involved with her hired hand? All he knew for certain was London Fiss was a formidable man who would protect her with his last breath. He shivered. Facing such a man was not something he wished to do.

"Here's what I want you to do, Hangar." Lady Holt was focused on the lawman again.

She began to pace, rattling off what she expected. Hangar was to get Judge Opat to issue a warrant for Rule Cordell's arrest and wire the governor to have Cordell's pardon revoked. After that, he was to go to the town's newspaper editor and tell him about the outlaw coming to town and being a part of Emmett Gardner's rustling operation. She made it clear Hangar was to insist on the story being run. What wasn't said was that Henry Seitmeyer, the editor, was his own man.

Hangar looked as if he had been slapped in the face. Why did he have to do all the dirty work?

Lady Holt's directive to Meade was simple. "Find this A. J. Bartlett and kill him. I'll pay you the same as the other Ranger."

Meade nodded, stood and nudged Hangar to respond the same way. As they started to leave, she said, "Wait. Where does this Rule Cordell live? Do you know?" Her smile was radiant, her eyes wide and bright. "That's where Emmett Gardner and his stupid sons are hiding. Has to be."

Hangar and Meade stood in the hallway, both unsure of what she wanted.

"Ah, Hires said the deed was written up in . . . ah, Clark Springs," Hangar said.

"That's it, then. Eleven, I want you to ride there," Lady Holt demanded. "You can be there by morning." She nodded agreement at her own thinking. "Find where he lives. Then wire me. I'll decide what happens next. Don't kill him 'til I tell you to."

Hangar was relieved. His assignments seemed easier by contrast.

Meade straightened his cravat. "You're going to have to be more clear, m'lady. Is this project in addition to the Bartlett assignment—or instead of? Either way, what are you going to pay me for this search? It might be quite time-consuming."

Lady Holt's expression transformed from enthusiastic to vengeful. Her eyes narrowed as her gaze homed in on the hired killer.

"Maybe I should just have Ranger Captain Jaudon arrest you for murder?" The snarl reappeared at the corner of her mouth.

Meade's first impulse was to challenge the statement with his own threat. "Well, now, what's to keep me from shooting you—and your darling star packer here—taking my money and leaving?" He rested his right hand on the pearl handle of his holstered gun. "What would you say to that, m'lady?"

"I would say turn around. Real slow. Elliott doesn't like quickness."

"*Cor aut more.*" The phrase came from behind the killer.

"That's Latin for 'heart or death.' Interesting choice of words, huh? In case you didn't look, Elliott is holding a shotgun. Is it cocked, Elliott? Ah yes, it is."

Meade chuckled. "Touché, m'lady."

"Find where Rule Cordell lives—and I'll pay you five hundred dollars."

"For that, I'd kill him."

"I'll remember you said that." She smiled and ran her fingers through her hair. "Oh, Elliott, please give Mr. Meade his money—and after you've seen them out, please find Mr. Moore. Have him come and see me. I need his report on his meeting with Charlie Carlson." Her smile was lustful.

Chapter Twenty-six

It was midmorning when Eleven Meade pulled up in front of the first saloon he saw upon entering the town of Clark Springs. He was tired and dirty. He couldn't remember when he last drove so long in such a short time. Something about Lady Holt made a man do things he didn't want to do. Ah, but the money was good. Very good.

A drink, something to eat and a bath were his priorities. After that, he would check into finding Rule Cordell's home. He didn't think it would be hard to do. A nap would also be wonderful, but he wouldn't allow himself that pleasure. Not yet.

Unlike Lady Holt, he didn't expect to find much there. Anything, actually. He figured Emmett Gardner had taken his sons and gone on, probably heading toward New Mexico. Santa Fe, likely. And not Nebraska as the fool Hires had reported. He smiled. If Lady Holt wanted him to do so, he could return there and find them.

His apartment in Santa Fe wasn't much, but it was home when he wasn't working. Like now. He wrapped the reins of his tired horse around the hitching rack and strolled inside,

telling his cat to remain in the carriage. The happy noise of
the saloon always pleased him. Comforting.

An open table caught his eye and he moved to it, slid into a
chair and let his body relax. Soon a Mexican waitress came to
find out what he wanted; she was also offering herself in the
back. He snorted and said he was too tired and just wanted a
drink and something to eat. Then he changed his mind.

"Say, I'm looking for Rule Cordell. He's an old friend.
Heard he lived here. In Clark Springs. Do you know him?" He
handed her a coin and she took it, slipping it between her
breasts visible above the wrinkled peasant blouse.

"Sí, senor. All know of ze great Rule Cordell. He ees a
pistolero. He ees a preacher. Ah, he ees, what you call eet . . .
a hoss man," she said, tossing her long black hair as she
spoke.

He handed her another coin. "Good. That's good. Do you
know where he lives?"

She thought for a moment and said she needed to check
with someone. After talking with a hard-looking vaquero
in the far corner of the long bar, she returned and told
him where to find the Cordell house. He paid her again
and asked for a bottle and whatever they were serving for
food.

After eating, he left, found the town public bath, a service in the back of the barbershop, and bathed. Completing
his initial self-prescribed tasks, he returned to his horse
and carriage. The animal looked tired, so Meade headed to
the livery and exchanged horses, paying in advance for the
stable manager to feed and water his horse.

There was no hurry. Lady Holt would be wired after he
went to the Cordell house and found it empty. Of that, he
was certain.

The directions were easy to follow and he soon found

himself overlooking a small house with three corrals, a windmill and several outbuildings. He reined the horse within a narrow crease in a mile-long ridge that yo-yoed across the prairie. Viewing the entire ranch yard would be excellent from here, he decided.

After laying out a saddle blanket carefully on the ground, he straightened it several times and stretched out on the blue-and-green fabric. He withdrew his two pistols and positioned himself to study the ranch and its empty yard through his field glasses. The guns were placed at his side to allow for more comfort as he lay.

No Rule Cordell. At least not in sight.

In his mind, he began drafting the wire he would send to Lady Holt. After an hour, he decided he had watched long enough. Only a few children had ever emerged from the house to play hide-and-seek. If the former outlaw was in the house, he was apparently not coming out. The only thing to do was to ride down there and find out.

He would present himself as a horse buyer from Austin. If Cordell was there, he would return here and wait to kill him. That would definitely please Lady Holt. The price would be fair, even though the act was done before she told him to do it. If he didn't get the chance—or Cordell wasn't there—he would drive back to town and wire her what he knew and ask for orders.

After returning his revolvers to their holsters, he stood and wiped imaginary dust from his coat and sleeves. He straightened his cravat and his hat. When this was over, he would go back to the saloon and have a nice time with that Mexican waitress. He deserved it. Grabbing the blanket and folding it carefully, he carried it back to the carriage and laid the garment on the carriage floor.

Where was his rifle? He left it in the carriage with his cat, he was certain. He looked at the ground on all sides of the stationary vehicle. This didn't make sense.

From behind a large boulder stepped a handsome woman with snapping black eyes and black hair pulled back into a single mane on her back. In her hands were two pistols. Silver-plated and pearl-handled. A few steps behind her came the vaquero from the saloon, holding the Evans rifle in his hands.

"You come lookeeng for *mío* husband." Aleta's words were a meanacing challenge.

Taking a deep breath, Meade introduced himself as a horse buyer from Austin.

"Do you always look from ze hidden place?"

Licking his lips, Meade took off his hat. "I'm sorry, ma'am. I know how it must look. But I like to be careful. Found it's easier to look at a man's horses . . . when he isn't standing right there, telling me how good they are. You know . . ." His voice trailed off.

"Is eet so important to carry so many guns when you do thees . . . thees horse buying?"

"Well, I've found it's better to be safe than sorry," Meade said, avoiding her eyes.

Actually he found her to be more fearsome than the silent man holding his rifle. There was something about her that made him shiver. He noticed the vaquero had not cocked the rifle in his hands. That was good. Very good.

"I've a letter from your husband. About selling me horses," Meade said. "Let me show it to you. I represent a large rancher there. He wants only the best mounts."

Without asking, he reached into his coat, smoothly drew the short-barreled Smith & Wesson revolver from its shoulder holster and brought it forward with his coat hiding his real intent.

This would be easy. After all, he was "Eleven," the chosen one. Eleven was a master number in astrology and numerology, he had been told by his parents. Others looked to those who were "Eleven" for inspiration.

He would kill her first, then the foolish man who had told on him. The gun had been named "Illumination" in honor of his special presence. The black nose of the pearl-handled gun with its strange markings and a left-handed loading gate cleared his coat.

Bam! Bam! Bam!

The impact of Aleta's bullets drove him backward. His bowler spun from his head as if it had its own life. He staggered and tried to fire his own gun. His eyes were blurring. What was wrong? No one could stop Eleven. He had known this since he was a child. His gun finally exploded, missing the woman before him.

Two more bullets, one from each gun in her hands, smashed into his chest, inches from the first three.

He staggered backward. His gun was too heavy and slipped from his fingers and thudded on the ground. Blood slipped from his mouth and he collapsed.

"I—I—I . . . a-am . . . E—Eleven. I—I am . . . L-Light . . . B-Bea . . ."

His eyes stared unseeing at the midday sky.

Aleta walked over to him, keeping her guns pointed at the unmoving body. She pulled his second revolver from its hip holster and tossed it. "You ees a murderer. It does not matter what number you ees." She stepped back. "*Mío* husband has never written a letter to anyone in Austin."

She spun on her heel and thanked the hard-looking Mexican in Spanish. He said again Rule had told him to keep a lookout for any strangers coming to town asking about him. She nodded and said they would go to the town marshal to report the attempt on her life. A wire to Rule would inform him of what had happened.

"What do you think he meant by saying he ees 'eleven'?" she asked.

"No *comprende*."

Aleta stared at the carriage. "We weel need to see if someone in town wants a cat."

Chapter Twenty-seven

Judge Opat was conducting a hearing about a leasing disagreement between two businessmen when Morgan Peale entered the small municipal courtroom from the main door. Morning light from the single window sought her maple-colored hair and danced with it.

"Sorry, ma'am, this is a closed courtroom right now. I'm conducting a hearing. You understand." Opat's face and manner looked more like a pompous rooster than usual.

The two businessmen barely turned to look at the woman in the doorway. All three men immediately noticed she was wearing a gun belt.

"That can wait. You're going to handle something more important," Morgan said, walking down the narrow aisle separating the courtroom's rows of planked seating.

After a glance at the men, Opat straightened his back. "Ma'am, I thought I made it clear. This is a closed—"

"And I thought I made it clear you have something more important to do," Morgan demanded, continuing her ascent. Her right hand rested on the handle of her holstered revolver.

"I'll take care of this, Judge." The taller businessman with the long sideburns stood.

"That would be a big mistake, mister." The words halted his attempt to have her leave even before he realized who said them.

From the courtroom's rear door, John Checker emerged.

"What? Aren't you John Checker? You're dead!" Opat almost choked on the words.

"No, I'm not, Opat," Checker growled. "And these two gentlemen will be happy to stand aside for a few minutes while justice is done." He looked at the two men. "Won't you?"

Opat waved his arms and shouted, "You're not a Ranger anymore, Checker. You're wanted for murder."

"No, I'm not a Ranger, Opat. That means I don't have to abide by the Ranger's rules. Understand?"

Checker's stare was too intense for the skinny magistrate. He shook his head, making his odd lock of brown hair shake.

Stepping farther into the anxious courtroom, Checker rested both hands on his gun belt. Sunlight stroked his Roman face, long black hair and hawkish nose.

"That murder charge is one of the things we're here for, Judge," Checker declared. "First, though, you're going to conduct a real hearing on the charge of rustling against Emmett Gardner. Then you'll do the same with that ridiculous murder charge against my partner and me."

He stopped and looked at the two businessmen, who were terrified, and asked again, "You boys don't mind waiting a bit, do you?"

"A-ah, of c-course n-not."

"N-no. W-we'll c-come b-back. Later."

Checker cocked his head. "You sit right there. You can be witnesses." He glanced at Opat reaching under his walnut bench where he sat. "If you're reaching for a gavel, that's fine. If you come up with a gun, it'll be your last hearing."

The rooster-haired judge froze. His narrow, curved nose whistled in alarm. Slowly, his hands rose away from the podium.

"Good, Opat. You're a smarter man than I thought," Checker said, and motioned toward the main door. "Come on in, Emmett. Bring our guest."

The grizzled rancher slipped inside. His lopsided grin reached his brightened eyes. With him came the editor of the *Claisson Recorder,* the town newspaper. Henry Seitmeyer's bow tie and fresh shirt made him appear more dapper than usual. In his hand was a pad of paper and a pencil. Both hands were stained with old ink, a constant part of the profession.

"Henry, I'm sorry you had to be brought here against your will," Opat said, trying to appear more confident than he felt. "I'll get this cleared up."

The stocky editor hunched his shoulders. "I came of my own free will, Judge. Sounded to me like a good story was going to happen. I'll just sit here and listen."

He took a seat near the front, resting his paper on his lap. Checker smiled and nodded toward Morgan.

She stared at Opat. "Judge, as a rancher in this area, I demand a hearing. Right now. On the rustling charge against Emmett Gardner and the murder charges against John Checker and A. J. Barnett." She folded her arms. "These are innocent men and you have been a conspirator to the will of Lady Holt. I expect real justice. Here and now."

Opat pulled on the lapels of his oversized suit coat and glared at her. "I ruled on that matter, the rustling charge, earlier. Mr. Gardner needs to give himself up—and stand trial." His Adam's apple bobbed as he swallowed.

"No, we're going to have a hearing. A real one. Not that jake leg thing you pulled earlier," Morgan said, pointing her finger at the surprised judge.

Checker shifted the weight on his boots to keep it from his wounded leg as best he could. His body was stiff and sore. It was far too early to be moving, but he knew it was necessary. He had been shot before. Silently, he had prayed to both the white man's God—and the Comanche Great Spirit—to help him.

"Opat, I don't think you get it yet," Checker said. "This Lady Holt is through making the laws around her. There's a small army of us planning to make it so. Call us *Fire*. She will know what it means."

Licking his lips, Opat said, "Well, we'll need to call witnesses. Sil Jaudon is out of town. He brought the charge—and he's on the stage, I believe. Coming from Austin." He twisted his neck, first to the right, then the left. "Mr. Jaudon is a captain of the Rangers now. A worthy appointment, I believe. Of course, he has the details on this case."

"No, that won't be necessary. We'll take care of Jaudon separately. He'll be brought in—again—for attempted murder. By that time, we'll have a real judge in place," Checker said. "There's no way he's going to stay a Ranger—much less a captain. But that's for another day, Opat. Nothing you need to worry about. This hearing will move on without him."

"But there has to be someone for the prosecution present."

"In your first hearing, you didn't have the defendant present, so what's the difference?" Checker's voice was heavy with sarcasm. "I'm getting real tired of you, Opat. Do this right, real justice for a change—and you'll be able to leave town a free man. Do it wrong, well, you get the idea. Either way, you're leaving."

"Are you threatening an officer of the court?"

"No. I'm telling a crooked henchman of Lady Holt's that his time in this town has ended. How he leaves will be his choice," Checker said. "I've been in a lot of courtrooms, but this is the first one I've seen with no idea of what justice is all about." He paused and looked at Emmett. "Is Rule outside?"

"Yep. An' he's got him wi'."

"Good. Have him come in." Checker returned his stare to Opat. "But you will have your prosecution witness present."

Rule Cordell pushed Sheriff Hangar inside. The hatless lawman looked half dazed and half scared; his empty holster spoke of an earlier confrontation. His cheek was reddened from a recent blow and his big mustache was pushed out of shape. His shirttails flapped below his coat on the right side.

He saw Opat, then Checker. When he saw the tall Ranger, his jaw dropped and bile slammed its way into his throat.

Swallowing, he managed to gulp. "Wh-hat's th-this all about?"

"You're going to be the witness for the prosecution, Hangar."

"E-Eleven M-Meade said you were d-dead. S-said he shot . . . at you . . . in your grave," Hangar spat. His eyes were wide.

"Sounds like Eleven likes to tell a good story," Checker said. "Kinda like the rustling whopper you tried to lay on my friend. And that charge of murder on A.J. and me."

"Th-hat wasn't my idea."

For the first time, Hangar realized Emmett Gardner was standing in the courtroom and then saw Seitmeyer. Cursing to himself, he should've known the British woman's ideas about handling the two Rangers—and Rule Cordell— weren't going to work.

"Sit down, right there, Hangar. You and Opat are through in this town. It's time the good folks had a choice about these matters," Checker said. "You're going to present the cases against Emmett—and me and my partner. That'll be your last official act here. In Claisson. Do it right and you'll be able to ride out of here." He looked at Rule, standing near the doorway. "Is A.J. all right?"

"Sure. He's with Hangar's two deputies. They're having a nice, quiet talk. Figure they'll be leaving town when this is over."

"Probably discussing a little Tennyson." Checker smiled.

"More than a little."

"Rikor's outside. Watching the back."

Rule saluted Checker and left. The Ranger grinned in spite of the situation. The two gunfighters were quickly becoming friends.

Hangar tried to catch Opat's attention, but the judge had no intention of looking at him. The onetime attorney was trying to think what he should do. He should have known this day was coming. No one would get to Lady Holt; she wouldn't be touched. It would be her hirelings who would take the brunt of the counterattack. She owned too much land, too much money and enough of the right contacts to withstand any assault.

Even from the likes of John Checker and Rule Cordell.

To avoid looking at Hangar, Opat studied Checker. There was a small circle of fresh blood on the Ranger's shirt, just above his belt, along his back. So the killer Meade hadn't totally lied; he *had* wounded the famous Ranger. Just not enough. Opat looked away. Maybe if he played this straight, the townspeople would let him stay. Would Lady Holt let him, if he bent to what Checker wanted . . . to do what was right?

Scuffling at the door became Rule Cordell with a handful of Claisson townspeople. The blacksmith, a freighter, a young general store clerk, the woman who ran the dry goods shop, two Triple C cowhands who worked for Charlie

Chance Carlson and several others. George Likeman joined them; he was the town undertaker and furniture builder. All had been selected by Morgan and Emmett. They weren't quite sure why they were asked to come to the courtroom, but there was something about Rule Cordell that made it seem smart to go.

"Is London outside?" Checker asked, motioning for the new people to come forward and take seats.

"He is—and I'm joining him," Rule said.

"Good. We won't be interrupted, then."

Turning his attention to the now-seated townspeople, Checker told them that they were going to be witnesses to a hearing, that although a hearing didn't require a jury—or even anyone witnessing it—he and his friends had decided the town deserved a look at real justice for a change.

The blacksmith shook his head affirmatively and said loudly, "We do thank ye, Ranger, for trying. Lady Holt, she has men over in the saloon. The No. 8. They're there every day. Just watching and waiting. They're over there now."

"Thanks. We'll settle with them later."

The dry goods store owner politely raised her hand. After being recognized by Checker, she asked, "Will this last long? I have a dress promised to Mrs. Haulprin by two."

Checker smiled. "No, ma'am. It won't, but you leave whenever you think you need to do so." He turned to Opat. "Start the proceedings, Opat. You know what to do."

With a tremor in his voice that wouldn't go away, Judge opened the proceedings with his usual statement that the purpose of a preliminary hearing was to determine if sufficient evidence existed for the accused to be bound over for formal trial. Licking his lips, he added that the first case to be heard was that of a charge of rustling against Emmett Gardner. The charge had been brought by Lady Holt's ranch.

He stared at Hangar. "Sheriff, you presented a number of Holt cattle that had their brands changed to Mr. Gardner's. Is that correct?"

Hangar glared at him. "Of course, you fool."

"Do you wish to add anything to your testimony at this time?"

"He's a guilty son of a bitch—and everybody knows it."

"I see. Will the defense make its statement please?"

Morgan testified she knew Emmett was not involved in such criminal act and only an idiot would think the revised brands would have been done by anyone, other than an attempt to make the rancher look guilty. She pointed out how complicated the rebranding had been and how rigged it looked. Turning toward the seated townspeople, she explained that the Holt brand was a jagged line with an H above it. She said most called it the "fire brand."

One of the cowboys growled, "We call it the hell brand."

Nervous laughter followed the remark.

She smiled grimly and continued. "The 'fire' had been blurred over with a running iron. Above it was a single line. The H had been turned into Emmett Gardner's EG with the backward E covering the H as best it could to represent his Bar EG."

Shaking her head, she declared, "Nobody could look at that mess and think Mr. Gardner did it. And, of course, he didn't." Her face became a frown as she glanced at Checker and continued. "Lady Holt wants his ranch. She wants mine. She wants all of them. And she'll do anything to get them— like buying the judge and sheriff."

One loud eruption came from the small group, followed by someone declaring that she was right and the judge should be run out of town on a rail. Both cowboys loudly agreed.

Without moving, Checker reminded them that they must

be quiet. He looked over at Morgan and smiled. Having her lead the cause for a new hearing was important; she would be perceived in the community as honest.

She smiled.

Opat looked pale. Down the right side of his face rolled a sweat bead bound for his collar. "Any cross-examination, Sheriff?"

"I don't know. Ah, no. Except I didn't have anything to do with this." Hangar looked back at the people sitting behind him. "Honest. As far as I knew, this was just rustling. Really."

Checker took control of the room. "Since this is a hearing, and not a trial, I don't see why we can't have questions from the folks in here. Anyone have a question they want to ask of Mrs. Peale, or Mr. Gardner, or the sheriff here? Or me, for that matter?"

Silence followed as the group stared ahead.

Finally, Henry Seitmeyer raised his hand and said, "I have a question. Well, sort of. I thought you were dead."

Checker nodded. "Well, a known killer from New Mexico, Eleven Meade, was hired to do that. Holt hired him. He bragged a little too soon, thanks to Mrs. Peale and Mr. Fiss."

"I see," Seitmeyer said. "Do you know where this Meade fellow is now?"

Checker grinned. "When I go outside, I'll look under the first rock I see."

Without further probing, Checker explained what had happened, that they were moving Emmett's family to a safe place after the attack by Holt's men, led by Jaudon. He said six Holt riders were trying to intercept their escape and he rode to stop them. He made the mistake of not watching his back. Meade had tried to kill him at that time.

Seitmeyer scribbled in his notebook, looked up and said, "I trust you are all right, Ranger Checker."

"I'm all right."

"That's good. For all of us, sir. Your reputation is known—and respected," Seitmeyer said. "I have a question for the sheriff, if you don't mind."

"Please go ahead. I'm sure Sheriff Hangar will be happy to help."

"This morning you told me Rule Cordell was an outlaw and was part of Emmett Gardner's rustling operation. You insisted I write a story about it." He paused and added, "You said Lady Holt wanted it done. Did I miss anything?"

Snickering followed and the closest cowboy whooped, slapped his thigh and apologized for the reaction.

Hangar turned white and waved his hands urgent. "I—I didn't have all the facts."

"Doesn't look like it," the editor said. "So, you don't want me to run a story about Rule Cordell being an outlaw—and a part of the Emmett Gardner rustling operation—is that correct?"

Laughter spat through the room and Hangar winced.

Opat shifted in the chair behind the bench. He glanced at the dry goods store woman and smiled his best smile. She ignored the attempt at connection, choosing the moment to say something to the blacksmith sitting beside her. He nodded and looked at Opat.

Damn, the judge thought. Why did he let Lady Holt talk him into coming to Caisson? He had built a nice legal practice in Austin. A profitable one. She had come to see him, paid for the visit and told him of her plans. When first hearing them, he wanted to laugh. King was building a cattle empire in middle Texas and this British woman wanted to make him look like a two-bit farmer. The opportunity was there, he saw that in her plan. For the right person with the right instincts—and the ability to destroy anyone in the way. Still, a woman? A woman from England, no less?

What finally convinced him to go with Lady Holt was the revelation of her relationship with Governor Citale. He knew the man was weak—and crooked. But she planned to turn him into a weapon. Opat's own checking supported her claim. He had come to Claisson, opened a practice and was immediately recommended for the open municipal judge position. Judge Diales had been shot and killed two weeks earlier. No one knew who or why.

Hangar had joined the conspiracy a month later. Opat seemed to be the only one in town who knew he was wanted for fraud in Tennessee.

It had been a good run, he told himself. If he was lucky, the Ranger would let him leave. That's what Checker had said. He didn't seem like a man who made promises lightly. John Checker was known throughout Texas. Fearless. Honest. Driven by something no one quite knew. And sometimes, he was violent. Opat had heard the stories. Who hadn't? Some said he was better with a gun than anyone in Texas. Better than Allison. Than Harding. The only gun warrior who might be as good—or better—was Rule Cordell. And he was working with Checker.

Opat shivered and wished the killer Meade had done what he bragged he had accomplished. He bit the inside of his cheek and forced himself to concentrate on Morgan's ending testimony.

". . . if a fellow was going to steal beef, he'd do it with mine. There's just me and a good friend helping me. Everybody around knows Holt has gunmen . . . everywhere. Nobody's going to be stupid enough to steal from her. Nobody. And you know it, Judge."

Hunching his shoulders, Opat said, "Anything further from the prosecution?" He didn't wait for Hangar to respond. "Hearing none, I rule in favor of the defendant. There is no basis for the rustling charge against Mr. Gardner. I declare this matter dismissed."

From the back of the room, Emmett grinned and said, "'Bout time we got some justice outta the bastard."

Several in the audience turned to congratulate him; loudest were the two Triple C cowboys.

"When we're finished here," Checker said, "we'll go to Hangar's office and pick up the wanted posters—and burn them."

One of the cowboys yelled, "We'll help ya tear down the ones they put up. Charlie'll be real happy to hear 'bout this."

"Wires will go out to surrounding towns. From you, Judge. And you, Hangar," Checker added.

Hangar nodded and leaned down to scratch his right leg. The movement reminded Opat that the crooked lawman carried a short-barreled Scofield revolver in a special holster built into his boot. Did they check him for hideaways? Should he tell Checker about the gun? The questions popped into Opat's mind. No one would expect him to know of such a weapon, so he wouldn't say anything. If Hangar got lucky and shot Checker, everything would change. At least until Rule came back.

The roosterlike judge banged his gavel and announced, "This court will now hear evidence concerning the deaths of . . . ah, three Holt . . . ah, cowhands. Accused of their deaths are John Checker and . . . ah, Bartlett . . . A. J. Bartlett." He leaned forward. "This court will now hear the prosecution's statement—and evidence. Sheriff Hangar, please proceed."

Chapter Twenty-eight

Wilson Tanner, the well-dressed attorney, strolled toward the courthouse. He and Opat were planning on lunch together, a frequent activity. It was an easy way to exchange information, something Lady Holt considered as important as gold. Both were in Lady Holt's employ; both were pragmatic about it.

As he walked along the planked sidewalk, he noticed two armed men standing outside the courthouse. A white man in a long black coat and a black man. They were talking quietly to each other while watching passersby. Resting in the black man's crossed arms was a double-barreled shotgun. He was vaguely familiar to Tanner. Where had he seen him before? Of course. He was Morgan Peale's hired man.

The other man? The white man. He didn't know.

Yes, he was certain. The black man was with the woman rancher every time she came to town. Of course, he didn't go into any of the stores. For a black man, that wasn't allowed. He just waited. What was he doing there? What were the two of them doing there? If the black man was in town, Morgan Peale would be as well. Was she inside the court? Doing what?

He touched the brim of his hat in greeting to the two passing couples and headed across the street. Sheriff Hangar would know what was going on. He always did. A fast-moving carriage made him stop and wait for its passing. He fumed but held his temper. It was one of his strengths, he told himself. On the far side of the main street, he headed for the lawman's office.

A glimpse through the window of Hangar's office warned him again. A man sat behind the sheriff's desk, drinking coffee. A shotgun lay on top of the desk. It looked as though Hangar's deputies were each sitting in a cell. He didn't see Hangar. What the hell was going on? Who was that man?

Tanner continued walking past the closed door and window, trying to think. The man had to be the Ranger who rode with John Checker. Had to be. Yes. Bartlett. What was he doing in town? He was wanted for murder. Was it just a coincidence that he and the Peale hand were in town at the same time, both at key locations?

Hardly.

Something was going on and it wasn't good. What should he do? He wasn't carrying a gun. Never did. Three or four Holt gunmen would be in the No. 8 Saloon. It was part of Lady Holt's strategy to keep pressure on the town. Quick responses, if needed. There wasn't much she didn't think of. Caisson was vital to her plans for control. Only three ranches remained in this region. He knew she was already thinking about expansion beyond. Twice he had heard her refer to herself as "Queen of Texas."

He pulled on his vest to straighten it and headed for the saloon. Once he reported the situation, he was done. Whatever Lady Holt's men decided to do was fine. He had more than done his job: providing information.

She would pay well for that. Perhaps with herself. He longed for that pleasure. So far it had only been a tease.

The saloon was gray and the wall oil lamps were struggling to provide light to match the outside. He entered slowly, letting his eyes adjust to the darker atmosphere. There shouldn't be any sense of distress. She never liked panic, or signs of it. She preferred careful, methodical action. So be it. At the back of the room were three men sitting at a table, playing cards. Luke Dimitry saw him and alerted the others.

Minutes later, the three Holt gunmen left the saloon with Tanner's information ringing in their ears. He moved to the bar and ordered a whiskey. Drinking this early in the day was not his style, but a drink seemed like a good idea. Afterward, he would check the telegraph office for any new wires and ride out to see Lady Holt. She would want to know about this. Of course, he would wait until her gunmen took care of the situation.

Inside the sheriff's office, A. J. Bartlett stood and headed toward the stove for another cup of coffee. Sheriff Hangar's two deputies sat in one of the cells. Neither looked up, or spoke, as he passed. When the courtroom hearings were finished, Hangar's two assistants would be released. Bartlett knew they were employed by the British woman; that was common knowledge. Still, they hadn't been involved in the attempt to destroy Emmett's family, so they would be allowed to ride away. Nobody expected them to ride any farther than the Holt Ranch.

Halfway across the busy street, the three Holt gunmen spread out and walked slowly, cutting in and out of passing traffic. After they took over the jail, they would head to the courtroom building. They moved easily. Confidently. Most likely this was some kind of attempt to retake the town. Lady Holt had expected it and ordered them to be especially on guard for strange-appearing actions. The promise of a bonus was added to the direction. It was clear she didn't have much confidence in Hangar's ability to handle anything stressful.

Wearing an old Navajo coat, Luke Dimitry slid behind a rumbling freight wagon, watching the two men outside the court as he moved. The half-breed knew who they were: London Fiss and Rule Cordell. He had no intention of facing them. That was suicide. Once they had retaken the jail, he would have the deputies go and ask them to move on. While that exchange was going on, he and his two comrades would sneak into the courtroom from the back door. There, they would be able to determine what was happening. Maybe Judge Opat was being forced out by some townsmen.

He didn't want anyone inside the jail to know they were coming until they hit the door. From what the fancy attorney said, there was only one man inside. The other Ranger, the educated one. They reached the planked sidewalk and Dimitry motioned for the skinny gunman with crossed bullet bandoliers to make his move.

The gunman slipped to the back of the jail as planned. Once there, he stood against the adobe wall and said, "Alex, this is Sonny. Is the Ranger close? Is he watching?"

"Naw. Drinking coffee. By the stove," the jailed deputy whispered.

"Good. I'm going to push a gun through the bars. You catch it. All right?" the skinny gunman said, glancing around to make sure no one was watching.

"Say when."

"Here she comes." He stood on his tiptoes, eased the handle of the revolver between the bars, holding it by the long barrel, and let it go.

"Got it. What's next?"

Looking around again, the skinny gunman told him to wrap something around the barrel to hold down the noise and wait, that they were coming in the front door in about two minutes. He walked away, stopped and coughed, holding his hand against his mouth to minimize the noise. The other two were waiting in the alley.

"He get it?" Dimitry asked.

"Yeah. He's ready. Waiting for us."

"Should've got one to Lamon, too." The gunman with the long scar on his face tugged on the brim of his flattened hat.

The half-breed responded with a curse and said, "Yeah, an' you might've handed off a gun right to that Ranger, too."

"Yeah, guess so."

"Give me one of those towels."

The scarred gunman distributed three towels taken from the saloon and each man wrapped one around his gun. Satisfied with their readiness, Dimitry jerked his head for the other two to follow him and went to the sheriff's locked door.

Knock! Knock!

"Sheriff! There's trouble in one of the saloons!"

He was certain the call for help would yield an immediate response.

"The sheriff isn't here. I'm sorry," Bartlett said from the other side of the door.

"Please, sir. You're a Ranger. We need your help. Please. It's Lady Holt's men."

"Coming. Hold your horses." Bartlett grabbed the shotgun from the desk.

"Please hurry. Someone's going to get hurt."

The heavy oak door swung open to the office.

Inside, the deputy with the sneaked-in gun fired. Bartlett grimaced and spun toward the cell and fired a barrel of his gun. He twirled back toward the door too slowly as the three gunmen pushed through the opening, pouring bullets into him.

The Ranger fired the second barrel as he fell. The skinny gunman screamed and grabbed his bloody face.

Pulling the smoking towel from his gun, Dimitry stomped on the garment to put out the flames. He shoved the second gunman. "Let's get outta here! Rule Cordell will be coming fast!"

"Rule Cordell? You're kidding," the second gunman said.

"He was standing outside the courtroom. That damn shotgun blast will bring him—and the black man. Do what you want. I'm leaving." Dimitry turned and headed outside.

"Hey! Let me out!" The deputy looked stunned by the suddenness of the attack and the immediate retreat. He stared at Bartlett and the skinny gunman and the widening circle of blood beneath both of them.

The second gunman hesitated and followed. As he stepped to the opened doorway, a blood-soaked Bartlett groaned and raised his arm, enough to draw his revolver. His hand shook as he fired. The scarred gunman staggered into the sidewalk. Bartlett's hand couldn't hold the heavy gun any longer and it thudded to the floor.

He gasped and said, "I—I a-am a Ranger."

From the courtroom building, Rule and Fiss came running. The street had already become empty as people realized the noise from the sheriff's office meant trouble. In six strides, Rule was ten feet ahead of Fiss, drawing his revolvers as he ran. From the front door of the courthouse, Checker emerged. The look on his face was tense. He, too, knew what the booming sounds from the jail meant.

"Emmett, stay here. Watch Opat and Hangar. Opat, finish this hearing. I'll be back," he yelled, and ran after the men halfway down the sidewalk.

The sudden movement made him light-headed and he grabbed his side as new pain struck the wound. His hand came away with fresh blood. He gritted his teeth and kept moving. He had a bad feeling they were too late to help his friend.

Reaching the opened sheriff's office, Rule wheeled inside with a cocked revolver in each hand. His gaze absorbed the awful results of the Holt attack, then studied the town for signs of movement. The only thing he saw, on this end of main street, were two dogs chasing each other. In the window of the barbershop, three men watched; one turned away as soon as Rule looked in their direction.

Nothing would be gained now looking for whoever escaped. He stepped past the groaning gunman with the scar on his face. The man held both hands to his stomach to hold in the blood that wanted out. Rule walked past the dead, skinny gunman, whose face was a red mask. He sought A. J. Bartlett.

"Oh, A.J.," he muttered, and hurried to the still, bloody body.

Laying his guns on the floor, Rule knelt beside the dying Ranger and cradled him in his arms. "My God, they set you up. From front and back—and you still managed to get three of them," he said. His next words were a whispered prayer to God to welcome the Ranger's soul.

Behind him, a frozen deputy finally managed to speak. "I—I d-didn't have anything t-to . . . do with th-this. H-honest, I d-didn't."

Rule's face was a hot snarl. "You mean your friends didn't have time to get you out. How many got away? One? Two? Don't lie to me."

"Ah . . . just one. It was one. Dimitry. Luke Dimitry. H-he works for L-Lady Holt."

"Where'd he go?"

"I—I d-don't know. H-he ran . . . south."

Rule's attention was drawn to Bartlett. The dying Ranger's eyes fluttered open and he tried to speak.

"Rest easy, old friend. We'll have the doctor in here."

Bartlett shook his head. "No. I-t's too late. T-tell John . . . I'm s-sorry I . . . c-can't stay around. I—I sure . . . would've liked to."

"Hang on, A.J. Hang on."

"Did you g-get the h-hearings d-done? I-s . . . Emmett s-still w-wanted . . . for r-rustling?" Bartlett grabbed Rule's arm.

Swallowing, Rule told him the hearings were over, that the charge against Emmett was dropped—and so were the charges against Checker and Bartlett. Then he added they had just received a wire and both men had been reinstated as Rangers. It was a lie, but one he wanted to say. Needed to say.

Bartlett patted his arm weakly. "P-pray for me . . . will you?"

Rule started to tell him that he already had, but realized Bartlett was dead. At the doorway, Fiss appeared, holding his shotgun.

The black man shook his head and stared at the various guns on the floor, all wrapped in towels. One was still smoking.

"Well, they figured on shooting whoever was here—and we wouldn't have known it until it was too late. A.J. . . ." Fiss didn't finish the statement.

Through the doorway came John Checker, almost out of breath. His dark eyes took in the scene and locked on to Bartlett in Rule's arms. "Is he?"

"Yes. Died in my arms. Told me to tell you that he was sorry he couldn't stay." Rule lowered his head. "Only wanted to know if Emmett's charge was dropped." The gunfighter looked up at the tall Ranger. "Told him it was—and I told him he was a Ranger . . . again."

Checker's mouth was a slit. He stared down at the wounded gunman and kicked him in the stomach. "Get that gun of yours, you bastard. You can forget the towel." He spat; his eyes were hard. "Let's see how good you are when you're *facing* a Ranger." He kicked him again. "Get up—or I'll shoot you right there."

Into his hand, the black-handled Colt appeared.

"No, John. A.J. wouldn't want that." Rule's voice was soft, almost a whisper.

Checker's shoulders rose and fell. Twice. He shuddered as he struggled to bring his rage under control. Fiss watched him from next to the dead deputy's cell. His shotgun was held at his side. He was almost motionless; only his cheeks showed movement as he bit them to hold in his feelings.

"I'm sorry, John," Fiss said. "He was a man to ride the river with."

Checker tried to answer but couldn't.

After easing Bartlett's head back on the floor, Rule closed the Ranger's unmoving eyes. He stood, saw his own pistols and leaned over to retrieve them, shoving one into its holster and the other into his waistband. He looked at Checker and his eyes asked what the Ranger wanted to do next.

Checker's return gaze was full of hurt as he walked toward Bartlett and knelt beside him. "I'll miss you, my friend. You kept me balanced. You always had my back." He took a deep breath. "I should've had yours." He bit his lower lip and recited, "'*Your* strength is as the strength of ten, because *your* heart is pure.'"

Rule nodded as he realized Checker changed the word *my* in Tennyson's "Sir Galahad" to *your*. A bittersweet tribute.

Fiss found a blanket in the small storeroom and brought it to Checker. The three men placed it over Bartlett's body.

After a few moments of silence, Checker stood. "Rule. London. Would you take care of . . . this . . . while I go back?"

Both men agreed. The tall Ranger made no attempt to explain what he wanted done. It was Fiss who suggested the editor be brought to the jail to see for himself what had happened.

From the cell, the deputy whined, "I—I'll leave . . . an' not c-come back. H-Hangar d-didn't say anything about . . . this . . . kinda stuff. I . . . ah, I'm sorry."

Rule glanced at him, but said nothing. Checker walked away as if he hadn't heard the deputy. He stepped across the body of the dead skinny gunman and over the body of the wounded scarred gunman. The gunman shut his eyes and pulled his legs into his stomach.

As the tall Ranger reached the door again, Rule said, "The deputy said there was only one who got away. Dimitry. Ran south."

"As soon as the hearing is over, we'll find him. I'll ask Seitmeyer if he wants to come here and see for himself what happened." He took a deep breath. "He's a good man, I think. A.J. thought so."

"John?"

Checker paused at his name from Rule. "Yes?"

"We need this town if we're going to stop her."

"I know that."

"Opat and Hangar should be arrested. Not shot."

Checker's eyes darted toward Rule as if they were bullets; then he nodded. "I know that."

All eyes were on the tall Ranger as he returned to the courtroom. Morgan Peale ran toward him, hesitated and knew what had happened without asking.

The blacksmith stood and said, "Is everything all right?"

"No. No, it's not. Lady Holt's men tried to take over the jail. They killed one of Texas's best Rangers, A. J. Bartlett. He stopped three."

Opat watched the tall Ranger and knew this was a particularly dangerous time. John Checker was on edge, feeling the death of his friend, aching to fill the hole in his heart. With anything. Anything.

The small group of townspeople had grown since Checker left. The room was half-filled with stern-faced men and women. Lady Holt's fist had driven them into submission for a long time. Now there seemed to be hope. It rested in the tall Ranger and his gunfighter friend.

"Ah, Ranger, sir, while you were gone, Sheriff Hangar tried to take over." The blacksmith rubbed his big hands together. His face was streaked with black to match his clothes. He was a small man, but his upper arms and chest would have made it difficult for any man to best him.

"Had a hideaway gun in his boot," the blacksmith continued. "Emmett Gardner's boy came in from the back—and several of us took it from him."

For the first time, Checker noticed a subdued Hangar standing in the corner; his hands were lashed together in front of him. His right eye was swollen shut with redness streaking from it. A few feet away stood Rikor with a rifle and a deep frown. On the other side of the tied lawman were the two Triple C cowboys; neither were armed.

"We're gonna take our town back," the blacksmith announced proudly. "Get ourselves some real law and order. A real judge. A real sheriff. Yes, sir, that's what we're gonna do. An' we thank you for making it so."

Morgan completed her advance and hugged the Ranger and he returned the emotion. "I am so sorry, John. So sorry." Her eyes sought his for comfort and more.

"I know. It's awful hard, Morgan. Awful hard. I wish that British woman was a man. I'd know what to do." Checker's face twisted with agony.

"Treat her no differently than anyone else who breaks the law," Morgan said, and motioned to the sitting townspeople. "A lot happened here, John, and you—and A.J. and Rule—made it happen." She wiped a tear trying to escape from her eye. "I almost forgot. The murder charges against you and A.J. were dropped."

Checker listened without speaking. His gaze indicated he was a long way away. When he first met A. J. Bartlett at Ranger headquarters, the gentle Ranger had greeted him with a Tennyson quote, the one he had said a few minutes ago.

"So, what are you expecting from me?" Seitmeyer asked as he walked toward the Ranger.

"Newspapers are supposed to print the truth, aren't they?"

"That's what I try to do." Seitmeyer's answer was more confident than he felt.

"That's all I want."

"Well, I'll certainly report on the hearings—and their outcome," the editor said. "You know I can't go directly accusing Lady Holt—just on your say-so, or anybody else's," Seitmeyer questioned, his brow furrowing. "No offense, but I wouldn't do that to anyone."

"Of course not," Checker said. "But I also know the town isn't going to take a stand against her—and her hired guns— unless the truth gives them strength. A town needs a backbone. You can give them a backbone."

"I'll do my best." Seitmeyer's face was flushed. "You know the mayor's her man. Alex Wilkerson. I'm pretty certain she owns the bank."

"The truth'll be plenty."

"What are you going to do . . . with the sheriff—and the judge?" Seitmeyer's eyes focused on Checker's hard face.

"I'm going to make a citizen's arrest. Of both of them. A real court can take it from there."

From his bench, Opat yelled, "You said I could leave!"

Cocking his head to the side, Checker said, "That was before Lady Holt's men killed my friend." His eyes narrowed. "You can thank God that Rule Cordell was there at the jail with me. I was coming back to kill you—and Hangar. He told me my friend wouldn't want that."

Opat looked as if he was going to vomit.

"You and Hangar have been doing the bidding of Lady Holt ever since you boys hit town," Checker growled. "That's why you came to town in the first place, isn't it, Opat?"

"Ah, I didn't have . . . any choice. I really . . . didn't." Opat's face went white and he swallowed twice before finding any words.

"I don't have any choice, either," Checker said. "Both of you are under arrest."

The dry goods store woman stood and spoke. "Ranger, sir, who will be our sheriff? Our judge? Who's going to protect us when that awful woman hears about this? She has all kinds of bad men working for her." She folded her arms over her ample chest.

"As soon as I bury my friend, we're going after her," Checker said. "Pick someone you trust to be the sheriff—and someone to be judge." He rubbed his chin. "I think you'd make a fine judge, ma'am, but that's just my opinion."

She smiled in spite of herself. "Ah, I haven't had any training."

The blacksmith blurted his support. "I think you'd be a good judge, too, Mrs. Loren. A good one."

Several voiced similar support.

"Where are your council members?" Checker asked. "They can make this decision. Unless you don't trust them."

"There's one I don't. Wilson Tanner," the blacksmith said, waving his arms. "He works for Lady Holt. I know it."

"Sounds like you need an election. Why don't you get them in here?" Checker said. "We'll take Opat and Hangar to jail."

"I'll go get 'em," the blacksmith said, moving toward the door. "Who's gonna help me?"

Three men and a woman jumped from their seats and headed toward him.

Chapter Twenty-nine

It was nightfall before Wilson Tanner rode up to the Holt Ranch. His horse was lathered and streaked with sweat. Even though he hated this kind of riding, he knew she would want to know. He was also excited about his new appointment as the municipal judge.

Yes, Caisson was alive with change!

Opat and Hangar were in jail; the remaining deputy had been relieved of duty and allowed to leave; he was last seen riding south. The blacksmith had accepted the job as sheriff until a countywide election could be held. Tanner had been asked to become the municipal judge to replace Opat, primarily because he was the only other attorney in town.

Initially, sentiment for Margaret Loren, the dry goods store owner, to become the judge had run strong, but the town council decided to seek help elsewhere. It helped that Mrs. Loren told them that she really didn't want the responsibility. His mind kept rehearsing the need to not sound sarcastic about the silliness of a woman becoming a judge. Lady Holt would not take kindly to that, to put it mildly. The owner of the No. 8 Saloon was advised to leave by an armed committee when it was discovered Lady Holt actually owned the establishment. As far as Tanner knew, no one objected to Alex Wilkerson's position as mayor, even though it was well known she owned the bank. Two council members resigned on their own accord, each stating that he didn't want to be seen lining up against Lady Holt and touting her importance to the region.

A tired, but exuberant, Tanner was greeted at the door by Elliott, who bowed graciously and invited him in.

"Welcome, Mr. Tanner. Madame will join you shortly. She is . . . occupied at the moment," the black servant declared, and motioned for the attorney to wait in the library.

"Sure. Sure. This is important or I wouldn't have come. Took it out on my horse."

"I'll see your mount is cared for. *Maximus in minimis*."

"Thanks. I could use a whiskey if you've got one."

"Certainly, sir." Elliott took the attorney's hat and placed it carefully on a hat rack next to the door.

"Tennessee, if you have it."

"We do, sir."

Inside the library, Tanner paced back and forth, barely noticing the three walls of bookshelves lined with books. He had been in this room several times, but not recently. The fourth wall of adobe featured a huge wood carving of a phoenix. Soft gaslights on the wall, above the carving, gave the room a golden glow and happy shadows. Another lamp rested on a shiny walnut table along with a stack of magazines and newspapers.

He knew well of Lady Holt's fixation on the legend; at some point, he thought it might be used to his advantage. Sometime. Not now, though. Now he had information, important information. It had been a wild day, a strange one, to say the least.

The only good things about the day he could think of were that none of his railroad clients were in town—and no one suspected him of a connection to her. He walked over to the carving and ran his forefinger along its edges. Primitive, he thought. Something a Mexican peasant had done.

Elliott returned with a crystal glass half-filled with brown liquid.

"It is Tennessee," he declared proudly, and handed it to Tanner.

"That will be fine. Thank you, Elliott."

"You are welcome, sir. Please make yourself comfortable." The servant spun and retreated from the room.

Sipping the whiskey, Tanner tried to make himself relax. The situation was not bad, actually; she had lost a foothold in Caisson, but it could be corrected when Jaudon returned. Or whenever she decided to send her gunmen there. As an aside, his railroad clients might like the idea of dealing with a magistrate who could expedite matters.

He smiled and took another drink. The hot liquid slid down easily. Yes, this thing could turn out quite fine. For him.

Walking over to one of the tables, the attorney picked up a magazine. *Harper's Bazaar*. He flipped through the pages, stopping at an article about Texas gunfighters. Rule Cordell was one of the featured names. He shivered. The gunfighter was apparently paired up with John Checker. Why he didn't know, yet. Ah yes, John Checker. Alive. He smiled savagely. Eleven Meade was full of it.

A few minutes later, Lady Holt entered with her own glass of whiskey. Her hair was disheveled and her blouse was buttoned incorrectly, as if put on hurriedly.

"I trust this is damn important." She stood in the doorway.

"John Checker is alive," Tanner said, returning the magazine to the table and responding without any greeting. "He and Rule Cordell are working together."

She sipped the whiskey, used her forefinger to stir the brown liquid and asked, "And you know this how?"

Tanner explained what had happened in town: the hearings, the shootings, the new appointees, John Checker's appearance—and his appointment as the town's judge.

"So one Ranger is definitely dead."

Her response surprised him. He thought she would be excited about his new position. He managed to respond, "Definitely."

She took another sip. "And the town has a new judge." Her eyes flashed.

He knew she would like that news. Then she fooled him by asking about Margaret Loren.

"Well, she owns a small dry goods shop. Makes dresses for—"

"Have her make six for me. You pick the colors—and the fabrics."

Tanner took a deep breath. "Ah, she'll need your . . . ah, specifications."

Lady Holt's glare was more than he wanted and he glanced down at the magazine.

"Sometimes I'm surprised at what your railroad friends see in you. Can't you tell what you need by looking? At me."

He cocked his head and said, "I deliver information—and results."

Downing the rest of her whiskey, she yelled for Elliott to bring more and asked Tanner what Checker and Rule were doing when he left town. He told her they were mourning Bartlett's death and were in the undertaker's office when he left. He didn't know where they intended to bury the dead Ranger.

"Here's what I want you to do. Get that fool telegrapher out of bed. The one with the awful breath." She walked over to the phoenix wall carving and stared at it. "I want a wire sent to Citale. Tonight. From you, as the new judge and town council member." She stopped and looked back at him. "You are still on the council, aren't you?"

"Oh yes, the others looked to me."

"How wise of them."

He wasn't sure if her remark was an insult or a compliment, but decided the latter was a smarter choice for him.

She rattled off what she wanted the statement to the governor to say. The town had been taken over by an outlaw gang led by Checker and Cordell, the sheriff and judge were being held against their will and that Ranger Captain Jaudon would need wide authority to subdue the situation as soon as he arrived by stage.

Tanner didn't like the idea and told her so. The whole town would know he was part of her effort and that wouldn't set well with him as the new judge. Besides, the telegraph was closed down for the night. He added that Jaudon could act as needed without such direction. If she felt such a wire was needed, it should come from Wilkerson as mayor.

Spinning toward him, she licked her lower lip, enjoying the taste of the whiskey there. He braced himself for her rage at being told she wasn't correct.

Her response was surprisingly mild. "You're right, Wilson. You're right. I like that in a man. Brings good information— and good counsel.

"Let's try this instead," she continued. "We'll lull those silly little people into thinking their stupid little town is doing well. As soon as Jaudon arrives, he can lead a force of Rangers in there and clean things up." She smiled. "And then we can get back to getting the rest of my land." She turned her head to the side. "Did you say that Peale woman was in town, too? With Checker and Cordell?"

"Oh yes. She testified on Emmett Gardner's behalf . . . on the rustling charge," Tanner said. "At least, that's what I heard. I wasn't in the courtroom—until later. They made the council meet right there. Right after the shooting at the jail."

"Who's 'they'?"

Tanner blinked. He hated her when she did this, challenging each word, each nuance. " 'They' is the group of people who sat through the hearings. Townspeople. From what I heard, it was a handpicked group."

"Handpicked by whom?"

He smiled. Should've seen that one coming, he thought. "By the people who forced the hearings. Checker and Cordell."

She walked across the room and straightened a book on the fourth row. "How did they know who the right people were?"

He explained Emmett Gardner and Morgan Peale did the selecting, or so he thought.

"Of course." She straightened another book. "Ever read *The Odyssey?*"

He was surprised by the question. "Ah . . . *Odyssey?* Ah, no. Ah, should I?"

"Never mind. The written word is powerful, isn't it?" It wasn't really a question. "I want to buy the Caisson newspaper. Is this Seitmeyer open to being bought—one way or the other?"

"I don't think so. He seems like a man hell-bent on goodness and mercy," Tanner said. "Understand he really went after Hangar in the hearings. Did you ask Hangar to get a story published about Rule Cordell being an outlaw—and involved in Gardner's rustling?"

"I did. Hangar never was very good at that sort of thing. Maybe Seitmeyer doesn't understand how good and merciful

I can be—once I take over the region," Lady Holt said, and turned to the side. "We will take it, won't we, Iva Lee?"

"I'm sorry. Iva Lee? I don't understand."

Her eyes blinked, and for a moment, she was flustered and red-faced. She coughed into her fist to give her time to think. "I'm sorry. It's been a long day. Iva Lee used to work for me—before Elliott. A sweet woman. She died two years ago."

Tanner decided it wasn't wise to pursue the matter further and swallowed the rest of his drink. He put down the empty glass on the small table adjacent to a long brown sofa.

"Don't put it there. It'll leave a ring," she demanded, the nostrils in her nose flaring in anger.

He grabbed the glass as if it were in need of saving. He must be careful; she was on edge—or getting close to being drunk.

"You need a refill." She turned her head and yelled, "Elliott!" She looked at the attorney, laughed and said, "Almost said Iva Lee again. She's really been on my mind today."

"Yes. m'lady. Coming, m'lady. *A fortiori.*"

"Bring the whiskey." She grinned to herself; there was yet a stronger reason to come.

She seemed only mildly interested in Opat and Hangar being arrested. Her eyelids blinked four times and she snarled, "I was supposed to get a wire from Eleven Meade. He went to Clark Springs. Yesterday. Rule Cordell lives there somewhere." She smiled wickedly. "Or so I've been advised."

"Well, obviously he's waiting for him to return." Tanner glanced at the magazine at the table and looked away quickly.

"More'n likely he's headed back to New Mexico—with my payment for killing John Checker in his pocket. That bastard." She noticed her blouse was badly buttoned, smiled, faced the books and rebuttoned it.

Tanner watched with interest, hoping she might turn around to give him a tease. He was, after all, a handsome man. She might even ask him to spend the night. He straightened his cravat and brushed his coat lapels. The slender servant glided into the room, holding the whiskey decanter on a silver tray. When she spun toward the servant's entrance, her blouse was correctly buttoned. She noticed the attorney glance at her corrected blouse and what it hid, and smiled.

She nodded toward Tanner's glass and held out her own. Elliott poured whiskey into Tanner's glass, then refilled Lady Holt's and left.

"Oh, I almost forgot. Has that half-breed come back to the ranch?" Tanner asked, waving his arm.

"Dimitry? I don't know. Why?"

Tanner explained about the killing of Ranger Bartlett and Dimitry being the only one who got away. He smiled and suggested she keep him out of sight for a few days.

"We haven't toasted your new position, Judge," she said, and held up her glass to salute him.

He grinned and clinked his glass against hers and both took a drink. Feeling confident, the attorney said, "M-y horse, he's worn out. I beat him up getting here."

"Elliott will have the boys saddle one of ours."

"I—I could wait here and ride back tomorrow morning." He gulped most of the whiskey.

She matched his gulp and studied him as a wolf studies a lamb. "Sure. Good idea. I'll ride in with you. I've changed my mind. I'm going to send some men to get Jaudon off that coach and bring him here. So we can go over things." Her eyes brightened and she ran her hand through her hair.

"We're going to turn this into a triumphant takeover—and get rid of these pissant ranchers forever."

Giggling, she declared, "He can wire Citale. Get full authority to do whatever is needed . . . to quell the insurrection in Caisson." She finished the glass. "You can ride with my boys—as an official of the city. To get the great Ranger captain." She laughed long and loudly. "After we straighten out the town, he'll take a band of Rangers to the Gardner Ranch—and the one that belongs to that damn woman. And Carlson's, while we're at it. We'll finish it. I've got more important things to do, you know."

His glass halfway to his mouth, Tanner stopped. "What band of Rangers?"

"Jaudon will swear in my men as Rangers, of course. I even have badges ready. Made of silver."

Chapter Thirty

Only the sky's pink underbelly signaled a new day. Five riders on four horses and a buckboard were black shapes against a brightening prairie. With Checker leading the way, Rule Cordell, Emmett, Rikor and Morgan Peale rode silently. London Fiss had volunteered to stay behind in town to see what might happen.

A cold wind intimidated any clouds from the sky, making the moment seem more depressing than it was. Checker was drawn sadly to memories of his best friend and the realization that they didn't matter anymore.

The old rancher drove his buckboard carrying the wooden casket with the wrapped body of A. J. Bartlett. The casket had been donated by the undertaker. Checker had bought a new suit—and new socks—to bury his friend in. Bartlett's journal had been placed in the casket as well, along with a book of Tennyson's poems.

Their destination was a shallow rock pond the two Rangers had discovered when they had ridden from town to help Emmett. The pond was on the eastern corner of Morgan's land. She had readily agreed to the burial there.

Checker tried to stay focused on what was ahead of them,

instead of letting memories wash away his thinking. As usual, no one disagreed when he said where he wanted Bartlett buried. Rule's eyes were clouded with his own anguish. Emmett glanced at his son, shook his head and cursed at the awfulness of the day.

As they rounded a patrol of boulders, Checker pointed at a glistening small pool twenty yards ahead, crowded with two cottonwoods, a mesquite tree and a patrol of bushes. The water itself was only a sometime thing, resting on a bed of white and brown rocks. A jackrabbit skirted from the green protection as they approached.

"This hyar be a ri't purty place, John." Emmett stopped the wagon and admired the tree-clustered pond. "Too small for herd use." He rubbed his unshaven chin, as if deliberating his statement, and wrapped the reins around the brake stick.

Morgan smiled thinly and nodded. "Yes, it is. Quiet. Peaceful. I've always liked this place. I think A.J. will, too."

Birds of red, brown and yellow were gathered in the trees, discussing their next meal and where it might come from. As the four men drew close, flapping wings made all of them reach for their guns.

Behind the shallow pond a few feet were three large, flat rocks piled upon each other with a fourth lying next to them. Rikor stared at the rock grouping and thought it was a grave; he sniffed away his runny nose, keeping his face away from the others.

"Rode by here when we were on the way to your place," Checker said. "A.J. thought it was pretty. Reminded him of his home. As a kid. Back in Ohio." He swung down and looped his reins around a low mesquite branch.

"Probably quoted Tennyson," Rule said with a wry smile, reining his horse and dismounting.

"Yeah, something about 'the white flower of a blameless life.'"

Rikor pulled his horse alongside the wagon, jumped down and spun his reins around the wagon's brake stick.

"Any folks we need to be tellin'?" the young man asked, staring at the casket.

Checker explained there were two brothers and a sister, all back in Ohio. Ranger headquarters had the addresses, he thought. He would get them when he was in Austin. Emmett glanced at Rule, who was tying his reins to a cottonwood branch, but said nothing.

"What about a lady? A wife?" Rule asked without turning.

"No wife. There was a lady he mentioned several times." Checker twisted his chin and tried to recall the name. "Harriet. Yes, Harriet. I should write to her as well."

Rule glanced at Emmett and decided this wasn't the time to ask the Ranger if he knew the woman's last name—and where she lived. Morgan bit her lower lip and looked away.

"Hand me the shovel," Rule said.

"I'll dig the grave." Checker's tone was thunder.

Sternly, Emmett told the Ranger that he wanted to share in the work. So did Rikor, almost apologizing. Rule said he did, too. It would be his honor. After a few minutes, they selected a level place between the two oldest cottonwoods. Checker dug for twenty minutes, then handed the shovel to Rule. The tall Ranger was pale and gasping for breath. The four men rotated the digging and completed the task quickly with Rikor doing most of the final dirt removal.

Standing around the freshly mounded grave with its wooden cross in place, Checker spoke first, holding his hat in both hands. "A.J., ride easy, my friend. I put your notebook with you. Figured you and St. Peter will have some things to go over. Like you always did with . . . me. You're ready to see him . . . with a new suit . . . and socks." He choked back the emotion." His hands tightened around his hat brim. "You have my word I won't stop until this evil woman is finished. Or I join you."

With that he walked over to his horse and produced a small book of Tennyson poems. He flipped open the pages and read the first three stanzas of "The Charge of the Light Brigade." "'All in the valley of Death rode the six hundred. . . . Someone had blunder'd; Theirs not to make reply . . . Theirs not to reason why, Theirs but to do or die . . . Cannon to right of them, Cannon to left of them, Cannon in front of them . . . Into the jaws of death, Into the mouth of hell . . . Rode the six hundred.'" He put the book down to his side and knew he couldn't read more.

Silence grabbed the small group until Rikor began to sing "What a Friend We Have in Jesus." Morgan joined him, then Emmett and Rule. Checker tried, but couldn't.

When it was finished, Morgan stepped beside the grieving Ranger and took his hand.

Rule glanced at his new friend and said, "Let us pray. O God, our Father, whose very breath gives life to the world and whose voice is heard in the soft breeze of the morning and the great thunder in the evening, whose very touch gives color to the sunset and the birds of the land; hear us now. Our voices are small, but steady, for we mourn the passing of our great friend, A. J. Bartlett.

"He is coming to you now. You will know him by his great brave heart, his love for his friends and his enjoyment of poetry. He comes to you without shame, with clean hands and without fear, but he leaves us with many tears. It was too soon, O Lord. We need your strength and wisdom to understand.

"Direct us to ride in strength. Your strength. Help us learn the lessons you have hidden in every leaf and every rock. Help us to remain steadfast against those who would destroy us. Ever give us the song of A.J.'s laughter in our hearts. We ask this in Thy name. Amen."

Morgan's face was laced with tears as she murmured, "That was beautiful, Rule."

Checker took her to him and held her. Tightly. Letting his hat drop to the ground. Then he walked over to Rule and hugged him, then the others, patting each on the back. His eyes were filled with wetness.

It was Emmett who finally broke the spell of the moment. "Well, we need to be movin'. A.J. wouldn't have wanted us a-mopin' over him. No, he wouldn't'a."

Picking up his hat and returning it to his head, Checker said, "You're right, Emmett. We need to ride." He walked over to the cross and adjusted it. "Adios, my friend. I will miss you."

Softly, Morgan said, "Let's go to my place for some coffee and breakfast. We need it, I think. Mr. Fiss should be rejoining us soon."

Checker turned and his face was hard. The words from his mouth were Comanche. A commitment to death to his enemies or to his own in trying. Only Rule understood and whispered the same Comanche promise.

Chapter Thirty-one

Six mules pulled the inbound heavy stagecoach from Austin along the rutted road. It was nearing noon on the day of A. J. Bartlett's burial.

As the heavy vehicle rocked and bounced like a ship in a stormy sea, Sil Jaudon wiped his forehead with a handkerchief, brushed off dust from his coat sleeve and cursed softly in French. The other passengers had given up trying to keep dust from their clothes and sweat from their faces and had disappeared within themselves. The heavyset man laid his head against the leather-upholstered row with the wall of the carriage and shut his eyes. His third gun, carried in his belt in back, was causing him discomfort no matter how he sat, so he finally withdrew it and laid the gun on his lap, apologizing in French.

On his coat lapel was a Ranger captain's badge. Already it had brought him much attention and the interest of one of the women passengers. The woman had a birthmark that covered most of her left cheek. She had approached him at the last stage station. He guessed she was a whore headed for Caisson. When he got to Caisson, the first thing he intended to do was eat; then he would take advantage of her offer.

Already he could envision a big steak and potatoes at Lourdeson's, his favorite restaurant in Caisson. Lady Holt could wait. Besides, he already knew John Checker was dead; Sheriff Hangar's wire had informed him. Of course, that would make Eleven Meade her favorite for the moment, maybe even more than Tapan Moore, her current lover.

So be it, he told himself. *I am ze Ranger captain and he eez not. When I kill ze bastard, no one will care. Except her.* He smiled. *Maybe I will kill Tapan, too.* He glanced outside, pushing aside the window's shade. No more than three hours from Caisson.

Above the thunder of the road, the driver's shouts to his team—and the crack of the nine-foot whip—were a constant reminder of the stage line's emphasis on speed. When climbing aboard, Jaudon had noticed the stage was carrying express freight and mail, along with passenger luggage. Only three men passengers had been allowed to sit on top; there was no room for more.

Concerned, the driver and guard were exchanging thoughts about what they were seeing ahead. He caught part of the conversation. "Looks like a bunch of them. They carryin' a flag. Never seen the like before."

"Do you know 'em?"

"They ain't soldiers."

"It's wide-open country, Buster. Nobody's gonna try to hold us up here."

"Maybe."

"'Sides, I ain't takin' on no army. Must be twenty or so."

"You just keep that scattergun pointed at that fella with the flag. I don't like this."

"You're getting jumpy in your old age."

"I'm a-gonna keep them mules a-goin'." The driver snapped his long whip over the top of the team to reinforce his intent.

Gripping his hideout gun, Jaudon leaned out the window and saw one silhouette coming closer to the coach.

For the dramatic impact of the passengers, Jaudon flipped back his coat to reveal the two additional ivory-handled, gold-plated pistols carried in formfitting holsters at his waist. But he knew immediately it was Tapan Moore, Lady Holt's curly-haired gunman with the toothy smile and square jaw. He was leading a band of Holt gunmen. As if leading a cavalry unit, he held a red flag bearing the design of a phoenix. The banner fluttered as they neared the coach.

Jaudon leaned out as far as he could and yelled to the driver, "*Arreter!* Stop ze coach. Stop ze coach. Those are my men."

"Hold up, mister. No need for trouble," Tapan said, grinning. "We're here to escort Ranger Captain Jaudon to the Holt Ranch."

A second rider emerged from the pack. Dressed in city clothes and obviously uncomfortable, Wilson Tanner declared, "I am the new municipal judge of Caisson. We have an emergency in town that will require Ranger Captain Jaudon's immediate attention."

"Well, that's where we're a-headed," the driver said. "What kinda trouble?"

The stage jerked and bounced as the driver pulled the mules to a stop.

"Do what he says," the shotgun guard said. "This ain't no holdup."

"Hey, Jaudon. They wanna take you to Lady Holt's. Instead of going on to town. Says there's trouble there. Sound all right?" The driver's voice was gruff but worried.

Jaudon took a deep breath. "*Oui* . . . ah, yah. That is *bien.* Ah, good."

He leaned out again, but could only see part of Tapan,

who touched the brim of his hat in greeting. "Good to see you, Sil."

"*Bonjour*, Tapan. What is going on?"

Jaudon liked the young gunman, even if Tapan was currently Lady Holt's favorite. He had seen them come and go. His own involvement with the British leader was strictly financial—and that's the way he wanted it. They had made an agreement in Houston when he met her.

"Lots going on. John Checker's alive—and riding with Rule Cordell. The other Ranger's dead. Hangar's out as sheriff. The blacksmith's wearing his badge. For now. Opat's out as judge. Tanner's in," Tapan said, looked up at the driver and smiled widely. "Your stage isn't in any danger, mister. It's political stuff."

"Oh. Well, if'n you're sure. Don't want to be takin' these folks into some kind of shootin' trouble."

"You won't."

Jaudon sat back in the seat and straightened his cravat. His mind made no attempt to settle on Tapan's news, except for Checker being alive. *Damn, that fool Meade's a bald-faced liar!* he muttered. *Just like that bitch to make me come directly to ze ranch. Wonder if she'll have anything good to eat.*

From outside again came Tapan's voice, more urgent this time. "Come on, Jaudon. Lady Holt's waiting. I'll tell you about it on the way."

"*Oui. Oui.* I am coming. I am coming."

The heavyset Frenchman slowly opened the coach door and stepped outside, shoving his hideout gun into his back waistband. He glanced back at the blotchy-faced woman, arched his shaved eyebrows and smiled. The doorway clipped his hat with the pinned brim and sent it spinning.

"What about your luggage?" the driver asked. "It'll take a while to clear it from the others."

"*Non. Non. Merci beaucoup, monsieur.* I vill get it later. At ze station in Caisson." Jaudon picked up his hat and shoved it back on his head.

"Good enough."

The shotgun guard sat with his weapon on his lap and studied Tapan Moore. "Don't I know you from somewhere, mister? The war, maybe? I rode with Longstreet."

"Could be. Were a lot of us in that awful thing." Tapan grinned without answering directly.

"Yeah. Sure 'nuff," the guard responded, and rubbed his thick mustache.

A bearded gunman brought forward a saddled, riderless horse. Tapan took the reins and waited for Jaudon, leading the horse beside a large rock. Awkwardly, the fat man pulled himself into the saddle, using the rock as a stepstool. Tapan waved at the driver and guard, swung his horse around and kicked it into a gallop without waiting for the Frenchman. The band of gunmen followed.

Annoyed at the suddenness of it all, Jaudon stared after them, then kicked his horse into following.

"I know who that was, Buster," the guard said. "Just came to me."

"Yeah, who?" The driver snapped the reins and yelled at his team to start moving again.

"That was Tapan Moore."

"Tapan Moore? The gunfighter from down around El Paso?"

"That's the one. Hear tell he's a bit crazy in the head."

The shotgun guard shifted his weight as the driver restarted the team. "He is. That's where I remember him from. He was yelling and screaming. In a Rebel army hospital. In Tennessee, it was. During the war."

"Sorry to see he's working for that Holt woman."

"Reckon she's the only one hiring guns. They say she brought in that half-breed . . . ah, Dimitry."

"Damn. He's a bad one. Heard tell somethin' about Eleven Meade comin' this way, too." The driver snapped the reins again.

"Heard that." The shotgun guard settled back against the coach frame. "Don't understand how that Frenchman got to be a Ranger captain, do you?"

The driver yelled again, snapped the reins again and said, "No. I don't wanna know, either. Stay as far away from that Holt woman as you can. She's pure devil, boy. Pure devil."

"Didn't he say those boys were Rangers?" The guard frowned.

"Yeah, guess he did."

"Guess that means Tapan Moore's a Ranger."

"Damn."

As the stage bounced over the ridge, Tapan, Tanner and the other Holt man eased their horses to a walk to wait for Jaudon. Already the Frenchman's horse was laboring under the man's weight.

"What's going on?" Jaudon demanded as he caught up. "Do *vous* have *nourriture* . . . ah, any food? I am starving." His horse, thankful for the rest, spotted some blades of grass that looked interesting and began to nibble on them.

"You'll have to wait, Sil." Tapan fiddled with the flagpole resting in a special saddle sheath and pointed toward the closest ridge.

From over the rolling land came another rider, riding sidesaddle on a black horse. Lady Holt's long red hair danced on her shoulders. She was dressed in a dark red riding suit with a matching hat highlighted by a crimson feather. Black boots, decorated with beading around the top, reached past her knees. In her black-gloved hands was a coiled whip.

"*Bonjour*, Madame Holt. *Tres heureux de voux*," Jaudon declared loudly, removed his hat and bowed from the saddle.

She nodded in return. She loved the sound of French and knew he had said he was delighted to see her.

The pig-faced Frenchman in the dust-laced, three-piece suit opened his mouth, shut it and finally asked, "*Comment allez-vous?*"

"*Assez bien, merci,*" she responded to his polite question of how she was doing.

Tapan's face reddened with jealousy, but he kept telling himself that she was interested in the fat man only for business.

"Let us ride, Sil," Lady Holt said. "I'll tell you on the way. The rest of your men are waiting outside town."

"I thought we were going to, ah, your place," Jaudon said.

"Not now. We have work to do."

The Frenchman's stomach growled.

Late afternoon brought new fear to Caisson.

Riding down the main street of town came Lady Holt with thirty-two armed riders strung out behind her. Beside her was Sil Jaudon. Behind him rode Tapan Moore holding the red flag. They rode slowly down the street like a cavalry unit taking a predetermined position.

People stopped and stared. Word sped through the stores and offices. Lady Holt had come to town. Traffic in the street disappeared magically. A stray mongrel dog dared to bark and was shooed into silence by three men.

No one noticed Wilson Tanner returning to the livery a few minutes later. He shook his head, watching the Holt army take control of Caisson just by entering it.

In front of the telegraph office, Lady Holt reined her horse and swung down from her sidesaddle rig and handed the reins to Tapan. Jaudon dismounted in awkward stages and handed the reins to Tapan as well.

She stood, letting the drama of her appearance be absorbed by the townspeople. She enjoyed the effect and decided she must do it more often. She commanded Tapan to hold the men in the center of the street until they returned. With that, she went inside the telegraph office with Jaudon a few steps behind. The telegraph operator almost stumbled, attempting to greet them. He was shaking from nervousness.

"A-afternoon, L-Lady Holt. Ah, C-Captain Jaudon. H-how may I help you today?" The greasy-haired operator rubbed his sweaty hands on his wrinkled pants.

"He needs to send a wire to the governor. Now."

"Of course. Of course. I'll get you some paper—ah, and a pencil," the operator declared, turning around and banging into his own desk.

"I have no need of either. Here." She held out a folded piece of paper. "Send this."

"I—I certainly w-will, ma'am. H-hope you are d-doing well today," he said, his hands shaking. "W-we don't have the h-honor of your presence . . . in town . . . often enough."

Her smile was one of disdain. "Send the wire."

Methodically, he unfolded the paper.

TO GOVERNOR CITALE:
    RETURNED TO FIND ANARCHY IN CAIS-
SON. SHERIFF AND JUDGE HELD. OUTLAWS
IN CONTROL. DEMAND FULL AUTHORITY
TO RETURN ORDER. AWAIT YOUR ORDER.
CAPTAIN JAUDON

She watched him read the message and snapped, "What's the matter?"

"Ah, nothing, I guess." The operator sniffed nervously.

"Do you disagree with this assessment?"

"Ah, no. No. Of course not. Glad Captain Jaudon is here to . . . help."

"Send it."

Jaudon sneared as the operator sniffed again, unlocked the telegraph key and began sending the message.

"I know Morse code." She folded her arms and one eyebrow arched triumphantly.

He nodded and ignored the sweat bead rolling down from his forehead and finding the end of his nose.

On the corner of the operator's table was a folded paper, a message received but not delivered. Jaudon looked closer. Rule Cordell's name was written in the upper corner. Without asking, he picked it up, unfolded the paper and read:

ELEVEN MEADE DEAD . . . STOP . . . TRIED TO AMBUSH US . . . STOP . . . HE DID NOT SUCCEED . . . STOP . . . ALL WELL . . . STOP . . . LOVE, A

He handed the paper to Lady Holt, who read and returned it to the fat Frenchman, who laid it back on the table. If the operator noticed, he didn't say.

"At least that explains why he didn't wire me," she said. "I thought he had run off with the money I paid him." She paused and her eyelashes flitted as if out of control. "Where is that money now? I want it back."

Turning toward Jaudon, she told him to wire the Clark Springs marshal and follow up. He should claim the money was stolen. Without waiting for his response, she took a sheet of paper from the desk, wrote a short note about retrieving the "stolen" money and laid it beside the operator tapping out the initial message. He would know who to send it to in Clark Springs. On top of the sheet, she left several coins.

Minutes later, Lady Holt emerged from the telegraph office. Jaudon came behind her, waving the return message.

"I am authorized to take ze control," he yelled to his men.

"*Vous* know what to do." He waved the paper again for emphasis.

Tapan nudged his horse forward and led the Holt men to the sheriff's office. All of them drew rifles from their saddle scabbards, cocked and aimed them at the sheriff's door. The blacksmith-turned-sheriff emerged, holding a cocked Winchester. Scared, but determined, he stood in the doorway as the armed riders lined up in front of him. Muscles in his arms twitched with nervous energy.

"Wh-hat can I d-do for you, gentlemen?" he said in his best voice, hoping to keep the fear from bubbling over.

"The governor has just given Captain Jaudon military control of this town," Tapan declared, and pointed at Jaudon standing beside Lady Holt outside the telegraph office.

He pushed the flagpole forward in its leather holster. "We have been deputized as Rangers." He pointed to the badge on his shirt and grinned.

"I d-don't u-understand."

"Understand this, then. Resign as sheriff now or die . . . now."

The blacksmith choked back the fear climbing in his throat. A wet spot appeared at his groin, bringing chuckles from the string of riders facing him. He wasn't certain he could even walk. Finally, his hands let the Winchester drop and it thudded on the planked sidewalk, barely missing his boots.

"The hell with this. I—I r-resign." He yanked the badge from his soot-covered shirt and dropped it. Without looking at them, he walked away.

"Smoky. Ben. Go inside and bring out Hangar and Opat," Tapan commanded. His half smile was confident and cruel. When this was all over, Lady Holt might make him her number-one man, instead of Jaudon. Or her husband. He smiled and muttered, "Lord of Texas has a nice ring to it."

No one appeared on the street. It was as if the entire town had become an oil painting. The bravado built from the hearings had evaporated like a wisp of smoke. Smoky and Ben reappeared a few minutes later with a smiling Hangar and a tentative Opat. Both gunmen quickly remounted.

"Thanks, boys. We were in a bad fix!" Hangar yelled. "That damn John Checker—and Rule Cordell—sneaked up on us. The bastards! Meade lied about killin' the Ranger!"

Tapan glanced at Jaudon and Lady Holt, then back to the two released men. "You two failed. Lady Holt doesn't like failure."

"Hey, wait a minute!" Hangar held out his hands.

Opat shook his head and bowed it.

A stream of rifle shots tore through Caisson. Both Hangar and Opat crumpled to the ground.

"Smoky, get the undertaker," Tapan yelled, examining the aftermath of their firing. "Tell him the state of Texas is paying. For the boxes an' the diggin'. I want those bodies out of here. Quick."

He liked the feeling that came with leadership. Would Jaudon be a problem now that he had returned with his captaincy? He knew there was no romantic interest between the Frenchman and the English duchess. Maybe Jaudon's responsibilities as Ranger captain would take him away.

"Drinks are on the boss at No. 8," Tapan yelled. "Cause trouble in town and you're fired. Same if you're too drunk to ride when we leave."

Grunts of approval and statements of agreement followed as the Holt gunmen wheeled and galloped toward the saloon. They vanished inside in seconds. Tapan looked around and saw Jaudon and Lady Holt standing in the middle of the street. He swung his mount toward her and took a position at her right, holding the flag of the phoenix upright. Jaudon looked at him and Tapan produced one of his best smiles.

The fat Frenchman actually giggled as he began a loud pronouncement to the quaking town. His horse snorted and shook its head. Jaudon yanked hard on the reins.

"Ze citizens of Caisson, hear me," he yelled. "Ze governor has given me, as ze Ranger captain, ze complete authority to bring law and order to ze region. He is very concerned about ze outlaws attempting to take control of zee town. *Bien entendu . . .*" Jaudon caught his lapse and continued. "Ah, *certainly*, ze governor has ze need to be so concerned. But I—and *mon* fellow Rangers here with me—will change theez bad thing."

He stared in both directions of the quiet main street. A boy on a bicycle went by, not paying any attention. He didn't notice the black man watching from the alley. The speech was exactly as Lady Holt had written. He had promised to leave out any French words or she would have Tapan deliver it.

Loudly, he began again, explaining Hangar and Opat had been executed because they were found to be working with the outlaws. The mayor and town council would be disbanded until order was reestablished. Tanner would remain the municipal judge and Tapan Moore would be the acting sheriff until an election could be held.

Tapan held up the sheriff's badge and put it on, just under the Ranger badge on his leather vest.

Warrants would be issued for John Checker, Emmett and Rikor Gardner, Morgan Peale, London Fiss, Charlie Carlson and Rule Cordell. Rewards would be established for each, dead or alive. He finished his proclamation with the statement that it would be printed up and placed on display throughout the area.

Hearing his declaration, Margaret Loren rushed from her dry goods store and hurried toward them. Her face red with anger, she screamed at him. "This is insane! That Holt woman is trying to ruin our town! *Our* town!" She looked both ways. "Come out! Come out! We don't have to take this nonsense. Come on!"

Jaudon moved his hands toward his holstered revolvers, laughed and told Tapan to take care of the matter. He spun his horse and headed toward the newspaper office, where Lady Holt was already waiting.

Margaret followed him, screaming for others to come and help her.

Holding the flag in its saddle boot, Tapan swung his horse toward her, kicked it into a gallop and rammed the running animal into the woman before she had a chance to get out of the way. The horse's shoulder hit the side of her face as she stumbled and fell.

He rode past her without looking back.

She lay in the street. Unmoving. From the alley across the street, the black man came running.

Jaudon shook his head, stepped inside the newspaper office and slammed the door behind him.

Chapter Thirty-two

The lone window rattled with the force of Jaudon's entry. Lady Holt was already inside, delivering a combined offer and threat to the young publisher.

Henry Seitmeyer stood behind his desk with his arms crossed; his shirt was blotched with black. Neither it nor his bow tie had been changed since the hearings. His expression was easy to read: he didn't like either Lady Holt's words or the deliverer of them.

A large, metal printing press stood silently behind him, its job finished for the moment. Seitmeyer had had it shipped from Finsbury, London; it was "an improved Coumbia press." The small office was cluttered with paste pots, type trays, ink bottles, stacks of paper, a dozen books, two coats, a stack of printed posters and a large ashtray holding a cold pipe. A sack of loose tobacco rested against the tray.

Piles of the latest edition of the *Caisson Reporter* lay on his desk piled with other exchanges, research papers and ad layouts. The front page headline read COURT DECLARES GARDNER, CHECKER INNOCENT. The subhead was RANGER KILLED IN RELATED INCIDENT.

"You should be ashamed of printing such garbage." Lady

Holt pointed at the newspapers. "Did the outlaws make you do this?"

"Ma'am, freedom of the press is guaranteed. By the Constitution," Seitmeyer said. "I will publish what I want, when I want."

"How much for this silly place?" Lady Holt asked, waving her arms.

"The newspaper is not for sale, ma'am. Neither am I."

She glared at him, but her intensity was more than matched by his own. "I don't think you understand, Mr. Seitmeyer. Progress is coming to Caisson. I am bringing it. Soon this land will be completely under my authority. Behind that will come the railroad and barbed wire. Riches will follow." She cocked her head. "Some will have the wisdom to see what I bring—and some will not."

"What happens to that second group?" Seitmeyer growled.

"Oh, nothing, I suppose. Although most likely, they will decide other places are more comfortable." She reached out and touched the top newspaper with her forefinger, leaving it there.

"You mean like Gardner, Peale and Carlson?"

"No. Those people are guilty of breaking the law. They will be tracked down and punished." Lady Holt's mouth curled into a long sneer that made her look more like a sinister man than a woman.

"The court just conducted a hearing on the charges against Emmett Gardner and found him innocent of rustling. The same for the big Ranger, John Checker—and his murdered partner."

Jaudon walked over to the printing press and studied it. "That was ze illegal court. And John Checker is no longer ze Ranger. He is ze murderer."

Seitmeyer licked his lower lip. "Jaudon, he's a lot more of a Ranger than you'll ever be. So is A. J. Bartlett, who was murdered by your men, Mrs. Holt." His jaw tightened; a glimmer of fear flickered in his eyes, but he had no intention of backing down. "You can't try a man for the same thing twice. That's double jeopardy. That, too, is against the law."

The Frenchman glanced at Lady Holt, who explained the charges were new ones; new rustling had been discovered—and Checker's initial murder charge did not cover the killing of a deputy and two more of her men. Morgan Peale and Charlie Carlson were charged with attempting to impede justice.

"You mean Mrs. Peale testifying at the hearing was illegal?" Seitmeyer said; his face was full of disgust. "Mr. Carlson wasn't even there." He waved his right arm. "The men you say were murdered by Ranger Checker were actually killed by Ranger Bartlett, who was defending the jail against their assault."

Lady Holt's retorts were thorough and completely distorted, but delivered with intense passion. "No, Carlson wasn't there, but employees of his were, acting on his behalf. The Peale woman was helping the outlaws. And I have it on good authority that it was Checker who did the shooting at the jail. He was attempting to break out and my men tried to help the deputies there."

"I see. That's quite a twist of the truth, ma'am."

Jaudon rubbed his nose. "I need ze poster. Now. It is ze proclamation for ze town to understand."

"Find someone else." Seitmeyer rubbed his nose. "I'm too busy."

Lady Holt motioned Jaudon away and smiled warmly at the editor. "I understand how you feel, Mr. Seitmeyer. You see us as unmerciful—and uncaring." She waved her finger. "But that is not so, sir. I intend to donate the money to build a church for Caisson. The money will be turned over to the council as soon as this terrible lawlessness, this rustling, the murdering, is ended."

"That's a very generous offer, Mrs. Holt."

"Yes, it is, but I am a very generous person. And caring. When I take hold of this entire region, many will benefit," she said. "Certainly the *Caisson Reporter* will grow and prosper."

Without responding, the editor walked over to the table next to the wall. It was stacked with papers, books and envelopes. He shuffled through one stack, then another.

Finally, he found what he was looking for and yanked the newspaper clipping free of the others.

"I wrote this last year. You should read it, Mrs. Holt." He handed the crumpled paper to her. "I haven't changed my mind—and won't, no matter how many churches you pay for."

She took the clipping, looked at it and crumpled the paper in her fist. The headline read HOLT PLANS TO CONTROL ENTIRE REGION BY ANY MEANS NECESSARY. Her face transformed into purple hate.

"You stupid little man. I will squash you like this piece of paper." Lady Holt looked over at the Frenchman and nodded.

Returning the subtle directive with a grin, Jaudon stepped closer to Seitmeyer.

"I want you two out of here. There's no outlawry in Caisson—except for you. Get out." The editor shoved the bigger Jaudon away.

"*Oui, vous* are through." The Frenchman drew a revolver and raised it

Seitmeyer's hands rose too slowly to stop the barrel slamming against his head. "No . . ." he gasped, fell against the printing press and collapsed on the floor. A thin trail of blood eased from his head and slid along the wood planks.

Without examining the downed editor, Lady Holt ordered Jaudon to send a rider to bring Elliott. The black servant would know how to set type, she was certain. Her men were to work through town, picking up every issue of the latest *Caisson Reporter* they could find. She intended to publish a new edition immediately.

After her band of gunmen were finished with retrieval, she wanted them to make a swing through the remaining ranches, burning all the buildings, stampeding the herds and killing anyone they found.

"I'm sick and tired of this," she snarled. "This is my land. My land."

Jaudon returned his gun to its holster, straightened his coat lapels, wanting to ask if he could get something to eat first.

"*Vous* want Tapan to lead this—or me?" he asked, keeping his hunger to himself.

Stepping toward the door, Lady Holt smiled. "Get yourself something to eat. I know you're starved. I want you good and ready to lead the men. You're the Ranger captain—and they're the Rangers. We want that cover of legitimacy."

"*Bien.* How about Dimitry and Tapan going with us? We could use their guns if we run into Checker and Cordell."

"That is fine. Tapan is the new sheriff and, logically, should be with you," she said.

"*Sacre blue!* It is too bad we don't have Meade with us. We could use his gun. Who is this 'A'?"

"I don't know and right now I don't have time to worry about him—or Meade."

Jaudon frowned. He didn't like things he couldn't control any more than she did. "Too bad. We could have used him." Jaudon glanced at his holstered revolvers. "I vould like ze bastard's guns. They very nice, *vous* know."

"Bull. He lied about killing the big Ranger. I don't like people lying to me." Her face contorted into a scowl. "Tapan wired the marshal there—to get my money back," she said, glancing out the window at the street where a black man was helping an older woman to her feet.

"*Vous* think this A is helping Gardner—and them?" Jaudon's large belly rose and released.

Running her finger across her lips, she replied, "I have no idea. What does one man matter?"

"Speaking of ze one man, what do *vous* want with him?" Jaudon motioned with his head toward the unconscious editor.

"If he's dead, get the undertaker. If he's not, get the doctor." She smiled and grabbed the doorknob. "There's a black man outside. Looks like some old woman fell down."

Chuckling, Jaudon explained about the owner coming from the sewing store and yelling at him—and Tapan running at her with his horse. Realizing who the woman was, she told him the woman had been considered as Opat's replacement for municipal judge.

"*Cela va sans dire . . .* ah, of course."

From the alley, London Fiss ran to the knocked-down woman. He laid his long-barreled saddle revolver on the ground as he knelt beside her and slowly helped her to stand.

"Thank you, sir, thank you," she said, patting him on the arm as she gathered her feet. "I'm all right. Knocked the wind out of me." She took a deep breath. "You work for Mrs. Peale, don't you? You'd better get out of here. They want all of you." She patted his arm again. "I appreciate your kindness. There weren't any white men who were brave enough to help me. But please go."

After retrieving his weapon, Fiss glanced down the street and saw Tapan wheel his horse away from the saloon hitching rack. He had gone there after knocking down the dry goods owner with the intention of joining the other men.

"Ma'am, step away. Trouble is coming," the black man said. She hesitated, saw the horseman galloping toward them and hurried to the sidewalk, knowing it was too late to tell him to leave. Running now would only get him shot in the back.

Fiss didn't move. Tapan shot and missed. The black man raised his gun and fired. Twice. Tapan's horse squealed and stumbled. Tapan flew over the horse's neck as the animal skidded and collapsed. Still holding the reins in his left hand and his pistol in the other, the gunman hit the street, bounced once and didn't move. Only his gun bounced a second time from his opened hand.

Fiss looked at the older woman, touched the brim of his hat and spun back toward the alley.

The gunshots outside made Lady Holt jump.

"What the hell?" she said.

"Stay here!" Jaudon ran toward the door, yanking free his revolver again, shifting it to his left hand and drawing the second with his right. His thick stomach wobbled with the fury of his movement.

He opened the door just far enough to see the street in front of them. Holt gunmen were pouring from the No. 8 Saloon. Tapan lay unmoving in the street, not far from his dead horse.

The black man drew his holstered second gun as he ran toward the alley.

Jaudon fired through the crack with both guns.

Fiss jerked and his left arm twitched as one of Jaudon's bullets tore into it. The gun in his left hand popped free. He half turned and shot at Jaudon. His bullet thudded into the building wall a few inches from the opened door. Jaudon jumped back. Fiss fired again at the oncoming horde of gunmen up the street. A stunned Margaret Loren screamed for him to run.

At the far end of the alley, London Fiss jumped on his waiting horse and spurred it into a hard run. He had left the animal there, readied, just in case. He hadn't planned on getting involved at all, but he couldn't just let that poor woman lie in the street. He raced into the open plains, leaving the town behind him. There was a possibility some of Holt's men might follow, so he wouldn't ride directly to the Morgan Peale Ranch. Or go near the small pond where they were going to bury the dead Ranger, either. He would make it look as if he were leaving. For good. He swung his smooth-running horse to the south, running across soft ground wherever he could find it.

"Tapan! Tapan?" Jaudon finally stepped through the door and onto the sidewalk.

The handsome gunfighter didn't move.

Four Holt gunmen caught up with Jaudon and three more moved to check on Tapan.

"What's going on?" Lady Holt yelled from inside.

"I do not know, m'lady. Tapan is down," Jaudon yelled back.

"My God! Is he shot?" she screamed.

"I do not know. Yet."

"Get the bastards!"

"*C'est ca.*" He caught himself. "Right. There is only one. He is gone. Up ze alley. Had ze horse waiting."

Lady Holt screamed, "I want him hanged."

Jaudon holstered his guns and yelled for his men to ride after the escaping Fiss. He turned back to Lady Holt, who was clearly distraught. "*Oui,* it vas ze darkie working for ze Peale woman."

"I want him hanged. Let all the bastards see it—and know the rage of . . . me." Lady Holt stamped out onto the sidewalk.

"No! No, you will not."

The challenge stopped Jaudon and his men. They turned to look at Margaret Loren. "He didn't do anything except help me get up—after your man tried to run over me with his horse. That awful man in the street there. He came after him, too. Shooting."

"Hell, lady, it's just a darkie," one of the Holt gunmen said.

That brought chuckles from the rest.

"Tapan's coming around," another said.

Jaudon looked back at Lady Holt for direction. If she wanted this bothersome woman killed, so be it. The cattle baroness licked her lips and turned her head slightly to the right.

"What, Iva Lee? Let the woman go? Why? Oh, sure."

Jaudon and his men weren't sure what they were hearing. He motioned for his men to get their horses. Margaret walked down the sidewalk to Lady Holt.

Lady Holt stared at her as if not seeing. Her face paled, then turned red, then normal again. She pointed at Tapan, who was now sitting with Jaudon talking to him.

"Get a doctor for him. And for this man . . . inside. He fell down and hurt himself." She spun and went inside the editor's office without waiting for Margaret to reach her.

The dry goods store owner grabbed the doorknob. From inside, Lady Holt screamed, "I'll kill you if you come inside. Me an' Iva Lee."

Chapter Thirty-three

Hesitating, Margaret Loren opened the newspaper office door and stepped inside. "Mrs. Holt, I need to talk with you. I was hoping you'd see that this isn't the way to build a community."

Lady Holt stood a foot away from the printing press. Her eyes were wild, her complexion crimson once more.

"I told you to get out." The words blurted from her mouth, leaving spittle on her lips.

The energetic store owner took a half step backward, refound her courage and walked closer. For the first time, she saw the unconscious editor on the floor.

"Oh my! Henry . . . is he . . . ?" She rushed to his side.

Haughtily, Lady Holt said, "I have no idea. He slipped and hit his head. I called for a doctor to come." She glanced away as if hearing a voice and looked back, "Oh yes, Iva Lee wants me to tell you that you have on a pretty dress." She blinked twice. "I want to buy . . . ah, six custom dresses from you."

Either Margaret didn't hear the comments or didn't care. "Find me a towel. Anything! Hurry!"

Lady Holt stared at her, not believing she had heard correctly. This woman had dared to command her to do something. She turned away and sat down at the editor's desk. Taking a pen and stroking it in the inkwell, she began to write. At the top of the paper, she wrote:

The Caisson Reporter, scratched out *Reporter* and wrote *Phoenix* next to it. Below the heading, she scratched *Town Enjoys New Peace as Ranger Captain Sil Jaudon Combines Forces with Major Rancher.*

Taking a second sheet of paper, she wrote *Arrest Warrants Issued for Emmett Gardner, Charles Carlson, Morgan Peale, John Checker, London Fiss and Rule Cordell.*

Smiling, she grabbed a third sheet, dabbed her pen into the ink again and wrote *Lady Holt Agrees to Take Over Three Small Ranches After Owners Are Killed.*

She would write the stories later. It was important to get the overall sense of them down. Elliott would know how to set type, she told herself. Her most important task, right now, was getting the stories ready for a special edition. She had already written the proclamation of emergency law Jaudon had announced in the street. Elliott would set it first.

A knock on the door, answered by Margaret, brought Jaudon and the town doctor. The Frenchman barely noticed the store owner, moving to the editor's desk to report Tapan Moore was going to be fine; he had merely had the wind knocked out of him.

Her eyes flashed and she mouthed, "Thank you, Great Phoenix."

He ignored the supplication; legends were for people with too much time on their hands. He also reported one of his riders had left for the ranch and Elliott. All of the new newspaper copies had been collected and were being burned.

"All of them?" she asked, turning her head to the left.

"*Oui.* All that we could find, m'lady." Jaudon bowed slightly. Lowering the pen, she straightened her back and stared at him. "That is not *all*. Didn't I say that I wanted *all* of them collected and destroyed?"

The Frenchman listened without speaking. He hated this kind of rebuke. How the hell would he know if they got all of the copies? Somebody might have one hidden somewhere. What difference did it make? He smiled and said he would personally check out the situation.

"Good. I will expect a report of perfection."

Outside, he saw Luke Dimitry walking toward him from across the street. His horse had just been tied to the hitching rack.

"Couldn't find the darkie," he said. "Didn't look like he was headed for Peale's place, more like due south. Maybe he's running."

"How bad was he hurt?"

"Don't know that. Never saw him," Dimitry said. "The way he was riding, I'd say he wasn't hurt bad."

Jaudon resisted asking how he knew that. Lady Holt would have asked the question, but he wasn't Lady Holt. The Frenchman stepped down from the sidewalk and onto the street. "I want the blacksmith dead. He might cause trouble. Later."

"Got it. I'll do it myself."

"A knife would be the best."

"I would like that."

Smiling evilly, Jaudon said he wanted all of his men ready to ride out after that. They would hit the Peale Ranch first, then the others. This would be the day.

"What happened to Henry?" the doctor said as he entered, ignoring both Margaret and Lady Holt.

"I have no idea." Lady Holt snorted. "Fell against something, I guess. Can you get him out of here? We have work to do."

The young, slim physician's eyebrows cocked in reaction

as he slid beside the unconscious editor. He opened his large black bag, took out a stethoscope and listened to Seitmeyer's breathing. Lady Holt returned to her writing, as if the room were empty and this were her own domain. Jaudon stared over the doctor's shoulder, occasionally making a comment, sometimes in French.

Margaret leaned over and asked if she could do anything to help.

"I'm going to need hot water and cloths," the doctor said. "I can't move him like this. It's too big a risk."

Margaret was on her feet quickly and headed to the back room of the newspaper office, an odd sort of part kitchen and part storeroom, grabbed the only container she could find. An old pot. A towel and a shirt lay on a cluttered shelf. She took them, too. Hurrying past Lady Holt, who was writing furiously, she handed the towel and shirt to the doctor and left. Minutes later, she returned with the pot filled from the city well and placed it on the stove to heat.

"There's not much I can do for him," the doctor announced. "After I clean his wound, we'll just have to let him sleep—and see what God wishes."

Lady Holt looked up from her writing. "You're not serious, are you, Doctor? We're going to need room to get the next edition out." She waved her left arm to demonstrate the need for space.

Angrily, the young physician glared at her. "I am quite serious, madam. A man's life is at stake." He glanced past her toward Margaret standing by the stove. "Mrs. Loren, is the water hot? It doesn't have to be boiling."

Chapter Thirty-four

At Morgan Peale's ranch, the small group of defenders ate silently. Rikor reluctantly agreed to stand watch down by the first ridge. Sending along some of Morgan's donuts—and the promise of stew later—made it easier for him to go. Anyone coming from town could be seen for miles from that vantage point.

John Checker said he wasn't hungry and resisted anyone looking at the wound on his side, even though it had bled through his shirt. He insisted that he was fine, doing so gruffly. The death of his friend lay heavily on him and it was obvious. He stood by the fireplace, drinking coffee and staring into the yellow coals.

After eating, Emmett said, "Ya know, I'd sure like to be a-seein' my boys. The rest o' 'em. Reckon yu're a-missin' your family, too, Rule. Think we could take a ride down thar? To yur place?" He put the last bite of stew into his mouth and savored it. "Like to see mine, too. See if my beeves are still happy. Got a lot of things to do there. That barn roof's in need of fixin'."

"That's up to John," Rule said, sipping his coffee. "Mrs. Peale, that was a fine meal. We thank you. Best stew I've had in a long time."

"You're welcome—and please call me Morgan," Morgan said, removing some of the used dishes from the table and heading to the small kitchen.

From the counter, she looked back at the tall Ranger, drawn to him in ways she hadn't felt since her feelings for her late husband. They were feelings she didn't think would ever arise again. Or should. Yet she wanted to go to him. To comfort him, she told herself. Of course, to comfort him. He was a lonely man; any woman could read that. A man difficult to reach. Would he allow her close? To his soul? Had a woman ever done so?

She placed the dishes in a large bowl filled with hot water, cut off some soap shavings from the large bar and massaged the water to create a thin line of suds.

In the main room, Checker studied the tiny dancing flames within the hot coals. His mind danced with them, along yesterdays: A. J. Bartlett recited Tennyson from one corner of his mind; his little sister reminded him of his promise to return in another. In between were the shadows of Jaudon, Tapan, Dimitry and Meade. He couldn't bring himself to think about what had to be done. He tried, but his thoughts kept curling back to other times.

Touching the small pouch under his shirt, Checker couldn't help thinking about Stands-In-Thunder's views on death, on the afterlife. The old war chief was convinced all Comanches went to live in a magnificent valley, where everyone was young and virile. At some point, each would return to the earth and be reborn, to help keep the People strong. There was a beauty in his words.

Would he ever see Stands-In-Thunder again? Or A.J.?

It took Emmett to pull him—and all of them—back to the day.

"Thought London would be back by now. Said so," the old rancher declared. "What if that evil woman's guns all came to town after we done left? When was that Jaudon supposed to be back? Soon, I reckon." He took another gulp of coffee. "Why don't them other Rangers come an' help us?"

Checker turned from the fireplace. "Citale would've fired all the Rangers in the Special Force. Jaudon'll make Rangers out of his men."

"What about that thar regular bunch of Rangers, then? Ain't there more than just yur bunch, John?"

"Yes, the full force. But they're spread out all over Texas, Emmett. Besides, Captain Poe knows which side his bread is buttered on," Checker said. "I imagine he's stayed out of this. And will. He can't go against Citale and stay in his job. He'll keep his men out of it. Or try to." He shook his head.

"Ya mean he's gonna let them do whatever to . . . ah, yur captain?"

"It wouldn't surprise me, Emmett." Checker moved from the fireplace to the table.

Leaning forward at the table, Rule rubbed his hands together and stared at them. "What about this Spake Jamison? A.J. told me he was a tough old warrior."

Checker was surprised Rule knew the older Ranger. "He is. Be a good hand to have on our side." He slammed his fist on the table. "But he's not here. None of them are. We can't plan on wishes."

"Wonder why we haven't seen Eleven Meade," Rule said, changing the subject. He held up three fingers. "Guess it doesn't matter. She's got three really bad ones, besides him. Sil Jaudon. Tapan Moore. And Luke Dimitry."

"Figure we're going to see all of them soon enough," Checker said. "Might not see Meade unless we're watching our backs." He pointed toward the kitchen. "I'm going to get some more coffee. Anybody need some?"

"Naw. Done coffee'd out."

"No, thanks, John."

The tall Ranger headed into the small room and was greeted by Morgan with a warm smile.

"What do ya think, Rule?" Emmett's tired face was a question.

At first, Rule thought the old rancher was talking about the attraction between Checker and Morgan. Then he realized the gunfighter was talking about their situation. "We bought a little time." He shrugged his shoulders. "I don't know how much. I'd say we're going to have to leave here as soon as we can. My guess is they'll hit tonight."

"'Member when ya fooled all them Yanks?" Emmett stroked his unshaven chin as if he wasn't listening. "Wha'd they call it? Masquerade Battalion, I think. Yah, that's it. How 'bout we try somethin' like that?"

Rule winced, trying to think of some gentle way to tell the older man that it was a different situation in a different time with a different objective. All he was trying to do then was to slow down the Union sneak attack long enough for the Confederates to prepare for the advance.

Shaking his head, the gunfighter explained, "Not sure how we could do anything like that, Emmett." He pointed out that his scouts had taken advantage of an abandoned breastworks with left-behind uniforms and gear.

"We even had some cannonballs," he said. "No cannons, but we faked those. It's not the same, Uncle. All we were trying to do was slow them down so our boys wouldn't be ambushed. We knew exactly where the Yanks were heading."

"Well, ya faked out them Regulators, too. With that 'Sons of Thunder' stuff. That big boy . . . ah, 'the Russian' . . . the travelin' trader tolt me 'bout it. Said he did some helpin'."

Rule shook his head, watching Checker come back into the room, sipping a filled mug. "Yes, Caleb Shank was a big part of bringing them down. Still . . ." He stopped talking and looked at Checker. "You know, Uncle Emmett, we're not even sure where they'll hit first. They should come here, but they might not."

"You're right, Rule. But a smart play is that they will." Checker walked over to the fireplace where he had been before. He took another sip. "Ever been around Luke Dimitry or Tapan Moore?"

"Can't say as I have." Rule ran his fingers along the table. "How good are they?"

"We aren't going to like facing them."

Checker turned toward the fire and drank his coffee. Rule and Emmett gathered the rest of the used dishes and took them into the kitchen. The old rancher took charge of washing, in spite of Morgan's insistence that she would finish the chore. With a backward glance at Checker, she took an old watering pot outside to fill at her well and water a string of struggling flowers on the east side of her house.

"I'll be right back, Uncle Emmett," Rule said. "Want to tell John something. Before I forget it."

"Sure. I'm an old hand at this . . . since my li'l lady up an' died on me." He bit his lower lip and looked away.

Rule spun back toward the main room. His own thoughts were huddling next to his wife, Aleta. He missed her very much. And Ian and Rosie. And Two, for that matter. In his mind, his children hugged him every night before he went to sleep. His dog, Two, joined in the warmth. Being separated, sometimes, was the cost of liberty.

Lady Holt seemingly had every advantage going for her against the three small ranches. She had money and influence, the governor, a gang of gunmen and now she had the Rangers. That meant the law. Like Checker, he had no illusion about what they had accomplished in town. The overturn of the charges against Emmett and the two Rangers would only last until Lady Holt heard about them. The townspeople couldn't be expected to stand up against her power.

Pausing, he laid a hand on the back of the closest chair. John Checker had his back to him, lost in yesterdays.

"John, may I bother you?" he said, walking closer.

"What? Oh, of course, Rule." Checker turned toward him and waved his hand. "I was just . . . doesn't matter."

"Sure it does. A.J. was a great friend," Rule said. "He died fighting . . . for a better Texas. That's what he wanted." The gunfighter stood next to Checker and laid a hand on the tall man's shoulder. "It's our job to make it happen."

There was a hesitation before Checker agreed.

"I think you ought to go outside now," Rule said, removing his hand and looping both thumbs into his gun belt. "I think a certain young lady would like that. A lot."

Checker stared at Rule, then frowned. "Rule, I can't. This isn't the time. You know what we're up against."

The gunfighter took a step back and looked out the window. He could see Morgan watering her flowers.

"Don't figure she sees it that way, John. The heart doesn't carry a watch." He smiled. "I only know life started for me when I met Aleta." He turned away and headed back to the kitchen. Over his shoulder, he yelled, "You do what you think best, John."

Checker shook his head and chuckled. The time for mourning was over. He put down his cup on the table and headed outside. Taking a deep breath, he eased toward Morgan, who was pretending not to notice his coming.

"Flowers do something special to a place," he said, shoving his hat back on his forehead.

Glancing at him and smiling, Morgan said, "Wouldn't think someone like you would notice."

"You don't think Rangers like flowers?" His returning smile equaled hers.

Their eyes met and danced briefly.

"I—I w-wish things were different," he managed to say. "I'd do things different."

She stood and stepped closer to him. "How different, John?" Her voice was soft.

Putting his hand on her arm, he pulled her to him.

Their mouths met.

As they kissed, the silhouette of a rider appeared from the west. Their moment of intimacy interrupted, Checker and Morgan stepped back from each other. Their hands held each other's arms to keep the instant from fleeing.

"That's got to be London. Otherwise Rikor would be warning us," Checker said.

"Something's wrong! Mr. Fiss has been hurt!" she yelled, and headed for the incoming figure.

The black man reined up; his left arm hung at his side.

"Mr. Fiss, what happened? You've been shot." She pointed at his bloody sleeve.

Rule and Emmett joined her with Checker a few strides behind.

The three men helped him from the saddle and he told them what had happened in town.

Checker's face matched Rule's in intensity.

"Rode south out of town. Like I was scared, headed for the border. Left plenty of tracks," the black man said, trying to catch his breath and ignore the steady ache in his arm. "They quit following me. Saw them turn back. An hour out, I'd guess." He took a deep breath. "One of them was Dimitry. I'd recognize that old Navajo coat anywhere."

"So Jaudon and Lady Holt are both in town," Checker said.

"And Tapan Moore and Luke Dimitry," Rule added.

"Let's go inside. We can talk there," Checker said. "Morgan made a fine stew for us. Maybe I'll have some, too. I'm getting hungry."

Rule grinned to himself.

Holding the reins of Fiss's horse, Emmett said, "If'n you don't mind, London, I'll borrow yur hoss an' ride down to Rikor. He'll be a-wantin' some o' that stew." He shook his head. "Fact, you boys better git yur fill afore he comes. That boy kin eat somethin' fierce."

The black man warmly agreed. They continued walking to the house while the old rancher swung into the saddle and headed back. Checker looked at Morgan and smiled. Her return smile made him want to take her in his arms right there. Her eyes said she would like that, too.

As they walked into the house, Rule asked Fiss if he had seen Eleven Meade. The black man hadn't seen him.

Fiss looked at the three men and the woman walking beside him. He should feel strange. White people didn't like being around black people. For any reason. But not these four. They thought of him as a friend, an equal. And he wasn't just a colored man, he was a former convict. It didn't matter. Not to them. It hadn't mattered to Morgan, either; she respected his skills. Of course, he lived in the special bunkhouse built from the barn, which was empty except at roundup when she hired short-time riders. At her insistence, his meals were always taken in the main house.

Inside, Morgan insisted she should clean his wound.

"There's no lead in there. I checked. And it's my left arm. It'll have to do."

"Better let her have a look anyway," Checker said.

"Look who's talking," Fiss replied.

Morgan took his arm. "Hold out your arm, Mr. Fiss."

"Sure. Sure." He shook his head, but complied.

Checker handed him a fresh cup of coffee.

She began to cut away the bloody sleeve, pulling slowly on the garment where it had embedded itself in the wound.

"I'll get some hot water going." Rule headed for the

kitchen. Over his shoulder, he yelled, "Where's a big pot, Morgan?"

After the wound was treated and wrapped with a white bandage, Fiss finished a second cup of coffee. Morgan returned with a new shirt.

"It was my husband's. I think it'll fit, Mr. Fiss."

In spite of his suggestion that she call him "London," she always insisted on the more formal designation.

"I can't wear that, Mrs. Peale."

"Put it on. Now, how would you like some stew?" Morgan asked.

"Thanks, Mrs. Peale. I'm hungry as can be." He looked at his left arm; it was stiff and hurting badly. John Checker wouldn't stay in bed with a wound much worse than this; he couldn't show any sign of weakness. He removed the old shirt with Rule's help and put on the fresh one. It was a dull brown. It fit.

"And you, John, are you ready . . . for some stew?" Morgan smiled.

"Yes, ma'am. I am." Checker sat down next to Fiss.

Quickly, she brought iron utensils and cloth napkins that had once been bright blue. Rule moved close to the table and touched the silver cross and medicine pouch around his neck.

"How do you want to play this, John?" he asked.

Checker watched Morgan set the white ironstone bowls in front of both men and asked if they wanted more coffee. They did and she left to get the pot.

"Not sure, Rule. Except they'll come," the tall Ranger said. "Most likely tonight. I think they'll head here first, move on to the Carlson Ranch, then to Emmett's. Their objective will be to destroy us. All of us. Time isn't on their side. The state of Texas isn't going to let Jaudon stay a Ranger captain."

After watching Morgan in the kitchen, Checker looked at Rule. "There are some big ranchers who'll scream about no Ranger help along the Rio Grande. That'll end Jaudon's time as a Ranger captain." He licked his lower lip. "It'll come too late to help us, though."

"I don't like waiting for trouble," Rule said.

Checker put a spoonful into his mouth, savored it and swallowed. "Me, neither. What say you and I ride to town."

It wasn't a question.

"I like that idea." Rule put both hands on the back of the end chair.

Returning with the coffeepot, Morgan raised her free hand to signal a halt. "Wait just a minute. This is my fight. Mine and Emmett's. Not yours." She poured fresh coffee, took the pot back to the stove and returned, standing in the kitchen doorway. Her arms were at her sides, her legs spread in defiance.

Checker thought she was the most beautiful woman he had ever seen and wanted to tell her so. Her earlier kiss lay on his lips—and mind—like a butterfly on a flower.

"I ride with Mrs. Peale," Fiss said, not daring to bend his wounded arm. He shoved another spoonful of stew into his mouth to emphasize his commitment.

Checker reminded them Jaudon would be bringing a force of nearly forty men, all experienced fighters. Among them would be Tapan Moore and Luke Dimitry—and maybe Eleven Meade. Tapan, in particular, would be hard to handle. The tall Ranger shook his head, pushing away the weakness in his body that wanted control. Not now. There was no time for giving in to the ache from the wound.

Only Rule and Morgan noticed. She wanted to hug him; Rule wanted to tell him it was all right to feel the bullets that had tried to kill him.

"I don't like the idea of taking on forty," Checker said,

"when we're really just after three." He stared at the stew, then took another spoonful.

Rule rubbed his chin. "Holt. Jaudon. Citale."

"Right." Checker washed a third spoonful down with coffee. The movement brought a pain to his wounded side that he tried to ignore. He added Jaudon would likely lead the Holt gang if they attacked, then asked Fiss what Lady Holt was doing in town. Fiss responded that she was in the newspaper office when he left; Jaudon had been there, too, firing at him from the doorway.

"Hard to miss that big boy, but I did." He forced a grin and continued eating.

"That means Henry Seitmeyer is in trouble. Or worse," Checker said. "He was going to bring out an edition telling about the hearings."

"Didn't see him. But I heard a couple of businessmen talking about the story." He turned his head to the side. "Probably should have gotten a copy."

"Mrs. Loren was all right when you left?" Morgan asked, leaning forward in her chair.

All of them complimented Margaret Loren for her courage. He retold what had happened, expanding it to include the resignation of the blacksmith as temporary sheriff.

Checker thought he had shown both courage and judgment. "Not much wisdom in going up against forty guns—by yourself."

Hoofbeats signaled Rikor's return. The young man entered the house with a question. "What's goin' on?"

Checker summarized the situation while Morgan rose and went to the kitchen again, returning with a filled coffee cup, tableware and a napkin.

"Sure did like those donuts, ma'am," Rikor exclaimed.

"You have some stew and I'll see if we have any left." Morgan set a bowl filled with stew in front of him.

"Oh my, that looks mighty good. You sure can cook, ma'am. Bet your husband liked coming home." He stopped, realizing the insensitivity of his statement, and apologized.

She smiled and told him an apology wasn't necessary and quickly asked if the others wanted more coffee. None did.

Checker stared at his empty cup for a moment before looking up. "Let's go to town—and arrest her. Citizens' arrest."

Rule's face brightened. "Well, we can't protect the ranches. Trying to do that puts all the advantage on their side. And puts us . . . dead." He turned to Morgan. "Are you ready for this? They're going to burn this fine home. Run off your cattle."

"I can rebuild a house. I can round up cattle." Her response matched the fierceness in her eyes.

"All right, let's do it," Rule said. "Got a thought, John."

"Of course."

"We need to ride like the guerrilla fighters did. During the war. Carry lots of weapons. Bullets. Food. Water. With us. Stay on the move. Until this thing's over."

"You're right. Whatever happened to that packhorse with food and bullets I brought to your place, Rikor?" Checker asked.

The young man grinned and looked more like a wolf than a man for a moment. "Ah, sir, we brought it along. What we ain't done et anyway. Packhoss is in the corral. With our other hosses."

Smiling, Morgan set out a plate of donuts.

"Oh, ma'am, are those fer me?"

"Enjoy. There's more stew in the kitchen. That's all of the donuts, though. Would you like some more coffee?"

"Yes'm." He grabbed a donut.

"Got another suggestion," Rule said, looking at Checker. "Let's hide out up the trail a mile or so—some place where we can sting them when they come. Tonight. Then leave for town." The gunfighter ran his forefinger along the table. "Might make them think twice about coming for the ranches. Especially if we make them think there are more of us."

Checker looked at him. "I can't shoot men who can't defend themselves. Even Jaudon's bunch."

The return gaze from Rule was an understanding one. "I can't, either. But maybe we could scare the hell out of them. Make them think other Rangers had joined us. Might make them make a mistake. Give us time anyway."

"Hot damn! That's what Pa were a-talkin' about," Rikor said with a mouthful of donut. "Doin' the masquerade thing all over."

Nodding at the young man, Checker said, "It's risky. What if they don't bite—and stay to fight, instead?"

"We'll set ourselves up to get out of there. Quick. Leave them wondering." Rule drew a circle with his finger on the table, then moved it swiftly away.

Checker was silent a moment; his eyes sought Morgan's, then returned to Rule. "I'm ready, if the rest of you are."

The location of the ambush was Morgan's suggestion. A short valley on the eastern edge of her grazing land, and not far from town. The main road from Caisson went right through there. There were plenty of boulders and ridges to hide behind. They would be able to hide their horses close by, fire down at Holt's men and ride away before they could reorganize.

"Wal, I reckon that thar's a good 'nuff plan," Rikor said as he raised a spoonful of stew to his mouth. "Whar do we head after?"

"Lady Holt."

"Ya mean her ranch?" Rikor drawled.

Checker cocked his head. "No. I mean her. Wherever she is. We're going to take her to Clark Springs. For trial."

"That'll be somethin'."

"Yeah. Maybe so," Checker said, and drew the handgun he carried in his back waistband to check its loads.

Chapter Thirty-five

After repacking the packhorse, filling canteens with well water and gathering every weapon they could find, the small party left the Morgan Peale Ranch and headed toward town. It was important to stay out of sight until they got to the valley where Morgan thought they should wait for Holt's men.

Fiss and Rikor took the point, knowing the land better than the others. Narrow ravines, an occasional stand of trees, a string of ridges and even a herd of grazing cattle provided the screening they desired en route. They didn't intend to go far, at least not now. Just far enough.

Nightfall found five of them hidden in separate shooting positions along the road from town, settled on both sides of the shallow valley. Two on the south side, three on the north. The positions were selected by Checker and Rule. Each was picked for its concealment from the road—and its easy escape to their horses. Each shooter was to come to the horses as soon as possible after firing on the Lady Holt gang. Shooting was to be over their heads unless the gang started firing back.

Located fifty yards behind the shooting positions, their saddled horses were tied to branches among a grove of pecan, mesquite and cottonwood trees. A shallow pond was the reason for their growth. Fiss was put in charge of the horses. He didn't like the job, but accepted it when Checker quietly explained they needed someone savvy there in case of trouble. Both Checker and Rule knew the man was hurting and unable to use his arm. This would be a good place for him.

Checker expected the Holt riders to come through this part of the road riding easily and unsuspecting. It was a good location for an ambush. The hardest for him was to leave Morgan in a firing site above him and Rule. The gunfighter told him that he had to do it—and to treat her like a man. She would insist on it.

Her shooting location was within a rock cradle above and to the left of where Checker and Rule intended to wait. In her hands was a rifle. A Colt rested in her belt. "Morgan, I . . . I'm not comfortable with you . . . being here," Checker said, feeling awkward. His long black hair rustled along his shoulders.

"You don't think I'm good enough, brave enough . . . what?" Her mouth twisted into a half smile. "Or do you want me beside you?"

"You know what I mean."

"Yes, I do. Don't worry about me. This is my ranch. I don't intend to let that awful Englishwoman have it." Her face changed into a frown.

He made her promise that she would fire quickly and crawl away. Immediately. Then he suggested she cock the rifle now and ease the hammer back into place until needed. That would keep her gun from making a noise being cocked as the gang rode through.

"My daddy would've called this the rattlesnake code. Warn 'em first, he'd say, and then let 'em have it if'n they don't leave." She cocked her head.

"That's about it. Only we're the ones who are going to leave. Remember that," Checker said. "If they don't turn and run, we need to."

"I understand." She smiled. "Now I need something from you, John."

"Anything."

She gently insisted on a parting kiss, which he was happy to offer.

Reluctantly, he climbed down from her position to the main one where Rule waited.

"Wish it was darker, Rule. The darker, the better," Checker observed as he joined the gunfighter.

Rule assured him a full moon favored them; the old Medicine Man Moon had told him never to fear Mother Moon's gentle caring. He never did. Even during the war and the guerrilla fighting afterward.

"Still wish it was darker."

Rule grinned and reassured him the evening would go well.

As she sat down to wait, Morgan Peale's mind was wrapped around the man she had just kissed.

"He's good-looking in a hard sort of way, isn't he?" she said to herself. "I wonder where he got that arrowhead-shaped scar on his cheek. He almost looks like an Indian, doesn't he?"

She couldn't forget the longing in his eyes when they were close. It made her warm all over. Way down under his Ranger ways was a caring man, one who would back up a friend, regardless of the odds. The realization of this gentle core drew her to him as nails were drawn to magnets at the general store.

Her late father—and her late husband—she had understood. And men like them as well. She could almost read their thoughts. They were good men, or tried to be, as they saw goodness. Dependable. Stubborn. Yes, and narrow-minded, too. Neither would have understood her hiring London Fiss—or allowed it. The three things they couldn't stand were liars, cowards and people of a different color. Men like them would fight when pushed hard enough, but only then. From that point, the fight was your own, yours to handle, not asking for, nor expecting, any help. "Stand n' git 'er dun, boy." Or die trying. That was her father.

She was glad Checker had insisted on the same kind of warning her father would have done. But the Ranger was different from her father.

Men like John Checker—and Rule Cordell—she didn't understand. They were a breed of men Texas needed now, or the worst kind of men—and women—would take over. But what kind of life could a woman have with a man like Checker and Rule? She knew the gunfighter was married and had a small family. How had he done it? Why was he here? She already knew the answer, to help his uncle. He was a wild-looking man with his stone earring, long black coat and many handguns. He was what she had expected him to look like. Yet he, too, had a gentle way about him. A caring way.

On her lap lay her rifle, cocked and ready. The hammer had been eased back into place as the Ranger had suggested. She moved her legs to relieve them of stiffness and studied the road below. Her thoughts returned to John Checker. He was a killer of men; a Ranger, but a killer nonetheless. Just like Rule Cordell. She could see Checker's face with those penetrating eyes.

"We could never have a life together. Never," she admonished herself.

A man like him was always drawing danger. Such a man could be killed at any time. Eleven Meade had already tried. God knows how many other men with a gun had. The thought of John Checker dying made her wince and shiver. She squeezed her eyes tightly to get that awful picture to go away. Seeing him lying wounded in bed was bad enough. She knew he shouldn't be up so soon; she knew what the blood on the side of his shirt meant. He had to be weak from losing so much blood. Had to be. That stubbornness was just like her father, she admitted. Just like him.

She could see Checker and Rule below, setting up the barrage of guns below her to add to the appearance of a larger force. It was Rule's idea. On the other side of the road, lower down, she could make out Emmett and Rikor setting up a similar fake barrage. She wanted to call out to the tall Ranger, to tell him to come and see her again. To hold her and kiss him. That was foolish, she told herself. All of them could be dead when the night was over.

This wasn't the time; Checker had said that earlier. Still . . .

A sound behind John Checker! He spun with his cocked rifle in his hands. Standing twenty feet away was a calf. The wobbly animal looked at him and started bawling. From the darkness, the mother cow appeared and nudged her infant away, giving the Ranger a scornful look as she did.

"Well, I think you just got told off." Rule laughed.

Checker smiled. "You take him on home, mother."

He returned his attention to the trail. At least they had time to set up Rule's idea.

He left his Winchester and a box of cartridges on a flattened area where he would return when finished. Rule had already begun work on the fake gun barrage. A lariat, Sharps carbine, shotgun, four pistols and leather strings lay on the hillside where he worked. In this crook of a broken rock slab angling skyward like a giant arrowhead, Rule had wedged the Sharps snugly into place. It had been A. J. Bartlett's gun. A separate boulder was pushed against the gun butt to keep it from sliding backward when fired. The gun was aimed at a dark ridge guarding the far edge of the open trail.

About ten feet away, he found another rock holster for one of his backup pistols. Checker joined him in the placement of the guns. A few feet away was another small crevice for a Smith & Wesson revolver that had been Bartlett's and another long-barreled Colt. The Ranger packed both in place with heavy supporting rocks. Rule inserted a fourth handgun a few feet away. These smaller weapons would be the most likely to pop loose when the triggers were pulled from a distance. Both checked the gun arrangement again, adding more rocks.

After a second review of the terrain, they decided the shotgun would fit nicely in the cradle of a small wiry bush, another four feet from the pistols. Tying the weapon with one of the leather strings ensured a steady placement.

Nervous sweat on the foreheads of both men told of battle anticipation more than of hard work. Rule laid out the rope two feet behind the row of guns and more or less in the middle of the row. Holding the loop itself, he tossed the other end uphill toward a half-burned mesquite tree with three wild-looking branches searching for the sky. Each trigger was now tightly knotted with a separate leather thong; his spittle on the knot would shrink the closure farther. The strings in turn were tied to the loop hole in the rope.

Checker told him to stop, as if hearing something in the distance. No. His imagination.

"Nothing. Just my nerves."

"Yeah. I know the feeling."

Across the way, Checker saw Emmett and Rikor creating a similar rig with extra guns collected from the group and from the Peale Ranch. There was a second Sharps, Emmett's, and a shotgun Fiss carried regularly.

Wrapping the rope around the base of the tree would give them the leverage necessary to fire all of the guns at once when the rope was pulled. Or at least it should.

With the tiedowns in place, they retraced their steps to cock each weapon. They would leave slack in the rope for now to avoid a premature firing. The concept could easily fail, but if it did work, Holt's men might think there was a small army of men shooting at them from ambush.

Guttural was the sound of the heavy Sharps carbine being readied for firing as Rule cocked it.

Checker moved on to the first pistol; it had belonged to Bartlett. As he stepped back from locking the hammer of the pistol in place, a rock slab under his feet slid down the incline. The Ranger stumbled, fiercely grabbing at the larger boulder to keep from falling. His wounded leg gave way as his momentum took him to the ground, in spite of his attempt to hold himself away from pulling the trigger.

In the tranquil night air, the *click* of a hammer on an empty cylinder was pure music to his ears. Checker lay on the ground for minutes, not moving. Not even attemping to climb up. Instead, he tried to recapture some of the energy and confidence driven from him in the last maddening moment. Only five bullets were in the gun. His late Ranger friend usually kept just five in his handgun as a safety precaution, and Checker was thankful he did. A shot going off now would warn anyone within miles of the valley, as well as confuse his friends waiting for his signal.

Looking down from the gun area, Rule asked, "You all right?"

"Yeah. Just embarrassed. A.J.'s gun. Kept five beans in the

wheel. Said it would keep him from shooting himself. Glad he did," he said, and finally returned to his task.

"Glad you weren't hurt. Morgan would never forgive me." Rule grinned.

Waving off the teasing, Checker added a flat rock underneath the pistol barrel to ensure that it wouldn't point toward their friends on the other side of the road when the rope was jerked. Hammers were readied on the second pistol and the shotgun.

Like two generals, they discussed the stages of their ambush. The Holt gang would enter the valley through the tree-lined opening and stay on the trail paralleling the creek. They would be too far from the Peale Ranch to be alert. Their first position fifteen feet down from the battery would provide an excellent field of fire. They would announce their attention to the gang from there and open fire over their heads with Winchesters. Three or four shots. Morgan, Emmett and Rikor would also begin shooting.

After an opening salvo from his rifle, Checker would run uphill five or six strides to the end of the rope lying on the ground, pull it and keep on scrambling to a second position. Farther to the right and higher than the battery, behind a man-sized, hawk-nosed boulder. Rule would cover his movement from his site, above and left of the gun placement. Once at his second position, Checker would shoot again with his Winchester while Rule followed; then both would head for the horses, making certain Morgan had already left.

"'Half a league, half a league, half a league onward, all in the valley of Death rode the six hundred. Forward, the Light Brigade! Charge for the guns! He said; into the valley of Death rode the six hundred. Forward the Light Brigade! Was there a man . . .'"

Checker stopped. It was all he could remember. "They're going to pay, A.J."

"Yes, they are," Rule added.

Across the road, Emmett and Rikor waved to signal their completion as well. Both returned the wave; then Checker couldn't resist waving at Morgan. She stood and waved back.

Satisfied, they picked up their rifles and started back down the slope to their planned first firing sites, easing down the steep incline. From a clump of tall grass to their left came a small lark. It flew in front of them, startled from its sleep by their advance.

"Sorry, little brother. We didn't mean to bother you," Rule said.

Checker smiled and patted Rule on the back.

"Our Comanche friends would like this place for an ambush," Rule said.

"Not without a little peyote to see ahead. To see their enemies." Checker grinned and continued. "My old friend told me they used it as a war medicine. To see ahead."

"You ever take off that pouch?" Rule said, walking around a struggling chaparral.

Checker touched the pouch under his shirt with his free left hand, holding the Winchester at his side in his right fist.

"No, not really. Figured it gave me luck. Didn't want to challenge something I didn't really know," he answered. "How about you?"

"Same. The only thing I've added is that cross. Guess it's two ways of looking at . . . help beyond us."

Rule explained his pouch contained owl medicine, including a sliver of bone from the giant, prehistoric cannibal owl the Comanches believed existed at one time. The full bone was used to heal, drawing out the sickness.

They took a few more steps down the incline, letting the rock shale slide in front of them. Neither spoke, both drawn to their strong connections to the Comanche way.

Rule spoke first, glancing down at the road below. "Sometimes, I think his spirit is close. Moon's. He died the same day I met him. My best friend and I were headed for the war. Stumbled into a Comanche camp and they were good to us. Not sure why, but they were. Probably it was because of Moon. The old shaman said he knew I was coming."

Looking back and up at where Morgan was waiting, Checker couldn't see her. His mind caught up with Rule's observations.

"Funny how meetings like that change everything," he said. "Before I met Stands-In-Thunder, all I'd ever done with Comanches was fight them. He ended up being, well, a father, I guess. Mine didn't want to claim me—or my sister. Happens, I guess."

The hillside jerked into a small, flat ledge. Rule would remain here.

"Yeah, most of my preaching came from Moon—or what I learned later from studying the Comanche's view of . . . the Great Spirit."

Checker watched his friend get settled. "Did you know they believe there is an Evil Spirit? Something like our Devil, I think."

Stretching out behind a large rock, Rule adjusted his Winchester into position and said, "Lots of parallels. Only the Indians think every step on the earth is a prayer. They see miracles every day. Silence is a prayer. I like that."

Overhead, an owl drifted past in search of an evening snack.

Rule looked up. "The Comanche think owls are reincarnated souls, you know."

Checker nodded.

"Did you know some believe in a group of small, evil men who come out only at night? *Nanapi.* They're supposed to kill every time they shoot with their tiny bows and arrows," Rule said, making motions of shooting a bow and arrow.

"Hadn't heard that one," Checker said. "Hope those boys'll be on our side."

"I do, too. I'll see you later."

Chapter Thirty-six

Checker completed the return to his site, twenty feet lower. Sounds of the land were welcome to his apprehensive mind. Just like music. Following a long drink from his canteen, he looked for a good place to wait.

There was nothing to do now, except that. Checker propped himself against a crooked mesquite tree and stared at the silent ridge behind him. Young green plants were ganged up trying to act big as well. Darkness hid their true color and twisted their shapes. He hated waiting.

Loneliness came and sat beside the tall Ranger. Everything in him wanted to climb the rocks and be with Morgan.

Wind had intimidated any clouds from the sky, making the moment seem more desolate than it was. Ahead of him was a well-used road from town; behind him and on the other side of the road were ridges that helped create the short walls of the valley. Waiting was the only thing that made sense—and the hardest to do. Attacking was always easier. For him.

Tired of sitting, he stretched out behind a huge yellow boulder, rechecked the loads in his rifle and laid it next to him along with a box of cartridges. He felt his side and knew that he was bleeding again, but not too much, he decided. He was so tired. So tired. He shouldn't rest, but it would feel so good. The night sounds would warn him, he rationalized, and knew he couldn't do so. To keep himself active, he pushed the cartridge box into his gun belt. It wasn't just idle activity; he might have to move and shoot fast, and carrying a box would hamper his use of the rifle.

Scattered fragments of the past days were resting on the border between his conscious and unconscious mind. One fragment kept blossoming whenever he let go of the troubling news from town and what might lay ahead for his friends. And that was Morgan Peale. Morgan.

The owl hooted once more as if responding to his thoughts. It seemed as though his whole life was going to be spent this way—riding, waiting, fighting.

Why couldn't he live as other men did? Why was he the one who rode alone to help people he didn't even know? He hadn't recognized the truth of the assertion until now. Stands-In-Thunder, in his wisdom, said it would be this way, that the grandfathers would gradually reopen his soul—when he was ready for it—to let caring back into his life.

A long streak of lightning and a boom of thunder off to the south reminded Checker again of his late Comanche friend, Stands-in-Thunder. Among his tribe, thunder was considered a spirit god, like other natural forces, and few men would have dared to stand outside during such a storm. His late friend had, indeed, been a highly respected leader. Checker missed him and his distinctive wisdom. He reached into his pocket and withdrew the small white stone.

"Wish you'd sing to me. Tell what's ahead. What we should be doing," he whispered, staring at the stone. "You know I can't kill those men without warning. I can't. That's still murder. You know that. I'm still a Ranger." He held the stone tightly and returned it to his pocket.

Maybe he could climb and see Morgan. Just for a few minutes. Oh, how he wanted to hold her in his arms.

Tiredness lay upon Checker and sleep was flirting with his eyes, but he dared not let the temptation overtake him. His fingers pressed gently against his closed eyes to ease their strain. Then he must be ready. He hoped the Holt gang would be riding in a tight group; a spaced group of riflemen would be more difficult to scare and track. If he and his friends were to have any chance tonight, it would come in the creation of immediate fear in the minds of the attackers. If they didn't run after the opening barrage of gunfire, if they dug in instead, it would mean his friends would need to get away quickly. Hopefully, they would be able to do so.

Fights had always brought a change within him. He was aware of the transformation now, but he hadn't been as a younger man. A cold intensity took over his actions. Everything was enlarged, as if under field glasses. And in slow motion. There was something that hadn't changed; only he was more aware of it. As if a thick moss had grown over his heart. It had been necessary to carry on after leaving his sister, his only family, behind. A clinging moss keeping out all feelings, all fears, all life.

Until now and Morgan.

Oh, he knew a bullet could be his sometime, somewhere. No one lived a charmed life; bullets didn't mind who they struck or why. He had seen too many good men, like A.J., die for no reason at all to believe he was invincible.

It was more as though he didn't care. Not a death wish, nothing like that. Or maybe it was, deep down inside where he never allowed himself ever to probe. Probably for fear of what he would find there. Something was lodged within him that hadn't been there before he realized his mother's situation. And his. Was his sister still alive? Would she even remember him?

Like a stone skipping across water, Checker's mind skipped back to Stands-In-Thunder, his late friend. How good it would be to see him again. To smoke a pipe and share the world from the old man's perspective. There was a mental cleansing just in the remembrance. Maybe the old war chief would have some suggestions about what Checker should do against Lady Holt and her many advantages. Maybe he should walk away from the reputation of a "deadly man" when this was over.

One long sad inhaling of the night's grayness returned him to the danger yet to come this quiet evening. Would one of his friends die? Would he? Right here in these rocks? He couldn't bring the question of Morgan dying even to his lips.

Stands-In-Thunder said the greatest warriors gave when no one would ever find out. And the greatest warriors fought alone against many to protect a friend who didn't even know he was in trouble. No matter the cost. That was the way it should be. That was the way it would be for him. No matter the cost.

After this was all over, if he was alive, Checker would ride away from this part of the country, from being a Ranger. Go where no one knew him, a place where he could start over. Where there were no nightmares chasing him. Would Morgan go with him? What did he have to offer? Nothing. Except weapons and the skill to use them. She could do so much better.

Night sounds disappeared into an eerie silent tension. A strange, yet familiar, chill rolled up Checker's back and settled in his head. He was alert. Gray shadows along the dark valley entrance introduced the coming of night riders.

Checker took a deep breath, drawing in the velvet cool air. In a low, hoarse voice, he reassured his friends to wait.

"Here they come. Wait for my shots."

He wasn't sure they could hear him, but it felt good to say it. Poised like a wolf, he lay flat on the slope, his rifle aimed in the direction of slowly advancing shadows. He wiped each hand on his pants, as if to help him pierce the night to determine the size of the approaching enemy.

What was that? Muffled sounds across the road. Emmett—or Rikor—must be moving to a new position. He wished they wouldn't. But he didn't dare call out. Not now. Everything grew quiet again.

Less than fifty yards away from his position, shadows were moving through the trees, fanning out as they rode to surround the ranch. Twenty-five riders. No, more. Twenty-eight. They were talking quietly among themselves. An occasional laugh punctuated their easy ride. Checker could tell the riders had exchanged bridles for rope hackamores. They weren't wearing spurs, either. There would be no jingling of a bit, or a spur, to give them away.

Moonlight washed stingily across the riders; purchased Ranger authority gave them a cloak of legality. Dry air crackled with tension. Two men were riding out front, twenty yards or so. Sil Jaudon led the force with a rider beside him carrying the strange phoenix flag. He didn't see Tapan Moore, or Luke Dimitry, or Eleven Meade. Checker's scalp curled. Where were they? In Caisson? Coming from another direction? He forced himself to wait for all of the riders to move into the middle of the valley and alongside them.

Satisfied the gang were as close as he dared to let them, he called out, "Drop your guns and ride out. You are surrounded by Rangers."

From Rule's site above him came the gunfighter's supporting challenge. "Jaudon, you have a chance to live. Turn around—and don't try to attack these ranches again."

Neither expected the gang to disarm themselves, but they hoped the unexpected challenge would force a turnaround.

"What the hell?" Jaudon snorted, and drew one of his gold-plated revolvers and yelled something in French.

Without waiting for more response, three times Checker's rifle cut through the night. White flowers of smoke broke the raiders' unspoken confidence. Both advance riders flew from the frightened horses, driven by Checker's bullets at the horses' hooves. His fourth shot missed Jaudon completely, ripping only shadow.

As the others opened fire from their different positions, Checker fired at one rider attempting to shoot and dashed for the rope's end and its multiple-gun surprise.

Again, he yelled, "Spake, move your men over there. Cut them off!"

Rule answered, "I've got them covered. They can run—or die."

Without pausing, he knew the appearance of more guns had to be terrifying, probably looking like twenty. He yanked the rope and the guns roared in unison. Shotgun slugs sounded as if they had torn into the opposite ridge. The Sharps slug ricocheted and ran off into the night.

Behind the first blast of multiple guns came the second from Emmett and Rikor, roaring as loudly as the first. Above him, he could hear Morgan firing. To the raiders trying to control spinning, wild-eyed horses, it had to look as if they had run into hell. Or so Checker hoped. If they regained their poise, this fight would be over in a hurry.

With his rifle in one hand, he crawled swiftly to the battery of silent guns. Reloading where necessary, he fired each weapon as he came to it, without trying to aim. With his left hand, he also fired his rifle. Hearing the awesome boom of the big Sharps carbine again had to be the breaking point, if there was to be one.

Like a covey of flushed quail, the raiders began leaving, yelling at each other. A few riders fired wildly toward the hillside where Checker and his friends had launched their special ambush. From below, Rule's rifle silenced one of the shooters and the others fled. He could hear Jaudon cursing in French at his men to stand. Scrambling to a new position, Checker fired as he moved and another of Holt's gunmen spun from his horse, firing in the air.

Gunshots from Emmett and Rikor were steady and over the heads of the fleeing riders. He didn't hear any shooting from Morgan.

Checker couldn't resist the temptation and yelled out, "Sil Jaudon! You're a dead man if you try this again."

Only the disappearing rhythm of fleeing horses answered his challenge. He had no idea whether the fat Frenchman heard him or not. But the shouted threat felt good just the same. Alive with shadowy movement of its own, the opposite hillside indicated Emmett and the others were trying to make sense of the retreat and whether it meant the battle was over or just beginning.

Standing up beside a downed tree that was resting its soul against the hillside's gravel and ironweed, Checker shrugged his shoulders in a slow celebration of the successful moment. He joined Rule at the fake battery.

"Well, John, I think it worked."

"Looks like it. Some would say we left them to fight again," Checker said.

"We did the right thing." Rule said, producing a pocket knife. "They've got to be worried now about who's helping Emmett and Morgan." He opened the blade and added, "We didn't kill anyone who wasn't facing us, either."

Gathering the tied-up battery was done swiftly. Rule cut the leather strips holding the various triggers, letting the remaining tied end tangle from the triggers. The weapons would be unknotted later. Checker shoved two of the handguns into his waistband, above his gun belt and the box of cartridges held there, and took the Sharps and his Winchester, one in each hand. Rule recoiled the lariat and placed it over his shoulder. Then he pushed the remaining two handguns into his belt, picked up his own rifle and the shotgun.

"Looks like Emmett and Rikor are ahead of us," Checker said, looking across the road.

"Good. That uncle of mine moves fast for his age. You and I should be so lucky," Rule replied, and grinned.

"Another line of work would help."

"Or fewer bastards trying to do in our friends."

Quietly, they climbed the darkened hill toward Morgan.

"Good. She's gone on to the horses," Checker said as they neared her shooting site.

Rule agreed. "That's quite a woman, John. She'd make a fine wife."

"What kind of woman would marry me?"

"A good kind. The kind that stands beside you, not behind you," Rule said as they continued climbing the ridge. "The kind that understands this fight. And supports your involvement in it. A woman like my Aleta."

"I'm looking forward to meeting her."

Chapter Thirty-seven

They reached the top of the ridge and saw the dark shapes of horses ahead of them as planned. No one called out, but Checker thought that was smart. At this point, they couldn't be certain if the entire gang had fled or not.

Wind had intimidated any clouds from the sky, making the moment seem more desolate than it was. The top of the ridge flattened out into a large spoon of quiet land. They passed a shallow pond. A struggling cottonwood stood not far from its life-giving water. Nearby was a squatty bowl of land where buffalo once rolled. Rule stared at it and remembered playing in something like that as a child. His best friend jumped into mind. Ian Taullary. They had protected each other growing up and fought beside each other during the war. Sadly, Taullary had gotten caught up in the wrong things in life, but had died trying to protect him. Again. He reminded himself that it was important to remember his friend's good ways, their good times together.

He was tired and knew Checker had to be. Once a fight was over, energy left quickly, leaving the body drained. He glanced at the Ranger, but Checker was studying the silhouettes ahead of them. Ahead, their horses were grouped around three trees. Shapes of men were knotted against the dark sky.

Checker said, "Something's wrong, Rule."

An invisible voice was cruel and demanding. "Come on, Checker. You, too, Cordell. Walk easy toward us. Don't try anything funny. Or the Peale woman and these two Gardners die."

Without saying anything, Rule and Checker separated and walked toward the horses.

"Drop those rifles. Do it now."

Both men let the long guns in their hands slip to the hard earth. The thuds of weapons hitting against the ground were four heartbeats. They dropped their hands to their sides, standing mostly in shadow.

The gray shapes in front of them became four Holt men. Luke Dimitry. Tapan Moore. And two men Checker didn't know.

Tapan had his arm around Morgan's neck, holding her close to him. In his hand was a cocked revolver. Dimitry stood, nonchalantly, pointing a rifle on Emmett and Rikor. The other two gunmen stood near the horses, holding rifles. Beside them, Checker saw the motionless body of London Fiss.

"Come on in, boys. The party's just getting started," Tapan said, motioning with his gun. "That was a good stunt you pulled on the Frenchman. What a stupid sonvabitch! Lady Holt should've had me become the Ranger captain, not him." Tapan laughed. "Reckon he won't stop running 'til he hits town. Him an' his men."

Checker and Rule stood with their arms at their sides.

Tapan's eyes brightened. "I see you boys brought along all your big toys." His smile reached only half of his mouth. "Luke an' I had a hunch you might try something. So we went a different route."

Dimitry glanced at the dead Fiss. "Ran into that colored boy and figured we'd just sit tight an' see who came along. Lo and behold, all kinds of folks Lady Holt wants to see dead came wandering in."

"Didn't want to do that before we had a chance to talk with you two. Besides, you would've heard the shots," Tapan explained. "That colored boy wasn't so lucky. He got his while you all were firing up a storm."

The curly-headed gunman smiled widely, his white teeth glistening in the moonlight, and continued, "Fact is, we would've shot you two when you came up the hill . . . but we wanted to know something."

Morgan struggled against his tightened arm and he shoved his gun into her side.

"Stand still, lady. Or I'll shoot you first."

"Sorry, John, we done jes' walked ri't into this," Emmett said, waving his arms in frustration.

Rikor's expression was impossible to read. Was it anger or fear?

"I see you boys are carrying lots of iron. Ready for a war, huh?" Tapan motioned with his gun. "Unbuckle the gun belts. All of it. Real easy, now."

Checker unbuckled his double-rowed cartridge belt and let it slide down his legs. The cartridge box tumbled ahead of it. Without being asked, he drew Bartlett's pistol from his waistband and tossed it on the ground. The leather string attached to the trigger fluttered in the air. He drew the other revolver used in the fake barrage with his fingers holding the butt and dropped it as well.

At the same time, Rule unbuckled his gun belt and let it fall. Both of his barrage handguns followed; one had been the backup Colt carried in his front waistband.

Checker said, "You won't get away with this. We've got Rangers . . . real Rangers . . . coming. Lady Holt is done."

"Save that crap for the town newspaper," Tapan snarled. "I want to know something. Eleven Meade was a friend of ours."

"Where is he? Waiting to shoot us in the back?" Checker answered, and looked behind him.

"You know where he is. He's dead. In Clark Springs."

The tall Ranger looked at Rule on his left.

Shrugging, the gunfighter said, "Last time I saw him, he was on the saloon floor. From my fist. He didn't die from that, I hope." His remark snapped with sarcasm.

"I didn't know that, Moore. When did it happen?" Checker said, hoping the conversation would keep going until he thought of something.

Tapan frowned and licked his lower lip. "Your friend here, he got a wire from Clark Springs about it. Someone named 'A' said Eleven was killed. There in Clark Springs." The curly-headed outlaw jutted out his chin. "Lady Holt sent him there. To see where you were living. You, Cordell. She wanted you dead. Since you own the Gardner Ranch—or whatever that little game was." The outlaw grinned again. "We want to know who 'A' is. Gonna pay him a little visit when this is over."

Rule shrugged his shoulders again. "You must be more stupid than I thought. Just when do you think I would have seen this wire? We haven't been to town. Or haven't you been paying attention?" His eyes narrowed. "I don't know any man like that."

"You don't know who 'A' is? Come on, Cordell."

"I sure don't know any man with the name that starts with an A. Wait, I know a grocery store clerk . . . in Clark Springs . . . he's Andrew. Andrew Gates." Rule shook his head. "Don't think he could've killed anybody. Andrew doesn't even own a gun." He rubbed his chin. "Well, wait a minute, there's old Amos Pillar. He's about seventy, I think. Spends most of his time in a rocking chair."

"Well, you aren't much help."

"Sorry. I'll keep thinking."

"No need. There's no reason you boys should live any longer, is there?" Tapan challenged.

Dimitry tugged on his Navajo coat and examined a particular large hole near its right-hand pocket. "This is quite a day. We kill two of the best there is, Checker and Cordell. And we get rid of two of the ranchers Lady Holt wants out of the way. I'd say we'll have a big bonus coming." He tugged on the coat again. "Reckon I'll just see how that fancy tunic of yours fits, Checker. Be a nice way to remember this."

"Mind if I have a last smoke?" Checker said.

Chuckling, Tapan said, "Sure, why not? Make it fast, though. We've got a long ride back to town. Lady Holt'll want to hear this. Probably make some changes in that newspaper edition she was working on. When we left. Her and our colored boy, you know." Tapan motioned with his pistol. "He knows how to set type, you know."

"Thanks. Nice of you."

"How about you, Cordell? Reckon it's the right thing to do," Tapan said.

"No, thanks. Tobacco and lead don't set well with me."

All four of the gunmen laughed.

Checker reached slowly inside his tunic and brought out a tobacco pouch and papers. He took a paper, creased it and began to pour tobacco shreds along the line. His hands shook and he dropped the paper.

"Kinda nervous there, aren't ya, Checker?" Tapan said, watching the Ranger bend over to retrieve the paper.

The other gunmen's attention went to the paper and the movement, chuckling at the Ranger's obvious nervousness.

Checker came up firing his backup revolver carried in his back waistband. His first two shots hit Tapan in the face.

The outlaw screamed. Morgan shoved her elbow in his side and dove. Blood covering his face, Tapan Moore fired his revolver as he fell. His shot sang past the tall Ranger's head. Checker fired his gun twice more at the bearded gunman to Tapan's left. Leaning over, the Ranger picked up the closest pistol, Bartlett's, with his left hand.

The bearded gunman grabbed his stomach and groaned, dropping his rifle.

Rule's own backup Dean & Adams revolver, also carried in his back waistband, was barely an eyeblink behind. His shots blasted into Dimitry and into the other gunman beside him. Dimitry spun halfway and tried to bring his rifle toward the diving Emmett. From a crouching position, Rikor pulled a handgun hidden in his back waistband and fired at the other gunman. The gunman's rifle roared into the night and ripped along the top of Rikor's shoulder. The young Gardner released his gun and grabbed for the searing pain.

Rule emptied his handgun into all four gunmen and grabbed one of the discarded weapons.

"They're done, Rule," Checker said, stepping closer. "Morgan, are you all right?"

Rule walked over to the dead gunmen, kicking their weapons away. He retrieved his gun belt and buckled it, adding his backup Colt to his waistband. He stood without talking, reloading the Dean & Adams gun.

Emmett was examining his son's wound. It wasn't serious, only a burn along his shoulder.

Quietly, Rikor confessed, "Pa, I saw Uncle Rule and John carry extra guns in their belts. In back. That's what I did. Nobody thought I was carrying."

"Smart o' ya, son."

Morgan was in Checker's arms moments later. Tears covered her face. "They killed . . . Mr. Fiss. London. They shot him . . . in the back. Oh, I hoped you wouldn't . . . come. They wanted to kill you and Rule so bad."

Breath hissed through Checker's clenched teeth. "Lady Holt has killed two very good men."

She buried her head against his Comanche tunic and sobbed.

Rule was already heading to the horses. His face was frozen in fury.

Looking at the fast-moving gunfighter, Emmett said, "The one who done kilt Eleven Meade . . . that were Aleta, weren't it? Ya figger her an' the kids is all ri't?"

Swinging into the saddle, Rule said, "I'm riding to town to find that wire. And see a British lady."

He whirled the horse and galloped into the darkness, slapping its withers with the reins.

The tall Ranger stepped back from Morgan. "I must go with him. You and Emmett . . . and Rikor . . . ride back to your place."

"Reckon we should go wi' ya, John," Emmett said, and looked at the grieving Morgan. "I'm sorry, li'l lady, but . . ."

"Not this time, Emmett. Please take London back to their ranch." Checker looked at Morgan. "Maybe you'd like to bury him in the same place where . . . A.J. is."

Walking toward him, the wounded Rikor said, "I'm going with you. They can't do this to us."

Checker shook his head. "Not this time, Rikor. They need you with them."

The young man stared at the Ranger. "You figured they wouldn't think of asking about backup guns—with all those irons you were carrying. Right?"

"That's what I was hoping, Rikor."

Wiping the tears from her face, Morgan walked over to the tall Ranger. "You come back. To me. You hear, John Checker?"

"I will. I promise."

Saying the words made the image of his little sister fly through his mind. He touched Morgan's cheek. "A long time ago, I gave that same promise to my little sister. When I had to leave Dodge. She took a button from my shirt. To remember me by. Didn't have anything else." He looked away. "I haven't kept that promise, Morgan. Not yet anyway."

She grabbed his shirt under his tunic and yanked a button free. "Whenever you're ready, I'll help you keep it."

Chapter Thirty-eight

Late night in Caisson found the lamps burning in the newspaper office. Even the saloons had quieted. Inside, Lady Holt wrote furiously.

Her face was flushed with the energy of creation. Behind her, Elliott toiled at setting type. Tomorrow would bring a brand-new world. Her empire would be established, and what better way to announce it than with a special edition of the newspaper?

Outside, lounging on the sidewalk, were four of her gunmen. The rest had gone with Jaudon to rid the region of the last of the interference to her empire. They would sweep through the Peale Ranch, then the Carlson place and lastly destroy Emmett Gardner's ranch house, burning and killing. Tracking down any of the remaining ranch owners who lived would come next. Another day.

She chuckled when she recalled Tapan and Dimitry coming to her, asking for permission to ride a different direction. They were concerned John Checker and Rule Cordell might set a trap. How could she resist! She had kissed the curly-headed gunman and told him to hurry back. She would stay in town, at her apartment, after the newspaper edition was finished. They could celebrate. Together.

Rubbing her hands together to rid them of writer's cramp, she examined the page before her. She had already finished the articles headlined TOWN ENJOYS NEW PEACE AS RANGER CAPTAIN SIL JAUDON COMBINES FORCES WITH RANCHER and ARREST WARRANTS ISSUED FOR EMMETT GARDNER, CHARLES CARLSON, MORGAN PEALE, JOHN CHECKER, LONDON FISS AND RULE CORDELL and LADY HOLT AGREES TO TAKE OVER THREE SMALL RANCHES AFTER OWNERS ARE KILLED.

Halfway finished was the story headlined GOVERNOR CITALE PRAISES RANGER CAPTAIN AND MAJOR RANCHER FOR FAST WORK IN QUELLING OUTLAW REBELLION.

Lying to her left was a blank sheet of paper with only the headline scratched on its top: BRITISH NOBILITY BRINGS WEALTH TO REGION. It would be a piece about her—with liberties taken as to accuracy. A third sheet contained the beginnings of a poem, entitled "Iva Lee, I wish you were here." Several lines had been furiously scribbled.

> O Iva Lee   O Iva Lee
> In the morning mist, I see thee.
> In the afternoon dusk, I call your name
> O Iva Lee   O Iva Lee
> You are with me
> Even when you are not
> You are part of me
> Even though you cannot be
> O Iva Lee   O Iva Lee.

She thought it would make a nice inset piece and planned to finish it later.

Elliott had created a new masthead as she requested. The

Caisson Reporter was now The *Caisson Phoenix*. Under the large typeset heading was a Latin phrase he had suggested. *Emitte lucem et veritatem*. He said it meant "Send out light and truth."

She had loved it. Jaudon wouldn't return for several days and she hoped to have the newspaper on the streets of Caisson before he rode in victoriously.

A knock on the door brought her alert.

"Yes?" she asked without moving.

"It's Wilson. Wilson Tanner. Thought you might like to take a break." The voice from the other side of the door was syrupy. "I've got some fine Tennessee whiskey. For toasting."

She smiled, rose and then stopped. "No, Iva Lee. I won't drink until I'm finished. Yes, I know this is important." Brushing her hair with her hand, she turned toward Elliott. "I'll let him in, but now is not the time to celebrate."

"*Ab inconvenienti,*" he muttered without looking up.

"Exactly."

Opening the door, she smiled her most magnificent smile. "Come in, Wilson. As you can see, we are hard at work. It will be my grand announcement, so to speak. The grand announcement of my becoming the Queen of Texas."

Looking disheveled, Tanner bowed and stepped inside, holding a bottle of whiskey in his hand. His own face was flushed from several hours of drinking.

"Well, I thought . . . perhaps, you'd like to take a break . . . from your writing. It is, indeed, a grand night—and one worth celebrating. Your greatness will soon be known throughout Texas—and beyond." He made an exaggerated gesture, then quickly held his fist to his mouth to conceal a hiccup.

"Your kindness is most appreciated, Wilson," Lady Holt said, returning to her desk. "Why don't you leave the bottle and Elliott and I will toast . . . when the newspaper is done?"

She smiled. "I've renamed it the *Caisson Phoenix*. Do you like that?" She motioned toward Elliott. "And dear Elliott, he has given it the perfect, ah, what do you call it? Ah yes, slogan. That's it, slogan. *Emitte lucem et veritatem*." She lifted her chin and added, "It means 'Send out light and truth.'"

She pointed at the edge of the writing table. "You can leave it there, Wilson. That would be a sweet boy."

The attorney-judge wasn't certain how to react. He had hoped she might be interested in a more romantic time in the back room. Or at least, the promise of a clandestine meeting in her apartment later. Instead, he had only gotten a rather cold dismissal.

"I like it." *Hiccup*. "Very much," Tanner said, and held his hand to his mouth again to deflect another hiccup. "Very much." He swallowed and placed the bottle on the table and started to leave.

"Wilson?"

His heart pounded and he turned around. "Yes, m'lady?" *Hiccup*.

"What do you hear . . . around town? How are . . . my people taking all of this?" Her face was full of joy.

He wiped his hand across his mouth. "Ah, what do I hear around town?" *Hiccup*. "How are your people taking all of this?"

Repeating her questions gave him time to think, but his hiccupping wasn't helping his concentration. What should he say? That Margaret Loren was trying to raise a posse to run her out of town? Should he tell her that Dimitry's killing of the blacksmith earlier had almost started a riot? That the only thing keeping a lid on things was the obvious fear of her retaliation against anyone who crossed her?

"I think . . . ah, I think the town is very pleased you have taken control." *Hiccup*. "You and Jaudon. There is praise for his swift action," he said, pulling on his collar to provide some relief from its tightness. "I would say many see . . . in you . . . the leader so needed in this region." *Hiccup.* "The word *queen* has been mentioned."

"Oh, very good, Wilson. Very good." She looked down at her writing. "You may leave now."

Outside, an attractive Mexican woman rode a spirited horse down the main street, heading for the hotel. Her ample bosom, covered by her blouse and a sarape, bounced with the movement of her horse. A sombrero, lying against her back, accompanied the rhythm and hid most of the trailing braid of long black hair.

Chapter Thirty-nine

"Hey, lady! We'd like some company. Come on over," one of the Holt gunmen yelled from the sidewalk.

A disappointed Tanner stepped outside as the four hooted at the passing woman.

"Who is she?" he asked, admiring her shape as she rode toward the hotel.

"Who knows? Never seen her before," the tallest gunman in a derby hat said, shrugging his shoulders.

"Probably a new whore." The heavily sideburned gunman licked his lips.

"Let's go over an' welcome her to Caisson," the third gunman with a thin mustache and a calfskin vest said, and laughed. "Get a free sample or two."

The four men shook off the hours of boredom and focused on the newest distraction.

"Yeah, let's do. I got firsts," the sideburned gunman declared.

The mustached gunman in the vest said, "The hell you do, Charlie. I'm in charge here. I'll decide who goes when."

The tallest gunman moved closer. "Who says you're in charge?"

Turning toward him with a thick sneer on his face, the gunman in the vest said, "Tapan, pecker-head. You wanna challenge him?"

"What will Lady Holt think?" the youngest gunman asked, slowly standing from his slumped position against the building wall.

"She won't care. Not if we stay close. We can do it in the alley." The sideburned gunman was already headed into the street.

Tanner started to object, hiccupped and decided it didn't matter. He went the other direction, toward the closest saloon without looking back. The laughing and jeering grew louder as the four gunmen crossed the street and hurried toward her. In the lead was the gunman with the massive sideburns, boasting of what he was going to do with her.

"Hold up there, missy. We're Rangers. We're the law," he commanded.

The others laughed and reinforced his claim.

"Look at our badges!"

"Yeah, they're made of silver. Real silver."

"You're under arrest, lady," the youngest gunman yelled, waving a Winchester in the air. He was the only one with a rifle; the other long guns had been left propped against the newspaper building.

The others yipped agreement and the sideburned gunman, in the lead, repeated the command. "Lady, you're under arrest. Stay right where you are."

Without paying attention to the advancing foursome, the Mexican woman pulled her horse to the hitching rack outside the hotel. Slowly, she flipped back the trail serape worn over her clothes. Revealed was a bullet belt with two holstered pearl-handled, silver-plated revolvers. She turned toward the advancing foursome and drew one of the guns.

Its distinctive *click-click* was a shocking sound in the quiet night.

The sideburned gunman skidded to a stop. "Hey, lady. I said we're the law. You don't want to get yourself in trouble, now, do you? Put that away and climb down. Nobody's going to hurt you."

Without moving, Aleta Cordell said, "Eet would not be ze smart thing for you hombres to come closer. I have ridden ze long way. I am tired. Go back to whatever you were doing. Adios."

From behind the sideburned gunman, the tall gunman pushed his derby hat forward on his head and urged his companion forward. "Come on, Spencer. She's bluffing."

Nodding agreement, the sideburned Spencer resumed his advance.

A bullet spat into the street in front of his boots.

"Ze next bullet ees for your head. *Comprende?*" She recocked the gun and aimed it at him.

Fearful, Spencer stopped again. The tall man behind him kept moving and collided into him. Both stumbled forward into the street. The derby hat floated in the air for a few feet, dropped and skidded to a stop in the street. She drew her second revolver with her left hand and pointed them at the four men. The last two were helping the first two get back up. The youngest retrieved the derby and handed it to the tall gunman.

She fired the left-hand gun and its lead spat a few feet in front of the foursome.

"Adios," she said again and recocked both weapons.

"This is crap," the mustached gunman in the vest said. "We're Rangers. She's a whore. A damn Mex whore. Are we gonna let her do this?"

From the shadows of the building between the hotel and the general store, an older man appeared. He held a sawed-off shotgun in one hand, as if it were a pistol. A black eye patch covered his left eye.

He stepped halfway between the mounted Aleta and the alley.

"You bastards aren't any more Rangers than horse dung," he growled. "Get your asses back across the street. I'm not as nice as the pretty lady here. I won't shoot to warn you." He motioned with the shotgun. "Now. Be gone." He hesitated and yelled, "No, wait. Don't any of you move."

Awkwardly, the four men staggered to a stop, waved their arms, grabbed each other and froze in various positions of retreat. Looks on their faces ranged from fear to anger. Mostly fear.

"You boys leave your iron. Right there. In the street." He cocked his head to the side. "And take off those Rangers badges. Leave 'em. None of you bastards has any right to be wearin' something like that. Kinda sacred, they are."

Frowning, Spencer stared at the shadowed man. "Who are you, mister? This ain't a town to be tellin' us what to do. Don't you know who we work for? Lady Holt, that's who. Lady Holt. She's right in there." He motioned toward the lighted newspaper office.

"Oh, really?" The man with the eye patch fired a barrel of the sawed-off shotgun.

The shot tore into the bearded man's leg and he fell, groaning.

Smoothly, he popped open the gun, tore out the empty smoking shell and slipped another in its place. His lone eye never left the terrified gunmen.

He cocked both barrels. "Now, which one of you peckerheads still doesn't understand?"

Immediately, the youngest gunman with the rifle threw it to the ground and stepped back. The other two unbuckled their gun belts and let them fall. The youngest gunman pulled Spencer's pistol from its holster and tossed it. Moonlight flickered on badges being yanked off and dropped. They helped the sobbing Spencer to his feet and half carried him back toward the newspaper office. His lower leg was mostly crimson.

Lamplight appeared in the upper window of the apartment above the general store. Window curtains wiggled. Spake glanced in its direction, then back to the street.

"Better let a doc take a look at that real quick," the eye-patched man hollered. "Hate to see such a fine fella lose his leg."

Forcefully, the door to the newspaper office opened. Lady Holt slid into the doorway, squinting into the night.

"What's going on out here? Spencer, is that you? Are you hurt?" she called.

"Yes'm, he's been shot. Shotgun. By that stranger across the street." The report came from the youngest gunman. He skipped the part about the Mexican woman riding into town and their attempted quest of her.

"We can't have challenges to my authority," she declared. "An insult, that's what it is. Kill him and be quick about it. Her, too." She glared at the four men. "Don't you know I'm creating in here? Leave me alone!"

She slammed shut the door.

Spake Jamison watched the men across the street. Without taking his gaze from them, he said, "Ma'am, I'm Spake Jamison." He touched the brim of his weathered hat in greeting and yelled, "You heard her, boys. Come an' get some more."

He watched the four talking and said quietly to Aleta, "Used to be a Ranger. 'Til that idiot governor—an' that English lady there—decided to rig up their own brand of law."

"*Muchas gracias, amigo.* I have come to find *mío* husband. I am worried he may be in trouble."

A wolflike smile took over the gray-haired former Ranger's wrinkled face. The leathery skin was laced with long lines; many were gathered at the outside edge of his good eye.

"If he's anything like you, ma'am, not sure trouble would want him. Don't think you needed my help," he said. "You handle those fancy guns like they were real friendly."

It was her turn to chuckle. "I am Aleta Cordell. Rule Cordell ees *mío* husband."

"Rule . . . Cordell? The Texas gunfighter?"

"*Mío* husband knows how to use ze gun, *sí.*" She shoved new cartridges into the revolvers as they talked.

He nodded. "I understand your husband—and John Checker—are ridin' together. Tryin' to stop this Lady Holt."

"*Sí.*"

Jamison pushed the hat back on his forehead. "Sounds like we're headin' for the same war, ma'am."

Returning her reloaded guns to their holsters, she glanced at the sidewalk in front of the newspaper office. The four men had disappeared. Their absence didn't seem to bother the old lawman.

"Don't worry about them, ma'am. They've gone somewhere to get some courage. An' get away from her."

He chuckled and said he had just arrived in town with the plan on finding out what was going on.

"I was headin' for the livery when I saw those clowns," he said. "There are thirty Rangers waitin' for me. Outside of town. Real ones. Or they were." He pushed the quiver back farther on his shoulder. "Just found out that phony Ranger captain . . . ah, Sil Jaudon . . . rode out with his gang. They were headin' for one of the small ranches left. Only three, I reckon. Don't sound like it would be hard to find. Looks like the Brit woman wants to get this over with."

His shoulders rose and fell. "Reckon us Rangers'll head that way. Come back for her later."

Her tired eyes brightened; then a film of worry dulled them. She told about sending a wire telling Rule about Eleven Meade's death and that her husband hadn't responded. Friends of theirs were watching their two children—and Emmett Gardner's two boys. She explained why the latter were at their house.

"Can't tell you anything about any telegrams," Spake said, shaking his head. "This town has been hit real hard by this English lady and her thugs." He pointed in the direction of the dark telegraph office. "There's where it be. You can go there in the mornin' and see if your man has been in. Bet he hasn't, ma'am. Bet he an' Checker are ri't where that gang's headed."

He returned the shotgun to the quiver on his shoulder and started walking again. "A bunch o' us came to help some friends. They were Rangers, too. A. J. Bartlett an' John Checker."

Rubbing his unshaved chin, he said, "Story we got in Austin was this killer name of Eleven Meade had killed John. Heard tell in that saloon just now . . . that he was alive—and A.J.'s dead." He shook his head. "Had me a hunch Checker wasn't dead. Bastard's too tough. No backshooter like Meade's gonna make it happen. Mighty sorry about A.J., though. He was a good'un. Loved talkin' poetry, ya know."

Swinging her horse to walk alongside the sidewalk as Spake headed toward the livery, Aleta explained Meade was the one who was dead and that she had killed him.

The old Ranger chuckled. "Them four idiots had no idea of what they had tangled with. Glad to hear Meade's dead. He was a sick one. Real sick. All that eleven mumbo jumbo." He looked at her for a moment and asked, "If I remember rightly a good-lookin' woman used to ride with an outlaw name of Johnny Cat Carlson. Right after the war."

"*Sí*, there was such a *senorita*. I weel ride weeth you. *Mío* Rule weel be there. I can feel eet. He and thees John Checker."

"Well, that'll be a pair to draw to." Spake hesitated. "Sure. Come on. You'd better switch hosses at the livery. That fella's too good to run into the ground. An' he's looking mighty tired. No offense, ma'am."

"*Sí*. I push heem. More than I should. He ees *bueno* hoss."

"Well, let's go. There'll be hot coffee at the camp. Johnson makes it good 'n hard. Puts an egg in it. Says it's Swedish." He withdrew a sack from his coat pocket. "Would you like some licorice? It's mighty tasty."

Chapter Forty

John Checker and Rule Cordell rode hard toward Caisson, keeping mostly off the main road, along the surrounding ridges, through narrow arroyos and across hushed open land. Night air helped lower their fierceness to allow them to think about their next actions. Riding down the main street of Caisson would only get them killed. They had to assume Jaudon and his men returned there.

They cleared a spongy stretch of bottomland, stubbled with grass and flanked by thickets of mesquite, ash, walnuts and persimmons. Crossing a wandering creek, the reason for the lower land's wetness, they reined up to let their horses drink and rest. Around them stray cattle were in search of grass. In the distance, coyotes were attempting to communicate with the moon.

Both men were weary and trying hard to concentrate.

"Right about now, A.J. would up and recite," Checker said. "He loved his Tennyson. Seems real strange not to have him riding with me." He glanced at the gunfighter. "No offense, Rule. That didn't come out quite right. I'm proud—and thankful—to have you with me. You know that."

"I understand. You'll always have the memories," Rule

said. "I lost my best friend a few years ago. Grew up together. Went to war together. I have those memories. They're good ones."

Checker nodded and his shoulders shivered. Rule glanced at the Ranger's side and saw streaks of blood, old and new.

Rule changed the subject, withdrawing his boots from his stirrups and straightening his legs. "You know, John, we're likely to be facing men we could've killed earlier tonight."

"Yes, and you wouldn't have had it any other way."

"Maybe. Maybe not."

"Guess it doesn't matter now."

Checker studied a narrow path heading up an embankment to the left. Definitely an Indian pony trail.

"We could move along that trail for a while. What do you think?" He pointed at the barely visible pathway. "Keep us out of sight as we get closer to town, in case Jaudon left any snipers behind."

"Makes good sense. Looks like an Indian trail. Ever see any man ride better than a Comanche?" Rule asked, twisting his head back and forth for relief.

Checker smiled. "No. You look at a Comanche walking—and here's this short, slow, awkward-looking man. Get him on a horse and he's awesome. Like some Greek god."

"What if Tapan had told you to take out the backup gun?" Rule asked without looking at Checker.

"Not sure. Probably tried to stumble. Something, anything to give us an opening."

"Did you know I still had a gun?"

Checker smiled again. "I can count."

Rule nodded. "You ready?"

"Ready as I'll ever be."

They swung their horses toward the bank, up and onto the pony path. Slowly, they began to discuss what they would do when they reached Caisson. Their horses picked easily along the path, but neither man chose to urge them beyond a trot. An unseen hole would mean a broken leg and change every thing. Both took turns napping in the saddle as they rode. After a mile zigzagging along the ridge on the packed-earth pathway, largely bare of grass or weeds, they swung down onto a grassy swale, cradled by the same creek on the right and by a line of trees on the left. Six Holt steers looked up as they passed.

They weren't more than a mile from town and had decided on a plan. When they reached Caisson, they would split up and enter from different directions. It was simple. Risky. Mostly, it depended on Lady Holt's men not expecting such a bold move. The two gunfighters would find where Lady Holt was staying, get her on a horse and out of town before Jaudon and her men realized what had happened. Checker would get fresh horses for the three of them at the livery; Rule was going to the telegraph office and see if Aleta's wire was there. They would take Lady Holt to Clark Springs and hold her until a circuit judge could get there. A real judge.

If they weren't lucky, it was going to be a long, hard day.

Both rode almost mechanically, badly needing sleep, but not daring to nap anymore. Rule's mind crisscrossed through memories, pausing to hear his father tell him that he hoped the young man would rot in hell, to the frozen battlefields of Virginia and onto the dusty Texas plains where his father had told the weeping child that the reason their black colt had died was the boy's sinfulness, to preaching his first sermon about loving the land as the Reverend James Rule Langford, to the Sons of Thunder. He shook off the darkness in his mind and touched the rose stem on his coat collar and thought of Aleta and their children. He missed them so. It seemed like forever since he had left their home. Forever.

Beside him, Checker was telling himself again that life

was more than riding and fighting. His thoughts slid to a
month ago when he let the outlaw Cole Dillon escape. He
wasn't certain why. But the man had just lost his wife to
sickness. The Ranger had tracked him across the windswept
Staked Plains and caught up to him standing over her grave.
Cole had not asked for leniency; Checker had just given it.
Something in the outlaw's broken face told him the man
was about to change. Something said they were more alike
than different.

"Thank you, Ranger. I'm going to be the man she wanted
me to be. Cole Dillon is dead." Cole had galloped away,
swearing he was going to change. Checker reported Cole
Dillon as dead to Ranger headquarters. It made him feel good;
he hoped the man would take advantage of the opportunity.
But not all men could ride a new trail. Could he? Should he?

They passed a dry creek bed, one that escaped from the
main branch of water, only to die. A company of mesquites
were joined by scrubby oaks to watch over the empty stream.
They rode with their rifles cocked. Checker held his rifle in
his right hand, resting the butt on his thigh. Rule's rifle lay
across his saddle, his right hand holding it for quick use.

Gunshots ahead brought the two gunfighters to an alertness they hadn't felt since leaving.

"It's on the road." Checker pointed. "Do you think it's
Jaudon?"

"That doesn't make any sense, John."

"No. It doesn't." Checker motioned with his hand toward
a tree-lined bank. "Let's move up there and get closer." He
reined his horse toward the trees.

They rode in silence for two hundred yards, blending
with the trees and brush. Finally, they cleared the broken
ridge through a crease. Ahead of them, a shadowy mass of
men and horses milled in the open spoon of grassland. Here
and there a body lay on the flattened ground.

At first, Checker could only make out one man. "That's Jaudon. He's got his hands up. There, in the middle. Standing."

"Well, this can't be all bad, John."

They reined up to study the situation, and a wide smile hit Checker's face.

"Well, I'll be damned. That's Spake Jamison down there. And . . . Rangers. Real Rangers. Damn. Where'd they come from?"

Shaking his head in disbelief, Rule said, "I don't care. They've got Jaudon and his bunch surrounded. It's over, John."

"Wait a minute, Rule. There's a woman with them. Over there. See?" Checker pointed.

"Aleta!"

Checker looked at his friend. "Your wife's down there?"

"She sure is. Well, I'll be." He shook his head.

The tall Ranger was still savoring the scene when he realized Rule was already loping toward them.

"Spake! It's Checker—and Rule Cordell. We're coming in," Checker yelled, and kicked his horse into a downhill lope, trailing Rule's advance.

Minutes later, Checker was shaking hands with Ranger friends who were guarding the surrendered Holt gang. Rule was holding Aleta close; both were dismounted and holding their horses' reins.

Spake grinned. "Thought you boys could use a hand. You must've spooked this bunch something awful. They were runnin' like the Devil himself was chasin' them. Said a bunch of Rangers ambushed 'em." He shook his head. "Ran right into us. Didn't have much fight left in 'em." He motioned toward the downed bodies. "Reckon they didn't know how real Rangers act."

After a short exchange about Captain Temple's arrest, the governor's involvement with Lady Holt and the mass

Ranger firing, Checker told him about the fake gun barrage, that Tapan Moore and Luke Dimitry were dead—and their murder of London Fiss. He told them the Gardners and Morgan Peale had taken his body back to her ranch.

"Been a hard ride for you, I hear. Sorry about A.J. Gonna miss that ol' boy—and his poems." Spake's hard face softened.

Checker nodded, excused himself and rode over to a disgruntled Jaudon, standing with two mounted Rangers holding rifles on him.

Swinging from the saddle, Checker handed his reins to the red-haired Ranger beside him. "Hold these a minute, will you, Sawyer? Got something that needs doing."

Checker strode toward the fat Frenchman. "Jaudon, you and your men killed two good men. Good friends of mine."

Hunching his shoulders, Jaudon spat a French curse and glanced at his three gold-plated revolvers lying on the ground a few feet away.

As he stepped next to Jaudon, Checker slammed his right fist into the fat man's stomach. The blow's power was driven by pent-up fury and sorrow. Jaudon doubled over, gasping for breath that had disappeared into the night. He gagged and vomited on his own guns.

Stunned by Checker's sudden action, the Rangers and the arrested gang members watched in silence.

Stepping out of the way of the projected vomit, Checker delivered a wicked uppercut to Jaudon's chin that lifted the Frenchman off his feet and stumbling backward. The fat man collapsed on the ground. Checker grabbed his shirt with his left hand and yanked the stunned gang leader back on his feet. A right cross slammed into Jaudon's face, spewing blood and spinning his head sideways. A long cut opened along the Frenchman's right cheek.

Wild-eyed and desparate, Jaudon threw a windmill punch Checker stopped with his left arm and drove an uppercut into the Frenchman's already throbbing belly. Jaudon wobbled; his legs wouldn't hold him up. Grabbing him before he could fall, Checker held the half-conscious man by his bloody shirt, smashed a short jab into Jaudon's face and cocked his fist to strike again.

"No, John. Let him go. A.J. wouldn't like that. Neither would London." Rule's voice was clear.

Not even Spake Jamison added a word.

Checker stared at the blurry-eyed Jaudon and released him. The Frenchman crumpled to the ground. A whimper followed. The tall Ranger turned and asked for his reins.

"Better get those hands into water, John. They'll swell on you," the redheaded Ranger said quietly, as if advising someone to wash his hands for supper.

Almost without understanding, Checker looked at his raw and bloody knuckles.

He looked over at Rule. "I haven't met your wife."

Chapter Forty-one

Red streaks of a new day greeted a strange group of riders entering the quiet town of Caisson. Thirty Rangers surrounded Holt's gunmen, their hands tied in front of them, as they entered the main street. In the rear were five horses carrying dead Holt gunmen.

A barely conscious Jaudon, with his face blossoming in purple and yellow bruises, rode in the center. His horse was led by the redheaded Ranger. His hands were tied together and grasped the saddle horn.

At the front rode John Checker, Rule Cordell, Aleta Cordell and Spake Jamison.

An excited young boy ran into the street and alongside them. "What's going on? You aren't real Rangers, are ya? My ma says there's a bad bunch claiming to be Rangers."

Aleta was the first to respond. "*Buenos dias. Sí.* These ees real Rangers. They ees bringing ze bad ones in. To justice." She looked down at him and smiled. "*Como esta usted?* Ah, how are you thees morning?"

"I'm fine, lady. I gotta go now. Tell my ma. She'll be very happy."

"*Adios.*" She waved and the boy ran off.

Spake turned in the saddle back toward the other Rangers. "Let's take them to the city corral. Down at the end of the street. We can tie them to the poles. Any of 'em give us trouble, we'll shoot 'em. Be less to mess with. They can stay there 'til the circuit judge can get here. Ol' Judge Jones'll be just what we need."

Checker motioned toward Jaudon. The Ranger's hands were puffy and swollen.

Spake pointed. "Except for the Frenchman. He goes in the jail."

From the newspaper office burst a disheveled Lady Holt. She screamed, "I demand to know what is going on here! Those are my men. That is Ranger Captain Sil Jaudon. Unhand him, I demand it."

None of the Rangers responded, focusing on the street ahead and watching as townspeople were beginning to gather along the sidewalk.

"You don't understand. I own this town." She waved a large sheet of paper. "This is the first edition of the *Caisson Phoenix*! It tells what is happening here." She hurried over to the closest Ranger and shoved the paper toward him. "Here, read it. It's exciting. There's even a poem about Iva Lee."

He brushed it aside and rode on.

She ran toward the first riders, pointing and screaming, "That's John Checker—and Rule Cordell! They are wanted . . . for murder. Arrest them. Arrest them."

Turning toward her, Checker said, "Better start a new edition. I've got the headline. 'Lady Holt and Her Men Arrested for Murder and Attempted Land Theft.' How's that sound?"

She looked at him, not comprehending. "Shoot him, Jaudon. Shoot him." As the group rode past, she frantically looked at the arrested gunmen. "Where is Tapan? I don't see Tapan. Where is my Tapan?"

Rule pulled his horse from the group and rode over to her. "Tapan Moore is lying on the top of a ridge. Back where he tried to kill us. So is Luke Dimitry. They weren't good enough. Your men tried to wipe out some good people. Your men weren't good enough, either. You hired Eleven Meade to kill John Checker. He wasn't good enough, either." Cocking his head to the side, he said, "You aren't good enough, either, lady."

Aleta and Checker joined the gunfighter, easing their horses toward the wild-eyed woman.

"I'll triple what you're earning right now. Triple the wages!" She waved her arms and screamed, "I'm the Queen of Texas! Iva Lee, I've done it!"

Waving the Rangers to a stop, Spake joined Checker, Rule and Aleta in confronting the unstable English rancher.

"You're under arrest, Holt. You're going to jail. With your buddy here, Jaudon." Checker swung down from his horse.

"You're not the law. Tapan is the sheriff. Jaudon is. . . the Ranger captain. I'll wire Governor Citale. He'll put a stop to this nonsense. He'll—"

"Citale's about two weeks away from resigning," Checker snarled. "Either that or he can stand trial like the dog he is."

"No! No! He's the governor. My governor. I am the Queen of Texas!"

For the first time, she saw that townspeople were gathering. "My people! My people! How good you are here. I need your help. These awful men are trying to ruin us. You must help me stop them. Stop them! Our glorious empire depends on it." She stutter-stepped toward the closest group, crossing her hands over her heart.

"Glorious Phoenix, you ever are my guide. Lead me to your Father, the Sun," she cried out. "As it dies each eve and is reborn each morn, so you direct me to become invincible."

"This time, lady, we're the fire—and you aren't coming out of it. Your phoenix is just another dead bird." Checker grabbed her shoulder to stop her advance.

"Don't you ever touch me! I am the queen," she screamed, and spun toward him, swinging her right arm to slap his face.

He caught the oncoming swing, grabbing her arm with his left hand in midair. She pulled at his grip and cursed.

"Be glad you're not a man, Holt. I've never hit a woman, but I'd make an exception in your case."

Aleta came behind him, leading her horse. "Ranger Checker, these ees woman's work. Let me take her to jail. Ees *bueno*?"

"I'd like that, Aleta. Thank you. I've about had it with this piece of British crap."

The Mexican beauty stepped next to Lady Holt and delivered a savage slap across the evil rancher's face. Lady Holt staggered and grabbed her pained cheek.

"Now, senorita, do you want to go to thees jail easy—or hard? Eet makes no difference to me." In Aleta's other hand was one of her revolvers.

Holding her reddened face, Lady Holt bit her lower lip, whimpered and started walking toward the jail. Hurrying down the sidewalk came Margaret Loren, her own face flushed.

"Miss? Miss? May I help you? I own the dry goods place up the street—and I've waited a long time for this day." She motioned toward Lady Holt and produced a short-barreled revolver from beneath her apron.

"*Gracias*, senorita."

Aleta started again, with Margaret beside her, moving the distraught Lady Holt toward the jail with jabs of their guns in her back.

"Riders coming!" Rule said, looking behind them.

Emmett, Rikor and Morgan led another bunch of Rangers—and Charlie Carlson and his six cowboys—into Caisson. Checker and Spake waved at their Ranger friends, part of Captain Poe's main force. They had heard of the trouble and come to help, ignoring Poe's wire demands that his men stay out of the complicated situation.

Immediately, Emmett spotted Aleta and Margaret taking Lady Holt to jail. His worried exclamation about where his boys were was answered by Rule. Both sets of children were fine and with the Morrisons, who were staying with them at the Cordells' home. He explained they were a black family who had become their friends.

Emmett swallowed what he was about to say and, instead, asked what had happened. They had decided not to go on to Morgan's ranch, but to come to Caisson to help. London Fiss's body was left where it was, for later caring. They just couldn't ride away and leave the trouble to Checker and Rule.

Jumping down and leaving the reins on the ground, Morgan ran toward Checker. She flung herself into his arms. At that moment, Jaudon pulled free the holstered pistol from the distracted Ranger next to him. Morgan stiffened as the bullet hit her, instead of Checker, and she slumped in his arms.

Checker, Rule and Spake fired at the Frenchman at almost the same instant. The lead impact lifted him from his saddle and his frightened horse bolted down the street as Jaudon slammed against the earth and was still. The Ranger next to him jumped down and ran toward the dying Morgan. He was crying.

Spake yelled at three men to find the doctor and they galloped away. Rule went over to examine the bullet-riddled Jaudon. No one saw a hungover Wilson Tanner slip toward the livery. With him was Alex Wilkerson, the banker and mayor.

Checker knelt in the street, cradling the young woman he loved. Jaudon's bullet had struck her heart and he knew it. Tearing off his neckerchief, he wadded the cloth and held it against the seeping wound.

"M-Morgan, hold on. Hold on. W-we'll get the doctor here." He touched her cheek as his eyes welled with tears.

She grabbed his arm and her eyes fluttered open. "M-my d-dearest John . . . I—I w-wanted . . . a l-life with . . . y-you."

"Morgan, please! I love you," Checker declared as tears trembled down his face.

"I . . . I . . . l-love you." Her hand slid from his arm and she was still.

Chapter Forty-two

Two weeks later, a somber John Checker and Rule Cordell walked into the governor's outer office.

"We need to see Citale." Checker's growl was a bowie knife.

"Ah . . . ah, the governor is busy right now. May I tell—"

Neither paused as they pushed open the door and walked into the governor's office. The stocky assistant scurried from his desk, wiping back his hair as he moved. Rule's glare stopped him.

"I . . . ah, go in. P-please . . . sirs."

The gaunt governor looked up, his face rich with annoyance at being disturbed. Captain Poe was sitting across from Citale's desk. Next to him was a well-dressed businessman. Checker reached under his Comanche tunic and pulled free an envelope.

"What in the world? These two are wanted murderers. Arrest them, Poe."

"Don't even think about it, Poe." Checker's hard face attacked the Ranger captain with his eyes. "I've had more of you than I can handle." He walked over to the surprised governor's desk and tossed the envelope on his desk.

"Here's your train ticket. To New Orleans," the tall Ranger said. "You are resigning as of right now. Lieutenant Governor Morse will assume leadership. He's waiting outside—with half of Captain Temple's Ranger force. The other half are taking prisoners to prison. All of them are criminals you made into Rangers." The heat of his glare made the governor look away.

"What the hell are you clowns talking about? Get out of here," the balding, narrow-faced governor said. "Can't you see I'm having a meeting with one of my Ranger captains . . . and, and an important citizen of the state? They are asking me to run for the U.S. Senate."

Checker reached across the desk, grabbed the governor by his shirt and yanked him to his feet. "I only see a spineless son of a bitch who has no business in this office or any other—or the state of Texas."

"Ranger Checker, this is extremely out of order," Captain Poe said, waving his arms.

"Shut up, Poe—or you're leaving, too."

Standing in the doorway, Rule recited what had taken place in Caisson—and that the Rangers waiting outside, and in Caisson, were waiting to be officially reinstated. The new governor would be doing that. He would also be dropping the charges against Captain Temple and officially restoring him to his proper rank and authority

"Lots of changes in Caisson and around there," Rule said. "Town's looking for a new bank owner. New saloon owner, too. Could use an attorney—and somebody who knows about land titles and the like." His smile didn't reach his eyes. "They're going to vote on a new sheriff. Spake is serving as their lawman for now. Same with the mayor. Mrs. Loren's the acting mayor. I'm sure she'll be voted in. Going to get a new town council while they're at it. Oh yeah, the new city judge is, oh, I can't think of his name, he owns the gun shop."

The gunfighter glanced at Checker, returned his attention to Citale and Poe. "Holt's ranch is going to be split up. Pieces sold off. Emmett Gardner and Charlie Carlson are buying pieces. Others, too. Judge Jones is overseeing the effort."

Checker shoved his hands into his gun belt. "Holt's servants and chef have left. Gave each one a month's salary. From her account. Looks like there's going to be enough left over to build a church. My friend has agreed to be their preacher until they get one of their own."

"That big herd's being divided among the new owners," Cordell added. "Not sure what's going to happen to her foreman. He's not wanted, though. He and his men were real cowmen. Heard he was going to buy a chunk of her land. Don't know that for certain."

Rule's right hand slid from resting against the door frame to his gun belt. A stone earring wiggled below his ear. Poe and Citale saw the stem attached to the lapel of his long black coat and wondered what it was.

He continued with what had happened. Morgan Peale, a local rancher, and her employee, London Fiss, were murdered by Holt's men. They were buried in a quiet place where they had earlier buried Ranger A. J. Bartlett, who was also killed trying to stop the Holt gang. Lady Holt's men, under her direction, had also murdered Jimmy Benson, the blacksmith who served as the temporary sheriff. It appeared that Henry Seitmeyer, the newspaper publisher, was going to make it, in spite of a severe head blow.

Lady Holt had been tried by Judge Roebuck Jones, the district circuit judge and convicted of murder, rustling and land embezzlement. Sil Jaudon, Tapan Moore, Luke Dimitry and Eleven Meade, all hired by her, were dead. Her other gunmen were on their way to federal prison, escorted by Rangers.

The businessman coughed and stood. "I believe my business can wait. For the new governor."

"Wait a minute, Mr. Kreig. This is just a silly misunderstanding. These men have no authority to . . ." Citale rubbed his fingers across his fine mustache and looked at the envelope resting on the desk.

"We have all the authority we need," Checker growled, and drew his Colt. "Your greed has cost me the lives of two friends—and the woman I love."

Frantically, Citale pulled open the right-hand drawer of his desk, to reveal a gold-plated revolver with ivory handles. Checker's challenge stopped his movement toward it.

"Pick up that gun. Please. I want you to. I imagine Sil Jaudon gave it to you when you appointed him captain. He killed my lady." Checker leaned forward. "Pick it up, Citale. Come on, you bastard, pick it up. Or can't you handle doing evil things yourself? I'll get your assistant in here. Maybe he can try."

"Easy, John." Rule drew his revolver. "They were friends of mine, too," he said to Citale. "You and Lady Holt tried to run over some good folks. One of them is my uncle. I didn't like that, either."

"Wh-who are you?"

"I'm Rule Cordell."

His face dark with fury barely controlled, Checker nodded toward the gunfighter in the black long coat. "I asked my friend to come with me today, to keep me from tearing you apart. You're getting a break with that train ride, Citale. If I ever hear you've stepped onto Texas soil again, I'll find you—and kill you."

"B-but, but what'll I say? What'll I tell the newspapers? I've got state projects we're working on. Important things. For Texas. Tell them, ah, Kreig. I'm running for . . . the U.S. Senate."

The businessman paused at the doorway. "Nothing that can't wait. You aren't running for anything." He looked at Checker, then Rule. "I didn't know." He hesitated and continued out of the office. Outside, the frightened assistant was sobbing.

"Your health is the reason for the sudden resignation," Rule said. "That's what the new governor will tell them. You can tell them anything you want."

"But there won't be any time for that, Citale. The train leaves in an hour. We're taking you there," Checker said, slamming the desk drawer shut.

Citale's eyes blinked four times and it looked as though he was going to vomit. "Wh-where's L-Lady Holt now?"

"She's in the Caisson jail, waiting to be hanged."

"H-hanged?"

"Yeah, she asked to be burned, but Texas doesn't do things like that," Checker said. "Something about being a phoenix."

Captain Poe swallowed and blurted, "I almost forgot." With the two gunfighters' permission, he reached inside his coat pocket and produced a letter. "Came for you, John. From Dodge City, Kansas. It's from a Mrs. Amelia Checker Hedrickson. Know her?"

Cotton Smith

"Cotton Smith turns in a terrific story every time."
—*Roundup Magazine*

Tanneman Rose was a Texas Ranger turned bad. When he and his gang robbed a bank, he brought shame to the badge. A jury found him guilty, a judge sentenced him, but Rose swore he wouldn't die in prison. Instead he died while trying to escape. Time Carlow helped to capture his fellow Ranger that day at the bank, and now he's investigating a very odd series of murders. Each victim was involved in sending Tanneman Rose to jail. Could it be a coincidence? Or is Rose's gang out for revenge? Or Rose, himself? Time doesn't believe in ghosts—or coincidences. He's got to find the answers and stop the murders…before he becomes the latest victim.

DEATH MASK

ISBN 13: 978-0-8439-6200-0

COTTON SMITH

"Cotton Smith is one of the finest of a new breed of writers of the American West."

—Don Coldsmith

Return of the Spirit Rider

In the booming town of Denver, saloon owner Vin Lockhart is known as a savvy businessman with a quick gun. But he will never forget that he was raised an Oglala Sioux. So when Vin's Oglala friends needed help dealing with untruthful, encroaching white men, he swore he would do what he could. His dramatic journey will include encounters with Wild Bill Hickok and Buffalo Bill Cody. But when an ambush leaves him on the brink of death, his only hope is what an old Oglala shaman taught him long ago.

"Cotton Smith is one of the best new authors out there."

—Steven Law, Read West

ISBN 13: 978-0-8439-5854-6

The Classic Film Collection

The Searchers by Alan LeMay

Hailed as one of the greatest American films, *The Searchers,* directed by John Ford and starring John Wayne, has had a direct influence on the works of Martin Scorsese, Steven Spielberg, and many others. Its gorgeous cinematic scope and deeply nuanced characters have proven timeless. And now available for the first time in decades is the powerful novel that inspired this iconic movie.

Destry Rides Again by Max Brand

Made in 1939, the Golden Year of Hollywood, *Destry Rides Again* helped launch Jimmy Stewart's career and made Marlene Dietrich an American icon. Now available for the first time in decades is the novel that inspired this much-loved movie.

The Man from Laramie by T. T. Flynn

In its original publication, *The Man from Laramie* had more than half a million copies in print. Shortly thereafter, it became one of the most recognized of the Anthony Mann/Jimmy Stewart collaborations, known for darker films with morally complex characters. Now the novel upon which this classic movie was based is once again available—for the first time in more than fifty years.

The Unforgiven by Alan LeMay

In this epic American novel, which served as the basis for the classic film directed by John Huston and starring Burt Lancaster and Audrey Hepburn, a family is torn apart when an old enemy starts a vicious rumor that sets the range aflame. Don't miss the powerful novel that inspired the film the *Motion Picture Herald* calls "an absorbing and compelling drama of epic proportions."

To order a book or to request a catalog call:
1-800-481-9191
Books are also available at your local bookstore, or you can check out our Web site **www.dorchesterpub.com**.

Bill Pronzini &
Marcia Muller

The dark clouds are gathering, and it's promising to be a doozy of a storm at the River Bend stage station ... where the owners are anxiously awaiting the return of their missing daughter. Where a young cowboy hopes to find safety from the rancher whose wife he's run away with. Where a Pinkerton agent has tracked the quarry he's been chasing for years. Thunder won't be the only thing exploding along ...

CRUCIFIXION RIVER

Bill Pronzini and Marcia Muller are a husband-wife writing team with numerous individual honors, including the Lifetime Achievement Award from the Private Eye Writers of America, the Grand Master Award from Mystery Writers of America, and the American Mystery Award. In addition to the Spur Award–winning title novella, this volume also contains stories featuring Bill Pronzini's famous "Nameless Detective" and Marcia Muller's highly popular Sharon McCone investigator.

ISBN 13: 978-0-8439-6341-0

INTERACT WITH DORCHESTER ONLINE!

Want to learn more about your favorite books and authors?
Want to talk with other readers that like to read the same books as you?
Want to see up-to-the-minute Dorchester news?

VISIT DORCHESTER AT:
DorchesterPub.com
Twitter.com/DorchesterPub
Facebook.com (Search Pages)

DISCUSS DORCHESTER'S NOVELS AT:
Dorchester Forums at DorchesterPub.com
GoodReads.com
LibraryThing.com
Myspace.com/books
Shelfari.com
WeRead.com

✂

□ YES!

Sign me up for the Leisure Western Book Club and send my FREE BOOKS! If I choose to stay in the club, I will pay only $14.00* each month, a savings of $9.96!

NAME: _____

ADDRESS: _____

TELEPHONE: _____

EMAIL: _____

□ I want to pay by credit card.

□ **VISA**　　□ **MasterCard**　　□ **DISCOVER**

ACCOUNT #: _____

EXPIRATION DATE: _____

SIGNATURE: _____

Mail this page along with $2.00 shipping and handling to:
Leisure Western Book Club
PO Box 6640
Wayne, PA 19087
Or fax (must include credit card information) to:
610-995-9274

You can also sign up online at **www.dorchesterpub.com**.

*Plus $2.00 for shipping. Offer open to residents of the U.S. and Canada only. Canadian residents please call 1-800-481-9191 for pricing information. If under 18, a parent or guardian must sign. Terms, prices and conditions subject to change. Subscription subject to acceptance. Dorchester Publishing reserves the right to reject any order or cancel any subscription.